A PLACE TO BURY STRANGERS

MARK DAWSON

A PLACE TO BURY STRANGERS

WELBECK

First published in 2023 by Welbeck Fiction Limited,
an imprint of Welbeck Publishing Group
Offices in: London – 20 Mortimer Street, London W1T 3JW &
Sydney – Level 17, 207 Kent St, Sydney NSW 2000 Australia
www.welbeckpublishing.com

First published in 2021
This edition published by Welbeck Fiction Limited, part of
Welbeck Publishing Group, in 2023

Mark Dawson has asserted their moral rights to be identified as the author of this
Work in accordance with the Copyright Designs and Patents Act 1988.

A CIP catalogue record for this book is available from the British Library

Paperback ISBN: 978-1-80279-584-4

Printed and bound by CPI Group (UK) Ltd., Croydon, CR0 4YY

FSC
www.fsc.org
MIX
Paper | Supporting
responsible forestry
FSC® C171272

10 9 8 7 6 5 4 3 2 1

To my family.

PROLOGUE

Salisbury Plain stretched out beneath a slate-grey sky, the sun obscured by clouds that promised yet more rain after a week of wet days. It was just after dawn, and Jan Lewandowski had brought his dog to the Plain for a walk while it was dry. There had been no other cars in the lay-by where dog walkers often parked, and there was no one visible as far as he could see. The wide-open space was desolate, the emptiness interrupted by the occasional beech and stand of fir and clumps of saw-wort, ox-eye daisy and milkwort.

Lewandowski's dog, Coco, was an enterprising two-year-old spaniel who needed a lot of exercise to prevent her causing disruption at home. Lewandowski wrestled the tennis ball from her mouth and fitted it into the plastic launcher. He drew back his arm and fired the launcher out, sending the tennis ball arcing high through the air. It bounced once and then a second time against the damp ground and rolled to a stop beneath the branches of a hawthorn bush. Coco bounded after it, her tail wagging with unbridled enthusiasm. She reached it and then stood there, stock-still, ignoring it. She cocked her head as if taking a sniff of the air, and then launched ahead, leaving the ball behind her.

'Coco!'

The dog sprinted to the north, ducking beneath the slats of a post-and-rail fence and continuing into the field beyond. There was a flagpole next to the gate in the fence that allowed access to the field, and a red pennant flapped from the top. Salisbury Plain was owned by the Ministry of Defence and was used by the Army for training. The red flag denoted that live-fire exercises were possible.

'*Coco!*' Lewandowski yelled. 'Get back here!'

The dog ignored him, hurrying across the field until she disappeared into a depression. Lewandowski cursed, jogged over to the fence and clambered over it. The ground had been churned up by tank tracks, and he had to hop over deep troughs that were filled with muddy water. He scanned the landscape, looking for any sign that might indicate that an exercise was taking place. There was none, but, even so, he had served in the Polish army before he moved here and remembered his old corporal warning new recruits to be cautious in places like this; it wasn't impossible for rounds to land without detonating.

He took the dog's lead from his pocket and hurried across the field. 'Come *here*, Coco.'

The dog showed no interest in heeding his call. Her attention was clearly fixed on something else and, as Lewandowski watched, she dipped her head and picked it up.

Lewandowski reached the dog. 'What are you doing?' he said, reaching down to clip the lead to her collar. 'What have you found, girl?'

There was a long white bone in Coco's mouth.

Lewandowski guessed that it was forty or fifty centimetres long, with a cylindrical head at one end and a smooth, shallow trough at the other. He tried to take it from her, but she growled and tugged to keep it.

'Drop it, Coco. Put it *down*.'

The dog laid the bone down, locked it in place with her paws and started to gnaw at it.

Lewandowski knelt down so that he was closer to the bone. He had assumed it belonged to an animal, but, as he looked at it, he realised that he couldn't think of any animal on Salisbury Plain with a bone that looked like that. It was too long for a fox or a badger and surely too short for a cow or a horse.

He felt the first sting of panic and looked around, in the hope that there might be someone whom he could call out to, someone who might be able to persuade him that he had not discovered what he feared. He saw no one; they were quite alone.

He reached into his pocket with trembling fingers, pulled out his phone and dialled.

'Emergency services – which service do you require?'

'Police,' Lewandowski said. 'I think I've found human remains.'

PART I

MONDAY

1

Detective Chief Inspector Mackenzie Jones led the way across the uneven track, stepping over the ruts that had been left by the tanks that were regularly used in exercises on this part of the Plain. Professor Allan Fyfe, the Home Office pathologist, kept pace alongside her. The rain had turned the track into something of a quagmire, with ankle-deep puddles and long stretches of mud that threatened to suck the boots straight off her feet. At least she *had* her boots, she thought as she stepped around a particularly treacherous patch of mud. She always kept a pair in the boot of the car, just in case. Fyfe had not had the same foresight and was complaining loudly at the state of his brogues and the bottoms of his trousers. He was carrying a square case with a strap that he wore across his shoulder; the case bumped against his hip with every step.

'Where is it?' he asked.

Mack pointed to the hawthorn hedge. 'There's a depression on the other side of that bush.'

'I'm not really dressed for this kind of terrain.'

Fyfe was an irascible man who had not been pleased to have been called out on short notice. Mack had worked with him before and found him to be something of a handful; he was intelligent, although perhaps not quite as clever as he liked people to think, with a short temper and a sharp tongue that he directed against those who he felt were not following his instructions with the necessary speed.

Fyfe wasn't the only person to have had their diary upended. Mack had been due in court for the conclusion of the case against Allegra Mallender and Tristan Lennox. The proceedings had, as far as she could tell, been going well and had gone some way to making up for the farrago that had preceded it. It had been Atticus Priest who had unravelled the evidence she had assembled against Ralph Mallender; he had also provided the evidence that had led to the charging of those whom they now believed to be the true culprits behind the Christmas Eve Massacre. It was an important trial and had drawn the press to the court in numbers that had not been seen in Salisbury for years. Chief Superintendent Beckton had given clear instructions that Mack was to attend every day until the defendants were convicted; he had then countermanded his own orders when the bone had been found, realising that DI Robbie Best was on leave and that there was no one else of sufficient seniority to handle the discovery. It had to be Mack.

Fyfe slipped and almost lost his footing. 'Bloody hell.'

'Nearly there,' Mack said.

The dog walker who had found the bone had called 999, and uniformed officers had been sent to take a look. They had called CID, and those officers, suspecting that the bone might be human, had summoned the forensic medical examiner. She had shared their conclusion as to the bone's origin, and that had led to Mack and Fyfe being here now.

'Did you speak to the MoD?' he asked her.

'I did. They're not exercising today.'

They followed the track through the field until they could see the site of the discovery. The area had been secured, with uniforms guarding the boundary and a loggist taking down the details of those who went beyond the tape.

'Down there,' Mack said.

Their details were noted in the scene log, and they clambered down the sloping side of the depression. The bone was visible at the bottom, half of it in the puddle of water that had gathered there. The pathologist placed the box of equipment down, unlatched the lid and opened it. He put on a pair of nitrile gloves and carefully picked up the bone with both hands. He turned it over, examining it carefully.

'What do you think?' Mack asked him.

'Human,' he said.

'How confident are you?'

'I'll need to speak to Simon Chester to be one hundred per cent sure, but it looks like a femur.'

'Simon Chester?'

'Forensic anthropologist,' he said. He turned the bone so that the bulbous head was at the top and pointed to it. 'I'm a generalist – I'm not trained to analyse skeletal remains, although, if you pushed me, I could give you my uneducated first impressions.'

'Please.'

'It's a bone from the right leg. Slightly arched – convex at the front and concave behind. You see the head – here? It articulates with the acetabulum of the pelvic bone.' He turned the bone so that the head was visible. 'It looks like it's been scavenged. The scoring marks here and here were most likely caused by an animal.'

'It was found by a dog.'

'And it might have had a little chew before its owner rescued it,' he said. 'But some of the marks look older than the last few days.'

'Male or female?'

'That'll be one for Simon, but from the length of it, I'd put my money on female.'

'How long has it been in the ground?'

He shrugged.

'Best guess?'

'Years. Look at the state of it.' He held it up. 'I'll get it to Simon, and he can tell us what he thinks. But we'll need to find the rest of the body in the meantime. Nothing around here?'

'Nothing obvious, but we haven't looked properly yet. I'll arrange for reinforcements.'

She left Fyfe with the bone and clambered up out of the depression. Her sergeant, Nigel Archer, was making his way along the track towards her.

'Bloody hell, boss,' he said. 'It's like the Somme.'

'Fyfe says it's human,' she said.

Archer rolled his eyes. 'Wonderful.'

'We're going to need to get as many bodies here as we can,' she said. 'The rest of the remains must be here somewhere. Can I leave that to you?'

'Course, boss. I'll call the nick and have them round up a posse.'

'Fyfe was talking about finding a forensic anthropologist to come down and take a look. Make sure he gets everything he needs.'

'Will do, Mack.'

A light shower of rain started to fall, and, as they both looked up, Mack saw a skein of lightning crackle through the purple and black clouds.

Great, she thought. Stuck out on the Plain during a storm. They were going to get soaked.

2

The atmosphere in the courtroom was sharp with anticipation; counsel for the prosecution and the defence shared anecdotes about previous trials, the reporters scribbled notes on pads, and the family members of the two defendants – Allegra Mallender and Tristan Lennox – kept a scrupulous distance from one another, reflecting the schism that had opened up between the two former lovers as they had turned upon one another in desperate attempts to save their own skins. The room was quickly full to capacity; Atticus Priest took his seat in the public gallery and looked around to see if Mack was present. She wasn't. Ralph Mallender, the husband of the first defendant, was just in front of him, dressed in an understated but obviously expensive suit; Atticus saw that the nails of both Ralph's hands had been gnawed down to the quick, as sure an indication of his unease as anything.

There was a buzz of excitement as the defendants were led into the dock. It didn't take any great skill to read the hatred that burned between them. Allegra Mallender, dressed in a white shirt with matching blue skirt and jacket, sat at one end and grasped the rail so tightly that Atticus could see the whitening of her knuckles. Tristan Lennox sat on the other side of the box, as far away from Allegra as it was possible for him to be. He looked out into the courtroom, his eyes flicking over the people who had come to observe his fate.

The jury were led inside next. Atticus looked from face to face for anything that might give him an indication of the decision that they might have arrived at, but before he was able to reach a conclusion, the clerk instructed them all to stand. Mr Justice Somerville came inside and sat down, wearing the red robes that the judiciary wore during murder trials. The judge was a short-tempered septuagenarian who had been given the trial after the first prosecution had collapsed. The acquittal of Ralph Mallender had been front-page news, and Atticus was in no doubt that the failure of the case had led to difficult conversations between the Crown Prosecution Service and the judiciary. That Atticus was responsible for those difficulties might have amounted to a first strike against his name; his propensity for rhetorical flourishes and showboating during the delivery of his evidence had been another. Somerville had gone so far as to warn him against showing off. Atticus had apologised, but, of course, it had always been his intention to draw a little of the spotlight onto himself and his business and, as he had hoped, it had worked out rather well.

The clerk of the court stood and cleared his throat. 'Both defendants, please stand.'

Allegra and Lennox did as they were told.

The clerk spoke again. 'Members of the jury, will your foreman please stand.'

The juror at the end of the line of seats stood up. Atticus watched him and, to his surprise – and concern – he saw the classic signs of nervousness. He reached up to stroke the side of his neck in a typical demonstration of self-soothing, then brought his hands together and started to pick at his nails. It was possible that it was the gravity of the verdicts that he was about to deliver, but Atticus didn't think so. There was something else that was making him anxious and, for the first time, Atticus wondered whether the trial was going to go the way everyone had expected that it would.

'Please answer the following question yes or no. Have you reached a verdict upon which you are all agreed?'

The foreman nodded. 'Yes.'

The courtroom hummed with tension. Here it was: the investigation, the abortive and farcical first trial and now this one, with the two duelling former lovers. It was all about to come to an end.

'Please answer the following question with either "guilty" or "not guilty". On the count of conspiracy to murder, do you find the defendant, Allegra Mallender, guilty or not guilty?'

'Guilty.'

Allegra had no relatives or friends in attendance, but there were gasps from the section of the gallery that had been claimed by the surviving members of the Mallender family. Ralph sat stock-still, his jaw clenched, unmoving.

'Order in the court,' the judge said in a loud, stern voice.

'Do you find the defendant, Tristan Lennox, guilty or not guilty?'

'Guilty.'

'Are those the verdicts of you all?' the clerk asked. The foreman nodded. 'Yes.'

'Very well,' the judge said. 'We'll adjourn for sentencing. Take the defendants down, please.'

The female guard who was responsible for Allegra Mallender helped her to stand. Allegra tottered on unsteady legs and then collapsed back into the chair. Lennox was led down to the cells.

Atticus looked again for Mack, but there was no sign of her in her usual place behind the solicitor from the CPS. She had been in court every day so far, including for all of his evidence. He had told himself it was because she wanted to see him in action, but he knew it was because his testimony was too important to miss.

The state of their relationship had been at the front of Atticus's mind throughout. He knew that she and her husband were living apart and that, as far as he was aware, there was no suggestion that the trial separation was close to coming to an end. Atticus also knew that he was singularly ill-equipped when it came to how others viewed him, and had – with some difficulty – managed not to bring the matter up when their paths had crossed outside the court. He was self-interested, and he knew that she would see that; far better, he told himself, to let her raise the question of their relationship. It had not been difficult to hold his tongue, but seeing her in the courtroom every day – if only so that he could smile across the benches at her – had been a part of the experience of giving evidence that he had enjoyed.

* * *

There was a scrum of reporters outside the court. 'Mr Priest?'

'Atticus!'

He could have asked to leave by the rear door and avoid them, but he had found that he quite enjoyed the attention. He had given an interview to *The Sun* following the arrest of Allegra Mallender and Tristan Lennox in which he had not demurred when it had been put to him that his investigation had been responsible for freeing an innocent man and for the arrests of the two people who had subsequently been charged for the crime. He was not ashamed to admit that his motive for giving the interview had been financial; he had earned the chance to make a name for himself and, at a time when his practice had been close to bankruptcy, there was significant value in that. The interview had led to other opportunities, including a ten-minute feature on being a detective – lazily backed by the Dire Straits' track 'Private Investigations' – that had been broadcast on BBC *Newsnight*, during which he was his profession's representative. He had been given a modest advance to write a treatise on the art of deduction, and there was talk of a podcast that might accompany its publication. There had even been talk of a photoshoot with *OK* magazine. Atticus had mentioned that to Mack, and she had told him that was the most ludicrous thing she had ever heard.

The crowd bubbled around him.

'Atticus – what are your thoughts?'

'The jury made the right decision,' he said.

'How long do you think they'll get?'

'Well, the sentence for murder is life. They won't be out for a long time.'

'Would you say your evidence was the deciding factor?'

'I wouldn't say that at all. The jury had a lot to consider. I think they did an excellent job.'

He gave what he hoped was an enigmatic smile, bade the reporters goodbye and made his way through the crush to the pavement beyond. His recent minor celebrity had led to a spate of new business, including the prospective case for which he had arranged an appointment at four o'clock. He didn't want to be late.

3

Atticus needed a walk to clear the cobwebs from his head. He put on his waterproofs and drove Bandit out to an Iron Age hill fort, Figsbury Ring – a large raised circular bank which surrounded a central ditch. The views across to Salisbury and Old Sarum were spectacular, and the wide-open terrain offered Bandit space to race around at top speed. Atticus watched the dog as he dashed up one side of the bank and then straight down the other, scampering away into the inner enclosure with boundless enthusiasm.

He called the dog to him after thirty minutes, and drove back into the city. He parked in his usual spot and reattached Bandit's lead, and together they strolled to the office. It was half past three, and he was expecting his potential new client on the hour.

Things had changed over the course of the last few months. The exposure that had been generated by the court case had been a boon. He had anticipated the interest and had paid Jacob, his upstairs neighbour, to put together an improved website from which he would be able to advertise his services. It had been a wise move. Traffic to the site was plentiful and had included enough enquiries into the possibility of new work that he had been able to pick and choose the jobs he took on and let go. His previous slate of work had been slender and dull, with occasional work to expose cheating spouses and insurance claimants who fabricated injuries to bolster their payouts. That species of work – for the moment, at least – had been put to the side. He had been taken on by a large regional law firm to provide evidence in a civil case brought by a national bank against a local developer who had been accused of bribing planning officials in order to win permission to build on parcels of land that had been bought for peanuts and then sold for fortunes. The developer had lost the case, and now Atticus had been tasked with locating all of his assets so that the bank could seek orders to liquidate it in order to pay the damages that the court had demanded.

For the first time since he had set up his practice, he had a steady flow of money being paid into his business account. He had used that to clear his outstanding rent and his overdraft, and then had taken some of the rest and redecorated his office. The larger of his two rooms – the one where he met with clients – had been repainted in neutral tones and then refurnished. He had a large sideboard in artfully distressed wood and a leather luggage trunk that he used as a coffee table. There were new pictures on the walls and a bookshelf that he had filled with legal textbooks and works on forensics, criminology, psychology and investigation. Some of the books were out of date, but that didn't matter; he had not kept them for the benefit of his education, but for the impression of learning that they could impart to the clients who came to visit him.

He fed Bandit, then went into the smaller of the office's two rooms, where he slept, and collected the shirt and suit that he had had dry-cleaned in preparation for appointments. He undressed and spritzed himself with deodorant, then tore the plastic protective sleeves from the clothes and dressed, making sure to button his shirt cuffs to obscure the tattoos that decorated both arms. He checked his reflection in the mirror, made sure that Bandit was comfortable on the futon, shut the door and went through into the office just as the bell rang.

4

The bell rang again. Atticus went to the stairs and climbed down, opening the door.

A man was standing in the passageway outside.

'Good afternoon,' Atticus said.

'Mr Priest?'

'That's right,' he said.

'James York.'

'Good to meet you. Please – come upstairs to the office.'

The redecoration of the office had not extended to the common parts that he shared with Jacob, and, although he had a cleaner coming in once a week now, she had complained that the cord on her vacuum cleaner did not reach down far enough for her to clean the stairs. She had, at least, disposed of the menus from the pizza restaurants that had been shoved beneath the door and then trodden on over the course of several months, but the carpet was still dirty from the muck that was trodden into it every day. Atticus knew that first impressions were important, especially when someone was considering an investment in services, and resolved to get the carpet properly cleaned. Whilst he was at it, he would get someone to paint over the scuff marks on the walls.

'I'm just up here,' he said.

He led the way into the office and invited York to take a seat on the sofa in the bay window, observing him as he settled down. He was a large man with a flat forehead and greying hair that was cropped close to his scalp. He had large ears and small eyes. Atticus guessed that he was in his sixties.

He started to speak, but was overcome by an abrupt coughing fit. Atticus went and fetched a glass of water and handed it over. York sipped it, spluttered down another cough, and then sipped it again. Finally, the coughing stopped.

'Sorry about that,' he said, wiping his mouth with his handkerchief.

'Are you all right?'

'Tickle in the throat,' he said. 'It's nothing.' He folded up the handkerchief, but not before Atticus noticed a splotch of bright red on the fabric. 'Thank you for seeing me.'

'My pleasure. My secretary said it was urgent. How can I help?'

'It's my daughter. She's gone missing. I was hoping you might be able to find her.'

Atticus was a little disappointed. Missing persons cases were meat and drink for a private investigator, but it was hardly the most challenging or remunerative of work. 'I'm sorry to hear that.'

York looked at Atticus hopefully. 'Is that the sort of thing you might be able to help with?'

'Of course,' he said with a reassuring smile.

'I hope you don't mind me asking,' York said. 'I know that you've built a reputation after the case at Christmas, but you never know how much of what you read in the papers to believe. I suppose what I'm trying to say is that I need to know that you're as good as they say you are.'

'Of course,' Atticus said. 'I don't blame you. I'd be asking, too. There are a lot of sharks who'll happily take advantage of people when they're desperate. Let me see what I can do to put you at ease. You work on the land. A farmer, I think. You're originally from Birmingham, and you ring the bells on Sundays at All Saints' in Houghton.'

York frowned, as if annoyed to have been so thoroughly stripped naked. 'How could you *possibly* know that?'

'Your hands were strong when we shook, and I noticed that the fingers show a little dirt beneath the nails. Neither is definitive, of course, but both are suggestive of someone who works hard outside. I hope you won't be too offended if I suggest that you look a little tired, and, given that it is just after four in the afternoon, my supposition would be that you were up early – not many professions start earlier than those who work on the land.'

'I could be a light sleeper,' he demurred. 'And the dirt under my nails could be grease. I could be an engineer.'

'Possibly, although the other evidence points away from that. Your face is red and shows signs of exposure to the elements. I might have hazarded a guess and said that you've recently returned from holiday, save the fact that the skin of your arms is pale. Now, obviously it's winter, so it is unlikely to have been burned by the sun in this country. I suspect it's wind – the skin can become painful after exposure to wind, and it has been windy recently. It removes the natural oils from the skin, causing pain, redness, and dryness.' He gestured. 'Just like that. Also, I noticed a blue Ford Ranger while I was walking back to the office for this meeting. It was parked on the other side of the road. I didn't notice the occupant, but people often stop there when they're not quite sure where to park. And Ford Rangers – especially very dirty ones – are often found in agricultural businesses.'

'The bells?'

'Your hands, please.'

York spread his palms to reveal a set of red calluses and broken blisters on the pads of his hands and up and down his fingers.

'Again, this could be a consequence of working the land, but I think not. I've seen wear and tear like that before – the price you pay for playing the world's loudest musical instrument every week. The nearest churches to you in Broughton are St James's in Bossington and All Saints' in Houghton, but only the latter has bells, if I remember correctly.'

'You do,' York said.

'Combine that with the sign of the ichthus that I noticed in the rear windscreen of the Ford Ranger, and you have a compelling argument.'

'The sign of the *what?*'

'The fish. The Christian symbol.'

'Yes,' he said. 'Of course. And Birmingham? I don't have an accent.'

'Enough for me to notice. You've also got an Aston Villa sticker next to the fish. That one was easy.'

'I spent a lot of time there as a child.' York chuckled and shook his head. 'You really notice things like that?'

'It's a useful skill for someone in my line of work.'

Atticus was pleased with the reaction. It was a simple enough little parlour trick, but useful to deploy when potential clients came to call.

'Now – can I get you a drink before we work out how I might be able to help?'

'Thanks,' York said.

'I'm having coffee, but I guess you'd prefer tea?'

'How'd you know that?'

'Educated guess,' he said. 'I'd bet that most Brummie ex-squaddies in their sixties would prefer tea. It was a hunch – and my hunches are right more often than not.'

'Then I know I've come to the right man.'

Atticus went outside to the small kitchen. He boiled the kettle, scooped coffee into his mug and dropped a tea bag into the other and poured the water, returning to the office and depositing the mugs on the leather crate.

'Shall we get started?' he said. 'Tell me about your daughter.'

5

York coughed again, holding up a hand to say that he was all right as he waited for it to subside.

'Her name is Molly,' he said at last.

Atticus took a pen and paper and noted that down. 'Molly. How old is she?'

'Seventeen.'

'When did you last see her?'

'She left home a day ago, and I haven't been able to get in touch with her. I've tried calling and sending messages, but she hasn't replied.'

'And this is unusual for her?'

'She's never done anything like this before.'

'She lives with you at home?'

'That's right.'

'Are you married?'

'I'm not. My wife and I parted ways ten years ago.'

'I see,' Atticus said. 'What about brothers or sisters?'

'No. It's just me and her.'

'What does Molly do?'

'She's studying at the college.'

'In Salisbury?'

'She's doing a food technology course. She wants to be a cook.'

'What else can you tell me?'

'She's clever, although she doesn't have enough confidence in herself.'

'Independent?'

'Not particularly.'

'That's why this is so out of character?'

'Exactly,' he said.

'Have you filed a missing persons report?'

York paused for a moment, and Atticus could see that it was a question that he had anticipated. 'I'd rather not.'

'Why?'

'It's delicate.'

'I'll need to know.'

'She's been seeing a boy.'

'Isn't that par for the course for a girl her age?'

York shifted uncomfortably in his chair. 'Yes, of course, and I wouldn't normally interfere in her business, but he's not a good sort. She met him through a friend from college, as far as I can make out. I've patched as much of it together as I can from what she's told me and what I've been able to find out from her friends. The last thing Molly needs is for the police to find her with him. He's bad news. He's into drugs. He's been in prison for dealing – he's only been out for six months.'

'Name?'

'Jordan.'

'Surname?'

'I don't know.'

'Does Molly use drugs?'

'She started smoking weed,' York said. 'I found some last week. I sat her down and confronted her about it, and there was an argument. She climbed out of her window, and I haven't seen her since.'

'Where does the boyfriend live?'

'I don't know.'

Atticus drew a line under his final paragraph and closed the notebook. 'I'm happy to have a look for you.'

'But discreetly?'

'Of course.'

'I *really* don't want the police involved. If she gets a record now . . .' He shook his head. 'It'd ruin her life before it's even got started.'

'I understand.'

'What do you need to do first?'

'I'd like to come and have a look at her room, if that's all right.'

'Of course. And then?'

'I'll ask around. I used to be a police officer in Salisbury. It's not a big town.'

'Smallsbury,' York offered.

'Exactly. The drugs scene here is very limited. Someone will know where to find Jordan.'

York nodded his satisfaction. 'How do you charge?'

'An hourly rate plus expenses will be best for a case like this.'

'Whatever it takes. I just want her back.'

Atticus took down the details he would need for Stella to open a file, and arranged to come over to look at Molly's room the next morning.

'Thank you,' York said as Atticus let him out of the building. 'It's a relief to have someone looking for her.'

'Try not to worry. The overwhelming majority of people who go missing are found.'

'I hope you're right.'

'I will be. I'll see you tomorrow morning.'

Atticus went back up to the office, filled Bandit's bowl with biscuits and let him out of the bedroom. The dog mooched over to his food, lowered his muzzle and started to eat. Atticus scratched behind the hound's ears and then went over to his desk and woke the computer. His secretary – a woman named Stella who worked for him remotely – had sent over a dossier on James York, and he had neglected to open it.

He double-clicked. James York was listed as the director of Hatfield Farm Limited, a company with a registered address in Broughton, Hampshire. A search online revealed that he was a farmer, and that he held a position on the committee of the Salisbury and South Wilts Golf Club. He navigated to Google Maps and typed in the address of the farm, switched to a satellite view and looked down on a collection of buildings: a house and several barns and outbuildings. He zoomed in and saw a collection of what looked like agricultural machinery and, in the yard that fronted one of the barns, evidence of building work. He zoomed all the way out and saw that the buildings nestled at the centre of a network of large fields; some bore the neat tracks of a tractor that had passed left to right from top to bottom; others were untrammelled green fields left to pasture to feed herds of cattle that appeared as small white dots. The farm was not on a public road and looked to be accessed by way of a narrow track.

Bandit padded over and presented his muzzle for Atticus to scratch.

'Not much to go on, boy,' he said.

His phone rang. He found it in the pocket of his jacket and saw that it was Mack.

'Afternoon,' he said. 'Where were you today?'

'Busy.' She sounded distracted. 'What are you doing?'

'Just looking into a new case. A parent has negligently misplaced his daughter, and he's asked me to find her.'

'What about now? Can you spare an hour?'

'Why? What's up?'

'I need you.'

'Words I thought I'd never hear you say.'

'Don't be an arse, Atticus. I need to run something by you. How about dinner?'

'Sounds intriguing.'

'Come to the hotel restaurant. Eight?'

The White Hart was two minutes away from the office. 'I can do that.'

'Good. I'll see you tonight.'

6

Atticus wondered how he should feel as he passed from the cold, damp night into the warm reception area of the White Hart. He knew that Mack would be missing her kids terribly, and he did not wish her sadness; on the other hand, he had never given up hope that he and Mack might be able to rekindle their relationship. It was difficult not to focus on that as he unzipped his leather jacket and took it off, hanging it on a coat hook outside the restaurant. Mack was sitting at a table in the back of the room, a notebook open in front of her.

Atticus took a menu and thumbed through it. It hadn't changed since he had been here last and, uninspired, he ordered a burger and chips. Mack ordered the fried cod and a pint of lager for each of them.

'You missed the verdict today,' he said.

'I was otherwise engaged. Were you there?'

'I was. You should've seen Allegra's face.'

'That would have been fun.'

'Lennox's, too. I think he still thought he was going to get off. Have you spoken to Beckton?'

'Not yet.'

'He'll be happy.'

'He'll be *relieved*,' she said. 'It's been a weight on everyone's shoulders.'

The waitress delivered their drinks.

'Are you okay?' he asked Mack. 'You look tired.'

'I'm knackered.'

'What is it?'

'We've got a situation, and I wouldn't mind picking your brain.'

'Pick away.'

'This stays between us,' she said. 'It's not public yet. All right?'

'Understood.'

Mack reached down into the bag at her feet and took out an iPad. She unlocked it and then tapped and swiped until she had a photograph on the screen. She turned it around so that Atticus could see it. The photograph was of what appeared to be a shallow depression in the middle of a bleak and isolated landscape.

'Salisbury Plain?' he asked.

'Yes.'

Mack swiped through to the next photograph; this one had been taken closer to the depression, looking more directly down into it. Atticus saw what looked like a bone resting half in and half out of a muddy puddle.

'Oh,' he said. '*Now* I'm interested.'

'We were contacted by a dog walker yesterday morning,' she said. 'He was on the Plain when his dog ran off. When the man caught up with him, the dog had *that* bone in its mouth.'

'Human?'

'Yes.'

Atticus took the iPad from her and zoomed in on the bone. 'Looks like a femur.'

'Female, we think.'

He squinted at it. 'Young?'

'Still to be confirmed.'

'Found anything else? Any other bones?'

'None. We've started to widen the search, but nothing yet. The first question we have is how it came to be there.'

'An animal. The bone's been scavenged from somewhere else and brought there.'

'That's what we think.'

Atticus sipped his pint. 'I read a report once. Foxes and badgers are the only wild animals large enough to affect a set of remains through scavenging.'

'You read a report on animals scavenging remains?'

'*Human* remains,' he clarified. 'And, yes, I did. You know me – I read *everything*. I believe this particular dissertation was from a student at the School of Anthropology at Oxford. You never know when information like that might prove useful. I store it away and then, when it might be relevant – like now – I have it to hand.'

She eyed him sceptically, although he knew that she found his voracious appetite for new information partly amusing and partly daunting; she'd told him the same when he'd tried to argue that a treatise on botany that he had read meant he could offer a solution as to when a body found on the banks of the Avon had arrived there. He had offered her a bet that he was right and the pathologist was wrong, and she had taken it. The body, as he recalled, had been found on a bed of Himalayan balsam, a species that died back every winter to regrow in the spring. Atticus had examined the flattened stems and estimated the balsam was four months old, which meant that, judging from the regrowth that had taken place, it was likely the body had been lying there for two months. Subsequent investigation was to prove his supposition was correct. Mack had grudgingly accepted that she had lost the bet and bought him dinner.

'Let's have it, then,' she said.

'The researchers used dead pigs and deer when they were testing their hypotheses. Foxes were found to scavenge the deer more frequently than badgers. Individual foxes were capable of removing a whole deer, and moved smaller items – bones, for example – over long distances.'

'How far?'

'Miles. I'm sure that's not what you want to hear, but I think you might have to expand your search area.'

'You know how big Salisbury Plain is?'

'Three hundred square miles. But I think we might be able to narrow the radius a little. I'd be happy to come out and take a look.'

She winced. 'Might be a *bit* tricky.'

'Because of that little misunderstanding?'

'I'm not sure it was a misunderstanding. You were fired.'

'Semantics.'

'You were fired, and then you drove a coach and horses through the Mallender investigation.'

'Thereby preventing an innocent man from spending the rest of his life behind bars.'

'And embarrassing the chief superintendent in the process.'

'The man has thin skin. What can I say?'

She eyed him. 'Let's say I could swing it. You think you might be able to help?'

'Possibly.'

'Can't you just *tell* me what you think?'

'I'll need to have a look at where you found the bone before I put my reputation on the line.'

The waitress returned with their food. Atticus picked up the burger and took a bite.

'What are you doing tomorrow morning?' Mack asked him.

Atticus had planned to go over and see James York, but he knew Mack would be up early. He could go to see the dig site with Mack and still visit York before lunch. And, he knew, he would find a mystery like this much more intriguing than tracking down a missing girl. One task was mundane and ought to be easy; the other was interesting and given added piquancy by offering him the chance to help the police. It wasn't altruism; it was the opportunity to show them what they were missing.

He chewed and swallowed. 'Would have to be early.'

'Six?'

'Okay.'

'Do you have boots?'

'I do.'

'You'll need them. It's a quagmire with all this rain. I'll pick you up at six.'

PART II
TUESDAY

7

Atticus's alarm sounded at half five, and his first thought was to ask himself why he had agreed to meet Mack at such an ungodly hour. He didn't have a shower and had been using the facilities of the gym near the Maltings whenever he decided he was too fragrant to put it off any longer. No time for that today, so he filled the basin with warm water and used that to wash, drying himself off and dressing in a Tool T-shirt that exposed the sleeves of tattoos down both arms; the designs ran from his shoulders all the way down to his wrists.

He opened the cabinet and took out the plastic bottles of Ritalin and Cipralex, shook out his daily pills and swallowed them with a mouthful of tepid water from the tap. The bottles were both less than a third full, and he reminded himself that he would need to go to the doctor for a refill. He had learned, to his cost, that bad things happened when he was off his meds, and he was not about to sabotage the progress that he had made over the course of the last few months. He ran his fingers through his hair, trying to tease out the worst of the tangles, and, happy – or as happy as he ever was – with the way that he looked, he went back into the office for his leather jacket.

He found his boots in the back of the cupboard with his wet-weather gear. He looked out of the window, saw the sky was still dark with clouds, and decided to take it all with him. He changed into the boots and stuffed his waterproofs into a rucksack. Bandit bounced around him excitedly, mistaking his sudden activity for the prelude to a walk.

'Somewhere different for your walk this morning,' he said to the dog. 'Excited?'

The dog beat his tail happily.

'Me too.'

Atticus clipped Bandit's lead to his collar and led him down to the street just as Mack was pulling up in her battered old Range Rover. She pressed the button to open the back, and Bandit bounded inside, curling up and laying his head on his paws. Atticus unclipped the lead, ruffled the dog's fur and went around to get in next to Mack.

'He'll be a good boy,' he said. 'You never know – he might find another bone.'

She put the Range Rover into gear and pulled out. 'I just called the station,' she said. 'We've had a couple of lads out on the Plain all night.'

'Any developments?'

'It was too dark to search,' she said. 'They've just been making sure the scene is secure.'

Mack drove them out of the city. She turned on the radio, punching the buttons on the old unit until she had found

Radio 2. The forced jollity of the DJ and her guests felt incongruous given the dark skies and what they would find at their destination.

* * *

Mack turned off the B390 at Chitterne Anstey and drove north. They passed signs indicating that the land ahead of them was restricted but Mack ignored them and followed a narrow aggregate track onto the Plain. The Range Rover handled the terrain without too much difficulty, although Atticus could see stretches of mud to the left and right that might have proven to be more of a challenge even for a four-by-four. There was a collection of vehicles by three large beech trees, and Mack parked there, next to a van with a stencil that identified it as belonging to Wiltshire Police Forensic Services. She killed the engine just as the rain started to fall, and pointed out through the windscreen.

'We're going just behind the hawthorn over there.'

They got out. Atticus put on his waterproofs, went to the back of the Range Rover and opened the door to let Bandit out. The dog looked left and right, his tail wagging vigorously, no doubt enthused by the prospect of all of this space in which he could run and explore. Atticus clipped the lead to his collar and held on tight as Bandit strained at it.

Mack led the way. They passed around the edge of the hedge and then descended into the hollow where the bone had been found. It was now being treated as a major crime scene. The boundary had been extended, with blue-and-white tape tied to a series of metal posts that laid out a wide perimeter. Mack signed the log for them both and held the tape for Atticus to duck beneath.

'Where's the bone now?' Atticus said.

'The mortuary. Fyfe is running tests to date it.'

'But it was found down there?'

'Yes.'

'Did the dog walker say if the dog had moved it?'

'He said it didn't. He was clear about that. He saw the dog come down here without the bone, and then she had it. If she moved it, it wasn't by much.'

A man wearing a protective forensic suit came over to meet them.

'Simon Chester,' he said. 'You must be DCI Jones?'

'That's right. And this is Atticus Priest.'

Chester looked at him. 'What do you do?' he said, a little sniffy.

'The DCI asked me to come down to help. Now – what are your conclusions so far? Is it human?'

Chester looked to Mack for approval; she nodded that he should answer the question. 'We believe so.'

'And how did it get here?'

'That's what we're trying to ascertain.' He paused, confused. 'I'm sorry. You didn't say what you do.'

Atticus didn't answer. 'Could you hold my dog for a moment?'

Chester was too bewildered to protest and took Bandit's lead. Atticus took out his phone, selected the compass and found north. He made his way around the edge of the hollow, slowly moving between the ferns and bushes, all of his attention focused on the muddy ground at his feet. Mack and Chester watched. The mud became irrelevant, save that he was careful where he stood. The ground was damp and muddy, and Atticus doubted that he would be able to distinguish anything from the morass of prints that had been left by the officers who had attended the scene. Still, he swept left and right, up and down the slope of the hollow, at one point pushing his way between the branches of a hawthorn.

'What are you looking for?' Chester asked.

Atticus was too engrossed in his work to answer, and, before Chester had the chance to repeat his question, he stopped and pointed. '*There.*'

'What is it?' Chester said.

There was a collection of bushes, close together but with enough space between them to allow for a small animal to pass. Atticus dropped to his knees, splashing in a muddy puddle but oblivious to it. He lowered himself until he was directly over the tracks that proceeded from between the bushes and then down into the hollow.

Mack knelt down next to him. 'Atticus?'

Atticus was too engrossed by what he had seen on the ground to answer.

Chester tied Bandit's lead to the trunk of a sapling. 'What is it? What have you found?'

'Here,' Atticus said. 'Look.'

He pointed to a collection of prints that emerged from between the bushes, and gestured to the clearest print.

'See? Indentations made by four pads and, there at the front of the print, four claws.'

Mack nodded. 'I see it.'

'We won't be able to follow the tracks to where the bone was found because, alas, the ground has been churned up by the flatfoots who've been tramping around without thinking of what they're doing.'

'Wait *just* a moment,' Chester began to protest.

Atticus silenced him with an upturned hand. 'It doesn't matter. We know where the animal went *to* from this point: it went down into the hollow where it left the bone. The question is where it came *from*.'

'How do you know there's not another dog involved?' Chester said.

'It's a fair point,' Mack added. 'There are walkers out here all the time. Couldn't another dog have found it and moved it?'

'No. Look.' Atticus found a small, straight twig and placed it across the middle of the print, along the tops of the two outermost toes. 'Dogs and foxes both have five pads on their front and back paws: two in front, two to the side and one at the back. With a fox track you'd usually see a gap between the rear of the two front pads and the rear of the two outer pads – the line of the stick should run between them without touching, and it does. The outer pads of a dog usually overlap the front ones, so the line would run across them. This is a fox – one hundred per cent.'

'So a fox was here,' Chester said. 'That doesn't tell us anything.'

'You're not looking carefully enough. *Here*.'

He took another, longer stick and pointed it down, holding it just below the lowest branches. Mack dropped down to her knees and bent down enough so that she could look at what Atticus was indicating. A straight track had been scored through the mud next to the prints. It was too dark in the underbrush to see how far the mark extended into the brush, but the track was clearly visible in the opposite direction until it reached the lip of the hollow. From that point on, it, together with the paw prints, was lost in the mess and jumble of boot prints from the attending officers.

'What is that?' she asked.

'A fox would struggle to hold an adult femur in its mouth so that none of it touched the earth,' Atticus said. 'It would have to drag it instead, so that one end scraped along the ground.' He pointed at the track. 'Just like that. It was a fox, not a dog.'

'All right,' Chester said, not convinced. 'But where did the fox find the bone?'

'Indeed,' Atticus said. 'That is the question.'

He stood and went around the bush until he was able to find a clear space. He dropped down on his hands and knees and examined the grass and mud at close proximity, his face lowered so that he was just a few inches from the ground. He searched for several minutes until he let out an exclamation of satisfaction.

'*There,*' he said, pointing down. 'And *there* and *there*. See?'

Mack looked. Atticus indicated the indentations in the grass and mud: paw prints and, in the mud, the same scored line. He opened the map on his phone. He put his forefingers on the screen and dragged down, scrolling the map to the north and the wide-open green space of the Plain. He turned the phone around so that Mack could look at the screen.

'We're here,' he said, indicating the icon that denoted their location. 'The fox approached from the north.'

He switched to satellite view so that he could take the terrain into account. The Plain was crisscrossed by a lattice of seemingly random tracks, with rows of trees and hedges delineating the patchwork fields. He moved his finger across the map until he reached the only settlement that was visible. The legend on the map relayed the name of the settlement – Imber – and showed a collection of buildings gathered on either side of a road.

'I'd look there,' he said.

Mack looked. 'You know where that is, don't you?'

'I do,' he said. 'Have you been?'

'Never. The Army only opens it now and again.'

'I've been. It's a very interesting place.'

'But no one's lived there for years.'

'*Seventy* years,' he said, enlarging the map and then centring it on a building at the south-eastern edge of the village. 'But I was thinking, where might a human bone found in the middle of Salisbury Plain have come from? And then I remembered the church.'

'A church with a graveyard?'

'Yes.' He zoomed in closer, the legend on the map identifying St Giles's Church. 'Two miles to there from here.'

Chester shook his head. 'You think a fox dragged the bone for two miles?'

'They've been observed moving scavenged food much further than that.'

The anthropologist shook his head, making no effort to disguise his disdain. 'I *really* don't think so.'

'Fine. You stay and wallow in the mud, but you'll be wasting your time. Your body isn't here. I'll go and find it for you.'

Atticus stood and looked to the north. The Plain stretched away, climbing to a shallow ridge that rendered everything beyond it invisible. He unhooked Bandit's lead from the tree and turned to Mack.

'Coming?'

8

They went back to the Range Rover. The narrow track headed to the north, but Mack said that she had been warned about the increasing possibility of unexploded ordnance the deeper into the Plain one wandered. It was safer to take the B390 and then the A360 to Gore Cross and follow the road west until it reached the settlement of Imber.

Atticus listened as Mack telephoned the station and asked them to make contact with the Defence Infrastructure Organisation, the body that was responsible for maintaining the military's facilities on the Plain, so that permission to visit the settlement could be arranged. Atticus told her what he knew about Imber as they headed north.

'There's been a settlement since before the Iron Age. The War Office started purchasing parcels of land around it from the beginning of the twentieth century. Some landowners sold up; others stayed. They bought it all, in the end. Said they needed it for training during the Second World War. They used the whole Plain for D-Day exercises. The locals were promised the opportunity to return to their homes once the war was done, but, of course, they got screwed over.'

'And since then?' Mack said as she turned off the main road.

'The Army kept the village and used it to train soldiers in urban warfare. Most of the old buildings are still there – the church, the school, the manor house, the pub. The Army has put up other buildings to simulate modern built-up areas. There's a couple of blocks of council housing and other buildings they use to practise clearing houses. They use Copehill Down for that now, too, but Imber's still important.'

'When did you visit?' she asked him.

'Couple of years ago,' he said. 'They have buses take people from Warminster. I thought it might be interesting.'

They reached a junction. A series of signs had been erected on a metal pole: one warned of tanks, and another of unexploded military debris. A paved road curved off to the left, bending around to a series of farm buildings and then continuing to the village beyond. Mack rolled onto the road and continued south. They reached the outer perimeter of the village after another mile.

'That's where they park the buses,' Atticus said, pointing at a bus stop that advertised Warminster.

Mack pulled over next to the sign. Atticus got out and opened the back so that Bandit could leap down, then clipped on his lead and looked around. Imber was in the foot of a deep, wooded valley. Atticus had seen pictures from before the Army had taken over. There had been a post office, a smithy, a pub – the Bell Inn – and a church with a substantial vicarage. There were five farms on the Plain that had offered work to the inhabitants. There had even been a cricket team. He had seen photographs of the men and women who had lived here, folk in their Sunday best, smiling for the camera. That was *then*, though, and the story was different now. There was a feeling of sadness in the air, a sense of melancholy that a village that would once have been busy was now deserted and bleak and unloved.

'The church is over there,' Atticus said, pointing.

They were about to set off when they heard the buzz of an engine and turned to see a quad bike approaching them from the road that led into the village. The bike pulled over, and a man wearing waterproofs and knee-high boots stepped off it and raised a hand as they approached.

'DCI Jones?' he said.

Mack nodded. 'Morning.'

The man shook Mack's hand and then turned to Atticus. 'And you are?'

'Atticus Priest.'

'Police?'

'He's working with me,' Mack said.

The man put out his hand, and Atticus shook it. 'Major George Slaney,' he said. 'I work for the DIO. I'm the training safety officer responsible for Imber and this part of the Plain.'

'And you got the call?' Mack said.

Slaney nodded. 'You're lucky I was in the area. We've had hare coursers out on the range. I've been trying to catch them before they get themselves shot or blown up.'

'Are you firing today?'

'Not until your officers are safely out of the way.'

'Yes,' Mack said. 'Sorry about that.'

'No need to apologise. The Army is as keen as you are to get to the bottom of what's been found. A bone, wasn't it?'

'It was. There's not much more to say about it at the moment.'

'So why do you want to look around the village?'

'I think it's possible that the bone came from here,' Atticus said. 'Specifically, the churchyard. We'd like to check.'

'Well, we can certainly do that. This way.'

They set off, heading south through the village. The road around which the settlement had grown up was in the shape of a lazy S. The church was at the bottom of the S, and they had parked at the top. They passed a collection of unfinished brick-built two-storey houses, three rows with five houses in each row, their doorways and windows left open to the elements.

'What are they used for?' Mack asked.

'To simulate Belfast, originally,' the major said. 'Then it was Balkan villages, and after that Basra and Sangin. Nowadays it's Mali and South Sudan. It's been very versatile over the years.'

Atticus gestured to the sky. 'Not very African today.'

'We make it as realistic as we can. But there are some things we can't change.'

They continued along the road until they could see the tower of St Giles's Church. A narrow, paved pathway cut between two fields and then through yew hedges until they reached a chain-link fence and a gate that was fastened with a padlock. Slaney took out a hefty bunch of keys, unlocked the gate and stood aside to let them through.

'How old is it?' Mack asked.

'Eight hundred years,' Atticus said. 'The nave was built at the end of the thirteenth century.'

'Is it still used?'

'They have services here four or five times a year,' Slaney said. 'The church took over the upkeep. It's in pretty good nick.'

Bandit strained against the lead. 'Is it safe to let him off?'

'It's fine,' Slaney said.

Atticus unclipped the lead, and Bandit shot away from them, disappearing around the corner of the church.

'Do you know what you're looking for?' Slaney asked.

'Any sign that the ground has been disturbed,' Atticus said.

'Take as long as you like.'

Mack led the way into the churchyard. She went left, and Atticus went right. The building looked to be in good condition and, as he started to skirt around it, Atticus noted that the graveyard also looked well tended. The grass had been trimmed, and the gravestones and tombs, although often more than a hundred years old, were largely intact. He completed his half of the circuit without seeing anything that suggested that the graves had been disturbed.

He met Mack halfway around. 'Anything?'

'No,' she said, shaking her head.

Atticus frowned. This had always been a hunch, but he was disappointed nonetheless. Bandit trotted up to him and waited while Atticus reattached the lead.

Slaney was waiting for them at the gate. 'Did you find anything?'

'No,' Mack said. 'Nothing.'

They passed through the fence, and Slaney secured the gate with the padlock once again. 'Is there anything else you want to see?'

Atticus stopped and scrubbed his fingers through his hair. 'There's another church, isn't there?'

'There was a Baptist chapel, but the building was demolished in the seventies. There's nothing there now.'

'Did it have a graveyard?'

Slaney nodded. 'Still there.'

'We need to look.'

'We're going back that way to where we parked. I think I've got the key with me.'

Slaney led the way back to the road and then turned left, headed north-west. They passed the spot where they had parked their vehicles and continued, turning left again and descending a grassy slope to an area that had been sealed off with more chain-link fencing. Slaney took out his bunch of keys, sorted through it until he found the one he wanted, and then used it to open the padlock that sealed the gate.

Bandit was pulling hard again, and Atticus leaned down to let him off. The dog bounded off, quickly disappearing behind two tall yew trees that looked to have been growing there for years. Atticus stepped inside the gate and looked around. The graveyard here had been allowed to fall into a state of some disrepair, quite different from the churchyard at St Giles. It was difficult to guess how many burial plots there were; Atticus counted ten headstones that were still standing, but there was evidence of others that had fallen down or been removed. The stones were waist high with weeds and covered with moss and lichen.

'I don't see anything,' Mack said.

Atticus stepped closer to a gravestone and laid his hand atop it. The inscription was for James Daniels and Eliza Daniels, who had died in 1920 and 1926. He sucked his teeth and was ready to abandon their trip as fruitless when he heard Bandit's excited bark. It was coming from behind the stand of yew. Atticus led the way, pushing between a tangle of bramble that had grown up in the spaces between the trees. Mack followed, with Slaney behind.

Bandit was standing next to a patch of ground that had been disturbed. This wasn't the rummaging of an animal, but a much more significant displacement of earth. A shallow crater had been torn out, and clods of earth, still topped by vivid clumps of grass, had been tossed around in all directions.

Slaney shook his head. 'Looks like it's been hit by a mortar.'

Mack gestured to the crater. 'And that's not supposed to happen?'

'Certainly not. The whole village is off the range for that kind of ordnance. Something landing here could only be because of a serious mistake. There'll have to be an investigation. There'll probably be a court martial at the end of it.'

Atticus drew nearer to the crater. It wasn't deep – likely reaching just up to his knee – and not particularly wide, either. The mortar, if that was what had caused it, had struck it only a glancing blow, with the detonation firing laterally rather than straight down. A gravestone had been split in half, its jagged stump standing in place like a rotten tooth. Bandit was at the edge of the slope, his head pointed forward and one paw off the ground. His tail wagged excitedly.

Atticus went over to stand next to him and looked down. The earth was damp with moisture, and a puddle had gathered at the bottom of the pit. A handful of stones and rocks were visible, but it wasn't those that had drawn the dog's attention. Atticus saw a flash of white contrasting with the dull brown. It was a bone, long and slender, poking out of the fresh earth at a shallow angle. The visible end terminated in a bulbous shape that Atticus recognised as the head of the humerus, the long bone of the arm that ran from the shoulder to the elbow.

Mack arrived at the lip of the crater, and Atticus turned to her.

'Tell Chester that he can pack up and go home. We've found where your bone came from.'

9

Mack drove Atticus and Bandit back to Salisbury and dropped them off outside the office.

'Thanks for this morning,' she said.

He waved her gratitude away. 'What are you going to do now?'

'We can probably put this to bed. I'll speak to Fyfe – I'll need to get him out to confirm that the bone we found matches the remains in the cemetery, and that'll be that. What about you?'

'I need to go and visit my new client,' he said.

'The missing daughter?'

He nodded and opened the door.

'Let me know if you need anything,' she offered.

'It won't be hard,' he said. 'She'll be with a boy. You know how it is – I'll have found her by this time tomorrow.'

She said goodbye and popped the back for him to retrieve Bandit and his rucksack. The dog jumped down and followed Atticus to the passageway that led from the street. Mack pulled out, and Atticus raised a hand in farewell. It had been an interesting diversion, but he didn't kid himself; he had gone along in the event that there might have been an opportunity to spend a little time with Mack. More, he knew, he had wanted to impress her and, as he watched her drive away, he was satisfied that he had been able to do that. He wanted to revive their relationship, but didn't have the first clue how to go about it. Showing off might not have been the most adult of strategies, but it was all he had, and he'd never pretended that maturity was one of his special qualities.

* * *

Atticus changed out of his muddy clothes, cleaned his boots and left them next to the radiator to dry, and went to leave Bandit with Jacob. He said that he would be back in the evening, and that the dog had had his exercise for the day and would probably only be interested in sleeping.

He went to his car and looked up the address that James York had given him. His farm was outside Broughton, a small town just off the A30 on the route to Stockbridge. Atticus drove to the northern edge of the village, following his satnav's instructions to the narrow track he had seen when he'd googled the address. He bumped along the track until he reached his destination and looked through the bars of a wrought-iron gate at the property beyond. A sign next to the gate advertised the property as Hatfield Farm. The farmhouse and outbuildings were approached along a gravel driveway that was bordered by laurel hedges to either side. The drive widened in front of the property to provide space for parking and turning.

Atticus got out and buzzed the intercom set into the right-hand pillar.

James York answered. 'Hello?'

'It's Atticus Priest.'

'Oh, of course. I'll open the gates now. Just drive up to the house.'

The gates parted. Atticus got back into the car and edged through them. The buildings looked less impressive as he drew nearer to them. They were in a state of disrepair, with several of the barns close to total collapse. The farmhouse itself was in only slightly better condition; the roof was missing several of its tiles, and a ground-floor window had been covered with a plastic sheet. The drive continued around to the rear of the building, but Atticus turned into the parking area and slotted his Volvo next to the Ford Ranger that he had noticed the previous day. He got out just as James York emerged from the front door.

'Good morning, Mr Priest,' he said.

'Please – it's Atticus.'

'Of course. Good morning, Atticus. Thank you for coming over.'

'My pleasure.'

'How can I help you this morning? You said you wanted to see Molly's room?'

'Yes, please.'

'Can I ask why?'

'There might be something obvious that you've overlooked. It can be easy for parents to miss things that might be obvious to someone else.'

'Wood for the trees?'

'Exactly. I've been able to find people before by noticing little details that have been missed. And parents, I've found, tend to have a blind spot for those details.'

'Well, you'd better come this way.'

York led the way up a set of stone steps to a leaded, pillared entrance porch.

'Sorry about the state of the house,' York said. 'Money is tight at the moment. The last couple of harvests haven't been kind.'

'What do you grow?'

'Rape and wheat. It's not great this year, either. Did you see the fields on the way in? You could look at them and you wouldn't be able to tell if the wheat was a crop – it's so thin and patchy. The plants have got no roots. If we get a dry spell, they'll just wither away.'

'How long have you been here?'

'I've had the farm since 2000,' he said. 'It was my father's before. It's a slog. Foot-and-mouth disease nearly wiped us out the year after I took it on. The bank was a day or two from pulling the plug at one point. I've been thinking about whether I ought to diversify. I was hoping to add glamping facilities. There's an empty field at the back that'd be perfect for it. Molly was keen on the idea, before ... well, before all this nonsense.' He pointed to the stairs. 'Maybe when she gets back. Her room is up here.'

Atticus climbed the stairs and turned right into the bedroom immediately off the landing. It was large, with an en suite bathroom that Atticus checked first. He opened the cabinet above the sink and took out two bottles that were labelled with prescriptions: one was Seroxat and the other Roaccutane.

York was watching from the doorway. 'The Roaccutane is for her acne.'

'And Seroxat for depression?'

'She's a teenage girl. She has issues like any other teenage girl. The acne doesn't help.'

'Is she happy at college?'

'As far as I know. No one there has said anything to me.'

'And at home?'

York shrugged, a rueful expression on his face. 'Like I said, she's a teenage girl. There are issues every now and again, but nothing that you wouldn't expect.'

'Do you have a good relationship with her?'

'I'd always thought we did.'

Atticus put both bottles back in the cabinet and closed the door. He went into the bedroom and looked around. There was a piano keyboard on a stand, a desk that was stacked with books next to a notebook and pen, and a football in the corner. There were three framed pictures on the windowsill. Atticus looked at them one at a time: the first was of a teenage girl standing in front of Shakeaway in Salisbury; the second was of the same girl on an ice rink; the third was of the girl with two others of the same age. Atticus picked up the first frame, took out his phone and snapped a photograph of it.

'None of her with her mother,' he said. 'Why's that?'

'They didn't really get on.'

'Where is she now?'

'No idea,' York said. 'We haven't seen her since she left.'

Atticus went to the desk and examined the things that had been left there.

'Anything useful?' York asked.

Atticus laced his fingers. 'I see a well-rounded girl in her mid-teens, religious, bilingual, right-handed. She's also careful with money.'

'How do you get there from that?'

'The well-roundedness from the fact that she has a keyboard that's clearly well used, given the smudges of sebum from her fingers on the keys, together with the football. Proficiency at both music *and* sport is unusual in my experience. She has a copy of *Tout commence mal . . .*, which, unless my knowledge of young adult fiction fails me, is a French translation of *The Bad Beginning*, the first in Lemony Snicket's A Series of Unfortunate Events – that she has the French edition over the English suggests that she's a fluent speaker.'

'She did a year in France,' York said.

'The framed quote – "Your beauty should be that of your inner self, the unfading beauty of a gentle and quiet spirit, which is of great worth in God's sight" – is a Bible verse – 1 Peter 3, I think. Plus, of course, you're religious – that'll be influential.' Atticus gestured to the desk. 'The pen is to the right of the notebook; therefore, she writes with that hand.'

'Very good,' York said. 'The money?'

There was an iPhone box atop a stack of books. 'Most people don't keep the packaging for things like that. I suspect she sells them on whenever she upgrades, and she knows that having the original box will help get the best price.'

'She does.'

'And although I would say she likes to read, I suspect that she's lost the habit recently.'

'How can you tell?'

Atticus picked up the empty iPhone box. 'This hasn't been moved for a while. There's dust around it.'

'I would've had the cleaner come in here and clean,' York said quickly, 'but she prefers people to stay out.'

'I'm not making judgements,' Atticus said with a smile.

'Does any of this help you?'

'It helps me to build up a picture. Can I ask you a couple of questions?'

'Of course.'

'Boyfriends other than the one you told me about?'

'None that I know of.'

'Close friends?'

'Not really. She prefers to keep herself to herself – she's always been like that. There are a handful of girls that she sometimes hangs round with – I've written down their addresses. There's a list downstairs.'

'Have you spoken to their parents?'

'Yes. And they say they don't know where she is.'

'Any other reason why she might have left home?'

York looked helpless. 'I've been thinking about that ever since she left. I can't think of anything – I wish I could, but there's nothing.'

'What about the drugs?'

He looked a little awkward. 'Just joints, I think, but who knows. It's been a while since I smoked, but it's not a smell that's easy to mistake. She was doing it in the garden. You could smell it on her clothes.'

'You said you spoke to her about it?'

'The night before she ran away.'

'You were angry?'

'I tried to be rational about it. I *was* angry, of course, and worried, but it wouldn't have helped if I'd lost my temper.'

'So your finding her stash might have been the reason she ran?'

'Might have been.'

'Do you know where she got it?'

He shook his head. 'She wouldn't say.'

'But you can guess?'

'It has to be the boy she's been seeing.'

Atticus took a final look around the room. There was a wastepaper bin in the corner that, judging by the detritus that had been allowed to gather inside it, had not been emptied for some time. Atticus turned it upside down and tipped the contents onto the floor.

He picked up a tissue between thumb and forefinger and held it up. It was stained red.

'Does she suffer from nosebleeds?' he asked.

'Yes,' York said. 'But only recently. The last couple of months.'

Atticus picked through the rubbish, checking each item and then depositing it back into the bin. He found what he was looking for: a square of glossy paper torn from a magazine. The top third of the paper was folded down and the bottom third folded up, the left and right sides folded together to make a wrap. Atticus palmed the paper before York could see it, and finished cleaning up his mess.

'Why are the nosebleeds relevant?' York said. 'What are you looking for?'

'Anything, really,' he said vaguely. 'Something that could give me a line of enquiry.'

Atticus decided not to mention his suspicions now. He supposed that he might be wrong, although the evidence suggested that he was not. The mood swings and nosebleeds, all relatively recent, suggested that Molly might have graduated from weed to cocaine; the wrap confirmed it.

Atticus made his way to the door.

York closed the door and followed him onto the landing. 'What's next?'

'I'm going to go back to Salisbury and ask around a little. Someone will know where she is.'

'You'll let me know if you need anything?'

'Of course.'

'And if you find her?'

'I'll call you straight away.'

'Yes, please,' York said. 'She'll be annoyed if you approach her. I'd like to be there if you do.'

'I understand, Mr York. Thank you for showing me her room. I'll call you as soon as I have any news.'

10

Atticus drove back to the city but, rather than parking his car in its usual place, he diverted to the Friary. The area of the city had, at various times, accommodated a pesthouse, a smallpox hospital, and, until the middle of the twentieth century, the local sewage treatment facility. The sewage works had been moved and houses built in the sixties and seventies; since then, the estate had gathered a not altogether unwarranted reputation as a place that attracted difficult families.

He parked in Greyfriars Close and stepped outside. His dealer, Finn, sold from one of the three-storey blocks. Cars were crammed against the kerb on both sides of the road, and dog mess was smeared across the pavement. Atticus made his way to the entrance and pressed the buzzer. There was a pause, a hiss of static, and then a voice asked who it was.

'Where's Finn?'

'I don't know who you're talking about, man.'

Atticus swore and reached down to try the handle. He pushed the door, but it was locked. He raised his fist and slammed it against the wood panel. He heard the sound of raised voices from inside and someone clattering down the stairs. The door opened. There was a security chain, but it wasn't fastened, and Atticus was able to peer through the gap at the confused woman with a pale, sweaty face who was standing on the other side.

'Hello,' Atticus said. 'I'm here to see Finn. I'm a friend of his. He's probably on the top floor.'

The woman stared at him, befuddled. 'Finn's not here,' she said, with no conviction whatsoever.

'Excuse me,' Atticus said, and pushed the door open. The woman was slight and bounced out of the way as he shouldered his way through.

'Hey! You can't just barge in here.'

Atticus knew the layout of the house from previous visits, both as a patron and as a police officer. His introduction to Finn had been to arrest him, but he had soon returned as a customer. There was a sitting room and kitchen on the ground floor, with a staircase that ascended to two bedrooms on the first floor. There were a further two bedrooms on the second floor and a small bathroom on an abbreviated third floor above that. The front door opened directly onto the sitting room. Mattresses had been placed over the floor, and Atticus counted four junkies laid out across them. The blinds were drawn, and the air was heavy with the sweet smell of heroin. Atticus stepped over and between them, made his way to the short corridor that connected the front room with the kitchen, and went up the stairs.

He stepped over an emaciated cat that, for some reason, had decided this was an excellent place to sleep, and reached the first-floor landing. He picked a path through the stolen goods that had been swapped for drugs and climbed to the second floor.

One of the bedrooms on this level had been turned into another shooting gallery. There was no furniture – Finn didn't use the house for its intended purpose; instead, there were more mattresses. There was an en suite bathroom, but the two one-litre Coke bottles lined up against the wall, each of them filled with urine, suggested that visitors often preferred not to leave their repose when they needed to relieve themselves.

Finn, an Irishman who had migrated to London to work as a builder before finding his way south to Salisbury, was sitting with his back against the wall. A small camping stove was on the floor, and a man Atticus had not seen before was cooking up in its flame. Atticus looked at the clear fluid that was bubbling inside the spoon and the clean syringe, still packed in plastic, that would be used to deliver the hit. Once upon a time he might have been tempted to indulge, but he had done his best to put those days behind him. Still, he thought, it would not serve him to stay any longer than he had to. Temptation was a tricky thing, and he didn't mean to give it a chance to persuade him to partake.

'Hey,' Finn said in a thick brogue. His accent was always more pronounced the higher he was. 'I wasn't expecting you. You here to get some?'

'No,' Atticus said. 'Not for me.'

'You sure? It's good.'

'I'm sure it is, and I'm sure I don't want any.'

'So how can I help you?' Finn nodded down at the spoon and the flame. 'I'm busy.'

Atticus reached into his pocket and took out his wallet.

He opened it, picked out a couple of banknotes and held them up. 'Couple of questions.'

Finn's eyes narrowed. Suspicion was a dealer's default setting, and Finn had lasted as long as he had because he was particularly careful. He knew very well that Atticus had been a police officer before he had set up his new business, and that informing on others to the Old Bill was a sure way to land yourself in trouble.

'That's not me. You know not to ask me about my work. I'm not a grass.'

'No one's saying you are. You're not going to grass anyone up. And it won't take long.' He held the notes up and rubbed them together. 'Come on. Just hear me out.'

Finn looked at him, his eyes still narrow. 'What?'

Atticus took out his phone and navigated to his photo album. He found the picture of Molly York that he had taken in her bedroom and held the phone out so that Finn could see it.

'Do you know who this is?'

Finn stared at the screen. Atticus watched his face carefully and saw how his right eyebrow kinked up almost imperceptibly. Atticus had known Finn for long enough to be able to identify one of his tells.

'I don't know, man. Maybe. Might've seen her around.'

Atticus reached out and gave him one of the notes. 'Her name is Molly York. She likes to smoke, and she recently started to do cocaine. I need to find her. If she doesn't get it from you, you can give me an idea where she *does* get it.'

Finn looked meaningfully at the second note. Atticus gave it to him.

'Molly,' he said. 'Yeah. She's been here before. Used to buy off me, maybe six weeks ago. Like you say – weed. She used to come in with this guy.'

'Name?'

Finn scrunched up his face as he tried to remember. 'Jordan, I think. Jordan Lamb. He's only just got out of Winchester for dealing. Thinks he's a big shot, but thick as two short planks. The two of them came in together, maybe six weeks ago. They bought a bag and lit up downstairs. There was another guy here, long-standing customer of mine; he said that Jordan had grassed a couple of his mates up to the police in exchange for favourable treatment. Jordan didn't take well to that, and it got violent. I had to tell Jordan he had to go. Haven't seen either of them since.'

'So where would they have gone if they didn't come here?'

'The last I heard, he was getting it straight from London.'

'He was going to London to get it?'

'No, man, the dealers are down here. County lines. There's a gang from East London – Hackney, Bethnal Green, I don't know. They've got connections in the city now. You know how it works.'

Atticus *did* know: gangs in London sent dealers to provincial towns and cities on account of the fact that there was more demand and less competition than they would see at home. The locals were also less used to the violence and intimidation that were a stock-in-trade in the capital.

'And Jordan is caught up with them?'

'I heard they cuckooed his flat.'

Atticus started to feel a little more uneasy on Molly's behalf. If Molly had fallen in with a crowd like that, then getting her back might be more difficult than he had anticipated.

'Anything else?'

'That's it.'

'Where's Jordan's flat?'

'I don't know. He never told me.'

'You sure?'

'I have no idea.'

Atticus nodded and stood.

Finn reached out and took Atticus by the ankle. 'How's the dog?'

'Very good.'

'You don't mind having him?'

'He's excellent company.'

'I was thinking,' Finn said, eyeing him. 'Maybe you want to have him for good? I can't offer you money to take him off my hands, but I could let you have a bag of very excellent weed.'

'You don't have to pay me.'

'That's a weight off my mind,' he said. He reached into his pocket and took out a clear plastic baggie that was full of a fibrous, greeny-brown material. He handed it to Atticus. 'Seriously, take it. You're doing me a favour.'

Atticus took the bag, gave it an appreciative squeeze between thumb and forefinger, and slipped it into his pocket.

'If you insist.'

11

Mack spoke to Professor Fyfe and updated him on what they had discovered at the graveyard that morning. He said that he would do his best to expedite the matching of the bone with the remains and that he would let her know when it was done.

It had been a good couple of days. The Christmas Eve Massacre could, finally, be put in the rear-view mirror, and she had disposed of the question of the bone much more quickly than might have been expected. She had a long list of outstanding work that needed to get done, but at least she had a clear run at it now. She realised that she was thirsty and went to make herself a cup of coffee. The kitchen was empty, but there were three people in conversation outside it. She recognised two of the lads from the drugs squad in Melksham: DS Simon McPherson and DC Jules Horne. They were with a third person – a woman – whom Mack hadn't seen before.

'Morning, lads,' she said.

'Morning, boss,' McPherson said. He gestured to the woman. 'This is DC Jessica Edwards.'

Mack held out her hand. 'Don't think I've seen you before.'

'Metropolitan Police,' she said.

'Jessica is with Operation Orochi,' Horne said.

'What's that – county lines?'

'Yes, ma'am. We've had intelligence that a particularly unpleasant gang in East London is setting up shop down here.'

'We've got an address by the ring road,' McPherson said. 'We're just about to head over there and take a look.'

'I hope these miscreants take good care of you,' Mack said.

Edwards shook Mack's hand and followed McPherson and Horne to the exit. Mack went into the kitchen and flicked the switch for the kettle.

12

Atticus inhaled deeply to clear his head. Finn's house was thick with narcotic fumes, and the simple act of breathing the air had made him a little high. He went back to his car, opened the door and lowered himself inside. He took out his phone and called Mack.

'Find your runaway?' she said when she picked up.

'Not yet. What about your bone?'

'Still waiting for the tests to come back.' She paused, and Atticus could hear the muffled sounds of conversation in the background. 'Sorry – I'm busy. What's up, Atticus?'

'I need a favour,' he said.

'Oh dear.'

'Come on, Mack. You owe me. You'd still be looking on the Plain if I hadn't helped.'

'Go on, then.'

'It's not *strictly* legal.'

'What is it?'

'The girl I'm looking for either is or was having a relationship with a local dealer. The boyfriend went down for dealing, apparently – did time in Winchester. He'll have a probation officer. There'll be an offender assessment report. I'd be very grateful if you could take a look at it for me.'

'God, Atticus.'

'Just his address. The odds are good that my misper is with him.'

She sighed.

'Look,' he said, 'I know I shouldn't ask, but my client doesn't want the girl to get into trouble.'

'She should've thought about that before she shacked up with a dealer.'

'True. But she's seventeen. She made a mistake. Wouldn't it be nice to give her a second chance?'

Atticus heard the sound of conversation again.

'Okay,' Mack said. 'I've got to go in now, but I'll see what I can do. What's his name?'

'Jordan Lamb,' he said.

* * *

Atticus didn't have to wait long. He had only just parked the car again when his phone buzzed with an incoming WhatsApp message. He tapped the screen to wake it and saw that it was from Mack. There was no preamble, no salutation, nothing except the address of a property on Payne's Hill.

Atticus checked the map: it was just a short ten-minute walk away.

No time like the present.

He set off.

* * *

Payne's Hill sat just inside the ring road that encircled the city. It was a narrow street, just wide enough for a single car to pass, and set on a steep incline. The house on the corner was a grand two-storey residence from the late seventeenth century with a hipped tiled roof, dormer windows and an imposing six-panelled door with a rectangular fanlight. But that was not the address that Atticus had been given. The terrace that adjoined that grand building could not have been tawdrier by comparison; it was brick-built, with miserly windows and satellite dishes fixed to the walls. It was next to the subway that ran underneath the ring road and faced a row of six garages, their corrugated metal doors defaced by graffiti and the unkind ministrations of the elements.

There were windows at street level, and, as Atticus walked along the terrace in the direction of the subway, he took the opportunity to look into them. Some were covered by cheap net curtains, while others revealed spare and austere interiors: a kitchen with stacks of unwashed plates and dishes in the sink, a sitting room with an enormous flat-panel TV and children's toys strewn around. He reached the bollard that marked the end of the road and the start of the slope that descended beneath the ring road and turned back. Mack's message had said that Jordan Lamb's address was number 59; the recessed doorway was set back from the pavement and reached by a short flight of three brick steps. Numbers on the outer door indicated that it was for flats 57 and 61; number 59 had fallen off.

There was a panel set into the door to the right with three buttons and a speaker grille. Atticus pressed the button for 59.

'Hello?'

'Delivery.'

'What?'

'Delivery. This is 59 Payne's Hill, right?'

'Yes.'

'Jordan Lamb?'

'I don't think I—'

'I've got another dozen parcels to deliver before I knock off, mate. You want to take this one or not?'

'Hold on.'

Atticus stayed close to the door. He heard an internal door opening and closing and then the sound of footsteps. The door opened, and a young man looked out.

Atticus smiled. 'Jordan?'

'What? You said you had a delivery.'

'Sorry about that. I doubt you'd've opened the door otherwise.'

'Piss off.' He went to close the door, but Atticus was too quick for him. He jammed his foot into the opening. 'Hey!'

'I'm looking for someone,' Atticus said.

'Didn't you hear me? Piss off.'

'Molly York.'

'Who's that?'

He was a dreadful liar; Atticus did not need a careful observation to see that.

'Come on. I know you know her. Her father is worried. He's asked me to see if I could find her for him.'

'You're police, then?'

'No. I'm not.'

'You *look* like police.'

'I used to be, but not any more – I work for myself now. You're not in trouble – not yet, anyway. Let me come in and ask you a couple of questions, and then I'll be on my way. If you don't, I'll go to the police and say that you've been selling dope.' He reached into his pocket and held out the bag that Finn had given him. 'Like this. You wouldn't want them to find that when they came knocking, would you? I'm pretty sure that's going to be against the conditions of your parole. Right?'

Jordan shuffled nervously behind the door. 'Questions about what?'

'About Molly.'

'It won't take long?'

'Five minutes,' Atticus suggested with a smile. 'Promise.'

'Okay. Fine. Come inside.'

13

Atticus stepped inside the door and closed it behind him. The communal hallway was tiny, with the doors to the individual flats set out around him. The door to 59 was ajar, and Atticus followed Jordan inside. He found himself in an entrance hall with three internal doors. They were all open, and Atticus quickly assessed the layout: bedroom to the left, sitting room ahead of him – the kitchen must be through there, too – and bathroom to the right.

He glanced into the bathroom; it was in a disgusting state, with mould growing on the floor and a discarded tourniquet next to the toilet.

'Hey!' Jordan exclaimed as Atticus stepped around him and looked into the bedroom. It was barely habitable. Atticus saw a photo of Jordan with a couple whom he took to be his parents and concluded that this was where he slept. There was nothing of any immediate interest, so he left it and continued to the final door at the end of the hall.

'You can't just go where you want.'

The space had been converted into another bedroom, with a mattress on the floor and a cheap set of drawers that had clothes spilling out of them. The mattress was a mess of crumpled clothes and plastic bags, and the floor was littered with the dog ends of cigarettes and empty cans of cheap lager. The carpet was stained and scorched with burn marks.

The kitchen was to the left. Atticus went inside and saw that it had been left in an awful state. Rubbish had been piled on the work surfaces, the sink was full of dirty crockery, and one of the cupboard doors had been yanked off, leaving stacks of used newsprint to spill out onto the floor. Atticus saw a scrap of paper on the counter that looked familiar. It was a wrap; he could see a little cocaine residue gummed into the folds. He took out the wrap that he had found in Molly's wastepaper bin and compared the two; the typeface of the text that he could see was the same, suggesting that the wraps might have been made from the pages of the same magazine.

'Stop!' Jordan complained.

'I'm sorry,' Atticus said with a reassuring smile. 'Let me just ask you those questions, and then I'll be out of your hair. Do you live here alone?'

'Get *out*,' Jordan said.

Atticus held up the bag of weed that Finn had given him. 'Answer the question, or I'm going to lose this somewhere.'

'You'd fit me up?'

'It would be so much easier for both of us if you'd answer the questions.'

Jordan's eyes glittered with animosity. 'Fine. Yes. I live here alone.'

'Really? This isn't just you – all this mess? It was the guy who came down from London. Right?'

'How do you know about him?'

'I asked around, Jordan. I know other dealers – I arrested most of them at one time or another. You get a London gang moving into a quiet city like this and it's going to make waves. It's bad for local business. This guy – he told you that he was moving in?'

Atticus was fishing, but he was confident in the conclusion that he had drawn. Jordan was exactly the kind of person who fell victim to cuckooing. The London gangs looked for vulnerable locals who could be exploited, and Jordan ticked all the boxes: he lived alone, he had a habit, and he didn't have the money to feed it. His parole made him susceptible, too; he could be blackmailed, just as Atticus had demonstrated.

Jordan shook his head. 'Don't know what you're talking about. I think you should go.'

Atticus didn't move. He had been watching Jordan's face for a reaction, and the young man was too naïve and guileless to be an effective liar, especially not to someone as perceptive as him.

'Come on,' Atticus said gently. 'I know he's been here. He's been using your flat to sell drugs.'

Jordan glanced away. 'You said that you're not police?'

'I'm not. And I'm not here to cause trouble. I just want to find Molly. Help me out and I'm gone.'

The second mention of her name caused a flicker of pain to pass over Jordan's face.

'You and Molly had a relationship, didn't you?'

He nodded.

'And you liked her.'

Jordan bit his lip and nodded again.

'How did you meet?'

'I'd just got out of prison. I had a connection down here, and I started selling again. I sold to one of her friends.'

'And Molly liked a smoke, too?'

He nodded. 'The two of them used to come here. She's nice. Really pretty. We'd get high and listen to music.'

'How often did you see her?'

'A couple of times every week, after she was done classes; then she'd go back home.'

'Is she happy there?'

He shrugged. 'I know she had arguments with her dad. He caught her with a joint, and she said he lost his shit. She said that she'd been thinking about moving out, but that she didn't have enough money. She was going to get a job and save up for when she was old enough.'

'She wanted to move out because he found her smoking?'

'There was something else, too. She got upset one night, said that she didn't want to go home – she asked to stay. Slept on the sofa. She never said what it was.'

'Next?'

'Pepsi came down from London.'

'Who's Pepsi? The dealer?'

'That's what they call him.'

'Real name?'

'Shayden, I think.'

'Last name?'

'Don't know.'

'And he moved in here?'

'He wanted to sell, and he said that I could get mine for free if I let him stay. I didn't know he'd be here for so long. Didn't know that he'd be selling the other stuff as well.'

'What other stuff?'

'Everything,' Jordan said helplessly. 'Cocaine, heroin, crack. I didn't think I could get rid of him; then I was thinking maybe I could but maybe I didn't want to . . . You don't know what it's like – you couldn't, not unless you're a user. It's like medicine on tap. He totally knew what he was doing, giving me just enough to keep ticking over. He said they didn't want me to be gouged out, so he gave me a little tickle, just enough to get a bit of a buzz a few times a day, a little bit in the morning to get me going. I needed that. That little hit in the morning, start the day right. He knew it.'

'Is Pepsi violent?'

'Didn't do anything, but he threatened me. He said that if I caused any trouble, he'd beat me up. What was I supposed to do? He had a knife. He used to show me it when he was telling me how things were going to go. It started to get really difficult. I lost my car, and I thought I was going to lose the flat.'

'Why?'

'Because when you're an addict, and when there's someone in the other room with drugs all the time, any time you get dole money, or *any* money, you keep going into the room and buying it. I did that until I was skint. Then I sold the car, my stuff, everything. Having the gear so close by was too tempting.'

'What about Molly? How does she fit in with Pepsi?'

'She came over this one time, and he started talking to her. He liked her. She liked him. There wasn't anything I could do.'

'You must have been gutted.'

He looked away again. 'She's too good for him.'

'What happened?'

'He got her smoking this really strong weed. Chemdawg – super high THC, melts your mind. She wasn't interested in doing anything with me after that – it was always *his* gear. Nothing else would do. She started coming every night. Sometimes they would go upstairs, and I'd see that she was still here in the morning.'

'She'd stay overnight?'

'Now and again.'

'Where is she now?'

'London.'

'They left together?'

'I don't know. Pepsi left on Sunday. He said the police were onto him. He took all his stuff and disappeared. He was right. Old Bill came yesterday. Drugs squad. They're still watching me.'

'Why would you say that?'

'There's a car outside with a woman in it. She's been there all day. They must think I'm an idiot or something.'

Atticus frowned. He hadn't seen anything. 'What – now?'

'She was there when you came in – I thought you must've been with her.'

'Where?'

'She's not stupid enough to park right outside. She's on Barnard Street. Down the hill.'

Jordan was getting agitated. Atticus was nearly done.

'Can you still get in contact with Pepsi?'

'No.'

'Do you have his phone number?'

'He changes it all the time. They use burners. I don't know the new one.'

'Social media?'

He hesitated.

'Jordan, please – I'm not interested in Pepsi, and I won't say that we've spoken. I'm just looking for Molly.'

'I know his Facebook,' he said, still reluctant.

'That would be a good start. Could you show me?'

Jordan went into his bedroom and returned with a beaten-up iPad with a cracked screen. He woke the device, opened Facebook and tapped out a search, selected one of the results and then showed the screen to Atticus. It was a Facebook profile for Shayden Mullins. The banner image showed an image with two hooded young men pointing handguns directly into the camera. The profile picture showed a young black man, a bandana tied around the bottom half of his face, staring straight out with cold, hard eyes. Atticus took out his phone, opened Facebook and made the same search.

'Thank you,' he said. 'You've been helpful. If you hear anything from Molly, would you give me a call?'

Jordan shrugged. 'If she says she doesn't mind.'

Atticus took a business card from his pocket and handed it over.

'Are you going to find her?'

'That's the plan.'

'Tell her to come and see me,' he said.

Atticus looked around at the flat and thought of what must have happened here for it to get into this sort of state, and about what James York would think if he could see where his daughter had been and the company that she had been keeping.

'Goodbye, Jordan,' he said.

14

Atticus stepped out onto the pavement and turned to the right. Barnard Street was over a crossroads, leading down the hill towards the centre of the city. There were marked residents' parking zones on the left and right with no spaces available. All of the cars, save two, were pointing down the hill. The exceptions – an old BMW with a dent in the right wing and a Volkswagen – were at the front of the parked queue, pointing up the hill towards him, and, although it was a little too distant to make out any details, Atticus could see that both cars were occupied.

He walked down the hill and crossed over the junction. The occupant of the BMW – a woman in her late twenties – opened the door as he approached and stepped out.

'Excuse me, sir,' she said.

Atticus stopped. She had long blonde hair and a face that was very slightly rounded, with expressive eyes and a slender nose. She was wearing a pair of jeans with black leather boots and a chunky cable-knit sweater. Atticus glanced into the car: the rear seats were untidy with clothes, an empty cardboard box, discarded fast-food packaging and at least two parking tickets that appeared to have been taken from the windscreen and tossed into the back. The vehicle would have been expensive when it was new, but it had not been cared for very well. Atticus concluded that she was a woman of untidy habits and careless. She was likely too young to have purchased a sixty-thousand-pound car on her own account, suggesting that she had a benefactor; the lack of a ring on her finger indicated against a rich partner, leaving him to conclude that the car had been a gift from her parents.

'Can I help you?' he asked her.

'What are you doing here, sir?'

'I could ask you the same thing. Police?'

She took a leather wallet from her pocket and flipped it open. The crest of the Metropolitan Police was embossed on the left-hand sleeve, and a warrant card, complete with a photograph of the bearer, an authenticating hologram and the signature of the commissioner, was on the right. Atticus looked at the card. Her name was noted as Jessica Edwards and her rank was listed as detective constable.

Atticus glanced over at the Volkswagen as the driver opened the door and stepped out. Atticus recognised him: DS Simon McPherson. He had worked locally before going over to the drugs squad.

'Simon,' Atticus said, 'hello. Who's that in the car with you?'

'Jules Horne,' he said.

Atticus held up a hand in greeting; Horne, who evidently had recognised Atticus too, raised his middle finger in response.

Edwards noticed and, confused, asked, 'Who are you?'

'His name is Atticus,' McPherson answered for him.

Edwards frowned in fresh confusion. 'What?'

'Atticus Priest.'

Her frown deepened.

Atticus spelt it out for her.

'First time I've met anyone called that.'

'Not an unusual reaction,' Atticus said.

'Atticus used to be a detective,' McPherson said. 'I used to work with him. Until he was sacked.'

Edwards ignored the little dig and gestured up the street. 'Can I ask what you were doing in that house?'

'Looking for a missing person. A girl – name of Molly York, seventeen years old. I was told she was with the occupant of the flat.'

'Jordan Lamb,' she said.

'That's right. I'm guessing you're looking for Pepsi? Lamb told me he'd been there.'

'Shayden Mullins,' she said. 'That's right. We'd like to speak to him.'

'He's in trouble because of drugs?'

She nodded. 'I'm on Operation Orochi. We go after dealers from London who sell in places like this. There's intelligence that suggests Shayden was sent here to set up the distributors.'

'I'm afraid you've had a wasted trip. He's not there. Lamb told me he cleared out on Sunday. He got wind that the local drugs squad was onto him and moved.'

She swore. 'Don't suppose Lamb told you where Mullins might have gone?'

'Back to London. But that's all he knows.'

The detective leaned against the side of the car. 'I might as well go and have a chat with him myself.' She paused, then took out a card with her details on it and handed it to him. 'If you find this Molly York and he's with her, I don't suppose you could give me a call?'

'Of course,' he said. He reached into his pocket and took out one of his own cards. He handed it to her. 'If you do the same.'

Jessica put out her hand, and Atticus shook it. 'Deal.'

'Bye, Simon,' Atticus said.

'Goodbye.'

Atticus raised a hand in farewell to DC Horne and was rewarded with a second middle-finger salute. He set off in the direction of the office. He paused on the corner of Brown Street and looked back: Edwards and McPherson were marching up the hill to Lamb's property.

15

Atticus walked back to his office. He sat down on the sofa in the bay window and took his phone from his pocket. He opened Facebook and pulled up Shayden Mullins's profile. The biographical details suggested that he was a student, studying at Mossbourne Community Academy in Hackney, London. His place of birth was listed as Accra in Ghana, and his newsfeed showed a picture of a black woman standing next to the back of a pickup truck that was loaded with cardboard boxes and black bin liners. The woman was smiling at someone off camera, and Shayden's accompanying comment thanked her for bringing him up and wished her a happy Mother's Day.

There was nothing else of interest; perhaps Shayden preferred to use Instagram or YouTube. He opened Instagram and found Shayden's account there. He scrolled down to the most recent update. It had been posted yesterday at six fifteen and showed Shayden and another young black man standing in front of what looked like a tower block. The shot had been taken from a distance away, meaning that a good chunk of the building behind them was visible. The first fifteen or twenty feet was composed of red brick, with the remainder clad in some sort of smooth white material. It was the sort of building that was ubiquitous in London, with nothing visible that would have allowed Atticus to identify it.

He scrolled down to the next update. It was an amateur flyer for a party with a thumbs-up emoji beneath it. The party was advertised as Tappy Turnup and that it would be the biggest night in Hackney. The music included hip-hop, afrobeat, dancehall and drill. The location was limited to just E9; a caption suggested that if you needed to ask where it was, you weren't cool enough to go.

Shayden had left a comment that he was 'back from Cunch' and that he would be going to the party. Atticus didn't know what 'cunch' was, but Google did. It was county lines slang for 'country'. Shayden was telling his friends that he had returned from Salisbury.

The post had been liked by seven people. Atticus clicked on their profiles and scanned through their updates. The first five offered nothing of interest, but the sixth was more useful. It was from another young man, similar in age to Shayden. He started each day by linking to a music video featuring drill artists: loud, aggressive and violent rap. His post included the flyer, and he had added an accompanying caption beneath it:

Buzzing. Going to the Kenton.

Atticus opened a fresh search and looked up 'E9' and 'the Kenton' and got lucky on his first attempt: the Kenton was a pub in East London. He opened Google Street View and dragged his fingers around the screen so that he could see the pub's surroundings.

He got lucky again.

The pub was pinched between the intersection of Kenton Road and Bentham Road. The latter ran along the northernmost side of the pub; its entire length, all the way to its junction with Bradstock Road, was taken up by six identical tower blocks. Each block was decorated in exactly the same way: red bricks nearest to the ground and then white cladding up to the top.

The same as the tower block from the background of the photograph with Shayden and the other youngster.

'Bingo.'

16

Atticus spoke to Jacob and checked that he was okay to look after Bandit for a little longer. Jacob said that he was – he said the dog was currently lying on his bed with his legs in the air in search of a tummy rub – and didn't protest too much when Atticus insisted on paying him another twenty for doing him the favour.

Atticus went back to the office, found his leather satchel and stuffed in the things that he thought he might need for his trip to London: his phone, his MacBook, a Sony 4K Camcorder, an Olympus digital recorder, and a GPS car tracker that he had purchased from an entirely disreputable eBay seller. He went to his bookshelf and took down David Bronstein's *Zurich International Chess Tournament, 1953*, the classic recount of the Candidates' Tournament that led up to the championship match between the author and Mikhail Botvinnik. He looked out of the window and saw that it was still cold and damp; he opened the cupboard and took out the stainless-steel hip flask that his mother had given him several Christmases ago. He had a bottle of Glenfiddich single malt on the sideboard and, with the aid of a plastic funnel, he decanted enough to fill the flask to the top.

He screwed the top back on, added the flask to the bag, closed the zip and made his way down to the street. There was a train in twenty minutes and, if he was brisk about it, he ought to be able to catch it.

*　*　*

Atticus made the train with three minutes to spare. The station was quiet; it was too early for the return of commuters and too late for many people to want to head into London. He bought a ticket and stopped at the concession for a coffee, then found a seat in an empty carriage. The coffee was watery and unpleasant; he unscrewed the hip flask and poured in a measure to add a little extra warmth.

He took out his phone and opened the chess app that he preferred. He had a number of open games, and he saw that all of his opponents had taken their moves and were waiting for him. He was about to open the game at the top of the list when he noticed an invitation to a fresh game.

> *JACK_OF_HEARTS wants to play.*

Atticus stared at the screen. Jack had been one of his regular opponents until sending a series of unsettling messages at the conclusion of the Mallender case. Jack had known too much about Atticus and the investigation. Atticus, on the other hand, knew nothing about Jack at all, and he had found that disparity unnerving and deeply frustrating. He had never encountered a problem that he didn't want to solve, and this one had been a continuing source of irritation that had been exacerbated by Jack's subsequent silence. Atticus had sent invitations for new games, and Jack had ignored him.

Until now.

He accepted the invitation and watched the screen as Jack's first move was played. He or she – Atticus had no idea as to his opponent's gender – was playing the English Opening, moving a pawn to 1.c4 in a dynamic strategy that would limit some of Atticus's favourite counters. Atticus pushed his pawn out to e5 in the Reverse Sicilian defence and waited for a moment to see whether Jack was online.

The board remained static.

Atticus put his phone away, took Bronstein's book from his bag and opened it to the first page. It was one of the seminal chess texts, a report on a championship that had featured some of the best games of all time: Euwe–Smyslov, Taimanov–Najdorf and Keres–Reshevsky, among the most reproduced and analysed games in history. Smyslov had won the tournament, and Atticus wanted to analyse his games for new strategies that he could bring to his own online encounters. He took out his earbuds and popped them into his ears, connecting them to his phone and selecting his David Gilmour playlist. He took a sip of the distinctly average but now slightly improved coffee and found his place in the book, and, as the train wheezed out of the station, he started to read.

* * *

Atticus reached Waterloo and transferred onto the Jubilee Line. He rode it to Stratford and then took the 277 bus into Hackney.

It was a short walk from there to Kenton Road, and he took the opportunity to get a sense of the area. Hackney had been, until a few years ago, one of the less pleasant suburbs of London. It was known for poverty, and after that, just as night follows day, came its reputation for crime and violence. But, just as with all of the inner-city suburbs that were within a short bus ride of the Square Mile, newly arriving workers looking for somewhere cheap and convenient to live had dragged it out of the doldrums. There were coffee shops and boutiques now, and the cars parked on the crescent that fringed Well Street Common were expensive.

He reached Kenton Road and followed it to the pub. The Kenton was a two-storey public house at the junction with Bentham Road. The exterior was painted bright yellow with half-height windows and square lights on either side of all three doors. The cornice was painted grey with the pub's name picked out in white. The first floor had two narrow windows flanking a wider middle window that had recently been smashed, the glass now covered by a wooden board. The light was beginning to fade, and the series of tower blocks that overlooked the area prickled with lights in the windows. The nearest block – identified by a sign on the wall as Ravenscroft Point – had attracted a clutch of young men to the communal space outside the main entrance. There were half a dozen of them; Atticus watched them for a moment, saw a phone being shared around, and heard hoots of laughter at whatever was playing on the screen.

He pushed the pub's door open and went inside. The Kenton was a typical East End boozer. At some point in its history, it had clearly been a well-loved local, but, just as seemed to be the case everywhere these days, the present proprietor had taken the decision to update it to reflect the changed demographic in the area. The walls had all been painted, rustic furniture tried (and failed) to look authentic, and flamboyant touches – a gilt mirror, ironic statuettes on the bar – had been added. The beers on tap were foreign and expensive, and the Sunday roast started at £15. This was not aiming to draw in the working class, but, rather, the middle-class wage slaves who liked to pretend that they were authentic Eastenders, but really were not. This was a theme-park version of the East End.

Atticus went to the bar and waited for the tattooed and moustachioed barman to notice him.

'Evening,' the man said. 'What can I get you?'

'A pint of Estrella,' he said.

The man took down a pint glass from the rack behind him and started to pour.

'It's all changed round here,' Atticus said.

'Tell me about it,' the man replied. 'You been here before?'

'Never been *here*, but I know the area. Haven't been back for years.'

'Different now, I bet.'

'Unrecognisable.'

'The pub was done up a couple of years ago,' the barman said. 'I suppose it's all right.' He finished pouring the drink and slid the glass across the bar. 'Five quid, please.'

Five pounds for a pint. Atticus ignored the impulse to make a comment, took out his bank card and waited for the barman to ring up the sale.

'Can I get you anything else?'

'You might be able to help me with something,' Atticus said. 'I'm looking for someone, and I think they've been in here recently.'

The man shrugged. 'It can get busy in here, though. I wouldn't expect too much.'

Atticus took out his phone and opened the photograph of Shayden Mullins that he had grabbed from the young man's Facebook profile. He put the phone on the counter and turned it around so that the barman could look down at it.

He gave a little snort of disdain. 'That's Pepsi. He was in here last night. He's in the LFB.'

'The what?'

'LFB – London Field Boys. It's a gang – one of the main ones around here. Bad news.'

Atticus swiped to the flyer for the party. 'Was he here for this?'

'Yeah,' the man said. 'We've got a room in the back we hire out.'

'I need to find him.'

The barman looked at him suspiciously. 'What are you? Police?'

'No. Why would you think that?'

'Because you're asking about him. He's bad news – we had to get the police out to deal with him and his mates.'

'Why?'

'He was selling things he shouldn't have been selling. Why are you looking for him if you're not police?'

'It's not him I'm looking for,' Atticus said. 'He's been hanging out with a girl who's gone missing from Salisbury. Her dad hired me to try to find her, and I think she's in London with him.'

Atticus took the phone back and swiped through his photographs until he found his picture of Molly. He laid the phone on the counter again.

The barman nodded. 'Yep. She was here, too. Both of them.'

'You sure?'

'Yes,' he said. 'I had to tell them to leave because of the drugs. There was an argument. It got heated. They were gone by the time the police came, but as soon as they'd left, someone put a brick through the window upstairs.' He shrugged. 'Not unusual around here, unfortunately.'

'I don't suppose you know where he lives?'

'I don't. Sorry.'

17

Mack had been busy. She had called the station and requested that uniformed officers be dispatched to Imber to keep an eye on the graveyard until they were able to confirm that the bone from the Plain could be matched to the disturbed grave. There was no reason to suspect that foul play was involved, but Mack wasn't minded to cut corners. She had called Professor Fyfe to update him and, once that was done, she had driven to school to pick up the kids.

It was her turn. Daisy and Sebastian both went to Greentrees Primary School, not far from the family home in Bishopdown. Andy worked late on Tuesdays and Thursdays, and they had agreed that she would be responsible for collecting them and feeding them before he returned to put them to bed.

She parked the Range Rover outside the gates and went out to meet the children in the playground. Sebastian came first, his school bag slung across his shoulder and his scarf haphazardly knotted around his neck. Daisy was older and, although still just nine, she was developing the kind of sassy attitude that Mack's mother reminded her that she herself had exhibited at the same age. Daisy was with two of her friends, and Mack knew better than to interrupt them until Daisy had had the chance to say goodbye and come over by herself. Daisy had made it obvious that her parents and friends were not to cross paths; the former, she had said, were 'embarrassing'. Mack couldn't *wait* for her to be a teenager . . .

'How are you both doing?' Mack asked as she led the way through the gate to the Range Rover.

'Can I play on the iPad when I get home?' Sebastian asked.

'If you're a good boy.'

'I want to FaceTime my friends,' Daisy said.

It was clear that neither child was going to answer her question. Mack got the children into the car and made sure that they were strapped into their seats, ignoring Daisy's observation that the car was filthy. She was right. The exterior was plastered in mud and dirt from the excursion on the Plain, and Mack had never been particularly good at keeping the inside neat and tidy. She started the engine and pulled away, ignoring Daisy's commentary about how it was so humiliating for her to be picked up in something that was so disgracefully dirty. Mack smiled as she continued her tirade, happy to be back with the kids and looking forward to spending some time with them.

*　*　*

Mack parked on the drive and told the kids that they needed to get changed and do their homework before they played on their iPads or spoke to their friends. She helped Sebastian to hop down to the drive and took out her key to unlock the door, pausing when she found that it was already open. Sebastian wriggled around her and dashed inside.

'Daddy!'

Mack took off her shoes as her husband, with Sebastian in his arms, put his head around the living room door.

'Hi,' Mack said. 'Have I made a mistake?'

'No,' he said.

'You're supposed to be at work.'

'They let me out early.'

'Why? It's my evening with the kids.'

'I wanted to have a chat with you.'

'You could've called.'

'I tried that last week,' he said. 'You said you'd call me back, and you didn't.'

Mack remembered the series of texts that he had sent her. He had been vague about what he wanted to discuss, but Mack was worried that it wouldn't be good and had decided that if she ignored him, then perhaps the conversation – or whatever he was percolating – could be avoided.

'Okay,' she said. 'We can talk. Shall we wait until they're in the bath or in bed?'

'I think we should do it now. Kids – go up to your rooms and get changed, please. Mummy and I need a little bit of time to have a chat about something. Okay?'

The children clattered upstairs, and Andy led the way into the dining room. He looked nervous, his face pinched and bloodless, and Mack could see that, whatever it was that was on his mind, it was going to lead to an unpleasant conversation.

Mack sat down, but he remained standing. Mack looked at the table and saw a letter on the headed notepaper of a firm of family solicitors.

Mack knew what Andy wanted to talk about. 'No,' she said. 'No. We're not talking about that.'

'We have to, Mack. There's no point in pretending that we can get back to how things were before. I've tried, and it's no good. I just can't get past what you did to me. To the kids.'

'How many times do I have to say it? I'm sorry, Andy. It was a mistake. I regret it more than I can say.'

'I know,' he said. 'I believe you, too – I believe that you're sorry. But it doesn't make any difference. I can't get what happened out of my head, and I know that's not going to change. It ruined everything, Mack. I know you don't want to hear it, but you can't pretend that it's not happening. I want us to get divorced.'

'What about the kids? Have you thought about them?'

He frowned. 'I have. I think about them all the time, and I think we'll end up doing more damage to them if we pretend that everything is okay when it obviously isn't.'

'I don't agree,' she said, her temper flaring just as she felt the weight of reality pushing against the hope that she had spent so much time nurturing: that they might be able to put their problems behind them. 'You're not thinking about them at all. They need a mum and dad. You're being *selfish*.'

'Please,' he said. 'Let's not talk about selfishness.' Mack thought he was going to rage at her, but, instead, he took a breath, and when he continued, it was with a calm detachment that killed what small residue of hope remained. 'I've spoken to the lawyers, and they've drawn up the papers. They're on the table – you should take them and read through them.'

'No,' she said.

'You said we should think of the kids. I agree – we should. The best way to make this easy on them is to do this like adults. I don't want sole custody, and I don't want you to come out of this looking bad. I've spoken to John at work, and he said he got through his divorce with a good relationship with his ex and with his kids both fine about what happened. That's what I want. No aggravation – let's just accept it's got to happen and get it done.'

'No,' Mack said.

She got up, perhaps a little too quickly; she felt a wave of dizziness as the blood rushed to her head, and she reached out for the back of the chair to steady herself.

'Are you all right?' Andy said, taking a step towards her.

'I'm fine,' she snapped.

She turned her back to him and went back out to the hall. Both children were standing there, both wearing expressions of confusion and concern.

Mack crouched down in front of them. 'Mummy needs to go.'

'Aren't you making our tea?' Sebastian asked.

'I can't tonight, darling,' she said. 'I've had a change of plans. Daddy will look after you, and I'll see you both on Thursday. Come on – give me a cuddle.'

They both stepped into her arms and allowed themselves to be drawn into a tight hug. Mack held onto them until she was sure she had mastered the urge to sob and then let them go. She was aware that Andy was watching, but she ignored him as she opened the door and hurried outside. She blinked back the tears, holding herself together until she had reversed off the drive and was on her way down the road, back to the hotel.

18

It was dark by the time Atticus came outside again. The sun had slipped down beneath the terraces, and the street lights had come on, some of them flickering as the bulbs warmed up, others dead. He looked over to the nearest tower block on Bentham Road and saw that the collection of young men had grown smaller, with just two of them left. He zipped up his jacket and crossed the road, passing between the stone bollards and making his way toward the metal bench where they were standing.

'Excuse me?'

The two men looked at him without bothering to hide their hostility. They were younger than Atticus had initially thought – late teens or perhaps early twenties – and dressed in bulky jackets, loose jeans and statement trainers. They were both wearing caps and hoodies, too, their faces cast in shadow.

One of them had a red bandana around the lower part of his face. He pushed himself away from the bench and squared up to Atticus. 'What you want?'

'Can I ask you a question?'

'What kind?'

'I'm trying to find someone.'

'So, what? You a fed?'

'Sorry?'

'*Po*-lice.' He enunciated each syllable slowly and with sarcasm. 'Are you a police officer?'

'No,' Atticus said. 'I'm not.'

This one, with the bandana, was evidently the senior of the two, or at least the one with the most confidence. His body language was obvious: he had his head up, his posture was good – shoulders back, chest out – and his feet were planted in an open, wide stance. The second man behaved with deference to the first, and, although he was confident enough to hold Atticus's eye for a moment, his attention was fixed on his friend.

The man with the bandana took a step towards Atticus. 'What you want, then?'

'Are you LFB?'

'Man's asking about LFB.' He laughed, and the second man followed suit. 'What *you* know about the LFB?'

'I don't really know anything.'

'So?'

'I heard that the gang runs things around here. Is that right?'

The man with the bandana shrugged.

'I'm looking for someone who I think might be in the LFB. He's not in any trouble, at least not from me.'

More caustic laughter. 'Like we'd care about trouble from you, man.'

'Exactly.'

'So what do you want?'

Atticus had no clever line and concluded that he might as well just tell the truth.

'I'm a private investigator.'

More laughter, harder this time. 'Like, what – some kind of Sherlock Holmes shit?'

'Something like that,' Atticus said with a self-deprecating smile, happy to laugh at his own expense if it led him a little closer to the answer that he needed. 'I've been asked to find a girl, and I think she might be with a guy who lives around here. I've got a picture of him. Would you have a look?'

'You want us to grass for you?'

'You're not grassing. I just need to find the girl he's with.' He made a show of reaching into his pocket and taking out his wallet. He knew that waving money around was perhaps not the most sensible thing that he could do in a place like this, that the two of them might just as easily take his wallet from him as listen to his offer, but he knew that he wouldn't get anywhere unless he appealed to their mercantile instincts. 'I'm happy to pay you for your help. And it wouldn't go any further.'

Atticus opened the wallet and took out a wad of twenties. He peeled off one, and then a second and a third, folded them and held them between thumb and forefinger.

The man with the bandana put out his hand. Atticus held out the money, and the man took it.

'Show me the picture.'

Atticus took his phone and found Shayden Mullins's Facebook profile.

'Here,' Atticus said. 'His name's Pepsi.'

He turned the screen so that the two of them could see it and watched their faces for a reaction.

'Nah,' the man with the bandana said. 'Never seen him.'

His lie was obvious. Atticus had seen the minute nod of recognition as he had looked at the photograph, a subconscious reaction of which he wouldn't even be aware.

Atticus took out his wallet again and counted out another three twenties, reminding himself not to forget to include the expense on his invoice to James York. He held the notes up. 'I know you know who he is,' he said. 'Where can I find him? That's all I want to know – tell me, and the money's yours.'

'Make that a ton.'

Atticus took out another two twenties and added them to the three between his fingers.

'There's a trap house on Amhurst Road. Pepsi'll be in there.'

'What number?'

'162.'

'How can you be sure?'

'You don't need to know why. But we was in there an hour ago, and he was there.'

'Did he have a girl with him? Seventeen, white, dark hair?'

'No idea,' he said. 'Didn't see no one like that, but we weren't there for long.'

'Thank you.'

'Money.'

Atticus handed him the money.

'Now – piss off.'

19

Atticus walked to Amhurst Road. It was a mile to the north-west, in an area of Hackney that had not yet been airbrushed to the same extent as some of the other streets nearby. Progress was coming – some of the terraced houses were in the process of being converted into flats, with scaffold clinging to their façades and builders smoking roll-ups in the street as they finished off for the day – but, for the most part, it was much as it would have looked twenty years ago. The gardens were overgrown with bushes and trees, wheelie bins had been left on the street, and satellite dishes from the nineties were still fixed to the walls.

Atticus found number 162 and continued down the street, crossing over to the opposite side and a spot from which he could watch the house without drawing undue attention to himself. It was a busy road, with traffic passing in both direc-tions. Pedestrians made their way, too, many no doubt arriving from or going to Hackney Downs station at the south-eastern end of the street. Atticus observed as one pedestrian – a man in jeans and a military-style parka – opened the gate to the house, climbed the steps to the ground-floor door and disappeared inside. He came out again shortly afterwards – Atticus timed it at a minute – and joined the pavement again, stepping aside at the gate to let a woman climb the steps. The woman had arrived in a taxi, and the driver waited by the side of the road as she went inside, returning just as quickly as the first person Atticus had seen.

Atticus assessed them both. The man was down on his luck, judging by the state of his clothes and his shoes, which looked as if they were falling apart. The woman was more prosperous, with shoes that matched her bag, and hair that had recently been cut and styled. They might have been from different social strata, but they had one thing in common: both were anxious. The man walked stiffly, and as he passed beneath a street light, Atticus saw that his face was frozen; the woman stood at the gate for ten seconds before she went up to the door, transferring her weight from one foot to the other with the result that she rocked from side to side.

Atticus didn't need any more evidence that the property was being used to sell drugs.

He crossed the street, pushed the iron gate aside and walked along the short path that led from the pavement to the flight of steps that ascended to the front door of the ground-floor flat. The path was cracked by weeds that had forced their way through the concrete over time, and fractured by the weather and the weight of the people who had used it over the years. There was a second set of steps to the left of the path; these, more vertiginous than those ahead of him, wound down into a tiny courtyard from where a door to the basement could be accessed. The courtyard was full of cardboard packaging that had been dumped there – Amazon deliveries, pizza boxes, juice cartons, broken bottles – together with debris that had been blown off the street. There was a black bin that had been filled with too many bottles for the lid to close. The basement windows were covered with a blanket, with just a sliver of light visible where there was a gap between the blanket and the window frame. Atticus squinted down at it, but the gap was not wide enough for him to discern anything inside.

He climbed the stairs to the front door. It was painted a lime green, but the last coat had evidently been applied years ago, and the weather had been allowed to batter it unimpeded, peeling strips of it away like dead skin. There were two glass panels in the door, but the view through each was blocked by squares of newsprint that had been stuck on the other side.

Atticus knocked on the door.

He heard the sound of voices inside, and then footsteps. The door was unlocked – Atticus heard three separate locks disengaging – and opened a crack.

'What?'

'I'm looking for some gear,' he said.

'You what?'

'I want blow.'

'Sorry. Can't help you.'

The door was closed in his face.

Atticus sucked his teeth, looked back to the street, then back at the door. He knocked again.

The rigmarole was repeated. 'Piss off!'

'Come on, man, hook me up. I'm *desperate*.'

'Wait.'

The door was closed, but, this time, it was not locked.

Atticus waited on the doorstep, a little anxious that he was very visible to anyone who might be passing along the street. They weren't making a very good attempt to be discreet, and if the police happened to have the house under observation, then he might end up with some difficult questions to answer.

The door opened again, wide enough this time for him to come inside. The place was in a dreadful condition, much worse than the flat in Salisbury. The hallway was long and narrow, with stairs leading up to the first floor to the right and two doors on the left that, Atticus presumed, were for the kitchen and sitting room. The wall bore faded posters with Rastafarian imagery, including the Lion of Judah and portraits of Haile Selassie. One of the photos was of the emperor meeting the queen. The air was heavy with the smell of cannabis and the sound of hard reggae.

The man who had opened the door was young – Atticus guessed in his late teens or early twenties – and had a sheen of sweat on his skin. Atticus recognised him at once: it was Shayden Mullins.

'How much you want?'

'A couple of grams,' Atticus said. 'How much is that?'

'Eighty.'

Atticus took out his wallet. He withdrew four twenties and handed them over. Mullins pocketed them.

'Stay here.'

He turned and went through the first door on the left.

Atticus waited a moment and then stepped forward enough so that he could see through both doors. The second door opened into a bedroom that looked as if it was used by customers who had just purchased drugs. Four people were lounging on the bed, one of them missing an eye and another with prison tattoos inscribed across his naked chest. They were passing around a glass pipe, and Atticus could smell the harsh chemical tang of crack. The floor was covered with plastic sheeting that had been left there, Atticus guessed, so that blood and vomit and excrement could be more easily cleaned away.

Atticus looked into the other room. It looked to have been used as the sitting room at some point, but now it had been taken over by whoever was selling out of the house. Atticus saw a leather sofa that was piled high with electronics that had almost certainly been pilfered and exchanged for drugs. He took a step to his left so that he could see more of the room. Mullins was crouching down next to a fireplace, pulling up on a piece of string that appeared to run down the chimney to the flat below. He gave the string a final yank, and a Coke can clattered out of the grate; the top of the can had been sliced off and the string looped into it; Atticus watched as it was upended and two small clear packets fell out into the young man's hand.

Mullins stood and turned, and, just as he did, Atticus caught sight of the two other people who were inside the room. There was a mirror on the wall above the fireplace, and he saw the couple in its reflection: two teenagers, a black boy and a white girl. The boy had his back turned so that Atticus couldn't see his face. The girl got up and walked across the room to a fridge in the corner. She turned to look at him as she passed the door.

It was Molly York.

'What you doing, man? I told you to stay where you were.'

123

Mullins had lowered the can back down into the basement flat and was staring angrily at Atticus.

'I want my gear.'

'Maybe you're getting nosy, sticking it where it don't belong.'

Atticus didn't need to feign discomfort; he knew that he was in a precarious position.

Mullins looked at him with fresh distrust. 'How you hear about this?'

'Dave,' Atticus said, thinking quickly.

'Who?'

'Dave – he drinks in the Kenton. He said he gets his gear here.'

Mullins frowned, but, rather than interrogate Atticus further, he decided to favour the easier approach. He held up the clear plastic bags and, as Atticus reached out to take them, he left his hand hanging. 'Don't come back here no more.'

'Understood.'

Mullins put the bags in Atticus's palm and then put his hand on his shoulder and shoved him towards the door. Atticus opened it and stepped outside. The door slammed shut, and the locks were fastened.

Atticus descended the steps, made his way over the path and stepped through the gate onto the street. He allowed himself a smile of self-congratulation. Molly's dad had only instructed him yesterday, and Atticus had found his daughter already.

20

Atticus crossed the road and took up the same spot as before; he was obscured from the house by a parked van but would be able to see if Molly left to go somewhere else. He took out his phone and found the number that James York had given him. He dialled it.

'Hello?'

'It's Atticus Priest.'

'Mr Priest,' said York, his anticipation evident, 'have you got any news?'

'I do. Good news, actually. She's in London.'

York gasped with relief. 'Where?'

'Hackney.'

'Is she with you?'

'Not yet. But I'm outside the house where I saw her.'

'Is she okay?'

'As far as I can tell. I haven't approached her yet.'

'What's she doing there?'

'She's with a lad she met in Salisbury.'

'What lad?'

'He's a drug dealer. Your daughter met him through some-one she bought drugs from in Salisbury. She's in a house where drugs are sold.'

'God,' he said. 'What do you know about him?'

'His name is Shayden. He's nineteen. I don't know a great deal more than that.'

'Right,' he said. 'I'm coming up now.'

'Tonight?'

'Of *course* tonight. I'm not leaving her there for a moment longer than I need to. Can you wait for me?'

'Of course,' Atticus said, thinking of the overtime that he was going to be able to charge.

'What's the address?'

Atticus recited it and said that he would wait outside.

'I'll be there as soon as I can.'

21

Atticus put his earbuds into his ears, scrolled down to his Dave Gilmour playlist and hit play. There was a bus stop fifty yards down the road, and he had decamped there; he was still able to watch the house from that vantage, but was now too far away to reveal himself to anyone inside who might be looking out.

There was a regular flow of customers in and out; he counted a dozen men and women who turned off the pavement and made their way inside. They were a motley bunch. Most were younger, with the suspicious aspects of people always looking over their shoulders; mixed in within their number were a handful of more incongruent patrons, better dressed and more fearful as they raised their fists to knock at the door. They were within twenty minutes of the City here, and it did not require a great feat of deduction to conclude that these were professionals venturing out to get their fixes. Each customer went inside and came out again in short order, pausing at the edge of the pavement to look left and right before scurrying away into the night.

He kept an eye on the time, and it was just before half past eight when his phone rang. It was James York, reporting that he had arrived in East London and asking for directions to the house. Atticus told York how to find him and waited for him to arrive. A few minutes later, he noticed the blue Ford Ranger driving slowly along the road. He stepped out and waved it down. York parked next to the bus stop and gestured for Atticus to get in.

'Mr Priest,' he said when Atticus sat down next to him.

'That was quick.'

'I might have put my foot down a bit more than I should have.'

'Perfectly understandable.'

'Where is she?'

Atticus pointed to the house. 'In there.'

'You're sure?'

'I've been watching since I called you. I haven't seen her come out.'

'What about him? The man she's with – what's his name?'

'Shayden Mullins. He's still inside, too.'

York looked out of the windscreen, across the darkened road and over at the terrace on the opposite side. He fidgeted nervously. 'I don't know what to do. Molly's nervous at the best of times. The last thing I want to do is frighten her.'

They stared at the door together for a moment.

'So what do I do?' York said.

'I'd reconsider the police.'

'No,' York said, shaking his head firmly. 'That's out of the question. You said they're selling drugs in there?'

He nodded.

'So I call the police, they go in, who knows what they find. I can't do that. That would ruin her life.'

'Then we need to think of a way to get her outside. We ...' He stopped and concentrated on the house. 'Wait.'

York was watching, too. 'Is that her?' he said. 'It is. It *is* her.'

Atticus watched the girl coming down the steps of the house. It was dark, but, as she passed through the glow of a streetlamp, he saw that it was Molly. She was on her own and, as she crossed the road and started in their direction, he saw that she was crying.

York reached for the handle and opened the door. Atticus opened his door and stepped out, too. Molly was coming in their direction, and her father stepped onto the pavement and blocked the way ahead. Atticus watched the girl's face. Her eyes were red, and her cheeks were shining with tears. She looked up and saw her father. Atticus might have expected surprise or annoyance, but, instead, he saw neither. There was a blankness to her expression that was strange and unsettling.

Atticus stayed a respectful distance from the two of them, but, even from next to the truck, he could hear James York's words quite clearly.

'Where have you *been*? I've been worried sick.'

Molly was seventeen, at the age where the idea of parental authority would normally have started to chafe. Her attitude towards her father had been evinced by the fact that she had run away from him, but now, as Atticus watched, instead of indignation at being found, there was just resignation.

'Sorry,' she said, her eyes cast down towards the ground.

'I'm going to take you home,' York said.

He wrapped his arms around his daughter and pulled her into a tight embrace. His shoulders gave a shudder and, when he unwrapped his arms and turned back to Atticus, his damp eyes caught the light from above. He took her by the arm and pulled her gently to where Atticus was waiting. She didn't struggle or protest, and, as York stepped around Atticus to open the door, she slid inside without complaint.

'Thank you,' York said to Atticus, reaching out and clasping his hand. 'I'm very grateful. I've been scared silly ever since she left. I can't tell you how relieved I am.'

'I'm happy I could help.'

'Drop me an email tomorrow with your account. I'll settle up with you then.'

'Of course.'

York got into the front of the Ranger and started the engine. Atticus couldn't see Molly's face, but she did not look out of the car as they pulled away. The Ford edged into the traffic and started to the south.

22

Atticus thought of DC Edwards. He reached into his pocket and took out the card that she had given him. He had said that he would give her a tip if he found Mullins, and he could see no reason not to do that. He reached for his phone and was about to dial the number on the card when the screen showed an incoming call.

'Hello?'

'It's James York.'

'Is everything okay?'

'I'm not sure,' he said. 'It's Molly. She says she left her bag inside the house.'

'Ah.'

'It has her things in it. Her phone.'

'That's not ideal.'

'Is there any way you could get it?'

'Where does she think she left it?'

There was a pause; Atticus could hear James asking his daughter the question and a quiet, inaudible reply.

'She says there's a downstairs flat. It's in there.'

Atticus sucked his teeth. 'I don't think that's going to be possible. That's where they keep the drugs. I won't be able to get inside.'

'I'm just concerned that someone will find the bag and work out that she was there.'

'It's unlikely. They'll sell the phone and anything else that's worth anything; then they'll get rid of the rest. It's inconvenient, but I doubt it'll be something that causes any problems for her.'

'You're probably right. I thought I'd ask.'

He thanked Atticus again and said goodbye. Atticus ended the call and looked over at the house. He wondered if there was any way that he could safely get into the basement, but quickly concluded that there was not. Molly would have to get a new phone.

He dialled Jessica Edwards's number. She answered. 'Hello?'

'Jessica?'

'Yes. Who is this?'

'Atticus Priest. We met in Salisbury.'

'Oh,' she said. 'Hold on.'

Atticus heard the sound of movement and then a door opening and closing. When she spoke again, there was much less background noise. 'Sorry. I was just watching TV. How can I help you?'

'I've found your suspect.'

'Really? Where?'

'In Hackney.'

'How'd you do that?'

'I nosed around. He's in a house that looks like it's being used to deal drugs.'

'Shit,' she said. 'He'll be with his brother. His real name's Joseph, but he goes by Bars on the street. He's bad news. There's a gang down here—'

'The London Field Boys?'

'That's right,' she said. 'Joseph's high up. Are you sure Shayden was there?'

'I went inside. I saw him.'

She cursed again. Atticus noticed movement from the property and saw two men coming up from the basement flat. They paused at the gate, saw him, then opened the gate and crossed the road.

'I'll come over,' Jessica said. 'What's the address?'

The two men started to jog. They split up so that one went to Atticus's left and the other went to his right. Two other men emerged from the house. Not all of the streetlights were working, but there was enough illumination for Atticus to recognise Shayden Mullins. The man next to him bore enough of a similarity for Atticus to draw the conclusion that they were related; it had to be the older brother.

The four men converged on Atticus: one on either side and two in front.

'I think I've got a situation here,' Atticus said. 'You'd better call for backup.'

'What? Why?'

Atticus ignored the question and quickly gave her the address.

Shayden's brother stepped up to him, a gold tooth gleaming in his mouth. 'Who are you?'

Atticus left the line open.

'Who are you?' Joseph repeated.

'None of your business.'

'You ask around about my brother and then you come into my place? It *is* my business, bruv. I want a word with you.'

'I don't know what you're talking about.'

'Stop flapping your gums. You're coming inside whether you like it or not.'

23

Atticus had nowhere to go. The two men to his left and right took him by the shoulders and tried to force him off the pavement and across the road.

'Don't make a scene,' Joseph Mullins said. 'You and me need to have a chat.'

Atticus had tried to hide the phone in his palm, but it was forced out of his hand.

The man who had taken the phone looked at the lit screen. 'He's calling someone, Bars.'

'So *kill* it.'

'And if I'd rather not have a chat?' Atticus said.

'I'm not asking.' Joseph pulled up the bottom of his hoodie to show the butt of a pistol that had been pushed beneath the red canvas belt he wore.

'I see,' Atticus said. 'In that case, I'd be happy to discuss things with you.'

The two men to Atticus's left and right were both bigger than him, and he knew he stood little chance of resisting them. They marched him across the road, pushed him through the gate and then angled him off the path and down the steps to the basement door. The door opened into a hallway that appeared to run down to a kitchen. There was a door to the left, and Atticus was manhandled down to it. He allowed himself to be shoved through the door and into the room beyond.

He looked around. The bedstead against the wall suggested that the room might have been used as a bedroom at some point, but it had taken on a different purpose now. The mattress had been removed from the bed and replaced with a wooden board. The makeshift table bore the product that was dispensed to the customers who came into the house through the ground-floor door. Atticus saw little bags of cocaine and heroin and weed, crystals of crack, pills kept in jam jars. This was evidently a serious operation. There were two wooden chairs, a television that was showing a boxing bout, and a small glass-fronted fridge that was stacked with cans of beer and Coke. Bottles of Hennessy were arranged atop the fridge. The fireplace had been torn out, revealing the opening for the chimney. The sliced-open can that Atticus had seen in the flat above was on the floor, the string that was used to hoist it up hanging there slackly. There was an intercom on the mantelpiece that he assumed was used to communicate with those upstairs.

The two Mullins brothers came inside. The younger sibling – Shayden – crossed his arms and stared at Atticus. The elder – Joseph – pointed to the wooden chair in the bay window. 'Sit down.'

Atticus did as he was told. The men here were all young – teenagers, most of them, with Joseph seemingly the oldest and not by much – but he had no doubt that they would be capable of unpleasantness if it came to it. The two men who had frogmarched

Atticus inside stood next to him, one of them unzipping Atticus's jacket and rifling through the pockets. He took out his wallet.

'Who are you?'

There was no point in lying; they were already going through his things.

'Atticus,' he said.

'What?'

Atticus sighed impatiently. 'Atticus.'

'What kind of name is that?'

'I know. It's unusual.'

'It's *ugly*,' Mullins corrected.

'I wish you could've told my parents that. It would have saved me from answering so many annoying questions.'

The second man found the business cards in the wallet and squinted down at one. 'Atticus Priest,' he said. 'Private investigator.'

Joseph grinned. 'For real?'

'That's right.'

'Let me guess – her dad hired you?'

'Who?'

'My brother's ting. Her dad.'

'Molly,' Shayden said.

'That's right,' Atticus said. 'Her father was concerned about her.'

'I was watching you out of the window,' Joseph said. 'Was that him? Her dad?'

'That's right,' Atticus said.

'You stuck your nose in our business? You thought that was a good idea?'

'She's a child,' Atticus said.

'She's nineteen,' Shayden corrected.

'Is that what she told you? No, she's not. She's *seventeen*. She's a minor.'

Joseph's jaw stiffened and, for a moment, Atticus wished he had chosen his words more carefully. Atticus thought that he was about to strike him, but, instead, he smiled.

'You got a lot of nerve, man,' he said, his gold tooth glinting. 'You want to think about how smart it is to have beef with me? It *ain't*. Not at all.'

'I'm sorry if I caused you any trouble. I didn't mean to do that. I was hired to return a child to her father, and that's what I did. I don't have any other reason to be here. I'm going to go now.'

He stood up.

'No, you ain't,' Joseph said. 'We're not done yet. Sit back down.'

Atticus felt hands on his shoulders, and he was dragged back down onto the chair.

'Mash him up, bruv,' Shayden urged.

'Easy.' Joseph turned back to Atticus. 'Let me tell you some things you need to know. I don't take no nonsense from some white piece-of-shit *civilian* who thinks he can stick his nose in my business and cause me trouble. You feel me? Molly was here because Pepsi wanted her to be here. I don't care what her dad says – she can make up her own mind. You come in here, giving it large, then you jack his girl from him. No way, man. No way. Now you start pretending like you can tell *me* what to do, and all I can think is that you've forgotten that I'm the one with the piece and you're just some poor white raasclaat who's about to get popped.'

'I have no idea what that means,' Atticus said.

Joseph reached down to his waistband and pulled out the pistol. 'It's all right – I'll show you.'

'*Okay,*' Atticus said, his hands held up, palms forward. 'There's no need for that. I said I was sorry.'

'I'll give you a chance to make up for that.' He stood up and pointed the piece down at Atticus's legs. He aimed at his right knee, then at his left. 'Which one? You decide. Which leg you want to limp on?'

Atticus tried to get out of the chair, but the two men behind him held him down.

The intercom on the mantelpiece squelched, followed by an anxious voice. 'Bars? You there, man?'

Joseph waved a hand at the intercom. 'Answer it.'

Shayden went over to the mantelpiece, but, before he could reach it, the intercom squawked again. 'Skate! It's the feds!'

Joseph cursed and hurried to the window. The basement was below the level of the pavement, but the blue-and-red strobe of police lights was visible against the trunk and naked boughs of the tree that stood in front of the house.

'Shit,' he said. 'He's right.'

The room was suddenly full of panic. That was bad. Poor decisions were made when people didn't think clearly, and Atticus was still vulnerable.

'Listen to me,' Atticus said. 'You need to be clever.'

'What?'

'Do you have a way out at the back?'

Joseph nodded. 'Door into the garden.'

'You need to go. *Now.*'

'They'll be waiting for us.'

'No, they won't. This isn't a drugs bust.'

'Course it is – feds are outside, man. Why *else* they be here?'

'No, it isn't. I was on the phone to a police officer when you came outside.'

Joseph's face twisted with anger. 'I knew you were a fed.'

'And I told you I'm *not*. It doesn't matter. They're here because they think I'm in trouble. I'd be very surprised if they've had time to stake out the back. If you go now, you'll be able to get away.'

Joseph stayed where he was.

'You don't strike me as being stupid,' Atticus continued. 'They catch you with that gun and you know the minimum: five years, probably longer. You add in all that' – he swept his arm out to indicate the drugs on the bed – 'and you're looking at a long time to think about how you *really* ought to have listened to me.'

They heard a banging against the ground-floor door above them.

'Police! Open up. Open the door!'

Joseph turned to the others in the room. 'Out the back,' he said. 'Go through the gardens. No waiting – just go.'

They had been standing by for his order to go and, now that he had given it, they turned and fled. Joseph turned back to Atticus and pressed the gun up against his forehead. He leaned in, close enough for Atticus to smell the sweat and the tang of the dope he had been smoking.

'Lucky,' he said. 'You put your nose in my business again and I swear to God you gonna get strapped.'

Atticus clenched, waiting for Joseph to underline his point, but he followed his younger brother out of the door and towards the rear of the flat.

24

Atticus heard more knocking on the ground-floor door. He got up and exhaled, allowing himself to relax. It had been awkward for a moment, to say the least; Joseph was clearly unpredictable, and Atticus knew that things might very easily have gone a different way without Jessica's intervention. He assumed that she had called for backup and that there had been a patrol car in the area. If she had not, or if the officers had been delayed . . . Well, he concluded, that was something that didn't really bear thinking about.

He remembered what James York had said about Molly leaving her bag inside the house. He had said that it was down here, in the basement flat, and he saw a bag in the corner nearest to his chair. He went over and took it. The zip was open and, as he opened it enough to look inside, he saw a phone in a bright pink case. He tapped the screen and a picture of Molly astride a horse appeared as the wallpaper. He dropped the phone back into the bag, zipped it closed and went to the basement door. He opened it and stepped out, the blue and white of the police strobe washing over him.

He tucked the bag under his arm and made sure that his hands were visible. 'Down here,' he called out.

The head and shoulders of a male police officer leaned out over the wall. 'Come up here, please, sir.'

Atticus climbed the steps. There were two police cars parked up against the kerb, their lights flashing. A small group of locals had gathered on the other side of the street, gawping at the spectacle. There were three officers on the steps outside the front door, with another standing on the street.

The officer who had called down to Atticus met him at the top of the steps.

'What's your name, sir?'

'Atticus Priest.'

'Ah,' he said, nodding. 'Mr Priest, we heard you were in trouble. That right?'

'It is,' he said.

The officer introduced himself as DC Hutchings. Atticus explained what had happened: how he had located Molly York, reunited her with her father, and then been accosted by her boyfriend and his older brother.

Hutchings scratched his chin. 'Is anyone still inside?'

'The ones in the basement went out the back. I'm not sure about the rest of the property.'

'They're selling drugs inside?'

Atticus nodded. 'The stash is in the basement. They send it up the chimney and sell it on the ground floor.'

Hutchings nodded his satisfaction. 'We've had half an eye on the place for the last few days – you've given us grounds to go in and have a look around. The lads from the drugs squad are on the way.'

The officer called down to the man by the cars and told him to go around the block and secure the property from that direction. Atticus opened the gate and leaned against the trunk of the tree as a car pulled up behind the squad cars, and Jessica stepped out.

'You okay?' she asked him.

'Thanks to you.'

'I called the cavalry.'

'And I'm very pleased that you did.'

'Where's Shayden?'

'With his brother. They went out the back.'

Jessica was about to reply when they both heard the sound of a phone.

'Nice ringtone,' Jessica said with a smile.

Atticus wasn't up on modern music enough to be able to identify the tune. 'What is it?'

'You don't know?'

'My tastes lie somewhere in the seventies,' he said as he unzipped Molly's bag and reached inside for her phone.

'It's The Weeknd. "Blinding Lights."'

'Popular with the kids?' he said, only half-joking. He reached into the bag and took out the phone in its pink case. 'Thankfully, this belongs to my client's daughter. She left her bag behind.'

'If you say so,' Jessica said.

Atticus looked at the screen and saw that the call was from Shayden. He held up the screen so that Jessica could see it. She indicated that she wanted to speak to him, so Atticus slid his finger across the screen to answer the call and then handed it across.

'Shayden?' she said. 'It's Detective Constable Jessica Edwards. Please don't put the phone down – your mother is worried about you.' She paused, perhaps waiting for a response, then frowned. 'Shayden? Are you still there? Hello?'

She lowered the phone.

'He'll turn up,' Atticus said.

'Once he's been arrested – and that'll be the end of whatever chance he had of doing something with his life. It's stupid – the whole thing. Just such a waste of potential.' Jessica handed the phone back to him. 'Where's your misper now?'

'With her father. He's driving her home.'

A police van arrived, parking in the middle of the street and blocking it as it disgorged the officers inside. There were six large men, all dressed in stab vests and wearing helmets and face masks. The final pair brought out a metal battering ram and hefted it across the pavement and up the steps. Atticus and Jessica watched as the officers held the ram in place, drew it back and then crashed it against the door. The lock was torn out of the jamb, and the door flew backwards, and the other four officers stormed inside.

'They'll want to take a statement from me,' he said. 'I'll miss the last train.'

'I could put you up if you like. I've got a spare room.'

'You sure?'

'Not a problem.'

'Thank you,' he said. 'That's kind of you.'

PART III
WEDNESDAY

25

Mack woke with a mouth that was sticky with sleep and a pounding headache. She lay still until she realised that it was the buzzing of the phone on the bedside table next to her that had woken her. She reached out and fumbled for it, knocking over a half-finished glass of wine and spilling loose change over the edge. She found the phone, wiped off the wine against the sheet, and put it to her ear.

'Hello?'

'It's Allan Fyfe. Did I wake you?'

'No, no,' she said. 'I was already awake.' She blinked the sleep out of her eyes and looked at the clock radio that sat on the table on the other side of the bed. It was six.

'I know it's early, Mack. I waited as long as I could. You need to come and see me.'

'What's the matter?'

'I've finished my examination of the bones we took out of the graveyard. We've found something – things aren't quite as straightforward as we thought.'

'Go on.'

'I'd really rather you came here so I could show you.'

Mack slumped back into the pillow. 'Is it important?'

'It is, Mack. Sorry.'

'Give me half an hour.'

She ended the call, reached over to put the phone back on the table, missed, and dropped it onto the carpet. She closed her eyes. She had ordered room service last night and had polished off a bottle of wine. *No*, she corrected herself, *two* bottles of wine. She remembered calling down for the second. She had been miserable. Getting drunk had seemed like a good idea at the time, but now she was still miserable, *and* she felt sick.

She bolstered herself against the throbbing in her head and, feeling like an old woman, sat up and swung her feet out of bed. She glanced around the room. The tray that her dinner had been served on was still on the table, but the metal cloche had fallen to the floor. The remains of the meal – a pasta bake of some description, she couldn't recall exactly what – were smeared across the plate, and there was a bread roll and a streak of butter on the chair.

Mack groaned, hobbled over to the table and cleared up the mess while the regrets of the previous night came back to her. She remembered the conversation with Andy. He was still *so* angry with her, and the separation hadn't helped him find his way to forgiveness. She didn't blame him for how he felt about what had happened with Atticus, but that was more than a year ago now, and she had apologised. She had done everything that she could think of to demonstrate that she considered the affair a mistake, that it hadn't happened again and that, as far as she was concerned, it never would. But it wasn't enough for him.

He had never *explicitly* told her that they had no future, but his behaviour had made it obvious that he didn't consider them to be a couple any longer, and that, as far as he was concerned, there was no chance of reconciliation.

He had made that abundantly clear last night.

She looked at the two wine bottles with disgust. She had the kids to think about now. She couldn't afford to drink away the self-pity. She was just going to have to deal with it, to make the best of a bad situation, if only for their benefit. She dumped the bottles into the bin and went into the bathroom to clean herself up for the day. She had always thrown herself into her work whenever she needed a distraction from the mundanities of real life, and, today of all days, at least she had Fyfe's news to uncover.

26

Mack drove over to the hospital and parked. It was still early, just after six thirty, but the wide space was already beginning to fill as staff arrived and made their way inside to start their days.

The remains that had been disturbed at the graveyard in Imber had been transported to the pathology department for examination. Fyfe's office was situated behind the mortuary, and, as usual, Mack felt a little shiver as she followed the signs to the nondescript rooms in the basement of the hospital. The forensic suite and mortuary were next to the two large furnaces that tended to the steady flow of medical detritus that needed to be destroyed: soiled bed linen and dressings joined organic waste, all of it poured down the chutes into the fiery innards of the incinerators. The units vented into the twin smokestacks that reached up into the dirty grey of the morning, creating trails of white smoke that were quickly dispersed by the wind. The chimneys and the cathedral spire were both visible for miles around; Mack had always found it grimly appropriate that they should dominate the city's skyline, markers of death in their own ways.

She made her way along an austere corridor, passing the morgue and the hospital's dead. She had seen her fair share of bodies in the course of her employment, but there was still something macabre about the thought of the corpses waiting to be examined or passed on to the funeral directors for disposal.

She made her way to the two post-mortem suites and held her finger against the doorbell. The lock buzzed and she stepped inside. Fyfe was waiting in the reception area that served the two suites. He was wearing his lab coat, nitrile gloves and a hairnet.

'DCI Jones,' he said, 'thank you for coming.'

'What do you have?'

'I'll show you.' He pointed to a box of disposable plastic gowns. 'You'll need to put one of those on. Gloves and hairnet, too.'

'Why? Has something changed?'

'Best if I tell you inside.'

Mack put on the protective gear and followed Fyfe into the examination room. There was another person waiting for them. She was similarly attired and, although it was difficult to be sure behind the protective gear that she was wearing, Mack guessed that she was in her late middle age.

'This is Detective Chief Inspector Mackenzie Jones,' Fyfe said to the woman. 'Mack, this is Dr Julie Williams, a forensic odontologist. What we're going to look at is a little beyond my expertise,' he went on as they shook hands, 'so I brought Julie in to help.'

Mack smiled to conceal her growing impatience. Fyfe had a habit of drawing out his big reveals for dramatic impact, but Mack had no time for that this morning. She was tired, she had a hangover, and she wanted to get on with the work that needed to be done. 'What are we going to look at? Can we get to the point?'

'Of course.'

The bones that had been exhumed from the graveyard were laid out on a stainless-steel examination table. The table had a groove in the centre that led to a drain at one end; Mack knew exactly what purpose the groove served and tried to put it out of her mind. Fyfe gestured to the skeleton. The bones had been cleaned and were alabaster white, much brighter than had been the case when Mack had seen them before. The skeleton had been reassembled as much as possible, and, now that it was together, Mack could see that it was perhaps five feet five from top to bottom. She was far from an expert, but she could see that not all of the bones were present.

'You're missing some,' she said.

'We are,' Fyfe said. 'Six bones, to be precise. Two ribs, the sacrum and three phalanges from the right foot.'

'Scavenged?'

'That does seem to be the most likely answer. I'm confident that the gnawing on the first bone that you found on the Plain was from a fox. The distance between the markings that were scratched onto the surface of the bones matches what we would expect to see from an adult fox. I'm confirming it with a zoologist I know, but I wouldn't expect that conclusion to change.'

'And the missing bones?' Mack said.

'The phalanges are small. The rib, too. They would have been easy enough to move. The sacrum is a little larger and more substantial, but if I were a betting man, I'd say it's been taken underground to a burrow.'

Fyfe went over to a tablet computer that was fixed on a stand on the desk next to the table and woke the screen. 'Let's start with what we have been able to establish. The bone you found on the Plain *definitely* matches the skeleton in the graveyard. I could have guessed that from the fact that the skeleton was missing her femur, but I decided to be sure and ran a DNA test. Bone is the best source of DNA from human remains – we can take samples from demineralised bones even after the flesh has decomposed. I took two samples – one from the leg and the other from an arm – and compared them. It was a match.'

'You said "her"? She's female?'

Fyfe nodded. 'We're calling her Amy for ease of reference. I estimate mid-teens when she died.'

'Good,' Mack said. 'That's progress.'

'"When she died,"' Fyfe said, repeating himself. 'Of course, *that's* the key question. I understand that there was no headstone near the body?'

'No. But that's not surprising. There are only ten headstones in the Baptist chapel's graveyard, but records show more than a hundred bodies buried there.'

'We don't need a gravestone to tell us when she died. Julie?'

The odontologist indicated that Mack should follow her to a smaller stainless-steel table at the side of the room. There was a metal object in a clear plastic forensic evidence bag. Mack bent over it so that she could look more closely. One end of the object was threaded, like a screw, narrowing to a point.

'We found that in the jawbone,' Williams said.

Mack looked more closely. 'An implant?'

'An endosteal implant,' Williams confirmed. 'The most common type that we see. Someone loses a tooth for whatever reason and goes to see the dentist – this kind of treatment is what probably happens. You have a titanium screw fused to the jawbone so a false tooth can be fitted. It has a rough, textured surface to increase the osteointegration potential of the implant.'

'Which means?'

'The likelihood that the bone will form a secure bond with the metal. The issue we have here is that *this* implant was etched by way of anodic oxidation. That's only been practical for the last twenty years or so. I did a radiographic examination of the implant to see if I could get a better idea, and my best estimate is that the work was done somewhere between 2000 and 2005.'

'No,' Mack said. 'Not possible. I've checked – the last body was buried in the graveyard in 1942.'

'Apparently not,' Fyfe said. 'That might have been the last official burial, but Amy went into the ground significantly later than that. At least sixty years later.'

Mack hung her head and exhaled. She had thought that the discovery would be easily explained, but now that bubble had burst.

'I'm sorry,' Fyfe said. 'It's not going to be quite as easy to dispose of this case as it first appeared.'

The first thought that struck her sucked the strength out of her; they were going to have to dig up the graveyard to see whether Amy was the only aberrant inclusion, or whether the disturbed ground was hiding other secrets.

27

Atticus opened his eyes and, for a moment, had no idea where he was. He was lying on his back on a bed rather than the futon that he was used to back at the office. The ceiling was higher, and the walls were painted a soft green rather than the neutral magnolia that his landlady insisted upon. The room smelled different, too; patchouli oil, he thought, rather than the fusty smell of clothes that really needed to be washed. He felt movement to his right, and, as he turned, he saw the shape of a second person beneath a single sheet. He saw a naked shoulder and a halo of golden hair that spilled over the cream pillowcase. He remembered: he had gone out with Jessica Edwards for a quick drink after he had given the police a statement about the drug house, and that drink had led to another and then another. The evening was lost in a fug of alcohol and spliff, but it wasn't difficult to put it all together.

Atticus heard a buzzing sound and, turning his head, he saw his phone on a bedside table. It was jerking left and right with the vibration of an incoming call. He reached over and grabbed it, holding the screen in front of his face until his eyes focused enough for him to read who was calling.

It was Mack.

He spoke quietly. 'Hello?'

'Atticus?'

Atticus looked over at Jessica, still asleep, and felt a ridiculous buzz of shame.

'Hold on.'

He carefully sat up, swung his legs around and got off the bed. The mattress springs creaked in protest, and Jessica stirred, turning over and mumbling something under her breath. Atticus froze, the phone still pressed to his ear as he waited to see whether she would wake.

'*Atticus?*'

Jessica sighed, stretched an arm towards the warm patch of bed where he had been, and drifted back into a deep sleep once more.

'I'm here,' Atticus whispered as he crept across the bedroom to the hall.

'Where?'

'London,' he said.

'Why are you in London?'

'The missing persons case.'

'And?'

'And she's not missing any more.'

'Why are you whispering?'

He crept down the stairs and saw his clothes – or some of them, at least – across the back of the sofa. 'No reason.'

'Are you *with* someone?'

He felt the shame again, as if he had been caught in flagrante, before chiding himself for it. Why? There was no reason for him to feel that way. He and Mack were not involved. It wasn't as if he had been unfaithful.

'I met someone last night.'

He listened for any note of regret in her response. 'You sly dog,' she said. 'Who is she?'

'Just someone I met,' he said, disappointed that she'd made no obvious reaction.

'Be nice to her.'

'I always am.'

'No, you're not.'

'Unfair,' he protested, but, before he could defend himself, Mack had moved on.

'I'm at the mortuary. I had an early meeting with Fyfe. You know it looked like we might be able to close that investigation down?'

'The bones in the graveyard?'

'Fyfe examined them overnight, and it's not what we expected. The last body that was officially buried in the graveyard was in the forties.'

'And this one?'

'Has dental work that can't be any more than twenty years old, give or take. Whoever it is, they died no earlier than the late nineties.'

Atticus lowered himself down onto the edge of the sofa. 'Shit,' he said.

'Exactly.'

Atticus went through into the downstairs bathroom and gently pulled the door closed.

'What's next?'

'I'm going to have to speak to Beckton.'

'Recommending what? Dig up the graveyard?'

'You got any other ideas?'

He shook his head. Mack's life was about to get a lot busier and more complicated. 'I don't think you have a choice.'

'No. But I'll admit I was hoping you might have something brilliant I could try instead.'

'I'm afraid it's too early for that. Look – I'm headed back now. If you need a second opinion—'

She cut him off. 'Go and be nice to whoever was foolish enough to get tangled up with you. I'll give you a call later – I wouldn't mind bouncing ideas off you once we know what we're dealing with.'

'Whenever you like,' he said. 'You know where I am.'

He ended the call and reached for his clothes. He had a hangover, probably milder than he deserved, and he was hungry. Had they eaten last night? There had been talk of it, but he suspected that they had limited themselves to liquid refreshment and the bag of dope that Finn had given him. He would grab something from the station and eat it on the train. He dressed, smelling the sweetness of the marijuana on his clothing. He didn't even know where this house was, so he took his phone again, opened the map and waited for the GPS to find him. It appeared he was in Bow.

He went back to look into the bedroom. Jessica was still asleep and snoring very lightly. Atticus told himself that he didn't have the heart to wake her, but knew that was just an excuse to save himself the possibility of an embarrassing conversation. He felt like a heel as he backed away, wincing as his feet found a loose board that squeaked in protest as he put his weight on it.

He crossed the room to the front door, stepped outside and followed the directions on his phone to the Tube station.

28

Mack parked in the car park behind the station. She got out of the car when she saw a man in a grey overcoat coming towards her.

'DCI Jones?'

'That's right. Who are you?'

He held out an envelope; Mack took it without thinking. 'I work for your husband's solicitor,' he said. 'You're served.'

He hurried away to a waiting car. Mack held up the envelope. It was addressed to her, the ink already running in the rain. She opened the top and pulled out the contents; she saw a petition with the royal coat of arms and a stamp that indicated that it had been issued and a form headed 'Acknowledgement of Service' that she was supposed to complete and return. She skimmed the petition and saw that unreasonable behaviour had been listed as the grounds for divorce. Mack knew how it would proceed from watching Robbie Best's divorce last year. Andy would apply for a decree nisi, and then the court would issue a decree absolute. The procedure was underway, and there was nothing that she could do to stop it.

Mack closed her eyes, fighting the urge to scream, and stuffed the envelope into her bag. She was too busy to worry about shit like this. It would have to wait.

* * *

Mack pushed open the glass double doors, held her Wiltshire Police ID against the scanner and waited for the lift. It arrived and she stepped inside, held her card against the reader and then pressed the button for the third floor. General CID was on this floor, with major crimes – and her own office – upstairs. She crossed the open-plan office, stopped in the kitchen to make herself a cup of coffee, and then passed along the corridor that led to forensics until she reached Chief Superintendent Beckton's office.

Mack could see him through the glass door. She knocked on it.

'Come!'

Mack held her coffee in her left hand, turned the handle with her right, and opened the door. The office beyond wasn't the largest in the building, but, thanks to its position, its window offered an excellent view of the cathedral. Beckton split his time between Salisbury and Devizes, where Wiltshire Police had its headquarters. As a result, this office was not furnished with anything that might reveal the character of its occupant. It felt unloved and unfinished, with just a single framed photograph of Beckton in full dress uniform accepting an award for good policing from a daytime TV presenter at an event in London.

'Good morning, sir. Can I have a minute?'

'Of course, Mack. Come in.'

She stepped inside and closed the door behind her.

'Everything all right with Mallender?'

'All good, sir.'

'Do you know when they'll be sentenced?'

'Next week.'

'It's a relief to have the bloody thing out of the way. I've never seen so many reporters in town. Maybe they'll all piss off back to London now the show's over, and we can get back to normal.'

'Couldn't agree more.'

He gestured for her to sit. 'What can I do for you?'

She took one of the empty seats opposite the desk. 'Did you read my email about the bone we found on the Plain?'

'I did. You traced it back to Imber?'

'Yes, sir. But it's not what we thought.'

'The bone *wasn't* scavenged?'

'It was, but that's not it. The last official burial in that grave-yard was eighty years ago. The bones we've found went in the ground no earlier than twenty years ago.'

Beckton groaned. 'God.'

'There was no one even *living* in Imber when the bones were buried.'

'I read about it – didn't some of the villagers who moved out want to go back?'

'They must almost all be dead now,' Mack said. 'Why?'

'There were villagers who said they wanted to be buried in the graveyard. Wives next to husbands, children next to their parents – you know.'

'There *have* been burials in the churchyard of St Giles since the village was abandoned,' she said. 'I checked. But this isn't the church – it's the Baptist chapel. There haven't been any additional burials there. It's not impossible that she's connected to Imber, and that someone buried her there because of it, but I wouldn't be comfortable betting too much on that.'

'She? It's a woman?'

'A teenage girl. Fifteen, we think.'

'Cause of death?'

'Fyfe is conducting a full PM today.'

'And you'll keep me posted?'

'Yes, sir. Of course.'

Mack made no move to leave.

'Why do I get the feeling you're about to ask me to do something that I'm not going to like?'

Mack smiled ruefully. 'I'd like permission to look for other bodies that shouldn't be there.'

'You want to dig it up?'

'I think we have to assume that might be necessary.'

'You know exhumations are a *nightmare* to arrange?'

'I've never done it, sir, but I can well imagine.'

'We'll need a licence from the Ministry of Justice. You need someone from Environmental Health on site, probably some from the council's health and safety team, too. And we'll have to tell the relatives that we're digging up granddad and grandma as well.'

'I wish I could think of an alternative, but I can't.'

'We'll need forensic archaeology on site. Ground-penetrating radar.'

Mack shrugged. 'I'm sorry, sir.'

Beckton exhaled, steepled his fingers and then rested his chin on them. 'Tell you what,' he said. 'If Fyfe tells you that there's any suspicion of foul play, I'll get the licence for you, and then we can put our heads together and work out everything you'll need.'

'Thank you, sir.'

* * *

Mack went through into her office and closed the door. She knew that she was going to have to brief her team about what they had discovered today, and found – to her annoyance – that there was only one person with whom she wanted to have that conversation. She had been thinking about Atticus since she had spoken to him that morning, and had realised – and this annoyed her even *more* – that she was jealous of whoever it was he had been with last night.

But she had something now that she knew he would find irresistible.

She took out her phone and called him.

29

Atticus took a seat at a table at the back of the restaurant. Salisbury wasn't blessed with a wide range of culinary destinations, but Anokaa was the best Indian in town, and he had never had a bad meal here. It had also been one of the places that he and Mack had frequented during their relationship. It was big, and there were plenty of places where you could be discreet, with tables that couldn't easily be seen by anyone who might be walking by outside.

He had just taken off his coat and sat down when he saw Mack at the entrance. He raised his hand in greeting. She smiled, said something to the waiter who had diverted to attend to her, and then made her way across the room to him.

'You look done in,' he said.

'It's been quite a day.'

The waiter, wearing traditional dress, brought them a bottle of wine. Atticus put his hand over his glass; the waiter poured for Mack and then left the bottle on the table.

'Not drinking?' Mack asked him.

'Still a little hungover.'

'I had a skinful last night, too,' she admitted.

'Why?'

'It doesn't matter.'

Atticus took his glass of water and touched it to her wine glass. Mack drank, then sighed and leaned back in her chair. She chuckled wryly to herself, and Atticus saw the tension release from her shoulders. She drank again, emptying the glass and then poured another.

'Easy, tiger,' Atticus said.

Mack winked and took another sip. Atticus was aware that she was looking inquisitively at him over the top of her glass.

'So,' she said.

'So?'

'The mystery girl. Who is she?'

'No one,' Atticus said.

'Come on – stop being coy. Tell me everything.'

'There's not much to tell. She's just someone I met.'

'Tinder?'

'What? *No!* I met her in London. Well,' he corrected himself, 'I met her here, actually. She's from the Met.'

'Doing what?'

'You heard of Operation Orochi?'

'County lines?' Mack said.

'She's a DC. She came down on a joint operation with the drugs squad in Melksham.'

'I think I might have met her. Is her name Jessica?'

'Yes.'

'She came into the nick. She's pretty.'

Atticus felt the heat rising in his cheeks a little. He didn't like the idea of Mack knowing Jessica, not after what had happened. 'The kid she was after was selling out of a house on Payne's Hill.'

'And your runaway?'

'She met the boy here and went back to London with him. I told Jessica where to find him. We went out for a drink to celebrate and—'

'I don't need *all* the details,' she said, stopping him with an upheld hand.

Atticus was a savant in many ways, able to read people for the most infinitesimally small reactions, but, when it came to his feelings for Mack – and especially when it came to *her* feelings for *him* – he was hopeless. He couldn't work out whether Mack was interested in him as a friend – because the interest in Jessica was what one would expect from a friend – or because she was jealous.

He decided to change the subject. 'What about you and Andy?'

'What about it?'

'You haven't made up yet?'

She finished the glass of wine and shook her head. 'I'm not sure that's an option.'

Atticus leaned in a little. That was the first time Mack had suggested that might be a possibility.

'What about the kids?'

'I see them twice a week. They're with him. It's better that way. He's better at being a parent than I am. He always has been.'

'That's not true,' he said. 'You're a great mum.'

She exhaled and shook her head. 'We both know that's not true. Me and you would never have happened if I were, would it?'

Atticus wanted to say more, but he could see that the subject of the conversation was difficult for her. The evening had the potential to descend into the maudlin, and he was grateful when the waiter arrived to take their orders. Atticus chose the chicken bhuna and Mack the pot-baked lamb biriyani. The waiter thanked them and made his way to the kitchen.

'What about Imber?' Atticus asked her. 'That's what you want to talk about.'

'I've been out there all day.' She stopped, then went on, 'This has to stay between us. We haven't gone public yet.'

'Of course.'

'As I said on the phone, the teeth show the remains are not as old as they ought to be.'

He frowned. 'And there's no possibility of this being an official burial?'

'None. The last burial there was in the forties. They still bury locals in the graveyard of the church now and again, but not at the chapel.' She nibbled at a poppadom. 'We searched the graveyard today to see if there was anything else that was out of place. There are a couple of spots that look as if they might have been disturbed in the last few months, but it's difficult to be sure without digging them up, and that's delicate. Fyfe's conducting a full examination. I'll have a better idea after that.'

Mack's phone buzzed on the table. She spun it around so that she could see who was calling. 'Speak of the devil.'

Mack got up and answered the call in the hallway that led to the bathrooms. Atticus loaded his poppadom with chutney and took a bite. He watched Mack as she spoke; she frowned, and that frown deepened into an expression that spoke of serious news.

Mack finished the call and came back to the table. 'Sorry,' she said. 'Got to go.'

'What's happened?'

'Fyfe says he's found something.'

'He tell you what?'

'No. You know what he's like.'

'Drama queen.'

She nodded. 'He wants to show me in person. I need to get over to the hospital.'

'You can't drive,' Atticus said.

'What? Why?'

'You'll be over the limit.'

She swore, then reached into her bag for her phone. 'I'll call a taxi.'

'I'll take you.'

'You don't have to do that.'

'It's not a problem. What else am I going to do tonight?'

His offer wasn't *entirely* altruistic. Atticus had been enjoying the evening and was not averse to continuing their conversation, even if it was in the car while he drove her to the hospital. And, beyond that, he was curious. What discovery could Fyfe have made that was important enough to drag Mack all the way out to the mortuary rather than discussing it on the phone? They both knew that the professor was prone to deliver information with theatrical flourishes, but there still had to be something of consequence, and Atticus was intrigued.

He had taken a day or two off from his work for the bank, but, now that he had located Molly York, he had no excuse for not getting back to it. Tracking down hidden assets was remunerative, but the fraudster he was pursuing was not particularly cunning, and the work was far from challenging. The bones that they had found in the graveyard were *much* more interesting, and, if there was a mystery as to how they had come to be buried there – plus whatever fresh tweak the pathology might discover – then Atticus definitely wanted to be involved.

He got up and laid a note on the table to cover the bill. 'All right?'

'Come on, then,' she said, slipping on her coat and leading the way to the door.

30

Atticus drove them to Oddstock. It was eight o'clock when they arrived at the hospital. He switched off the engine and turned to look at Mack.

'Let me know how it goes?'

She paused, weighing something up.

'What is it?' he asked her.

'Come in, too.'

'Sure?'

'It might be helpful. A bit of backup. And you did find the body.'

'This is true,' he said.

'Just don't make a tit of yourself.'

'As if,' he said, opening the car door before she could change her mind.

*　*　*

Atticus followed Mack as she led the way to the mortuary. Mack pressed the button to buzz the intercom and waited for the door to unlock. It did, and she pushed it open and went inside. Atticus came in behind her.

Professor Fyfe was waiting in the reception area. 'Good evening, DCI Jones,' he said.

'Evening,' Mack said. 'You remember Atticus Priest?'

He frowned with displeasure. 'How could I possibly forget?'

Atticus had always found it difficult to modulate his responses to other people, especially those about whom he had a low opinion. Atticus thought that Fyfe was a bombastic, self-aggrandising old fool, and he knew that Fyfe was aware of his opinion. The two of them had never really seen eye to eye, especially after – on their first meeting – Atticus had corrected the pathologist when he had erred about the cause of death of a man who had been found in the woods outside Tisbury. Fyfe had suggested that the man had been beaten before he'd died, but Atticus had disagreed, suggesting that the lesions upon which the conclusion had been founded were, in fact, the bluish discoloration that was sometimes caused by lividity. There had been an argument during which Fyfe had haughtily dismissed Atticus's objections as those of an amateur. The family of the deceased had insisted upon a second opinion, however, and Atticus's conclusions had been preferred.

Fyfe frowned at Atticus sourly. 'I heard you were sacked?'

'More of a mutual parting of the ways.'

'It was Atticus's suggestion that led to us finding the body,' Mack said, trying to maintain the peace between the two of them. 'He has a good eye for these kinds of things. I wouldn't mind having him here to listen to this – provided you are okay with that, of course?'

'It's irregular.'

'I won't say a thing,' Atticus said. 'I'll just stand here and watch.'

Fyfe looked as if he might complain, but, with Mack smiling pleasantly at him, he relented. 'Fine. This way.'

He took them through to the room where the bones had been arranged. Fyfe took a pair of gloves from a box and pulled them onto his hands. 'I've finished a preliminary examination. I have a much better idea about Amy at the time of her death.'

Atticus looked down at the skeleton and saw the open, circular inlet in the pelvic area. The hip bones were more outwardly flared, and the sciatic notch in the ilium was broad, both of which also indicated gender.

'Age?' Mack asked.

'As we thought,' Fyfe said. He pointed down to the skeleton's legs. 'To allow for growth, the ends and shafts of long bones are separated by cartilage plates. They disappear and the extremities of the various long bones fuse at different ages. By knowing the sequence of these bones coming together, we can estimate age. In Amy's case, the degree of fusion of the first and second sacral bodies and the medial clavicular bones suggests she's fifteen or sixteen.'

'Anything else?' Mack asked.

Fyfe moved around the table so that he was standing over the skull. 'This is more speculative, but the features we see here – the shape of the skull, the shape of the nasal region and orbits, the degree of protrusion of the jaw – suggest Amy was white.'

'Height?'

'Between five feet four and five feet five.'

Atticus moved closer to the table and bent at the waist so that he could look a little more closely at the remains. 'She was strangled.'

Fyfe started to speak. 'That's what—'

Atticus cut over him. 'The hyoid bone is fractured.' He took a biro from his pocket and pointed down with the chewed end to the small collection of bones beneath the jaw. 'There. It almost never fractures – it's protected behind the mandible and the cervical spine. It's only ever external pressure when it's been damaged like this.'

Fyfe folded his arms across his chest. 'Quite,' he said, indignant that his thunder had been stolen.

Atticus barely noticed it.

He turned to Mack.

'She was murdered.'

PART IV
THURSDAY

31

Mack got up at six and took a shower. She looked out of the window of the hotel and saw that the rain was coming down hard. She checked her phone and saw that rain was forecast until the evening, and the temperature was predicted to fall to just above freezing. Mack knew that she was going to be out on the Plain all day, that it was going to be dirty work and cold. She dressed in her warmest clothes and took her Wellingtons from out of the closet and stood them next to the door so that she wouldn't forget them.

She went down to the restaurant and had a larger than usual breakfast in anticipation that she might not get the chance to eat again until much later. She ordered eggs and bacon and checked her phone for emails while she waited for the food to arrive. She had reported the results of the forensic examination of Amy's body to Beckton late last night and then had been in touch with the station at Bourne Hill so that the preparations for a major incident room could be set in motion. The discovery of the fractured hyoid bone and Fyfe's conclusion of manual strangulation made murder the only possible conclusion. Beckton had arranged for an expedited application to the Ministry of Justice, and the exhumation licence had been granted just before midnight.

It was the green light for a lot of muddy, cold, unpleasant work.

The phone buzzed with a message. She checked: it was from Atticus.

Have fun today.

She smiled and tapped out a reply.

Fun? Have you seen the weather?

I'll think of you while I'm warm and dry.

Your concern is touching.

Want to take that bet?

She remembered what he had said as he had dropped her outside the hotel after running her back into town. He had predicted that Amy would not be the only murder victim that they found in the graveyard. Mack had dismissed the suggestion, telling him that there was no reason to think there would be more than one.

She typed: *What do I get if I'm right and you're wrong?*

Dinner with me.

And if you're right?

Two dinners with me.

Mack knew that flirting with him was a dreadful idea, but she couldn't help herself.

Agreed.

* * *

Mack walked from the hotel to the car park where she had left the Range Rover last night. It was a filthy day. Rain lashed the street, and the passing cars threw up curtains of dirty spray over pedestrians. The prospect of being out in the middle of the Plain on a day like this was not one that filled her with enthusiasm, but she knew that her presence out there – at least at the start of the day – was completely non-negotiable.

She had called Nigel Archer and told him to get the team together so that she could brief them before heading out to Imber to oversee the work that was starting there. There had been a lot of high-level negotiation with the Ministry of Defence to block the area around the village and to close off access to exercising troops. The Ministry were unhappy with developments and Mack knew that they would be exerting plenty of background pressure to bring the investigation to an end as quickly as possible.

She parked the car at the station, hurried inside and went to the bathroom, where she checked her reflection in the mirror. Her hair was wet, lashed by the wind and the rain and plastered to her forehead. She dried it as best she could, then took out her make-up bag and made herself presentable.

She looked in the mirror again. She still looked good, she told herself. Her skin was still supple, her nightly moisturiser replenishing it after days spent outside in all weather. A lifetime of regular exercise had maintained her trim figure. She didn't want to think about divorce, but she turned her face to look at both sides and told herself that she wouldn't be left on the shelf. She would start to take a little better care of herself in the meantime; she would show Andy that he had made a mistake.

She straightened her shirt, smoothing it down, and made her way to CID.

* * *

Mack went into the open-plan office and called out that the briefing was about to start. A conference suite had been secured as the location of the Major Incident Room, and she went inside and waited for the others to join her. They filed in and sat down around the long conference table. She took the chair at the head and looked from face to face.

To her right sat Robbie Best, Mack's second-in-command. Best was a doughty inspector with years of experience who, while a little slow on the uptake, was a hard worker who had succeeded by dint of diligence and determination rather than leaps of imagination or intuition.

DS Mike Lewis and DS Nigel Archer were next to each other. Lewis was an old-school copper who, by his own admission, was prepared to push the boundaries just as much as he could get away with. He had twenty years of experience and, thanks to that, owned an extensive knowledge of the criminal scene in Salisbury and the rural areas that surrounded it. Archer was younger than Lewis and had made the switch from uniform by dint of ferocious ambition and a work ethic that made everyone else feel guilty by comparison. Archer was smart and had hitched his wagon to Lewis in the hope that he might be able to short-circuit the acquisition of experience by soaking up as much of Lewis's as possible. His time at Lewis's side had seen him absorb some of his tutor's character, an irascibility that seemed to develop by osmosis. There were frequent jabs at the closeness of their relationship, with the less politically conscious members of the team suggesting that Archer was selling sexual favours in exchange for Lewis's tutelage; others just referred to them as Statler and Waldorf, the cantankerous elderly Muppets.

Mack's remaining two detective constables completed the team. Stewart Lynas was ambitious, but Mack feared that his aspirations outpaced his ability. He was a local lad from a wealthy family, educated at one of the city's private schools and then Bournemouth University, returning to Salisbury with an over-inflated sense of his own competence that Mack feared would not survive its first real skirmish with the practicalities of police work. He was in his mid-twenties and handsome, although he had a superciliousness that suggested he was simply marking time with the plebs while he waited for the brass to notice his talent; Mack suspected that he would be waiting a long time, at least until he found some humility.

DC Francine Patterson sat at the opposite end of the table to Mack. Her family had a long history of service in the armed forces, and she had not deviated from that path. She had been a redcap, a corporal in the 1st Investigation Company of the Royal Military Police based down the road at Bulford. She had made her name with the investigation of a private who had been killed during a live-fire exercise, eventually concluding that the lance corporal in the man's platoon who had fired the fatal shot had been high on LSD at the time. She was short and compact, with an athletic build that she nurtured on twenty-mile runs and hours spent at Parkwood, the health club just before the London Road on the way out of the city.

Mack took a seat and paused until they were all in place. She rapped her knuckles on the table and then ran through what they had discovered so far: the discovery of the bone, the location of the remains from which it had been taken, the dental implant that dated the burial, and then the suspicion that they were looking at murder.

'Cause of death?' Archer asked.

'Strangulation. Fyfe's full report should be with us this morning. But that's the headline.'

'How old does he think the victim was?'

'No older than sixteen.'

'Shit,' Archer said.

Mack nodded her agreement. She had been putting that to the back of her mind; the idea that they might find more kids in the graveyard was not something she wanted to think about.

Patterson raised a hand. 'What's the plan, boss?'

'We're going to go back to the graveyard today and look for any evidence that there are other remains that shouldn't be there.'

'How many bodies are *officially* buried there?'

'Around a hundred, although we'll want to be certain about that. We'll start near where Amy was found and work out from there.'

Patterson noted it all down. She was a dutiful officer with a bright future, and Mack reminded herself to give her a little extra responsibility if she could.

'And then what?' said Archer. 'Dig them *all* up?'

'Preferably not, Nigel. We'll take it as it comes. Fyfe is on standby, and we'll test the bones that we find as we go. The hope is that the remains we do find can all be dated to before the Baptist graveyard was closed.'

'And if they can't?'

'Then the odds are that we're looking at something that could get big. And then we'd have to keep digging.'

'The budget on that's going to be nuts,' Lewis said.

'It could be. That reminds me. Get on the phone to Simon Chester and make sure he's there.'

'Who?'

'Forensic anthropologist. There's a forensic archaeologist team already there – they're in charge of the excavation, of course, but the anthropologist's the one we need if we find more bones.'

'Beckton's not going to be pleased.'

'No, he's not. But he knows we don't have much choice.' She collected the clipboard that she had brought with her and referred to the piece of paper that was secured to it. 'We need to assign roles.'

She picked Robbie Best as deputy SIO, Archer as office manager and Lewis – although unhappily – agreed to serve as exhibits officer, responsible for ensuring that all the documents that were generated by the investigation found the right home. It would be a nightmare in a case like this, and Mack needed to be sure that it would be done right. Mack told Archer to appoint the rest of the backroom team – the action manager, disclosure officer, document reader and registrar.

'Robbie,' Mack said, nodding to Best, 'I want you out at Imber. There's going to be a ton of set-up work to do. Equipment, manpower – that's going to be on you.'

'Yes, boss.'

'Liaise with Fyfe. I know he can be a pain in the arse, but the two of you will need to be hand-in-hand on this.'

Best nodded.

'Francine,' Mack said, 'you're in charge of going through the missing persons reports. I'm thinking that you'll need to pull all the mispers from the city and the surrounding area between 1995 and 2005. Let's see if we can find out who she is.'

'What am I looking for?'

'Teenage girls. Any connection with Imber would be a start. A family in the Army who lost a child, maybe. I don't know beyond that. We don't have much to go on.'

Archer tapped the table. 'If the victim was a kid, we should look at local paedos.'

'Agreed,' Mack said. 'Stewart – get the records of anyone arrested for child sexual offences around the time she was killed. That won't be a bad place to start. And look at MAPPA for any perverts who might be worth a visit.'

Multi-agency public protection arrangements linked up probation and prison staff with social services, housing and health and helped manage registered sex offenders. Lynas said that he would give them a call.

'Everyone happy?' Mack said when she was done.

There were nods and the sounds of agreement. Mack corralled the pieces of paper that she had spread out over the desk and stood up.

'I'd better get out to Imber,' Best said.

'I'm coming, too,' Mack said. She pointed at Francine. 'And you. I'd like you out there today to get a feel for it.'

Patterson smiled, her pleasure at being given responsibility overpowering any reluctance she might have felt about spending the day in the rain and the mud. Mack smiled to herself. She remembered feeling that same enthusiasm as a young officer in the Met. Her first murder had followed the discovery of a man's body in an alley behind a supermarket in Brixton.

Mack had been one of the first detectives to respond and had played a key role on the team that followed the evidence back to a twenty-year-old who said the voices in his head had told him to kill.

'We're all good,' she said. 'Let's get to work.'

32

The graveyard looked very different to how it had been on Mack's last visit. A perimeter had been established, with crime-scene tape fastened around the trunks of trees and metal stakes driven into the soft earth. Two marked cars blocked the road twenty-five feet apart, with the entrance to the Baptist graveyard in the middle of the cordon. Blue-and-white crime-scene tape was knotted to their side mirrors and secured around a postbox at one end and a lamp post at the other. Uniformed officers had been deployed to guard the perimeter. Constable Dave Betts was the loggist at the gate, responsible for signing people in and out in the scene logbook.

Mack led Archer and Patterson to the gate. Betts nodded a hello and entered their details into the book. There were cardboard boxes containing Tyvek suits, booties, gloves and hairnets. Mack pulled on a suit, waited for Archer and Patterson to do the same, and then lifted the tape so that the three of them could pass through.

The path to the graveyard had been flattened by the passage of the archaeologists who had arrived to attend to the day's work. They had been busy: two large inflatable tents had been erected over the side of the graveyard where Amy's remains had been found. The tents were composed of semicircular ribs in alternating blue and white and were tall enough for the forensic officers inside to stand. There was activity outside the perimeter, too. Vehicles were parked up, including a four-by-four that bore the livery of a firm in Warminster that hired heavy equipment. A trailer had been hitched to the back of the four-by-four, and a miniature digger was being reversed down to the ground. Officers with bolt-cutters made their way across to the fence so that they could cut the chain-link and open a route inside. Next to the digger, a machine that looked like an oversized lawnmower was being rolled out of the back of a forensic van.

'What's that?' Patterson said.

'Ground-penetrating radar,' Mack said.

There was another cordon, this time marked out by yellow-and-black crime-scene tape and with a second log to sign before they could continue. Mack lifted the tape and slid beneath it, following the path behind the yew trees to the exposed grave that they had discovered two days earlier. One of the inflatable tents had been erected to protect it from the elements. Professor Fyfe was overseeing two CSIs who were on hands and knees, carefully examining the spot from which Amy's bones had been removed. He saw Mack, raised his hand in greeting and climbed up the shallow slope of the crater and stepped out of the tent.

'Good morning, Detective. Lovely weather.'

'Morning. You know Robbie Best.'

'Detective Inspector,' Fyfe said, raising a gloved hand in greeting rather than offering it for a shake.

'Not sure if you've met DC Patterson.'

'I haven't,' he said. 'Good morning, Detective Constable. Have you been to anything like this before?'

'No, sir.'

'It's not going to be pleasant.'

'Don't wind her up,' Mack said.

'Wouldn't dream of it. I was thinking it might help to know what to expect.' He gestured to all three of them. 'You two, as well – this'll be new to you, too.'

'I've seen plenty of stiffs,' Best said. 'Not quite like this.'

'What's the plan?' Mack asked.

Fyfe pointed to the bearded man in a Barbour jacket who was directing operations around the open grave. 'You'd better ask Professor Wilder.'

'The archaeologist?'

'Indeed. They're just waiting for the green light to start the dig. If we're lucky, all we'll find will be eighty-year-old skeletons. That's what we'd expect if the bodies here are the ones that were properly buried.'

Patterson bit her lip nervously. 'And if they're more recent?'

'Then the bodies will be somewhere along the spectrum of decomposition. Five stages. Fresh – when the cells begin to break down. Bloat – when the gases inside the body cause it to expand, turning the colour from flesh-coloured to green and then black.'

'Lovely,' Patterson said.

'Older than that and you'd expect to see active decomposition. Tissue liquefies, and maggots eat whatever they can get to. After that is advanced decomposition, where heavy-duty bugs go after the tougher material like ligaments and tendons. And last of all is skeletal decay, where bones begin to disintegrate. Hopefully that's what we'll see.'

'You're enjoying this,' Best said.

'Enjoying isn't the right word,' Fyfe said. 'Do I take pleasure from this? No. Do I find it professionally interesting? Of course. A job on this scale is a once-in-a-career opportunity.'

Lucky you, Mack thought.

'Robbie Best is going to be your liaison,' Mack said, 'but let Francine know if you need anything.'

'Very good.'

A team of crime-scene investigators arrived with duckboards, shovels and wheelbarrows. They watched as Professor Wilder briefed them, indicating that they should prepare to excavate in the area to the left of the open crater. The ground had been divided into squares with small pegs that were tied around with string. Each quadrant would be examined one at a time before the team moved onto the next. It was going to be a long and arduous exercise. The ground was soft – at least it would be easy to dig – but, on the other hand, it was already becoming something of a quagmire. The duckboards would give the investigators something solid to rest their knees on while they worked.

'Oh,' Fyfe said, 'I nearly forgot. We found something else. Come over here.'

He led the way to a trestle table that had been erected beneath the second tent. Lewis had taken up residence there as exhibits officer, and had arranged a stack of empty plastic evidence bags in a box, a Sharpie for marking them with new finds, and a logbook for recording them. Fyfe reached into a cardboard box and took out an evidence bag. He handed it to Mack. There was a watch inside.

'We found it where Amy had been.'

Mack held up the bag so that Best and Patterson could see it, too. The watch was a cheap Casio with an analogue face. It was filthy and caked with dirt. The dial bore a graphic with Mickey Mouse's face and oversized ears.

33

Mack was freezing, and Archer and Patterson looked thoroughly depressed. They had been out in the graveyard all day, and the rain had not stopped. It had slackened a little over lunch, falling as a gentle mist that was easy to ignore, but now, as the light began to fade and the temperature began to fall, it had become a deluge once more.

She pulled up her hood and looked at the work that was going on. A rough plan of the graveyard had been found online, and they were using that to avoid – as best they could – the existing graves. They knew that they might not be able to do that for ever, but it made sense to start looking in areas that were not *supposed* to have remains. The pit from which Amy's bones had been exhumed was in a stretch of the graveyard between two lines of headstones, and they had taken the decision to begin their search there.

The team assigned to the dig were members of the force's underwater search team, and each man proceeded with extravagant care. They were being overseen by Sergeant Keith Knight, a police search advisor from Trowbridge who had arrived at the scene before the substantive work had begun. Fyfe was still there, watching over their work with a critical eye and clearly fighting the urge to give them detailed instructions as to where they should and should not be working. The searchers worked one man or woman to each of the squares that had been marked with string, carefully removing the soil with trowels and examining anything else that they brought out. So far, their haul had been meagre: an antique bottle, stones, broken porcelain. The work was not restricted to the graveyard. There were administrators at Bourne Hill and Devizes who were responsible for making the job go as easily as possible. The Ministry of Defence owned the land and had made no objection to the search being carried out, but, nonetheless, an application to court under section eight of the Police and Criminal Evidence Act had been made, and a search warrant had been issued.

Yet, despite a day of hard work, they had found nothing. Mack was pleased. The longer they went on without discovering remains that shouldn't be there, the sooner the search could be brought to a close, and the sooner she could get back to the hotel for a hot bath and a glass of wine.

She stretched her legs. The paths that were cleared to use had been marked out with bright plastic cones, and she walked around the perimeter to the tent that had been erected over the spot where Amy's remains had been found. The bones had been buried close to the surface, but Knight wanted them to go down to five or six feet. The earth had been loosened by the rain, and, even though they had only dug down to knee height, it was obvious that going deeper would require the workings to be shored up. Knight had called for a supply of sheeting and hydraulic supports, and a local civil engineer was on his way to discuss the best way to complete the excavation.

'Coffee, boss?'

Mack turned. It was Francine Patterson. 'Yes, please. I'll come with you.'

More equipment had arrived during the day, including a second small mechanical digger, trackway to allow for officers with wheelbarrows to remove soil, and a pedestrian walkway to ensure that the ground was not disturbed by the police and support staff as they went about their work. Mack and Patterson followed the walkway to the hole that had been cut in the boundary fence, and they made their way across the sodden field to the incident support unit that had arrived courtesy of the Wiltshire Fire and Rescue Service. Two members of staff busied themselves inside the open-sided trailer, providing the search officers with hot food and drink.

'Two coffees,' Patterson said.

The woman behind the counter took two paper cups and filled them with hot water from an urn at the rear of the trailer. She added coffee and left them on the counter.

'You had anything from the press yet, boss?'

'Not yet,' Mack said. 'But it won't be long.'

'That's one of the benefits of working in a place like this,' Patterson said with a wry smile. 'You get the Army guarding the way in and out.'

'*Sarge!*'

The call was from back inside the graveyard. One of the diggers had stood up, his arm waving to attract the attention of Sergeant Knight. Mack and Patterson took their coffees and retraced their steps across the walkway and arrived next to the excavation at the same time as Fyfe. The officer in the pit was covered from head to toe in muck. He pointed down at a scrap of fabric that was visible amid the mud.

Mack crouched down and stared. It was hard to be sure from her vantage, but the fabric looked like denim, and, as the digger very gently used the tip of his trowel to scrape away the covering of earth that obscured it, she saw that it was more than just a scrap: it looked like the leg of a pair of jeans. The officer scraped the earth away from the bottom of the trousers, uncovering the unmistakeable shape of a shoe. There was a gap between the cuff of the jeans and the upper of the shoe and, as more earth was delicately moved aside, Mack could see the white of bone and the pallid grey of decomposing flesh.

'Stop,' Fyfe called down to the officer. '*Stop*. That's much more recent. We need to get it out carefully.'

The sight was grisly and, without the covering of earth to mask it, the smell of rot quickly became evident. The photographer arrived and, as the digger shuffled back to get out of shot, his camera flashed once and then twice and then a third time, the gloomy tent lighting up each time. Fyfe very carefully made his way down the slope so that he could take a closer look at the exposed remains. Mack stayed where she was. She was the senior investigating officer, but she preferred to let the experts do their work without having to worry about the DCI looking over their shoulders.

Fyfe clambered back up the slope.

'That *obviously* shouldn't be there,' he said.

'How long?'

'It's very badly decomposed, but it's much more recent.'

'Yes, but how long?'

'A couple of months.'

'God.'

'I'll need to sign a ROLE form,' Fyfe said.

It was one of the absurdities of the job that paperwork – a Recognition of Life Extinct form – needed to be completed in circumstances where it was patently obvious that the person was dead, but there it was.

She looked away, turning her face to the sky and the iron vault that spread out across the Plain all the way to the horizon. The bath and the glass of wine would have to wait.

34

The discovery of the body led to a flurry of additional activity. Fyfe made it clear that they needed to exhume the remains that evening, and, as darkness was closing in quickly across the Plain, Robbie Best had called back to the incident room and asked them to arrange for lights and a generator. A contractor had arrived at six, and now he was in the process of moving the generator into place so that the rest of the equipment could be powered. Stand floodlights had been placed around the edges of the site, plasterer's lights stood inside the tent, and a string of LED lights, their bulbs protected by metal cages, had been strung up between two temporary posts. The main cable was plugged into the generator, and the plugs for the lights pushed into splitters. The generator's engine chugged and spluttered as it was fired up, and then settled down into a steady thrum. The lights came on.

Mack's phone buzzed. She answered it.

'DCI Jones?'

'Speaking.'

'It's Mary Winkworth.'

Mack felt a twist in her stomach. Winkworth ran the media office for Wiltshire Police.

'I think I can guess what you're calling about.'

'I'm sure you can. I've had a call from a reporter at the *Mail*. She's heard that we've found two bodies on Salisbury Plain. Is that true?'

'It is. How did they find out so fast?'

'You know what it's like, Mack. How many officers have you got down there?'

'Lots.'

'So one of them fancies making a bit of extra on the side. Or maybe one of them says something to a girlfriend or a boyfriend, the girlfriend or boyfriend shares it with someone they know, that person shares it with *their* friends. Eventually it gets to someone who works in the press. It's impossible to keep a lid on it for ever.'

Mack turned away from the tent and followed the marked path back to the refreshment stand to get another hot drink. 'What do you propose?'

'We get out in front of it. Get them in for a press conference tomorrow, and you tell them whatever you can. Give them something to run with – it'll be better if we manage the flow of information. They're still going to root around, but it'll be better if we have them onside. You might need their help down the road. They're more likely to help if we cooperate at the start.' She paused. 'You okay with that? Is there something you can tell them?'

'Probably. It'll be vague, though – we don't know much yet. I can give them the top line.'

'That's all we need for now.'

'Clear it with Beckton,' she said. 'The last thing we need is to blindside him with something like this.'

'He's my next call.'

Mack reached the stand and asked for another coffee. 'When do you want to do it?'

'First thing. I'll be there to set it up. You just have to give the statement.'

'Fair enough,' Mack said. 'I'll see you in the morning.'

Mack ended the call, took her coffee and squelched through the mud back to the tent. The photographer had finished taking his pictures – for now, at least – and the careful excavation of the remains was continuing. The wet earth was slowly scraped aside, revealing more of the leg and, at the waist, a leather belt. The smell was worse; Mack had always thought that the odour of decomposition was like that of rotting meat with a drop or two of cheap perfume, a rank pungency with notes of sickening sweetness. The Tyvek suits were annoying enough to have been given a nickname by the police who wore them – Noddy suits – but Mack was grateful for hers now. The first dead body she had come across, a spinster with no family who had been left alone to rot during a hot summer, had left its stench on her clothes, and no amount of washing had been able to shift it. It had been a new suit from Monsoon, too; she'd given up in the end, taken it into the garden and burned it. The Noddy suit might mean that she rustled when she walked, but at least it ought to help keep the stink off her.

Fyfe was crouching down next to the officer who was excavating the earth around the remains. He looked up and caught

Mack's eye. He looked sombre. Mack knew what he was thinking because she felt it, too: someone had been using the graveyard as a place to bury their victims. Amy might have been buried twenty years ago, but this body – whoever it was – had gone into the ground recently.

Killers, in Mack's experience, did not leave twenty years between their murders.

She was uneasy about the secrets that the graveyard might yet divulge.

PART V
FRIDAY

35

Mack returned in her dreams to the field of bones in the abandoned village. She saw the dead, those who had been buried there a hundred years ago and those who had gone into the ground more recently than that. Sleep was fitful, and, as the clock on the bedside table showed four thirty, she gave up. She took her book and went to sit by the window, looking down onto the junction of New Street and Exeter Street. Even then, though, she was distracted. Atticus's office was just five minutes away, and she couldn't help thinking of him.

How would he have responded to the news of the second body last night?

What would he have done?

Thinking about him made her feel guilty and, tired and thoroughly annoyed with herself, she took a shower and prepared herself for the day. The press conference had been scheduled for nine, and, as senior investigating officer, she would lead it in tandem with Chief Superintendent Beckton.

* * *

Mack walked to the station. There were two outside broadcast vans with satellite dishes on their roofs in the car park, with technicians working on banks of equipment that she could see through the open rear doors.

Mary Winkworth was waiting for her in her office.

'Busy already,' Mack observed.

'We kept it local,' Winkworth said, 'but the news spread fast. The BBC and Sky have sent correspondents. It'll be on the news at lunch.'

'Right.'

'You okay with that? Mallender was big.'

She nodded. 'They hammered me after that, too – at least it should've toughened me up.'

'You'll be fine,' Mary said. She checked her watch. 'We start in an hour. I'd get down there twenty minutes before if I were you so we can run through what it'll look like.'

Mack said that she would. She got up, in need of a cup of coffee, but before she could follow Mary out of the office, she saw Professor Fyfe making his way across the CID room. It looked as if he was wearing the same clothes as yesterday. His trousers were crusted with dried mud that must have got inside the cuffs of his Noddy suit, and his shirt was crumpled and unironed. He looked exhausted.

'Good morning, Mack.'

'Have you been home yet?'

He shook his head. 'We haven't stopped. I'm going to go home after this, but I have an update for you – I thought I should come and talk to you in person. You're speaking to the press?'

'In an hour.'

'You'll need to know what we found last night, then.'

'I need a coffee first. Want one?'

He said that he did. Mack told him to wait in her office and went into the small kitchen. The kettle was already boiled. She took two cups and shovelled coffee into both, adding water but forgoing milk, and brought them back to her office.

She handed one cup to Fyfe and sat down. 'What do you have for me?'

'Another three bodies.'

'*Three* more?'

He nodded. 'Making five in total. We're testing them now. I'll let you know when I have results, but I think we should prepare for the worst. They all went into the ground in the last few years – closer in time to the body we dug up yesterday than to Amy.'

'It must be the same killer.'

'That would seem to be the most likely explanation.'

'Let's keep it to ourselves for now,' she said. 'I don't want that coming up at the press conference until we have a little more to say. I'll just be speculating until then.'

'Agreed.'

'What about the body we found yesterday?'

Fyfe sipped his coffee. 'He's at the mortuary.'

'Male? You're sure?'

'Definitely. And there's something unusual about him. He had a prosthetic leg. The prosthesis is missing, but the socket was still there.'

'Can we identify him from it?'

'I think it's quite likely. I've scheduled the PM for later. I need some sleep first.'

'And you'll let me know?'

He got up. 'Straight away.'

Mack thanked him. He zipped up his muddy jacket and left the room. Mack watched him cross to the lifts, and then took out her notebook and started to jot down the things that she wanted to cover – and the things that she could not – in preparation for her statement to the press.

36

Mack took the stairs to the ground floor. The press had gathered in the largest of the building's conference rooms. She looked inside through the glass panel in the door. The table had been removed and replaced by four rows of seats, five to each row. It wasn't really designed for an event like this, and the reporters, photographers and camera operators were jammed in tight. The seats were all taken and so was the space behind them. A long trestle table that had been covered with a white cloth faced the audience. Mary Winkworth had printed out their names on pieces of card and then folded them over so that they were visible to the crowd: Mack was on the left, and Beckton was on the right.

Winkworth stepped out of a room along the corridor and called Mack over. Chief Superintendent Beckton was waiting for Mack inside.

'Quick run-through,' Winkworth said. 'Chief Superintendent, it would be best if you opened the conference and then hand over to Mack.'

'Of course,' Beckton said.

'Keep it simple, Mack,' Winkworth suggested. 'Don't be tempted to give them any more than you're comfortable with.'

'Understood.'

Winkworth looked at her watch. 'A minute to go,' she said. 'Are you both ready?'

'I just need a moment with the chief superintendent,' Mack said.

'I'll see you in there, then.' Winkworth opened the door and went into the conference room.

'What is it?' Beckton said.

'I just spoke to Fyfe. They found three more bodies last night.'

Beckton swore.

'I know,' Mack said.

'Does anyone else know?'

'Outside the team? I'm not sure. The press found out about the others very quickly.'

'We play any questions on that with a straight bat,' Beckton said. 'We're not getting into details this morning. Understood?'

'Yes, sir,' Mack said.

'Ready?'

Mack said that she was. Beckton pushed the door and led the way inside.

* * *

Mack took her seat as Winkworth explained to the reporters how the press conference would work. She said that there would be statements from Chief Superintendent Beckton and then Mack, and then there would be a brief opportunity for questions to be asked. Mack looked out into the room full of expectant faces and found that her throat had gone dry. She had had experience of press attention during the investigation at Grovely Farmhouse, but she had never been able to conquer her fear that she would say something that she shouldn't. The Christmas Eve Massacre had been a cause célèbre, a multiple murder that had not turned out to be quite as it seemed. This, though, had the potential to be much, much more notorious.

Winkworth finished her introduction and handed over to Beckton.

'Thank you all for coming,' he said. 'As you know, two bodies have been discovered in suspicious circumstances on Salisbury Plain. We are currently investigating the discoveries, and I'll hand over to DCI Mackenzie Jones now to take you through what we've found so far. Mack?'

That was it? Mack had expected a little more of a lead-in, but that, apparently, was all she was going to get. She cleared her throat and opened her notebook.

'Thank you, sir.' Cameras whirred, and there was a volley of flashes as her picture was taken. She blinked the glare away. 'On Monday, a member of the public alerted us to what he thought was a human bone that he found while walking his dog on Salisbury Plain. Subsequent tests confirmed that it was, indeed, human. We searched the immediate area, but did not find any other remains. We then broadened the search to include the village of Imber, two miles from where the bone was discovered. There are two graveyards in the village, and it was in the graveyard that used to serve the Baptist community there that we found a grave that we believe had been disturbed by Army exercises. We believe that a mortar round exploded in the graveyard and exposed a set of remains. An animal – a fox, most likely – was responsible for moving the bone to the location where it was found.'

She looked down at her notes to compose herself; she knew that what she had to say next would ignite the story. There was nothing that she could do to change that, though. 'The Home Office pathologist examined the bones and concluded that they were buried no later than twenty years ago. Since the last burial in the graveyard was in the 1940s, it was immediately obvious that this was something that warranted further investigation. An examination was carried out and concluded that the skeleton showed evidence of violence, in particular that the victim had been killed by strangulation. At that point, a murder investigation was established.'

'And now you've found multiple victims?'

Mack looked up into the banks of reporters, unable to see who had asked the question. Flashes fired again, and she looked back down at her notes, blinking the light away.

Multiple victims?

They knew already.

She took a sip of water. 'The area in the graveyard where the body was found is now being examined in detail. Although there is not much that I can tell you at this stage, I can say that the forensic officers at the scene believe that they have uncovered a second set of remains that could not have been legitimately buried there. A post-mortem has been scheduled for today, and we will share any further updates as appropriate.'

'But you've found more than two bodies,' the same reporter called out.

'Is that true?' another said.

'How many bodies have you found?' asked a third.

Beckton held up his hand. 'Please be assured that we are doing absolutely *everything* we can to find whoever was responsible and try to understand exactly what happened.'

'It's more than two, isn't it?'

'I'm not going to be drawn into speculation at this stage,' Beckton said. 'Detectives are following a number of lines of enquiry. We're urging anyone who knows anything about the remains to get in contact as soon as possible.' He looked into the closest camera lens and addressed the watching audience directly. 'We think it is very likely that members of the public will be able to help. *Any* information that they might have could be crucial to our investigation.'

There was tension in the room, and Mack would have preferred to go back upstairs and get down to work, but Mary Winkworth stood up and announced that they would take a few questions.

A reporter near the front of the room raised her hand, and Winkworth pointed to her.

'Cheryl Rodgers,' she said, '*Salisbury Journal.* Question for DCI Jones. Are you still digging at the graveyard?'

'We are,' Mack said.

'And do you think you'll find additional remains?'

'That has to be a possibility.'

The reporter who had interrupted before now did so again. 'Ian Bird from *The Sun.* I've been told that you found more remains last night. How many bodies *have* you found?'

Mack shuffled uncomfortably. 'I can't comment on that at the moment. But, as I just said, we think it is possible that there will be more bodies. We are continuing to dig. If there are other bodies there that shouldn't be, we'll find them.'

Winkworth pointed to another reporter with his hand raised.

'Can you give us an idea of what you think might have happened?'

'It's too early for that,' Mack said.

'But it has to be likely that the same person who killed the first person is responsible for the second?'

'And the others!' Bird called out.

'As I said, it's too early to speculate.'

'One more question,' Winkworth said.

A woman at the back of the room whom Mack recognised raised her hand.

'Victoria Bishop, BBC Wiltshire. DCI Jones – you were in charge of the investigation into the Christmas Eve Massacre.'

Bishop had been responsible for a number of negative reports from the early days of the Mallender case, and Mack already knew where this was going to end up. 'I was.'

'The wrong man was initially charged in that case. Why should the public trust you to get it right this time? Shouldn't someone else be in charge?'

Mack glanced over to see whether Beckton would defend her, but, seeing him gazing cravenly down at the desk, she saw that she was going to have to deal with this herself.

'Mistakes were made in the Mallender investigation, but Allegra Mallender and Tristan Lennox were ultimately found guilty of all charges against them. We made errors, yes. But they were corrected, and the guilty parties were convicted. I can assure you that what happened last year will not be something that'll distract me from this investigation.'

'I wasn't asking about whether you'd be distracted,' Bishop pressed. 'I was asking if it was right – given that this is likely to be a significant investigation and that there are some questions about how the last investigation was conducted – that you should be in charge.'

Finally, Beckton came to her defence. 'DCI Jones is one of our very best detectives. She has my *complete* confidence.' He held up his hands to stifle the competing follow-up questions. 'That's all for now. This is already a fast-moving investigation, and we have several leads that we need to follow up. I'd just say again that if any members of the public have information that they think might be of use in understanding what has happened here, then they should call Bourne Hill police station or, if they'd rather speak anonymously, they can call Crimestoppers. Thank you.'

Winkworth thanked the journalists for attending, and they started to make their way outside. Mack knew that there would be many more of them than this the next time that a briefing was held. She hadn't mentioned the likelihood that the same person was responsible for burying the bodies in the graveyard. But the thought of a serial killer would be like catnip to the men and women now making their way outside. Mack knew, with a sickening feeling in the pit of her stomach, that the investigation was going to be challenging and that she was going to be its public face. That was a pressure she could have done without.

'Well done, Mack,' Beckton said as the room cleared.

'Thank you, sir.'

'That last question. There was something in it.'

'About my competence?'

'*I* don't have any doubts in that regard, of course, but it goes without saying that we can't afford mistakes.'

'You know what happened with Lennox had nothing to do with me, sir. It wasn't my mistake.'

'I realise that,' he said. 'But you were the SIO, and the buck stops with you.'

'You're right,' she said, not entirely able to dull the annoyance in her voice. 'It does go without saying.'

Beckton stood; Mack got up, too, and followed him towards the door.

'What you said about "several leads",' she said. 'You know we don't have anything, don't you?'

'You have to give these people *something*. Get out there and find a few bones we can toss their way – pun intended. At least give them the impression that we're making progress.'

37

Atticus had spent a quiet couple of days wrapping up his work for James York. He had felt guilty at not giving Bandit the attention he deserved, so, with that in mind, he decided to take him out for a long hike. He went to Grovely Woods and followed the Roman road to the Monarch's Way, the route reputed to have been taken by Charles II after his defeat at the Battle of Worcester. The clouds were heavy, and the gloom was oppressive as he passed beneath stands of conifers that blocked out what little sunlight there was. Bandit had spent the first mile or two dashing into and out of the trees, but, now that they were at the five-mile mark, he was content to trot out in front. Atticus had chosen a route that avoided Grovely Farmhouse, but now that he was among the trees again, he found that his thoughts led back to the Mallender case and to Ralph Mallender, who was now living alone in the house where his family had been murdered. He shuddered at the thought of it.

He was still thinking about that when his phone rang.

'Hello?'

'It's me.'

'Mack,' Atticus said, 'I was just thinking about you.'

'What are you doing?'

'I'm out with Bandit. Why?'

'I need to see you.'

'About what?'

'Imber. I could do with your help. How long will it take you to get to the hospital?'

Atticus looked around. Five miles to get back to the car . . . He guessed that if he walked at a steady pace, he could be back where he'd started in ninety minutes. It would take another twenty minutes to drive from Great Wishford to the hospital.

He looked at his watch. 'I could be there at five.'

'I'll see you in the mortuary.'

He asked why she wanted to see him, but there was no answer. She had ended the call.

Bandit trotted back to him and nuzzled his hand.

'What do you think she wants, boy?'

The dog looked up at him.

'Well, whatever it is, we need to get a move on.'

38

Atticus dropped Bandit back at the office and continued on to the hospital. He parked his car and made his way to the mortuary. He pressed the button for the intercom and looked up into the camera overhead. The lock buzzed; he pushed the door back and went inside.

Mack came out from the door that led to the mortuary. Her face was grim.

'It was on the radio,' he said. 'You found another body.'

She gave a bitter chuckle. 'I wish it were as simple as that. We found that one and another three after that.'

'Shit.'

Mack looked tired. 'Five bodies that shouldn't be there. That's one way of describing it.'

'How can I help?'

'There's one set of remains I want you to look at.'

'Why that one?'

'Just come and look.'

Fyfe was waiting for them in the same forensic post-mortem suite as before. The air extraction system had been turned on this time, the fans trying – and failing – to scrub the smell from the room. The professor was bent over one of the examination tables.

'Good evening,' Atticus said.

Fyfe shared a look with Mack that told Atticus that the two of them had discussed whatever it was that he had been brought here to see.

'Over here,' Fyfe said.

The pathologist stepped aside to reveal the remains of a body on the table. It was very badly decomposed. Atticus recognised the havoc wrought by the microbes that escaped the gut in the days after death. They moved from the intestines into the tissue, veins and arteries, and then the liver and gallbladder, where they caused bile to escape and flood the body. Yellow-green remains would have indicated staining by the bile; time of death in that case might have been between three or four months. But this body was brownish-black; the blood vessels had deteriorated enough for the iron inside them to disperse.

'Two months?'

'Give or take,' Fyfe said. 'We'll get a better idea when we get the lab results back.'

'Male?'

'Yes. Early sixties.'

Atticus stepped closer and saw that the left trouser leg flattened out to nothing just below the knee. The denim had been neatly cut along the hem and, with the aid of a metal rod, Fyfe reached in and flipped the fabric back to reveal a silicone liner with a metal pin at the end.

'A prosthetic?'

'That's right,' Fyfe said. 'That pin slots into the pole component of a false leg.'

'Where's the prosthesis?'

'It doesn't look as if it was buried with the body,' Mack said. 'We haven't been able to find it, anyway.'

Atticus felt the first stirrings of disquiet. 'Do you have an identification yet?'

'Look,' Fyfe said, pointing with the metal rod.

Atticus ignored the stench and bent over the body. The clothes had started to disintegrate as the release of acidic fluids and toxins broke the fabric down. The nylon waistband of the underpants and the reinforced seams of the jeans were still intact; the rest of the denim was still recognisable but starting to rot. There were wisps of cotton around the upper torso, but the acid from the body and the moisture in the ground had almost completely disintegrated the fabric. The flesh looked soft and pulpy, a watery mush that was well on the way to becoming grave wax, the soap-like substance that was formed by the decomposition of the fattier parts of the body. Clumps of liquefying flesh still stuck to the silicone sleeve where the prosthesis would fit; Atticus looked down to where Fyfe was pointing. He saw a series of letters and numbers that had been etched into the metal pin.

LOT 5 6635.6625.

'Orthopaedic prostheses have serial numbers linked to barcoded labels,' Fyfe said.

'Which are recorded in medical files,' Atticus said. 'I know. It makes it easy to match the prosthesis with the patient.' Atticus realised now why he had been brought here. 'You think this is Alfred Burns, don't you?'

Mack watched him carefully as she nodded. 'It is Alfred Burns. The serial number matches.'

Atticus cursed under his breath.

'I know you wanted to catch him,' she said.

'I *did* catch him.'

'You did,' she said. 'You're right. And you wanted him to face justice for what he did. Maybe this is what justice looks like.'

Atticus shook his head. 'Unacceptable.'

He turned away from the table and stalked out of the room.

39

Atticus went outside and started walking back to his car.

'Wait!'

He stopped to allow Mack to catch up.

'Burns needed to be tried and convicted for what he did to those kids. *That*' – Atticus gestured back to the mortuary – '*that* is not justice.'

Mack put her hand on his arm. 'So help me find out what happened to him. He ended up in a graveyard where he should not have been. I've got another four bodies buried there when they shouldn't be. Four teenage girls. Burns was a paedophile. You proved that.'

His head was swimming. He threw up his hands. 'But why would he have been buried with them? That makes no sense at all.'

'I know. It doesn't. That's what I need to know. Who killed him? Why?' She reached out and squeezed his elbow. 'You know him better than anyone.'

'I'm not a policeman any more. What are you going to do – deputise me?'

'No. I'll bring you in as a consultant.'

Atticus chuckled. 'Come on. Beckton will never go for that.'

'He's already approved it. I called him an hour ago.'

'No,' he said. 'I was caught doing drugs. I was *fired*. Apart from anything else, I'll never pass vetting.' He reached his car and pulled out the fob.

'We might have had a lucky break there. It appears that no one thought to tell the Vetting Unit what happened.'

'You're kidding.'

'You know what it's like – the admin's slipshod at the best of times. It was never reported. You've still got your old clearance.'

'Okay – wait until you try to pay me and see how quickly someone in accounts shops me.'

'Yes, well, there's a way around that, too. Set up a company and invoice us through that. Wiltshire Police pays the company; the company pays you. You know as well as I do that they won't check.'

Atticus couldn't help but chuckle again. 'You must be desperate.'

'And I don't mind admitting it. We've someone out there who's responsible for five murders. Maybe more. We're already being battered by the press because of . . . what happened at the Mallender trial. Beckton doesn't like you, but he hates bad PR even more. I think his view is that anything we can do to get to the bottom of this case is worth it.'

Atticus chewed on his lip and leaned his back against the car. 'Are you still digging?'

'We are. We'll dig it all up now. The whole graveyard. I wouldn't be surprised at all if there were more.'

It was cold, and there was more moisture in the air. It looked as if the respite from the rain might only be temporary.

Mack turned to look at him. 'Burns was your case. I want you to be involved.'

He looked out across the car park.

'Come on, Atticus. Don't make me say it.'

He grinned. 'I'm going to need to hear the words.'

'Fine,' she said. 'I don't just want you. I *need* you. There – happy?'

'You just want me to make you look good when you close the case.'

'What kind of monster do you take me for?' she protested.

'The ambitious kind,' he said.

'Hurtful.'

'Yet you're not denying it. What's in it for me?'

'Isn't taking Beckton's shilling again enough?'

'I'm doing all right for business now.'

'Fine. You *don't* want to know what happened to Burns?'

'I do.'

'And you'd be able to ignore the opportunity of finding out yourself?'

'I think we both know the answer to that.'

'We do. So?'

He pushed himself off the car and walked a few paces away from it. 'I'll need access to everything. The forensics, witness statements—'

'We don't have any witnesses,' she reminded him.

He stopped and turned back to face her. 'I'll find witnesses.'

'I can get you the files from the last investigation.'

'No need.'

'You copied them?'

Atticus said that he had. It was a very well-established rule that you were not to remove sensitive documents from the office, but Mack responded with the briefest roll of her eyes; she had known him for long enough to know that was a tiny transgression when held against some of the other things that he had done.

She looked up into his face. 'Are you in or not?'

'I'm in.'

'Come to the station tomorrow. Bright and early. We'll need to introduce you to the team.'

'Not all of them are my biggest fans.'

'Leave that to me,' she said.

PART VI
SATURDAY

40

Mack sent Atticus a text and told him that she would be waiting for him in reception at eight o'clock. There was an outside broadcast van parked next to the Greencroft, and a clutch of reporters, wrapped up warm yet stamping their feet against the cold, were standing within sight of the entrance. Atticus wondered how much they knew. The city had been the centre of the media's attention for the Mallender case, and now it looked likely that the caravan would return. At least, he thought, the bodies hadn't actually been discovered in the city itself. Imber was a good way off, and that distance would provide insulation. But the investigation would be led from here, and that would bring the Fourth Estate back in their droves.

None of them recognised Atticus, thankfully, and he was able to pass inside the building without issue. Mack was waiting for him. She signed him in and indicated that he should go to the lift. She held her badge on the reader and waited for the doors to slice open.

'I'll get you a temporary pass,' she said.

'Beckton's still okay with this?'

'His actual words when I suggested this were "over my dead body".'

'You didn't tell me that.'

'Because I worked on him. It turns out – and please don't let this get to your head – that he has a high regard for your work.'

'That's nice.'

'He was especially impressed with Mallender.'

'Even though I ruined it for you.'

'Better than if Ralph had gone to prison for ten years and *then* the evidence came out. The damages are going to be bad enough, but they could have been astronomical.'

'Speaking of money . . .'

'You get paid on a day rate. Get your company to invoice me once a month, and I'll make sure it's sorted. This is all conditional on two things.'

'Go on.'

'You charge a *reasonable* day rate.'

'Six hundred.'

'Three.'

'Plus expenses.'

'Reasonable, unavoidable expenses.'

'The second thing?'

'Don't be an arse. *Please* don't be an arse. I'm vouching for you. It'll reflect badly on me if you start upsetting people again.'

'I'll do my best,' he said.

'*Atticus . . .*'

'I'll be good.'

They reached the door to major crimes. Atticus raised his hand to push it open and then hesitated. He hadn't been in here for months, not since he had been fired. He had enjoyed his work as a detective constable, at least for the most part. His erstwhile colleagues had tended towards the pedestrian, and they had often frustrated him with their obtuseness, but the problems he had been asked to solve had occasionally been interesting. Some of them – the Burns investigation came to mind – had even been challenging.

He looked through the pane of glass in the door. He could see the other detectives: Francine Patterson and Mike Lewis at the coffee machine, Nigel Archer at his desk, Robbie Best speaking to someone on his phone. Working here had been where he had met Mack. He had memories tied up in the room beyond the door.

Mack was looking at him. 'You okay?'

'Feels strange to be back.'

'It's just temporary. Don't get settled.'

'Did you tell the others?'

She paused.

'Mack, you *said* you'd tell them.'

'Didn't really have a chance,' she said. 'Look – relax. It'll be fine. They don't *all* hate you.'

He rolled his eyes.

'And some of us are grateful for your help.' She smiled as she pushed the door open. 'Come on. The sooner they know you're on board, the sooner we can start to work out what happened to Burns.'

41

Atticus followed Mack into the CID room. He went by his old desk, now occupied by Mike Lewis, ignoring the looks from the other officers and resisting the urge to give them a cheery hello.

'Everyone into the incident room,' Mack said, pointing to the conference room.

Atticus went inside and took a seat at the far end of the table. He looked around. There were several maps tacked to the wall: an Ordnance Survey 1:50,000 scale Landranger map of Salisbury Plain; an OS Explorer map at 1:25,000 scale; a 1:5,000 scale Landplan map of Imber; and an MOD map of the Salisbury Plain Training Area. A digital projector shone a square of light at the wall, and a large whiteboard had been used to note the responsibilities that had been assigned to each member of the team. An investigation like this had the potential to be demanding when it came to resources, and he knew that the detectives would be stretched since existing investigations would still be continuing.

The others made their way inside and took their seats.

Atticus surveyed them: Best, Archer, Lynas, Lewis and Patterson. A decent team – solid if uninspiring – but at least they would be well marshalled by Mack. He would need help in gathering the evidence to test his hypotheses, and that ought to be well within their capabilities.

Professor Fyfe joined Mack at the front of the room.

She rapped her knuckles against the table to bring the room to order. 'First things first – you'll all remember Atticus.'

He looked around the room; the others regarded him with a mixture of surprise and curiosity. Atticus knew that some of his unpopularity was because of jealousy. He was a much more effective detective than all of the others, and many of them resented him for it. He knew, too, that he was difficult to work with, and that his impatience with mediocrity meant that the others had often complained to the brass when assigned to work with him. He knew he ought to have tried harder to fit in, to smooth down the more abrasive aspects of his personality, but he had persuaded himself that the game wasn't worth the candle. He didn't need to get on with anyone else in order to do his job, and, he had rationalised, concentrating on fitting in meant that he was less focused on getting things done. His dismissal had given him time to think about the wisdom of that attitude, but he hadn't really changed his mind. And now, when he had been asked to come in and do this investigation a favour? He didn't intend to make an effort this time, either; they could adapt to him rather than the other way around.

Archer frowned. 'With respect, boss, what's he doing here?'

Mack steepled her fingers. 'There have been developments overnight that mean that we'll benefit from his experience. You'll see what I mean by that once the professor has brought us all up to speed. But, for now, Atticus will be joining the team as a consultant, reporting directly to me. I'd appreciate it if you would cooperate with him and help him out with anything that he needs. Any questions?'

Atticus looked around the room. None of the others held his eye, and he could sense the tension in the air. He could tell that Mack felt it too, but she ignored it with a bright smile and a gesture to Fyfe that he should begin.

'Thank you, Detective Chief Inspector. As you all know, we've been digging at the Baptist church in Imber. We've been there since Tuesday, and I can't see us leaving for the foreseeable future. I wanted to come and tell you what we've found so far, and what we're concerned we might find as we continue to dig.'

He took a laptop out of his case and connected it to the projector. He took a clicker from the desk and pressed it to wake the screen. The first photograph to be displayed was a shot of the disturbed ground that Bandit had found, looking down on the remains of Amy.

'This is Victim A,' Fyfe said. 'A young woman, likely fifteen or sixteen, medium height. We think she's been in the ground for around twenty years.'

He pressed the button, and the photograph of Amy was replaced by a new one. It, too, had been taken from the edge of a pit and looked down on a second skeleton.

'This is Victim B. We found him on Thursday. He was buried more recently – two months ago or thereabouts. Whereas we haven't yet been able to identify the first victim, we've been more fortunate with him. He had a prosthetic leg that we were able to trace by way of its serial number. It's Alfred Burns.'

'The name should be familiar to you,' Mack said.

'We had him on possession of child porn,' Archer said.

'And he got off,' Atticus said.

Lynas squinted at the screen. 'We're sure it's him?'

Fyfe nodded. 'We have his DNA on file, and we were able to extract enough to test it. Perfect match.'

There was a murmur of surprise.

'How did he end up there?' Nigel Archer mused.

'We don't know,' Mack said, 'but you can see why Atticus is going to be helpful in this investigation. He ran the Burns case. No one knows him like he does.'

Archer looked over at Atticus. 'So? What do you think?'

'Too early to say,' Atticus said.

'A vigilante? The parent of one of the kids he was fiddling with?'

'Possibly. But it doesn't explain why his body would be found in the same place as the other victims. Unlawful burials in a village where no one is supposed to go. That doesn't make sense.'

'What?' Lynas turned to Mack. 'Other victims?'

Fyfe clicked through a series of images that showed the other sets of remains that had been discovered.

'Victims C, D and E,' he said. 'All female. I'm starting the PMs this morning, but they're all young. Teenagers, like Amy.'

Lynas swore, and others around the table exchanged looks.

'Robbie?' Mack said. 'Can you update on the dig?'

'They've only excavated a small fraction of the area so far,' Best said. 'They're using radar to map the rest of the graveyard and, although they're finding evidence of bodies – as we'd expect – they do seem to match the existing plots that we have been able to identify from photographs taken before the graveyard was closed.'

'So you expect them to find more?'

'There's plenty of space for more.'

The atmosphere in the room dipped. Atticus knew why: the officers were mentally striking out any plans that they might have made for when they weren't on shift.

Archer leaned back in his seat. 'So it's a multiple killer.'

'Or killers,' Atticus corrected.

Archer ignored that and kept his eyes on Mack. 'What's the plan?'

'We need to search Imber,' Atticus said before Mack could speak. 'Not just the graveyard. *All* of it. How did those bodies get out there? Were they driven out there and then buried? Or were they taken to Imber while they were alive and *then* killed and buried?'

'Motive?'

'They're all young. Burns was involved in whatever's been happening there in one way or another. Teenage girls were his preference. The most likely explanation is that the victims were abused and then murdered there. Imber would be perfect for that. It's miles from anywhere, and there are empty buildings where there would be no chance of being disturbed.'

Mack nodded her agreement. 'The graveyard is already covered, but fan out from there and look at the buildings. You'll need help – go downstairs and speak to Bob Bradley. Borrow some of his uniforms. Speak to the Army to get access.'

'Anything we should be looking for in particular?'

'Signs of recent use,' Atticus said. 'Doors that have been forced. Padlocks that are missing. You'll have to cross-reference it all with the Army to eliminate anything that they've been doing.'

'The military police have assigned a liaison from the Special Investigations Branch,' Mack said. She checked the email that she had received. 'Sergeant Matt Shelton. He's going to base himself in the village.'

'I assume someone's been looking through the local mispers?' Atticus said.

'That's me,' Francine Patterson said. 'I'm working through them. Nothing yet.'

'Keep at it,' Mack said.

'Yes, boss.'

Archer raised a finger, and Mack indicated that he should speak. 'What about local nonces?'

Mack turned to Atticus. 'Did Burns ever work with anyone?'

'Not to my knowledge.'

'Maybe he found someone else with the same tastes,' Archer said. 'They worked together until they had a falling-out. The other one tops Burns and buries him with the victims.'

'Atticus?' Mack said.

He shook his head. 'That wasn't the way he went about things. He was a loner. It was a struggle to find anyone who was prepared to admit that they knew him.'

'We don't have anything else, though, do we?' Archer said. 'Must be worth a look.'

Mack turned back to Patterson. 'Run another search and look for anything that might connect anyone with previous for sexual offences to what we know about Burns. We'll also need reader/recorders set up for everything we find. This has to be efficient. There's going to be a lot of information generated – we can't have any of it going in the wrong places.'

'No problem, boss.'

'Atticus,' Mack said, 'can you take Burns? Check his background and see if there's anything that we ought to be looking at. See if you can give Francine something to work with.'

Atticus was already well along that path, but he decided to keep that – and the angles he thought were worth pursuing – to himself. 'I'll get on it this morning,' he said, intending to do nothing of the sort.

'What about the press?' asked Best.

'We need to be very aware of the fact that this is going to be a big story. The conference yesterday was already busy – we'll have to announce the additional bodies soon, and it'll go through the roof. We're fortunate that the dig site is in a restricted area. But you will have noticed there are reporters outside the nick this morning. That's going to be standard from now on, and it'll get worse when they realise the scope of what we are dealing with. We'll all have to tread carefully. Goes without saying that nothing leaves these four walls. *Nothing*. I don't want to find that anyone's been talking out of school – Beckton will *not* be happy if that happens. Neither will I.'

Mack brought the meeting to a close, and the team dispersed to get to work on the tasks that they had been assigned. Fyfe told Mack that he was going to go back to the lab, and the detectives ambled out of the conference room and went back into the office. Mack waited for Atticus at the door.

'Run everything by me,' she said.

'Come on, Mack. I know what I'm doing.'

'Please?'

She knew him too well. Atticus had forgotten how frustrating it could be to have to get approval for everything that he wanted to do. It had driven him to distraction before, and the independence he had found as a freelancer had been one of the things he had enjoyed most of all.

'I've put my neck on the line for you,' she said when he didn't answer.

'I know. You don't need to worry. I'm not going to do anything that reflects badly on you.'

'Promise me.'

'I promise.'

42

Atticus walked back to the office. Bandit greeted him at the door, and Atticus ruffled the dog's fur before going over to his chair and waking his computer. He navigated to the folder where he had stored the information that he had gathered about Alfred Burns. He had obsessed about him for so long that he had memorised the details of his life, but he wanted to refresh himself.

It was all there: transcripts of the interviews that he had conducted, photographs of Burns's photographic studio where Atticus suspected that he had conducted most of his crimes, and a detailed biography that Atticus himself had written. He clicked through everything until he found the pictures that had been taken of Burns on his arrest. He flicked through the mug-shots, photographs of the suspect staring into the camera with the smugness of a man who was confident that his wit and guile would be more than a match for the provincial officers who would try to prove his guilt. Atticus recalled that contemptuous sneer; he had managed to wipe it off Burns's face during the interrogation, but it had only been temporary. Burns's disdain had returned after he had been acquitted, and his scornful expression had haunted Atticus's sleep ever since.

Because he knew: Burns would have been emboldened by his escape and would have returned to his perversions with the confidence that he was beyond the reach of the police.

But now he was dead.

Atticus had to find out what had happened.

He opened the biography. He had written ten pages following Burns's arrest and had continued to add to it as he had discovered additional information after the acquittal. It was thirty pages long now.

Burns was born in Surbiton in 1957, one of a pair of illegitimate twins who had never met his father. His mother was religious and had been so ashamed of her boys' birth that she had tried to have them adopted before emigrating to Australia to escape the stigma. The adoption never took place and, instead, Alfred and Derek were placed with foster parents.

The young Alfred was a loner who showed aggressive tendencies with the few friends that he had. He was bullied by children who were older than him, and reflected that behaviour onto those who were younger. Both twins had been abused by their foster parents and, after their deaths, the boys had been transferred to a children's home, where Alfred had subsequently been abused by a male member of staff. Derek Burns was less intelligent than his brother, but, lacking Alfred's inflated opinion of himself, was more apt to conform and at least leave school with qualifications. Alfred decided that school was beneath him and left with nothing and no prospects. There had been the idea of getting into photography, but without the money to set himself up, and with nothing else available to him, he had joined the Royal Green Jackets in 1976.

His first tour of Northern Ireland was in 1979, patrolling the streets of Ballymurphy. There were two subsequent tours, concluding with a final tour in Londonderry in the early eighties. It was brought to an end in 1982 – together with Burns's Army career – at a bar in Ballykelly when an INLA bomb exploded, killing seventeen people and leaving him badly injured. His leg was shredded by shrapnel and was amputated a day later. A medical discharge followed, and thereafter began the unravelling of his life.

Burns had been based at the garrison in Tidworth and, familiar with the area, he moved to Salisbury. There had been a number of jobs: an administrative position with the Ministry of Defence, a job at the council allocating funds to local groups, a short-lived business as a handyman and gardener. He had nurtured his interest in photography and, armed with a hard-won medical payout following his discharge, had eventually set himself up as someone who could take pictures of family events, portraits and the like.

He had been arrested in 2019 after the National Crime Agency received intelligence from abroad that the IP address associated with Burns's computer had been using encrypted services to host indecent images of children. Burns admitted after his arrest that he had always been interested in deviant pornography, although he would not speak of the paedophilic images that had been hidden in a locked folder on his hard drive. He insisted that he had no interest in those images and did not know how they had reached his computer. He argued that they might have been automatically downloaded into his system as part of other downloads, or as a result of the actions of others, suggesting in particular that people he met in chat rooms had occasionally posted indecent images. He also admitted to downloading packages of what he believed to be adult pornography, and suspected that some of the criminal images had arrived from those downloads.

His arguments did not prevent him from being charged. He appeared for trial in the magistrates' court and pleaded not guilty. His defence relied upon a computer expert who stated that it was impossible to say how the images had ended up on his hard drive. No one could prove when the images had been downloaded, and it was clear that nothing in their titles suggested their content. The judge doubted the strength of the evidence that had been adduced, and Burns was acquitted.

Atticus had been furious. He knew that Burns had benefitted from errors made by the prosecution, and that he was as guilty as sin. The case that he had spent so much time building had been botched, but that wasn't the reason for his frustration. It was because he knew that the charges laid were not commensurate with the real depth of Burns's depravity. He was convinced that Burns was guilty of more than just possessing the images; he believed that he had been making them, too. Atticus was sure that Burns had taken illicit photographs of the girls who passed through his studio. He had inspected the changing rooms in minute detail and found holes in the walls and floor that he suspected had been made in order to accommodate hidden lenses. But there was no evidence beyond the holes, and, without more, there were no charges that could be brought.

That was not the full extent of Atticus's suspicions. There had been reports in Salisbury for more than five years of a man who had been assaulting teenage girls. The suspect had always been careful; he struck only when there were no witnesses, in areas that did not have CCTV coverage, and obscured his face with scarves wrapped around his nose and mouth. Atticus had reviewed those cases and had been struck by a fact that had appeared in all the descriptions of the suspect: he was said to walk with a limp. That obviously wasn't enough to pursue a case against Burns, but Atticus *knew*.

It was him.

He knew, too, that predators like Burns progressed up a ladder of offending: they started at the bottom, with porn; they graduated to taking their own pictures of their victims; and then, when that wasn't enough, they began to be more active in their offending. Eventually, when repetition dulled the thrill of the illicit, they escalated further.

Atticus had known where that would lead, and had not been prepared to risk the death of a child because he had not been able to nail Burns.

Now, though?

Burns was dead, laid to rest in a graveyard with the bodies of four young women.

And Atticus needed to know why.

He opened the list of Burns's friends and family. There were precious few of the former, and, with both foster parents dead and his birth parents untraceable, Atticus was left with Alfred's brother.

He looked up Derek Burns's address and decided to pay him a visit.

43

Derek Burns lived in Idmiston, a village to the north of Salisbury. Atticus put Bandit in the back of the car and drove north, arriving at eleven o'clock. The town had grown over the years, swollen by its association with the military, and the village had been absorbed into it. Burns's house was in an estate near to All Saints' Church. The road was a cul-de-sac, climbing a slope to a turning circle that was choked with the cars of those who lived there. Burns's property was detached, with a garage at the front of the property, two large windows above it and a white fascia gable. Atticus had checked on Rightmove and saw that the house was advertised for just over £1,000 a month.

Atticus parked alongside and was about to get out when he noticed a man leading a dog towards the open fields to the north. The dog was a chocolate Labrador, and Atticus recognised him from the time he had interviewed his owner during the Burns investigation.

Atticus got out and went around to let Bandit out. He clipped the dog's lead to his collar, locked the car and followed Burns and his dog.

* * *

Bandit tugged at his lead, but Atticus held him back to give Derek the opportunity to get out of the estate. They continued north until they reached an open field. There was a metal gate that the Labrador was able to wriggle underneath. Atticus took out his phone and quickly recorded video as Derek clambered over the gate and hopped down into the mud on the other side. Atticus unclipped Bandit and climbed into the field himself, catching up with Derek as the two dogs sprinted towards each other and exchanged excited barks.

'Lovely dog,' Atticus said to Derek.

'And yours.'

The two dogs raced away into the field. Atticus smiled at Derek and waited for his expression to sour with distaste.

It didn't take long.

'I remember you,' Derek said. 'You're police.'

'That's right,' he said, not seeing any reason to correct the misapprehension – which was, after all, *nearly* correct.

'Not again,' he complained. 'This is about Alfred?'

'It is.'

'It was bad enough last time. You harassed him. You harassed *me*.'

'That's really Alfred's fault, isn't it?'

'They found him not guilty.'

'And we both know that was ridiculous.'

'No,' Derek said, 'we don't. It was a fit-up, from start to finish.'

'We'll have to agree to disagree on that. I need to ask you a few extra questions.'

'Am I obliged to answer them?'

'No. But I think you'll want to cooperate.'

'No, I don't think I will.'

Derek set off, following the edge of the field as the dogs continued to gambol around each other.

Atticus followed. 'When was the last time you saw Alfred?'

'Haven't you been listening? I'm not talking to you.'

'I'm not investigating Alfred this time.'

'Bullshit. I remember you – you were the one who had it in for him.'

'Really, I'm not.'

'Do you think I was born yester—'

'Alfred's dead.'

That stopped Derek in his tracks. 'What?'

'He was murdered.'

'No,' he said. 'That can't be right.'

'Sometime in the last couple of months. He was buried on Salisbury Plain. We dug up his body on Wednesday. It hasn't been announced to the press yet, but I doubt it'll be long before they find out.'

Derek's mouth hung open. 'I don't ... I mean ... I mean, who would murder him?'

'Come *on*,' Atticus said. 'There would've been a long line of people.'

'You think this is because of . . .' He waved his hand. 'Because of . . .'

'The child pornography?' Atticus finished for him. 'I don't know. That's what I'm trying to find out.'

'Jesus,' Derek said, exhaling. '*Jesus*.'

'That's why I need you to help me. I want to find out what happened to him.'

Derek looked stunned.

'He went abroad, didn't he – after the trial?'

'I don't know,' Derek said.

'Yes, you do.'

Derek walked off again.

Atticus followed once more. 'When did he get back into the country?'

'I wish I could help, but I can't.'

'You defended him before, Derek, and I always wondered why. Did you know more about what he was doing than you said? Were you involved?'

Derek looked back with anger in his eyes. '*No*. We were never close. I don't know where he went after the trial. I haven't seen him for months. That's it. I don't know anything else. I'm sorry, really, but I can't help you.'

Derek was no fool, but he was not a good enough liar to pull the wool over Atticus's eyes. He had managed to keep his face neutral, save the odd twitch, but it was the manner of his voice that gave the game away. Atticus had already established a baseline with his initial questions: Derek had been surly and defensive. There had been a definite change as he moved onto the more challenging, interrogative questions. He had become less defensive, as if he thought he might be more persuasive if he gave the impression that he was cooperating. That, combined with a more basic tell – he'd nodded his head 'yes' when he denied seeing his brother – was all Atticus needed to know that he was withholding.

'How's your health?'

Derek glared at him. 'What?'

'You were the victim of an assault, weren't you? I remember, from before. What was it – two years ago?'

Atticus saw the flicker of concern pass across Derek's brow; he covered it up with a scowl, but it was too late. 'Eighteen months.'

'But you're still claiming disability allowance?'

Derek didn't answer.

'I looked into your case before. You said that you'd been beaten while you were out walking the dog. Unprovoked. You didn't recognise who did it – that's right, isn't it?'

'Yes,' Derek muttered.

'You could only walk with a stick. You injured your back – that's what you said. The thing with back injuries, though, they're *so* hard to disprove. The amount of money the insurance industry loses to drivers who say they got whiplash after someone tapped them in the back – scandalous, isn't it?'

'What's your point?'

'You know.' Atticus smiled at him, as innocent as a lamb. 'You're out here exercising the dog, no sign of the walking stick. And you looked pretty spry climbing over that gate. I was surprised, given what you've said about how badly you were injured. I was *so* surprised that I took a video of it. I expect the Department for Work and Pensions would be surprised, too.'

'Are you threatening me?'

'I suppose I am. But if you help me out and answer some questions about your brother, then perhaps I could be persuaded to ignore that video and trust you to do the right thing about whether you should or shouldn't be claiming. But that's up to you.'

Derek walked on for a handful of paces before muttering a curse under his breath. 'What do you want to know?'

'Where did he go, after the trial?'

'Vietnam.'

'For how long?'

'He was there for six months; then he moved on to Thailand.'

'What was he doing there?'

'He said he needed a holiday.'

Derek looked across at Atticus, perhaps to gauge whether his answer was credible. Atticus saw anxiety and suspicion; Derek knew full well what his twin had been doing in Asia and was worried that it might blow back on him. Fear of incrimination was the reason for his reticence. Atticus hid his own disgust; he would extract the information he needed and then, when Alfred's murder was solved, he would poke into Derek's dirty secrets.

'And then? After that? When did he come back?'

'October.'

'Why?'

'He ran out of money.'

'And you helped him?'

He chuckled bitterly. 'I'm not exactly flush. Did you see where I live? I've got a shitty rented house, and I don't have a pot to piss in. I gave him what I could.'

'Which was what?'

'Four hundred quid to rent a place for a month.'

'Where?'

'Andover.'

'I'm going to need the address.'

Derek recited it.

'After that? When was the last time you spoke to him?'

'Not long after I gave him the money. He said he needed more.'

'For what?'

'He wanted to go back to Asia. I didn't have anything else I could give him. We argued, and he left.'

'No other contact after that? Phone call?'

'He texted me just before Christmas,' he said, stuffing his hand into his pocket and pulling out an old iPhone. He tapped the text icon, found the sender he wanted and read from the screen. '"It's sorted. Don't need you." That's it.'

Atticus held out his hand, and Derek handed over the phone. Atticus looked at the message, confirmed that Derek had read it accurately, and then checked to see when it had been sent. It was as Derek had suggested.

The dogs trotted over to them as Atticus handed the phone back.

'Did he say anything else? Something that might make sense now that this has happened?'

'No. Nothing.'

'When he said it was sorted – that was about the money he wanted. Yes?'

'That's what I took it to mean.'

'Thank you,' Atticus said.

'What now?'

Atticus clipped Bandit's lead onto his collar. 'Don't go anywhere,' he said. 'I'll be in touch.'

44

Atticus drove back into Salisbury so that he could drop Bandit at the office. The dog was tired and, after wolfing down the food that Atticus scooped out of the can for him, he settled down on the sofa with his head on his paws and went to sleep.

Atticus went into the bedroom and uncovered his leather satchel from beneath a pile of clothes. He tipped out the things that he had taken to London and repacked it with his multitool and his set of lock picks. He added a pair of latex gloves and overshoes, included the same camera as before, and then zipped it up. He undressed in order to change into black jeans, a black hooded top and a pair of black trainers with smooth soles.

He went over to pet the dog, slung his satchel over his shoulder and locked up. He thought about driving, but decided it would be quicker by train. Andover was two stops from Salisbury, and he ought to be able to get there in thirty minutes.

*   *   *

Atticus took out his phone and opened the chess app. He saw that Jack_of_Hearts had moved their knight to c3. Atticus stared at the board, plotting out his response, and was just about to make a move when a message arrived in his inbox.

> *Hello, Atticus. I'm pleased you agreed to another game.*

Atticus looked at the message and tried to put himself in the position of the person who had just sent it. He had no idea about Jack at all: they could be a man or a woman, young or old, and, although the flag by the avatar suggested that he or she was in the United Kingdom, it would have been easy enough to use a VPN to spoof that.

> *I've enjoyed playing with you. And I like a challenge.*
> *That makes two of us.*
> *I'll be honest, though – your last messages were unsettling.*
> *Why?*
> *You know more about me than should be possible. How do you know my name?*

Jack replied with a smiley emoji and then another message.

> *I'd rather leave a little mystery if you don't mind.*
> *I'm not sure what I think about that. At least tell me yours.*
> *Jack.*

Atticus stared at the message, wondering how best to reply, when Jack sent another.

> *I'm pleased that Alfred Burns is dead, although what happened to him isn't justice.*

Atticus found he was holding his breath. He typed.

> *How do you know about Burns?*
> *Our paths crossed several years ago. I had hoped that your first investigation might have found out a little more. You knew that he was guilty of more than the dirty pictures, didn't you?*

The cursor flashed; Atticus didn't know how to respond.

> *I know you'll find more this time.*

Atticus looked around, suddenly fearful that Jack was in the carriage with him. But he was not; it was late, and the carriage was empty save for him.

Atticus looked back to the phone.

> *Your move.*
> *JACK_OF_HEARTS HAS LEFT THE CONVERSATION.*

45

Atticus spent the remainder of the journey staring at the exchange and trying to work out how it was possible that Jack knew so much about him and the investigation into Burns. Again, just like before, he was thwarted.

It was half past nine in the evening when Atticus disembarked from the train and walked to the address that Derek Burns had provided. It was a flat above an off-licence on Bridge Street. The buildings on this side of the road were three storeys tall, with commercial premises on the ground floor. Number 13 was sandwiched between a door that led up to a unisex hair salon – 'A Cut Above' – and an off-licence. The door to the property was next to a bank of letterboxes that suggested that there were six flats behind it. There was an intercom next to the letterboxes with cardboard inserts that identified each tenant; the insert for Flat 5 was empty.

Atticus looked at the door. It was not particularly impressive, with a series of glass panels between thin wooden slats. He would have been able to force it, but it faced onto a busy street, and a group of youngsters had congregated outside a nearby burger bar. There was no way that he would be able to get inside without giving himself away.

He walked down the road a little, crossing over onto the other side and leaned against the wall of a passage that offered access to a parking space behind the shops. The kids outside looked as if they were settling in for the long haul, and a group of four older men – Atticus assumed from their buzz cuts that they were soldiers – got out of a cab and went into the Dragon Garden Chinese restaurant.

His phone rang. He took it out and saw that it was Mack. He was tempted to ignore the call, but couldn't rule out the possibility that there had been a break in the case.

'Evening,' he said.

'Where are you?'

'Andover.'

'What are you doing there?'

'Following up on a lead.'

'Go on,' she prompted.

'I'm looking into Burns, like I said. It's nothing yet – if I find anything out, you'll be the first to know.'

'Heard that before.'

'I promised – I won't do anything to embarrass you.'

He knew that the sensible thing to do would be to tell Mack that he had found out that Alfred Burns had only recently been back in the country and that he had been living just over the road from where he was standing now. But Mack would need to apply for a search warrant to legitimately get inside the property – none of the exceptions to the Police and Criminal Evidence Act would apply in these circumstances – and that would take time.

Atticus was impatient, and he had the advantage of being able to investigate Burns while the news of his murder was yet to break. Once that changed, things were liable to get unpredictable. Whoever was responsible for murdering him and burying him in the graveyard would be forewarned; outstanding evidence might be destroyed and the trail obscured.

He wasn't going to wait for that to happen.

Atticus's method wasn't legal, but that would only be relevant if he was found out. He would just make sure that he was careful.

'Can I ask you a question?' he said. 'Have you gone public with Burns's identity yet?'

'Not officially,' she said.

'Unofficially?'

'It might have leaked. There've been tweets naming him in the last couple of hours. We can't play dumb without looking like we're hiding something, so we're preparing a statement. Should go out in the next hour.'

He wondered whether he should mention Jack, but decided against it. He didn't really know what he could tell her – that he was being trolled by someone whom he couldn't identify who knew more about him and his work than ought to have been possible? Where would that get him? He needed to know more first.

'Anything to report at your end?' he asked instead.

'Two things, actually. The PM on Burns has come back.'

'Cause of death?'

'Unclear. There's a hole in the top of his head.'

'A bullet?'

'Fyfe doesn't think so. There's scorching around it, but he says the pattern isn't what you'd see from a gunshot at close range, and there's no foreign object – no casing or anything metallic – inside the hole. He's asking for a second opinion.'

'The second thing?'

'A bit more conclusive. We have a name for one of the victims. Abbie Ross. She went missing in 2005.'

'You're sure?'

'Dental records,' Mack said. 'Fyfe's confident.'

'What do we know about her?'

'Seventeen years old, broken childhood, ended up in foster care. Last seen at Grosvenor House youth club near the railway station. They had regular music nights there. She played bass in a band. They rehearsed, she left to walk home, and she was never seen again.'

Atticus closed his eyes and dug back through his memories. 'Burns was connected to Grosvenor House,' he said. 'He worked for the council – he was a caretaker, I think. See if you can dig anything out.'

'I'll check.'

'And try to find anyone who went there at the time she disappeared.'

'Already doing it.'

'What about the other victims?'

'Still looking.'

Atticus looked over at the building again; he had an idea how he might get inside. 'I'd better go.'

'Keep me posted.'

'Ditto.'

He ended the call.

46

There was a Domino's further along Bridge Street. Atticus went inside and ordered a large margherita. He paid for it and took it back to the door to the flats. He pressed the button for Flat 2, the one Alfred Burns had been living in before he died.

There was no answer.

He tried the button for Flat 1.

'Hello?'

'Pizza.'

'Wrong address.'

'No, I think this is the right one.'

'I didn't order pizza. Piss off.'

Atticus took a moment, then pressed the third button.

'Hello?'

'Pizza.'

'Sorry – what?'

'Pizza delivery.'

'I don't think we ordered pizza.'

'You're flat three?'

'That's us. But we didn't order anything.'

Atticus sighed. 'Must be a prank call. We've had them before here. Look – I've got a pizza, and I'm just going to have to throw it away otherwise. Would you like it?'

'I don't have any money.'

'No charge.'

'Go on, then. That's kind. We're on the second floor.'

The lock buzzed and the door opened. Atticus pushed it back and went inside, following the stairs to the first-floor landing. There were two doors, the one on the left marked with 1 and the other with 2.

Atticus crossed the landing and climbed the stairs to the second floor. The layout was identical, with another two doors. The door to the left, marked with a 3, was open, and warm light spilled out onto the gloomy landing.

Atticus tapped his knuckles on the open door. 'Hello? Domino's.'

He heard footsteps, and the door opened all the way. There was a young woman there, late teens or early twenties, dressed in black and with black make-up around her eyes. Atticus heard music in the background and recognised the Sisters of Mercy.

'Thanks again,' she said, taking the box from Atticus.

'Sorry to bother you,' he said.

'Free pizza?' She smiled. 'No bother at all.'

'I was in here last week,' Atticus said. 'The flat downstairs. The customer was really weird.'

'Really?'

'Flat two. There was something about him.'

'Sorry,' she said. 'Don't know the neighbours at all. We just moved in.'

The girl closed the door, and Atticus heard the sound of laughter from inside. He went down the stairs again and stood in front of the door to Alfred Burns's flat. It was thin and flimsy. The landlord had evidently taken the decision that he could afford to be stingy with the quality of materials inside, given that the front door would deter most unwanted visitors from accessing the building. That wasn't the soundest philosophy – it had been easy enough to get in, and now he could spend as long as he liked picking the lock – but he doubted the landlord was prepared to spend a penny more than strictly required.

Atticus reached into his bag and took out the gloves and overshoes. He put them on and then fetched his lock picks. The door was secured with a simple Yale lock; he took out a tension wrench and a pick, slid the former into the top of the keyway and the latter into the bottom. He raked the pins, jiggling them quickly, and used the wrench to ensure that they fell and stuck in place at the shear line. He turned the lock and the door swung open. It had taken less than twenty seconds and made very little noise.

He stepped inside the flat.

47

Atticus closed the door behind him and turned to look at the flat. It was tiny. The door opened into an abbreviated hallway, almost small enough for Atticus to be able to touch the walls to his left and right by raising his arms. He stepped forward, passing a door to a small bathroom with a shower and a toilet and a sink, and then a minuscule kitchen against the wall on the left. Atticus opened the fridge and gagged at the stench of rancid milk. He took the bottle and looked at the best-by date: it was two months ago. There were two cans of lager, a rotting apple and nothing else. He shut the door.

The main room, no more than fifteen feet by fifteen feet, combined the living room and bedroom. There was a bed jammed into a space that was only just large enough for it, and a settee faced a television that rested on a modest unit. The flat looked as if it had been recently refurbished, but there was no escaping the fact that it was compact.

Atticus started to look around. The bed was unmade, the sheets rumpled and stained. There were dirty plates in the sink, and an unfinished microwave lasagne lay discarded on the counter, still in its plastic tray, the cellophane film torn off and curled at the edges.

It felt strange. Atticus had investigated Alfred Burns for months – both officially and then, after he'd been sacked, on his own – and had built up a picture that was so comprehensive that it sometimes felt as if he were inside Burns's head. He had been involved in the search of Burns's Salisbury house and had found the stash of pornography that had been instrumental in building the case against him. That was months ago, and Burns had used the interim to disappear from view. To be inside his flat, to see his possessions, felt almost like reacquainting himself with someone he had once known. Some things were familiar: the framed picture of Burns and his brother from their childhood, feeding goats through the fence of a petting zoo; a green Army surplus greatcoat that Burns had worn when Atticus first arrested him, now dumped on the floor. Other things, though, were different. The furniture was cheap and disposable, most likely supplied by the landlord. The television still had the sticker from the British Heart Foundation affixed to the side, advertising the price and confirming that it had been given an electrical safety test. Burns had enjoyed a little money before, but it was clear that he had fallen upon harder times.

Atticus went over to a low bookshelf that stood next to the television. There was a collection of cheap paperbacks stacked side by side and, in a deeper shelf at the bottom of the case, a set of ring binders. Atticus took the first binder over to the settee and opened it. It contained bank statements from KBank. Atticus took out his phone and googled the name; it was an abbreviation of Kasikornbank, a Thai bank headquartered in Bangkok. Burns must have set up an account when he fled to Thailand in the aftermath of his acquittal. The statements were monthly and had been arranged in reverse chronological order; Atticus turned the pages to the first statement. The account had been opened with a deposit of five thousand pounds in December 2017. Atticus ran his finger down the separate entries and saw the activity that he would have expected to find: small cash withdrawals in Thai baht, payments to supermarkets in Bangkok and Chiang Mai, online shopping. The five thousand had not been topped up and looked as if it had been husbanded as carefully as Burns could manage. He had eked it out until, with six hundred pounds left, there was a payment of £468 to Lufthansa. Atticus could guess what that payment denoted, and a quick Google search confirmed it: a flight from Suvarnabhumi to Heathrow was between four hundred and five hundred pounds.

Could the fact that Alfred had needed money be connected to his death? Derek Burns had said that his brother had solved his financial problems. How had he done that?

Atticus put the folder back in the bookshelf and stepped back against the far wall so that he could look back into the flat in the hope that he might see something that would give him a better idea why Burns had been murdered.

There had to be *something*.

He lifted the mattress off the bed to see whether anything had been hidden between it and the slats of the frame.

Nothing.

He went to the kitchen and opened the oven and the microwave. He opened the cupboards and took out the meagre collection of pots and pans, then the crockery. He looked for any sign of loose tiles, then dropped down to his knees and pressed against the kick-board, pushing one side in so that he could pull it away and shine his torch into the void behind it.

Nothing.

He went back to the mattress and stripped the sheets. He examined it closely and, as he turned it over to look at the bottom, a flap of fabric fell open. He dragged it out into the middle of the floor – there was just barely enough space to set it down between the frame of the bed and the settee – and pulled the flap back. It wasn't wear and tear; it was deliberate. An opening had been cut, either with a knife or a pair of scissors. Atticus reached inside and felt the edge of a square or rectangular object. He closed his fingers around it and pulled it out: it was a brick of banknotes, sealed with an elastic band. The notes were twenties and, as he riffled the edge, he guessed there must be a hundred of them. He put the bundle down and reached into the mattress for a second time. He pulled out another brick and, reaching back inside again and again, pulled out another three. That made five in total and, checking them one against the other, Atticus estimated that there must be at least ten thousand pounds.

Here was the money Alfred had been seeking.

How had he come by it?

Atticus paused.

He had heard something.

Footsteps.

He waited, expecting to hear the sound of the other door on the corridor opening and closing, but it did not.

He closed his eyes and listened for the sound of footsteps climbing the stairs to the next floor up, but, again, he heard nothing.

He tried to remember if he had locked the door to the flat. He didn't think that he had.

He killed his phone's flashlight and looked for somewhere to hide. The bathroom was the only room that had the privacy of a door. The bed was screened from the kitchen by a short partition, and that, at least, would offer a place where he wouldn't be seen from the front door.

He stepped across the mattress, trying to avoid making a noise, and slid into the narrow envelope of space between the frame of the bed and the partition.

He heard the squeak of the door handle and then the creak of the door as it was pushed open.

48

Atticus heard the sound of footsteps and then the door closing with a gentle click. He heard the bathroom door opening, and the click of the light switch as the cord was pulled. The switch clicked again, and the bathroom door creaked as it was closed. He heard a gentle scrape as a pot or pan was moved on the counter, then a clink as a plate knocked against another one.

He saw the tight beam of a torch sweep out into the living space, follow the wall from left to right, then jerk away as the torch was pointed somewhere else.

Footsteps, drawing closer.

Atticus looked for something that he could use as a weapon, but there was nothing.

He crept to the edge of the partition and held his breath.

The torch shone out again, sweeping left to right against the wall.

A man stepped into the living space. He was big – bigger than Atticus, both in terms of height and build – and dressed all in black. He wore black trainers on his feet, the soles squeaking against the laminated floor as he pivoted.

He wore a pair of black jeans, a black bomber jacket, and gloves. He had a cap on his head and was facing away, the angle preventing Atticus from getting a look at him.

The man took three steps forward, leaving Atticus enough space to try to slip out from behind the partition and get back to the door. Atticus moved, but, as he did, he saw his reflection in the glass of the uncovered window that looked down onto the street.

The man saw it, too. He spun back around to face him.

It was too dark for Atticus to make out the details of his face. He saw glimpses: thick eyebrows, a squat, flat nose. The man didn't speak. Instead, and without warning, he closed the distance between them, drew back his fist and threw out a jab. Atticus managed to bring his arm up just in time, catching the inside of the man's right arm so that the punch deflected a little, his knuckles biting into Atticus's cheekbone rather than his chin. He felt a flash of intense pain and stumbled back into the kitchen. The man followed him, drawing back his fist again. Atticus bumped against the counter as the man uncorked a clubbing cross into Atticus's ribs, punching the air out of his lungs. He gasped for breath, raised both hands and shoved the man away from him. He felt heavy slabs of muscle beneath his shoulders and was dismayed by how little he was able to move him back.

Atticus reached out behind him, his fingers closing around the handle of a saucepan. He swung it, as hard as he could, but his assailant had seen what he was doing and stepped up, inside the arc of the swing. The saucepan missed the man's head and fell from Atticus's fingers, crashing against the floor with a loud clang. The man grabbed Atticus's jacket in both hands and drove him back against the counter; his elbow struck a stack of dirty plates and toppled them onto the floor, the plates shattering noisily.

Atticus slid his forearms between the man's arms and tried to force them apart, but the man was too strong. Atticus tried to knee him in the groin, missed, and, his attention momentarily distracted, didn't notice his assailant draw back his head and then bring it forward. The butt connected with Atticus's forehead and, for a moment, he saw stars.

He was aware of stumbling ahead and then falling to his knees.

PART VII
SUNDAY

49

Atticus opened his eyes and groaned. His head was throbbing and, when he reached up to touch his temple, he saw blood on his fingertips. He remembered: he had been attacked. He must have banged his head on something and blacked out. He was lying flat on his stomach, and, as he gingerly tried to raise himself, he felt a dizzying rush and the certainty that he was about to be sick. He lay back down and waited, closing his eyes again and concentrating on his breathing until he was sure that the moment had passed.

He tried to sit again and, this time, managed to push himself up. He shoved back so that he was leaning against the wall and, taking another breath, pushed himself to his feet. The dizziness returned, and he had to steady himself with a hand against the wall. He made his way over to the mattress. He had left the bundles of notes on the floor next to it, but now, as he looked down, he saw that they were gone.

He lowered himself to sit on the settee, took out his phone and dialled Mack.

'Atticus? What is it?'

He managed a grunt in reply.

'It's midnight. What's up?'

Atticus tried to speak, but his head suddenly swam, and he swallowed back another wave of nausea.

'Atticus – what is it?'

'There's been an . . . incident,' he said.

'What incident? Are you okay? You sound half asleep.'

'Someone . . . jumped me. Banged my head.'

'Jumped you?'

He made an affirmative noise.

'What are you talking about? Are you still in Andover?'

'Found . . .' He felt vomit in the back of his throat and paused until it receded. 'Found Burns's flat.'

'*Please* don't say you broke in.'

Atticus knew that what he said next would make Mack's job either harder or easier. He closed his eyes and tried to ignore the throbbing in his head for long enough to pick his words with care.

'I got inside the front door,' he said.

'You broke in?'

'No – it was open. The door to Burns's flat was open, too. There was someone inside.'

'Jesus, Atticus. Do you think I was born yesterday?'

'It's the truth,' he protested, although he knew – and didn't care – that Mack had seen through him; at least she could report what he had told her, and the search would be legal.

'I *asked* you not to do anything stupid. You *said* you wouldn't embarrass me.'

'I know,' he mumbled.

'Give me the address.'

'I found something, Mack. Burns was blackmailing someone.'

'Shut up,' she said. 'Enough. Give me the address. You can tell me when I get there.'

50

Atticus waited until he felt steadier on his feet and then conducted another search of the flat. The money was gone, and the man had also taken the files with the bank details. The books in the bookcase had been turned out of the shelves, and the drawers in the kitchen unit had been dragged out and emptied onto the floor. Scattered cutlery and the shards of the smashed plates glittered in the dim light. Atticus had no idea who had attacked him, but it was obvious that he had been looking for something. It wasn't *just* the money, or perhaps the money wasn't what he had been looking for at all; was it the bank statements? Or something else entirely? Had he found it?

Atticus heard a car pulling up to the kerb outside and looked down to see Mack making her way across the street to the entrance. He went to the intercom and pressed the button to speak.

'Up the stairs. I'll buzz the door for you.'

He pressed the second button and heard the sound of the door unlocking. Mack's footsteps followed and, a moment later, she arrived at the open door.

She was angry, but, as she looked at Atticus, the anger was replaced with concern. 'Shit. You look dreadful.'

'Do I?'

She stepped closer to him, reached up and gently touched her fingers to the side of his head.

'You can't keep doing this to yourself,' she said. 'This is the second time.'

'What?'

'Jimmy Robson?'

She had a point. Atticus had taken a beating after he had broken into the marijuana farm that Robson had been running in the cottage near to Grovely Farmhouse.

'You should see the other guy,' he said.

'Don't joke.' Mack's palm still rested gently against the side of his face.

'Sorry,' he said.

'I don't know what I'd do if anything happened to you.'

She left her hand there, her skin cool against his, and, for a second, Atticus thought she was going to kiss him. He froze, the same as he always did, caught between the evidence of her feelings for him and the crushing lack of confidence that he felt when it came to understanding what people thought. He saw all the proof – the parted lips, the flared nostrils, the slight upward kink of the eyebrows – but, even as he registered it all, his self-doubt undercut it and, just like always, he couldn't act.

He saw the flicker of doubt pass over Mack's face. She withdrew her hand, and the moment passed.

'Burns told his brother that he needed money,' Atticus said. 'He'd been in Asia. That's why he came back – he ran out of cash. The brother wouldn't give him any more; then Burns told him it didn't matter. Turns out he'd hidden a lot of money in the mattress.'

'How much?'

'Ten thousand – maybe more.'

'Where is it now?'

'The other guy took it. He took folders with Burns's bank statements, too. They were easy to find, though. I don't think they were what he was looking for.'

'Why?'

'Because he would have found those straight away – they were out in the open. But he kept looking. Look.' He indicated the mess the intruder had made. 'He emptied the kitchen drawers and the books in the bookcase. I don't know if he found anything or not, but, if I were you, I'd assume he didn't, even though he turned this place upside down.'

She nodded. 'All right. Even given the fact that your story is *total* bullshit, if we stick to it, we can argue that we're here lawfully. Anything we find is admissible.'

Atticus nodded, but, as she spoke, something caught his attention.

Mack noticed the change in his expression. 'What is it?'

Atticus pointed to a large sack that was inside the largest kitchen cupboard. He had pushed it aside in his earlier search and thought nothing more of it.

Mack went over to the cupboard and knelt down so that she could see what was inside. 'Cat litter. So?'

Atticus nodded. He felt dizzy again, so he sat down on the settee. 'Look inside.'

The bag was open, a corner cut away neatly at the top. Mack tore it a little so that there was enough room for her to reach her hand inside. 'It's full of litter.'

Atticus got up with a wince of pain and walked across. 'Let me,' he said impatiently.

She shuffled aside. Atticus reached for the bag and, before Mack could say anything, he upended it and started to pour the litter onto the floor.

'What are you doing?'

Atticus continued to tip the litter out. 'What *don't* you see here?'

Mack frowned, and then both eyebrows rose at once. 'Shit. There's no cat.'

'Or anything else that would suggest that he had a cat. No food bowl. No cat bed. Who would have cat litter without owning a cat?'

Atticus tipped out more of the litter, then reached inside. He felt something hard with a sharp edge and pulled out an oblong metal box, six inches by three inches, protected by a clear plastic bag. He opened the bag, withdrew a portable hard drive and gave it to Mack.

'Here's what he was looking for. Better tell forensics they're going to have to do some data recovery.'

51

The officers from Salisbury arrived soon after. Atticus waited in the corridor outside as Mack briefed them. She had left the hard drive in a kitchen cupboard for the officers to find; better, she suggested, that it was discovered and logged officially than have to deal with the potential problem of it having been found during the course of an illegal search.

Mack finished up with the officers and told them to call her first thing in the morning, or sooner if there was anything that they thought was particularly important. She took Atticus down the stairs and then out onto the street.

'Where's your car?' she asked him.

'I came by train,' he said.

She looked at her watch; it was three in the morning, and the first train wasn't for another couple of hours yet.

'I'll give you a lift,' she said. 'Get in.'

He did as he was told. She got into the car, started the engine and pulled away. They sat in silence as she picked her way through Andover's quiet streets. She reached forward to switch on the radio, jumped between channels and settled on Radio 2. The DJ was playing inoffensive pop and, after listening to it listlessly for ten minutes, Mack switched it off again.

She glanced across the cabin at him. 'What are you thinking?'

'I want to know what's on that hard drive.'

'They'll find out.'

She wasn't sure if he had heard her. 'There must be *something*. Why else would he have gone to the trouble of hiding it?'

A deer raced across the road fifty feet ahead of them, a streak of brown in the headlights. Mack dabbed the brakes in case there was another, but none followed.

Atticus ignored that, too. 'I mean,' he went on, 'it *has* to be why whoever it was who attacked me was there. Right? It wasn't a coincidence. Can't have been.' He stared out of the window at the dark fields on either side. 'Have you gone public about Burns being one of the dead bodies?'

'Not yet,' Mack said.

'That might've explained it,' he said. 'Whoever killed Burns hears that his body has been discovered, panics, and goes back to search his flat before we can get there.'

'Why now, though? Wouldn't they have done that *after* they killed him?'

'Maybe they did – maybe they went back to double-check. Or maybe they didn't know where Burns lived before.' He paused. 'Wait. Shit.'

'What?'

'What if they went to his brother, too?'

'Is that how you found out about the flat? You went to his—'

'Yes,' Atticus cut in. His mind was running ahead, faster than his words. 'I spoke to Derek Burns earlier. What if . . .' He paused again, then reached into his pocket and took out his phone.

'What are you doing?'

Atticus ignored her. He opened his videos and swiped to the one that he had shot of Derek Burns that afternoon. He tapped it to play, paused it, then let it play again. Burns was at the gate to the field, his dog straining against its leash. Atticus watched as a blue Range Rover drove between him and Burns.

'Atticus?'

'You need to send someone to check on Derek Burns.'

'Why?'

'I was followed today. This car.' He held up the phone.

Mack pushed his hand out of the way. 'I'm *driving*.'

Atticus closed his eyes. 'Range Rover. Dark blue. Dent in the front bumper.' He looked down at the screen, but the car that had passed between him and Burns had done so at a perpendicular angle, and the registration was invisible. He screwed up his face and tried to retrieve an image of the car from his memory, but he couldn't.

'Coincidence?'

He looked across at her and frowned. 'I don't believe in coincidences.'

'No,' she said. 'You don't.'

He pressed his fingers against his temples and concentrated. 'I think I've seen it near my office, too.'

Her phone was in a holder that was fastened to the window. She tapped it awake, called the Control Room and asked them to send an officer to check on Derek Burns.

Atticus reached into his pocket and took out a hip flask. He unscrewed it and took a draw of whatever was inside. He sighed and offered it to Mack. 'Whisky. Want some?'

'I'm driving,' she said again.

He took another sip and screwed the top back on again. 'You need to get onto the hard drive,' he said as he put the flask back into his pocket. 'You don't need a warrant for that.'

'*Please*,' she said. 'I know the law. Burns is dead, and we found the drive at his premises. I know we don't need one.'

Again, it was as if he hadn't heard her. 'And you have four dead girls in the graveyard who were likely put there because of something he was involved with. Burns didn't kill and bury himself, did he? You've got to move fast.'

He was getting agitated.

She said, 'I know—'

He cut in over her. 'Whoever else was involved is probably still out there.' He waved a hand in the air impatiently. 'Just . . . just *do* it, Mack.'

They crested the final hill and saw the city laid out in the valley below them. The spire's illumination had been switched off, but the red warning light still glowed at the very top. It was a welcome sight, and one that she had grown to love in the time that she had lived in the city.

She glanced over at Atticus. He had gone quiet. 'Okay?'

'Bit of a headache.'

'You've probably been concussed.'

'I'm fine.'

'I should take you to casualty to get it checked out.'

'No, Mack. Really. I'm okay.'

'I can't persuade you?'

He smiled and shook his head. 'I just need to sleep.'

'You shouldn't be alone,' she said. 'Where's the dog?'

'In the office.'

'And he'll be okay?'

'What?'

'Will he be okay if you don't go back tonight?'

'But I am going back.'

'You've got a choice. You either let me take you to A & E to get checked out, or you come to the hotel so I can keep an eye on you.'

'You don't have to do that.'

She reached across the space and took his hand. 'Will you do as you're told, for once? *Please?* Let me look after you.'

He squeezed her fingers. 'Okay. You win.'

52

Mack parked the car in the car park at the back of the hotel and led the way inside. She knew that what she was doing would lead to regret, but that wasn't enough for her to stop. She considered Andy, then dismissed him; her husband had made his thoughts on their marriage clear. She thought of her children, and that was almost enough for her to change her mind, but not quite.

They reached her room, and she pulled out her key, fumbling it into the lock. The room was clean. Mack was grateful that housekeeping had been in to tidy up after she had left it in a mess this morning. She guided Atticus to the bed. He sat down and, at her gentle insistence, lay back. She looked at his profile as he lay with his head on the pillow and his eyes pointed up at the ceiling; a livid purple bruise spread down from his scalp to just below his eye. She reached out a hand, stopped herself, and then, realising that she was too weak to resist, lay down next to him. She ran her fingertips through his hair, then let them fall down to his temple and across to his cheek. His skin was stubbled, the whiskers rough against her skin. She rested her head in the cleft between his neck and shoulder, nuzzling him, breathing in his familiar scent: a musk of perspiration and the deodorant that he wore.

She slid her hand down to the opposite side of his face and turned him so that she could look into his eyes.

'Mack,' he said.

'What?'

'Are you sure?'

'Shut up, Atticus.'

She braced herself with an elbow as she lowered her lips to his.

53

Atticus woke. The bed felt wrong – he was higher, and the mattress was softer – and, as he opened his eyes, it took him a moment to remember where he was. He turned – too quickly, triggering a twist of nausea – and saw that he was alone in bed. He reached out a hand and laid it in the indentation next to him where Mack had slept. The sheets were cool. There was a sheet of paper on the pillow, and he took it, sinking back into the mattress and holding it up above his head.

Gone to station. See you later. Don't forget your dog!

Atticus put the note down on his chest and closed his eyes. He remembered what had happened between them, that Mack had brought him back to the hotel and that they had been together again, like before, each of them frantic for the other. It had been as if the shackles that they had both agreed upon had been suddenly removed, and, without those chains to strain against, they had crashed into each other once again.

His phone was still in the pocket of his jeans, which had been discarded on the floor beside the bed. He reached down for them, collected the phone and checked for messages. There were none. He called Mack.

'Morning. Did you get my note?'

'I did.'

'How are you feeling?'

'Headache,' he said. 'It's not that bad.'

There was an uncomfortable pause. He wanted to speak about what had happened last night, but he had no idea what to say. He knew why that was: Mack might consider it a mistake, and that was not something that he wanted to hear. She didn't broach the subject, either, and that deepened Atticus's fear that she regretted it.

'I . . .' he began. 'I—'

She spoke over him before he could say anything else. 'Derek Burns is fine. They sent someone to check on him last night. Not very impressed about being woken at four in the morning, but, apart from that, nothing to report.'

'I still want to talk to him,' he said.

'Why?'

'Think about it: I find out from him where his brother was living, and then, as I'm looking around, someone else turns up. I need to know how that happened.'

'You think he told someone else that he'd told you?'

He stared at the wall, then shook his head in frustration. 'I don't know. There's too much I don't know.'

'One other thing,' she said, changing the subject. 'I spoke to forensics.'

Atticus felt almost relieved to have the subject changed. 'The hard drive?'

'They're working on it.'

'Still? We need to know what's on it.'

'I know.'

'It might tell us why Burns was killed.'

'I know that.'

'And then maybe we'll know what happened to the others.'

'I know, Atticus. I *know*. They're looking at it now.'

'Tell them to hurry. It shouldn't take this long. It's intolerable.'

'I will,' she said. 'What about you?'

'I need to walk the dog,' Atticus said.

54

Mack stood at the window of her office, looking out over the city. She was grateful that it had been a busy morning, and that she was able to throw herself into the investigation. The team in the incident room were working at a frantic pace, with conversation humming as the officers took and placed phone calls and discussed the contents of those conversations with one another. Mack had already had two detailed discussions: she had spoken with Robbie Best at Imber, and he had reported that another body had been discovered just after dawn, bringing the total to six, and Beckton, seemingly a permanent fixture at the station now, had called her into his office to be debriefed on the state of play.

There was work to be done, but, despite that, it was impossible not to think about what had happened last night. She had barely slept and, when she'd woken at five, tired and confused, she had decided that it would be best to come into the station and get started. Atticus was still asleep when she left the room. The bruise on his face had come out, a spectrum of blacks and purples and blues, but, if he had been concussed, there hadn't been any obvious consequences, and she had felt that it was safe to go. Looking at him sleeping like that had reminded her of the time when they had been together, sharing a room much like the one she was in now, and, most of the time, happy in one another's company. That memory had quickly prompted images of her children, and she had bitten her lip until it hurt; she had hastened away from the hotel, knowing that she would have to deal with what had happened, but later.

There was a knock at the door. Mack flinched, expecting to see Atticus, but, as she turned, she saw it was Professor Fyfe instead.

'Good morning,' he said. 'Do you have a minute?'

'Of course.'

'I have a development that I think you'll find of interest.'

Mack invited Fyfe inside and indicated that he should take a seat. He did, taking a document folder out of his bag and placing two pieces of paper on the desk. Mack looked at them: the first was a photograph of a piece of equipment with which she was unfamiliar, a long cylindrical tube with a trigger at the top. The second was a forensic photograph of Alfred Burns's skull, shot in close-up from the top and looking directly down.

'So,' Fyfe began. 'How did Mr Burns meet his end?' He tapped a finger against the cylindrical device. 'Do you know what that is?'

'I don't,' she said.

'It's a captive bolt gun. Usually used in abattoirs to kill cattle. Operation is simple. The operator secures the animal and presses the bottom of the gun against its skull. The propellant is a nine-millimetre-calibre cartridge without a bullet and, when the trigger is pulled, the powder ignites and pushes out a bolt. The bolt breaks the skull, usually going down about ten centimetres into the brain before a spring pulls it back. The bolt itself is concave, has sharp edges and is between ten- and twelve-millimetre calibre. Death is immediate.'

Fyfe moved the second photograph into the middle of the desk and tapped a finger against the image of the single hole that had been punched through the bone.

'I thought this was a bullet hole to start with, until I realised the powder burns were inconsistent with a gunshot wound and that there were no metal foreign bodies inside the skull. I was struggling until I remembered a suicide from years ago, back when I moved here from London. There was a worker at the slaughterhouse in Devizes. Poor bugger had clinical depression, not surprising given what he was being paid to do. He came into work one day, took his bolt gun, held it against his head and pulled the trigger. I remember looking at the wound when they brought him in. Witnesses said he'd held the gun to his head at a right angle. The sharp edge of the bolt cut the skin and pushed it into the wound like a plug. Skin, bits of hair, fragments of bone. The diameter of the plug was smaller than the bolt calibre, and the edges of the entry wound were sharp and pigmented with residue from the gas.'

Fyfe tapped his finger on either side of the wound. Mack could see discoloration against what was left of the skin.

'That was the key thing I remembered about the suicide: on either side of the wound, symmetrical to one another, we saw two powder tattoos that were created by gases venting through openings on the front of the gun. They were small and round, with the edges that were closest to the wound being sharp and clear and the outer edges less well defined. Just like this.'

'How would someone get hold of a bolt gun?'

'It's not that difficult,' he said. 'They used to be listed as firearms, but that changed. You need a slaughter licence to kill livestock, but you can buy the gun off the internet with no trouble at all.'

Fyfe stood and gathered up the two photographs.

'When will I have the full report?' Mack asked him.

'I'm aiming for just after lunch,' he said. 'I thought you'd appreciate an early look.'

'I do,' she said. 'Thanks.'

55

Atticus took advantage of the shower and dressed in yesterday's clothes, then went back to the office. Bandit was waiting for him by the door, his tail swishing back and forth in expectation of a walk.

'Sorry I'm so late,' Atticus said.

The dog trotted over to the table and stood there, his muzzle pointing to his lead and harness.

'Subtle,' Atticus said, clipping the harness on and then attaching the lead to the clip. 'Come on, then.'

He led Bandit outside, let him relieve himself in the grass, and then took him to the car. He put him in the back and set off to the north. He had hoped that the drive might earn him a temporary reprieve from the barrage of thoughts running helter-skelter through his head, but it didn't. They kept coming, rushing at him in a torrent that he was unable to stop: angles that they needed to investigate, possible connections, theories that might explain why Alfred Burns had been murdered and buried in the graveyard. None of his theorising did any good. The truth was hidden in a box that he couldn't open.

All he had were the vaguest hints.

Burns had hidden the hard drive because it contained sensitive information. That was the only possible explanation.

The man who had assaulted him had come to the flat to find it, and he hadn't.

Atticus needed to know what was on the device.

* * *

Atticus parked in the street near where he had stopped before. He let Bandit out and took him to Derek Burns's house. They climbed the sloping drive and turned right, making his way around the house to the entrance at the side. The property was larger than it looked from the front, with a second two-storey building connecting to form the shape of an L.

Atticus reached the front door and knocked. There was no answer.

He knocked again, with the same result, and then crouched down so that he could look through the letterbox. He saw an untidy hallway, with pairs of shoes scattered against the far wall and a muddy coat left hanging from the handle of a cupboard door. There were doors to the left and right, but both were closed.

There was a window to the right of the door. Atticus looked through it into the kitchen. It was tidier than the hall, with a clear counter and a neat stack of plates sitting on a table that was big enough for two. Atticus saw a fridge with notes and postcards stuck to it with novelty magnets.

'Hello?'

Atticus turned to the street. An elderly couple had stopped at the foot of the drive. They were dressed as if to go on a walk.

A terrier sat in front of them, his tail brushing against the ground as he looked at Bandit.

Atticus smiled warmly at them. 'Morning.'

'He's not there,' said the man.

'Really?'

'Left early this morning. What time did I say it was, Jenny?'

'Around five, you said.'

'That's right. I couldn't sleep, so I came downstairs to read. There was a police car outside. I remember thinking how odd it was, that time of day.'

'And after that? You say Mr Burns isn't here – how do you know?'

'The police car left, and ten minutes later I saw Derek put his dog in the back of his car and drive off.'

'Did he have anything else with him? A bag, maybe?'

'A suitcase. One of the ones on wheels. He put it in the back next to the dog.'

'Thank you.'

The woman squinted at him. 'You didn't say who you are?'

'I'm with the police,' Atticus said, hoping they didn't think it odd that someone in the police would bring a dog to work with him.

'He's not in trouble, is he?'

'No,' he said. 'Not at all.'

* * *

Atticus took Bandit out to the field at the back of the house where he had spoken to Derek Burns the previous day. He had run. Why?

His telephone buzzed in his pocket.

'Hello?'

'Mr Priest?'

'Mr York, how are you? How's Molly?'

'Not good. I've lost her again.'

'When?'

His tone was despondent. 'Last night. She went to bed, but when I got up this morning, she wasn't there. She's packed her things and gone.'

'What kind of things?'

'Clothes, some books – her suitcase, too.'

Atticus slowed his pace. 'She didn't do that last time.'

'No, she just went. Do you think you could look for her again?'

'Of course. Let me make a few phone calls.'

Atticus ended the call, promising that he would let him know the moment he found anything out.

Bandit had lowered his snout to sniff at something interesting at the side of the field. Atticus whistled to bring him in and clipped his lead to his collar. He turned and headed back to his car, navigating through his phone's memory for the number he wanted. This was going to be an awkward conversation, but there was no way around it; if he wanted to save himself another trip to London, he was going to have to ask for help, however uncomfortable that might be.

He dialled the number.

'Hello?'

'It's Atticus Priest.'

Jessica Edwards sighed. 'Oh.'

'How are you?'

There was a pause and, for a moment, Atticus thought that she had ended the call.

'You didn't hang around the other morning,' she said.

'I'm sorry about that. I had to get back to Salisbury.'

'You couldn't even have said goodbye?'

'You were asleep. I didn't want to wake you.'

'*Right*,' she said, and he could tell that she had seen through his excuses. She was right, too. He *had* bailed. They had both got very drunk, and he was embarrassed that he might have said something that he might have regretted. He was worried, too, that she might have regretted taking him to bed, and it had just seemed better to make a clean break. He knew that was cowardly.

'I'd like to say this was a social call, but . . .'

'You want something.'

'My misper has gone AWOL again. I wondered if she might have gone back to London.'

'To be with Mullins? I haven't heard anything like that. We arrested him – him and his brother. They've been charged with conspiracy to supply.'

'Remanded or bailed?'

'Joseph's in Pentonville, but they let Shayden stay out. He's supposed to be living with his mum.'

'Could you check? See if she's with him?'

'I'll call you back.'

'Thank you,' he said.

There was no answer. She had already ended the call.

*   *   *

311

Atticus had just put Bandit into the back of the car when Jessica called him.

'Any luck?'

'He isn't there. He told his mum he was going to stay with his dad. She spoke to him, and he says he hasn't seen Shayden for weeks.'

Atticus leaned against the side of the car. 'So, he goes missing at the same time as Molly.'

'It's not a coincidence,' Jessica said. 'I checked. He *has* been in Salisbury. His mum says he stole her debit card. She checked with the bank, and there was a transaction at Waterloo at nine fifteen on Thursday morning. The trains to Salisbury run from Waterloo, and the amount on the card is the same as a single ticket. The next charge was at a cash machine in the Old George Mall.'

'He came down to get her,' Atticus mused aloud.

'And breached his bail,' she said. 'He's supposed to stay in London. His mum's beside herself. I said I'd come and get him.'

'You want a hand?'

'Maybe,' she said, although her tone was still a little defensive.

'I haven't been over to see Molly's dad yet,' he said. 'That's probably not a bad place to start. I could introduce you to him.'

'What about this afternoon? If I leave now, I'll be there at lunch.'

That would depend upon whether the police were able to get into Burns's hard drive, but there was no sign of that happening just yet.

'That ought to be fine.'

Atticus gave her his address and said that she should give him a call when she was near so that he could suggest somewhere to meet. They finished the call, and Atticus opened the driver's door and dropped inside. He looked back at the house, wondering where Derek might have gone.

He started the engine, turned the car around and set off back to Salisbury.

56

Mack was filtering through a stack of outstanding emails when she heard a tap against the glass of the door.

She turned. It was Atticus.

'Can I come in?'

She gestured that he should, and that he should close the door behind him.

'How are you feeling?' she asked him.

'I'm fine,' he said.

'Your bruise is coming out nicely.'

He absentmindedly touched his temple. 'A little sore, but I'll live.' He stood just inside the door; Mack could see that he was nervous. She tried to think of what to say, but couldn't find the right words. She realised that she was nervous, too.

'I ...' Atticus began. 'I, um ... What happened last night. Look, I don't know what you're going to say, but I just want you to know that I don't see it as a mistake. I could probably make a pretty good case that you took advantage of me, but—'

'What? I didn't take advantage of you!'

Too late, she wondered whether he was being sarcastic. He was infuriatingly hard to read; being on the spectrum often meant that he said things that others would consider inappropriate, and the way that he occasionally spoke without inflection made it difficult to tell when he was speaking truthfully and when he was being sarcastic. Now was one of those times.

Atticus was about to respond when they were interrupted by a knock on the door.

'Come in,' Mack called out, grateful for the distraction.

The door opened to reveal a middle-aged man in a crumpled grey suit.

'DCI Jones?'

'Yes,' she said.

'Bob Oldfield. I'm the manager of the data forensics unit at South-West Forensics. You asked for a hard drive to be analysed?'

Mack had availed herself of the unit's assistance before. A suspect's mobile phone had been cracked, and a cache of illegal images uncovered. There were eight investigators together with examiners and technicians, and the team had a range of tools and software to extract and analyse data from electronic devices. Mack's previous case had been assigned to a young female investigator, and she had hoped that she might have been given this case, too; it seemed not.

Oldfield seemed to anticipate her disappointment. 'You dealt with Bella Wilson before,' he said. 'I'm her manager. I know the case you're investigating – all over the news, isn't it?'

'It is.'

'I decided, given that it's obviously sensitive, that I'd better take this myself.'

'Of course,' Mack said, already irritated with his presumptuousness.

Oldfield aimed a glance at Atticus. 'I'm sorry – you are?'

Mack looked over at Atticus and saw him bristle. 'This is Atticus Priest. He's working on the investigation.'

Oldfield shut the door and came inside. He was carrying a bag. He unzipped it, withdrew a flash drive and laid it down on Mack's desk.

'So,' he said. 'Here we are. We've transferred the data from the hard drive you gave us to this.'

'Was it encrypted?' Atticus asked.

'It wasn't.'

'So what took you so long?'

Oldfield frowned. 'We only got it early this morning. And it's not the same as taking it to a shop and asking for the data to be recovered. It's forensic data recovery. The clue is in the "forensic".'

'He wasn't suggesting otherwise,' Mack said, sensing that Atticus's temper was beginning to bubble up. Oldfield was clearly angling for praise, and Atticus would have no time for that.

Oldfield continued, oblivious. 'What we do wouldn't be obvious to a *civilian*,' he said, laying emphasis on the last word. 'The end result is the same – a list of files, of data – but the way we get there is different. It's important. If this were your hard drive and I buggered it up, the worst thing that could happen is you lose your data. If I bugger *this* up, maybe your defendant's brief finds an error and then, boom, the defendant gets off.'

'I appreciate the thoroughness,' Mack said, mollifying him as best she could. 'Perhaps you could tell us what you've found?'

'I'll show you. Could I borrow your machine?'

Mack nodded and moved out of the way. Oldfield inserted the drive into the port of Mack's computer and tapped the keyboard to wake the screen. Mack saw an open window that listed a single file.

160681/Drumcliff/RM.jpeg.

'It's a scan of a photograph,' Oldfield said. 'Have you looked at it?'

'Just briefly, to make sure it wasn't corrupted. It's not.'

Mack looked over at Atticus and saw a gleam of excitement in his eye. He wanted to look at it.

'Thank you, Bob,' she said, taking the hint. 'I appreciate how quickly you've turned this around.'

Oldfield bid them goodbye and left the room.

Atticus came around the desk to stand beside her and pointed at the screen.

'Open it.'

Mack closed the blinds and double-clicked the file, and a photograph appeared. They were looking at what appeared to be a modestly sized bedroom. There was a bed, a chest of drawers that held a lamp, an old-fashioned cathode-ray TV set and an open fireplace covered by a wire mesh guard. The walls were covered in floral-print wallpaper. The view out of its single window suggested it was on the first floor of a building, with rooftops and the spire of a church visible through the glass. It would have been unremarkable save for the two men standing in front of the window and the two people – a man and a woman – who were on their knees before them, facing the camera. The men were dressed in black, and both held pistols that were pressed down so that the barrels rested against the tops of the heads of the kneeling couple. The man and the woman had their hands linked behind their heads and stared into the lens of the camera with a mixture of fear and hatred. The men with the pistols were both grinning.

Mack turned to look at Atticus. He was staring at the photo intently. He leaned in closer to the screen, as if greater proximity might grant him the opportunity to identify the people in the shot.

He held his finger over the armed man on the left. 'Recognise him?'

Atticus withdrew his finger so that Mack could examine the man more closely. She guessed that he was in his early twenties, with a solid build and a mop of thick black hair. His grin was especially wide, an exultation that was incongruous given the plight of the couple in front of him.

'Alfred Burns?'

'It is,' Atticus said. 'Definitely. Much younger.'

'He still has his leg.'

'He lost it in Northern Ireland.'

'So you think this was taken there?'

Atticus pursed his lips as he examined the photograph. 'How old would you say he is?'

'Early twenties?' Mack suggested.

He nodded his agreement. 'He enlisted in 1976, when he was nineteen. He's older than that in the photo – right?'

She nodded.

'Burns did his first tour in Belfast in '79 when he was twenty-two, and the bomb was in '82 when he was twenty-five. On that basis, I think we can assume that this was taken somewhere in Northern Ireland between 1979 and 1982.'

'Fine,' she said. 'So who are the others?'

He shook his head. 'I don't know. We need to identify four people.'

'Four?'

'Yes,' he said, as if that was obvious. 'The man next to Burns, the two on the floor . . .'

'The fourth?'

'Someone took the photograph.'

'Of course,' she said. She pointed to the filename that ran across the top of the image. 'That's got to mean something.'

Atticus read aloud. '160681/Drumcliff/RM.'

'Sixteen, six, eighty-one,' Mack said. 'That must be the date.'

'That would make him twenty-four,' Atticus mused. 'It fits.'

'Drumcliff?'

'Don't know.'

'RM? Initials?'

Atticus shrugged. 'Don't know.'

Mack ran her fingers through her hair; it felt like they had made progress, but the way ahead was blocked. 'This is frustrating.'

Atticus didn't respond and, when he did speak, it was as much to himself as it was to Mack. 'What do we know? That's Alfred Burns, most likely in Northern Ireland in 1981. The photograph was on a hard drive that was hidden in Burns's flat. He'd just received a large amount of money, *and* someone broke into his flat looking for something. I think it is reasonable to assume that someone in the photograph was being blackmailed. My money would be on either the other man with the gun or whoever took the picture.'

'Or both of them,' Mack said.

'Yes – or both.'

'What about the man who attacked you in Burns's flat? Could he be one of them?'

Atticus paused, thinking. He pointed to the man next to Burns. 'How old would you say he is?'

'Mid-twenties?'

'Give or take. If we're right on the date, then that's forty years ago. He'd be at least sixty-five now. The man last night was much younger than that.' Atticus moved Mack aside, leaned over and opened her email browser and emailed the picture to himself. 'I'll look at it in the office. I have some software that I can use to clean it up a little.'

Mack ejected the drive and stood. 'I'll show this to the team. Do you want to be there?'

'Can't,' he said. 'My misper has gone missing again, and it looks like her boyfriend broke bail to come down from London to get her. The investigator who was looking for him is on her way now. I'm supposed to meet her at lunch.'

'The investigator from before? The same woman?'

Mack felt a blush of jealousy and was annoyed with herself for her inability to suppress it. Atticus looked for a moment as if he was going to say something, but then he seemed to change his mind. Instead, he got up and made for the door.

'Tell me if you get anywhere with the photo,' he said.

'Ditto,' she said.

He left the room and, as the door closed behind him, she realised that they hadn't finished talking about what had happened between them.

57

It took Jessica three and a half hours to drive from London to Salisbury. She had timed her departure to avoid the end of the rush hour, but there had been an incident on the A40 and then another on the M3, and it was just after one in the afternoon when she saw the spire of the cathedral poking through the damp mist that had not yet relinquished its grip on the hills and fields around the city.

She found a car park, slotted her car into a space and paid for three hours' parking. She took out her phone and checked the address that Atticus had given her. The offices of Priest & Co. were on the nearby New Street. The rain was hammering down on the windscreen and, despite what looked like a short walk, she knew that she was liable to get soaked if she didn't wear her waterproof. She hurried around to the boot and opened it, moving aside her kit – a pair of rigid cuffs, her MPS flak jacket, a can of dog deterrent spray – and fetched out her waterproof. She tugged it over her head, locked the car and, with her phone in hand, followed the map to New Street.

Salisbury reminded her again just how pretty it was.

There were ugly parts – the 1980s multistorey car park to her right was a dreadful addition – but the majority of the architecture, protected by council regulations that forbade anything tall enough to disrupt the view of the cathedral, was beautiful. She followed a line of centuries-old buildings until she reached a hairdresser's salon and a bridal shop. There was a passageway that led between the two businesses, and she turned into it, grateful for the shelter that it afforded from the rain. She passed through the passageway into a courtyard that was ringed by buildings, each accommodating a small business. There was a flight of metal stairs to her right that led up to an external landing, which, in turn, served two doors. She climbed the steps and looked through the door to the right. A dog started to bark from inside; she remembered that Atticus had mentioned that he had a dog, and guessed that she was in the right place.

She knocked on the glass.

The curtain was pulled back, and she saw him.

He opened the door. 'Afternoon, Detective Constable.'

'Sorry I'm late. Traffic. Can I come in? It's pissing down.'

Atticus stepped to the side. There was a mattress on the floor. She looked at it. 'Do you *live* here, too?'

'Now and again,' he said, evidently embarrassed.

She was diplomatic enough not to say anything else. The dog bounded over the mattress and launched himself at her, his tail wagging. Jessica knelt down so that she could make a fuss of him. 'What's his name?'

'Bandit.'

'He's gorgeous.'

He clicked his fingers, and Bandit detached himself, his tail still wagging as he went to Atticus. He told the dog to go back to his basket.

'The office is this way,' he said.

She followed him through the door into a larger space with a two-seater sofa in a bay window, a desk, a coffee table and walls that were fitted with whiteboards. There were cardboard boxes stacked in a corner, and documents had been dumped into the one at the top. There was a laptop with two extra screens on a large desk; Jessica went over to them and saw a photograph of two men standing in front of a couple kneeling on the floor before them. The two in the back were aiming pistols down at the couple's heads.

'What's that?' she said, pointing.

'The case I'm working on for the police here.'

'That doesn't look recent.'

'It was taken in 1981,' he said. 'I'm just trying to work out where. And who's in it.' He held up two mugs. 'Coffee?'

She said that that would be nice, and, at his invitation, sat down on the sofa while he disappeared out of another door to attend to the drinks. The dog padded over to her and nudged her hand until she scratched him behind the ears. She looked at the open door and wondered if she should bring up what had happened between them after Shayden and Molly had been found in London. She had the distinct impression that Atticus would be uncomfortable discussing it, and, with that in mind, she decided that her instinct was right: better to chalk it up to a drunken mistake and forget it ever happened.

She looked around. The set-up was not quite what she had expected to find. Atticus clearly lived in the room next to this one. She had googled him and had read about his success in the Mallender case; she had assumed that he must be prosperous, but could see now that she had been wrong. Who lived on a mattress in a room next to their office?

He came back inside with two mugs. 'Black okay? I don't have any milk.'

'Fine,' she said. He handed her a mug, and she took a sip. 'So – do you have anything on Molly?'

'Nothing more than I told you on the phone.'

'Shayden must have come to get her.'

'Looks like it,' he said. 'Where they are now is the question. London?'

'Not here?'

'It's not big enough for them to stay hidden for long.'

'You said you'd introduce me to her father.'

'I'd take you out to meet him myself, but I'm tied up on this.' He waved a hand at the photograph on the screen.

'Just call ahead and introduce me. You don't need to be there.'

He nodded. 'Thanks.'

'Feels like I'm doing your job for you,' she said.

'I found Shayden for *you* last time. You owe me.'

'True,' she said. She sipped the coffee and then laid it down again. 'I'll get over there now. Can you set it up?'

'I'll call him now.'

58

Jessica followed Atticus's directions, turning off the A343 and following Salisbury Road into the village of Broughton. The weather was filthy, but she could still see that the surrounding countryside was spectacular. The area was flat, with gentle hills rising to the left and fringes of forest to the right. Cow parsley whitened the verges on either side, stalks swaying in the wind. She turned onto the narrow track Atticus had identified and bounced along it for half a mile until she reached the farm.

She stepped outside and went over to the intercom next to the gate. She pressed the button.

'Hello?'

'Mr York? It's Detective Constable Jessica Edwards. I believe Atticus Priest has spoken to you?'

'He has indeed. Please – come in.'

A moment later, the lock buzzed and the gate swung open. Jessica got back into the car and drove along the gravelled drive to a parking area at the rear of the house. She saw barns and other agricultural buildings, none of them in particularly good condition.

She parked next to a Ford Ranger and got out as a man approached from the house.

'Mr York?'

'That's right,' he said.

She took out her warrant card, holding the wallet open so that he could look at it.

'Atticus told me you were coming,' he said.

Jessica looked at him. He was immaculately turned out, with salmon-coloured corduroy trousers, a checked shirt and Hunter boots.

He extended a hand. 'Nice to meet you.'

She shook it. 'Likewise. I understand your daughter has gone missing.'

'Last night,' he said.

'I think she might be with a suspect I'm looking for.'

'Shayden Mullins,' he said. 'The shit she was with in London?'

'That's right. He's in Salisbury again. We think he arrived on Thursday. Have you seen him?'

'No. But I don't think it's him this time.'

'No? Why not?'

'We had a visitor last night. She was seeing a boy in Salisbury. A bad lad – I understand that he was dealing drugs from a house in town.'

'Jordan Lamb?'

'Yes,' he said. 'That's right. He said his name was Jordan. Didn't tell me his surname.'

'What happened?'

'He said he wanted to see Molly. I told him that wasn't going to happen – I might have been a little more brusque than that – and he didn't take it well. He told me he was seeing her whether I liked it or not. I said I'd call the police unless he cleared off.'

'Did Molly see what happened?'

He nodded. 'She tried to go after him, but I managed to stop her. We argued. She told me she hated me and that she couldn't wait until she was eighteen.'

'And then?'

'She went to her room and locked the door. I left her there to think about things, but when I went to see if she wanted breakfast today, there was no answer. I panicked and forced the door.'

'And she wasn't there?'

'No,' he said. He pointed back to the farmhouse. 'That's her bedroom window. She must have climbed out and then gone down the drainpipe; it was loose when I checked it. She must have broken it on the way down.'

'Have you looked for her?'

'I've been to all the places she might have gone to, all her friends, but she was nowhere. The two of them – her and Jordan – are obviously together. I called the police this morning to report her as missing.'

'Atticus told me that you didn't want to involve us before.'

York exhaled wearily. 'I was concerned she would get into trouble, but it's as clear as day that she won't listen to me. It doesn't matter what I say – she's not going to pay any attention. I can't protect her from the consequences of her actions, and maybe my trying didn't do her any favours – there were no consequences before. I just brought her back so she could run away again. Maybe she needs to see that the real world isn't like that.'

'Even though she's associating with criminals?'

'She's made her choice. I've given her the idea that she can do whatever she likes and nothing bad will come of it.'

Jessica nodded her understanding. She could see the exasperation in York's demeanour and could well imagine that Molly's most recent disappearance – after all the trouble that he had gone to in order to find her – might have been the straw that broke the camel's back. She was certainly not in any position to judge; she didn't have kids and wasn't about to criticise a single parent who had been given a difficult set of circumstances to negotiate.

'It's not out of the question that Shayden is involved,' she said. 'I'll keep an eye out for her.'

'Thank you. I'd be grateful if you could keep her out of trouble, but if not ... that'd be her fault. I want her home – of *course* I do – but I need her to know that she can't keep behaving this way.'

* * *

Jessica drove away from the farmhouse and continued on to Broughton. She pulled over at a bus stop, called Atticus and put him on the speaker. 'Can you talk?'

'Just quickly,' he said. It sounded as if he was breathless.

'Are you okay?'

'I've had a breakthrough,' he said. 'I'm on the way to the station. What is it?'

'I saw James York.'

'What do you think?'

'I think he's had a tough time of it recently.'

'What about Shayden and Molly?'

'It's not Shayden.'

'Why not?'

Molly relayed what York had told her about Jordan Lamb's visit.

'I thought she'd moved on from him.'

'She's a teenage girl,' Jessica said. 'Maybe she had a change of heart. I'm going to go over to Lamb's place now. If I don't find her there, maybe I'll find him. If Shayden didn't come down here for Molly, then it would have had to be something to do with the drugs. Maybe Jordan owes him money.'

'Good idea,' he said. He was evidently distracted.

'Can you just check with the local police to see what they're doing about her?'

'What?'

'York's reported her missing.'

'He said he didn't want to get the police involved.'

'That was before she ran away again. He's at the end of his rope.'

'I'm nearly here. I'll see who's got the file. I'll call you if anything comes up.'

59

Mack was speaking to Stewart Lynas when she saw Atticus through her office window. He had just turned off the street and was half-walking and half-running to the main doors of the station, holding a newspaper above his head in what must have been a futile attempt to shelter from the rain. She woke her PC and busied herself with a review of the documents that had been generated by the investigation, knowing that Atticus would come straight up to her. He did, not bothering to knock as he stepped inside and took off his wet jacket.

'Out, out, out,' he said to Lynas, holding the door for him.

'You *what?*'

'You heard me. Out, please. *Out!*'

Atticus was buzzing with excitement, almost manic. Mack had seen him like this before, and knew that, first, he wouldn't care about whom he offended and, second, that whatever had animated him so much was something he would want to share, and she would likely want to know. She mouthed an apology to Lynas and gave a little nod that he should leave, following him to the door and closing it behind him.

'Manners don't cost a thing,' she chided.

'I need to talk to you.'

'I can see that,' she said. 'You're soaked. Go and dry off.'

'Never mind that,' he said, waving his hands in frustration. 'This can't wait.'

'Deep breaths, Atticus.'

'I know who he is.'

'Who?'

'The man standing next to Burns in the photograph,' he said impatiently, as if she was slow. 'I know who he is.'

He came around to Mack's side of the desk and swept her papers onto the floor. He opened the satchel he was carrying and took out a plastic folder. He opened it and laid down a printout, his palm slapping against the desk as he did. Mack looked down: it was the photograph that had been on the hard drive that Atticus had found in Burns's flat.

'We start with what we know,' he said. 'We know that Burns was in the Royal Green Jackets between 1976 and 1982. And we know that he served in Northern Ireland. Right?'

'We do,' she said.

'Specifically, we know that he was posted to Londonderry. Right?'

'If you say so.'

'I *do* say so,' he said. 'Look – *here*.'

He took another sheet from his stack and slapped it down. It was a printout from Google Maps; Atticus had picked out the name of one of the streets, ringing it in red ink.

Drumcliff Avenue.

'The filename,' Mack said.

334

'Exactly. *Drumcliff.* It's in Londonderry. Bogside, to be precise. The British Army was there during the Troubles. It's close to where the Bloody Sunday shootings took place.'

'How can you know that? There's only one Drumcliff in Northern Ireland? No Drumcliff Road? Drumcliff Street?'

'Sixteen, actually.'

'So, even assuming that the filename relates to where the photo was taken, how do you know which Drumcliff it is?'

He took the photograph from the bottom of the pile and put it on top. Atticus pointed to the bedroom window and then took out a third sheet of paper and laid that down next to the photograph. Atticus had isolated the window, zoomed in on it and then cleared it up. He had focused on the spire that was visible above the roofline of the surrounding buildings. Atticus took a fourth sheet of paper and laid that down on the other side of the photograph. It was a printout from Google Street View, from a vantage that appeared to match the sightline from the window. The spire was much more clearly visible.

'I googled every Drumcliff in Northern Ireland and looked for anything that might look like that spire. It took me a while, but I found it. It's St Columb's Cathedral in Londonderry.'

She shook her head in admiration. 'Okay. I'm with you so far, but how do you go from knowing where the picture was taken to knowing who the second gunman is?'

He held his hands together, the fingertips touching. 'A lot of patient work. I've been on the phone to the Army most of the afternoon. Took me a while to persuade them that I was authorised to search their records, but we got there in the end.'

'Atticus,' she began, '*please* don't say—'

'Doesn't matter,' he interrupted. He was speaking with an intensity that Mack recognised. He had the scent of his prey in his nostrils, and the excitement of the hunt was evident from the glitter in his eyes. 'Too important to wait. Remember the filename?'

'160681/Drumcliff/RM.'

'Exactly so. I got them to search the regimental records for anyone with the initials RM who served in Londonderry in June 1981. It's a common combination, and there were six hits. I took them and then googled for each name *plus* Alfred Burns, and I found this.'

Atticus slapped another piece of paper onto the desk. It was a printout of a newspaper website. The masthead identified the *Londonderry Sentinel*, and the story was dated from 2002. Atticus had ringed a passage in red ink, and Mack read it aloud.

'"A visit to Ballykelly was provisionally pencilled in for Margaret Thatcher's Christmas visit to Northern Ireland in 1982; however, the Prime Minister ultimately visited the Musgrave Park military hospital to visit survivors of the infamous Droppin Well bomb attack instead, newly declassified state papers reveal."'

'Last paragraph,' Atticus urged.

'Thatcher said: "We had a wonderful welcome in Bangor. From there we went to the Musgrave Park military hospital, very conscious that we were in the wake of Ballykelly. We found a few people there who had experienced that terrible tragedy. We also found some of the armed forces who had suffered whilst on patrol in Crossmaglen and others in Belfast. We were very much reminded how very much we owe to the courage and bravery of all of those in the security forces who are trying to eradicate terrorism from our lives. I would like to pay a special tribute to Captain Richard Miller and Rifleman Alfred Burns, both of whom were badly injured as a result of the bombing yet displayed great resilience and senses of humour in the face of what will be long and difficult recoveries.'"

Mack felt a buzz of anticipation. 'RM. Richard Miller.'

Atticus reached into his pocket and took out his phone.

He woke the screen, selected his browser and laid the device on the table next to the photograph taken in the sitting room of the house in Londonderry. The phone showed the website of Richard Miller, the Member of Parliament for Salisbury. His smiling face was offset to the left, beaming into the camera. Mack looked at the website, then the photograph, then back at the website. It was hard to be sure given the quality of the image, plus the time that must have intervened between the taking of the two photographs, but it could have been the same man.

'There's a resemblance,' she said.

'Open his biography.'

She tapped the screen and read the paragraph that described his career.

'"Richard was educated at Dauntsey's in Devizes from where he went directly to the Royal Military Academy at Sandhurst. He won the Sword of Honour and was commissioned into the Royal Green Jackets. He served for thirty-one years, completing five emergency tours in Northern Ireland and other campaigns before retiring into politics. He was present at the scene of the Ballykelly bomb in 1982, where he was seriously injured by shrapnel, and spent six months recovering from his injuries in hospital.'" She laid the phone down. 'Holy shit. It *is* him.'

Atticus nodded, a smile of satisfaction playing at the corner of his mouth.

'Fine,' she said. 'Burns and Miller knew each other. What were they doing in that house?'

Atticus had one more piece of paper, and he laid it down atop the others. It, too, was a printout from a newspaper website.

She read the headline. '"Police appeal for help in murder of local couple."'

'Keep reading.'

'"Enquiries remain ongoing following the discovery of two bodies in a Londonderry property last week. Saoirse Fairley and Seamus McCann were discovered by neighbours in their Drumcliff Avenue house after they had not been seen for several days. The couple were believed to have been shot to death. The RUC have revealed that Fairley and McCann had criminal convictions for drug offences, and officers believe that their murder might have been at the hands of local paramilitaries. Loyalist groups have been known to extort money from local criminals, while Republican groups have murdered those in an ongoing campaign against the drug trade."' She gaped at the paper. 'My God, Atticus. They killed them?'

'Because they knew the police would assume it was the loyalists.'

Mack's mind was racing. The case had jerked sharply off course, and she was instinctively aware that she was going to have to brief Beckton.

'There's one thing we need to know,' Atticus said. 'Who took the photograph?'

60

Jessica parked in the same car park as before. She would need her warrant card to identify herself to Lamb, but, as she reached down into the mess in the footwell of the passenger seat and took her handbag, she found that the wallet with her ID was not there. She closed her eyes and tried to remember what she had done with it. She had definitely had it at the farm; she had shown it to York.

She must have put it down somewhere. She would have to go back to get it.

Never mind.

She got out, locked up and made her way to Payne's Hill. The rain was falling heavily, and run-off was pouring down the gutters on both sides of the street, the drains already full. She was soaked by the time she reached Jordan Lamb's address, and it was a relief to be able to shelter under cover as she buzzed the intercom.

There was no answer.

She went back onto the pavement to see whether she would be able to get a look inside through the windows, but they were obscured by net curtains. She went back to the front door and buzzed the intercom again, holding her finger on the button for ten seconds.

Still nothing.

No Jordan Lamb and no Shayden Mullins.

Jessica waited there for ten minutes before giving up.

Neither young man was there.

Jessica went back to her car and got inside. It was cold, and she turned on the engine so that she could run the heater. The wipers swept across the windscreen, squeaking as the worn blades brushed the water off the glass. Jessica rested her hands on the wheel and stared out at the Methodist chapel on the other side of the road, watching the kids from the nursery that was attached to it as they ran around their tiny outdoor space in their raincoats.

She took out her phone and found the number for Ngozi Mullins. She dialled it and waited for the call to connect.

'Hello?'

'Mrs Mullins?'

'Yes.'

'It's DC Edwards.'

'Oh,' she said. 'I was just about to call you.'

'Really? Why? Have you seen Shayden?'

'He came home,' she said.

Jessica sat a little straighter. 'What?'

'He's very sorry for all the fuss he's caused.'

'What did he say?'

'He went to Salisbury, like you said.'

'Why?'

'He wouldn't say. I told him he was stupid – I think he actually listened to me for once. He's very sorry.'

'That's good to hear. I'm going to need to talk to him, though.'

'He's asleep.'

'It's not urgent. Please ask him to call me when he wakes up.'

'Why?'

'The girl he came down to see has gone missing. I promised her father that I'd keep an eye out for her.'

'She's not with him,' Ngozi said.

'No, I'm not saying she is. But he might have an idea where she's gone. And, apart from that, he needs to know that he has to follow the conditions of his bail. I can speak to him on the phone or send someone around to bring him to the nick. It's his choice.'

'I'll speak to him.'

'Thank you, Mrs Mullins.'

Jessica ended the call and stared through the rain-slicked windscreen, the wipers beating backwards and forwards with a metronomic rhythm. She dialled Atticus's number, but the call went to voicemail. She left a message explaining the new development and that she would tell York when she went to pick up her warrant card, ended the call and slipped the phone into the cupholder.

There was no reason for her to stay in the city, but she needed to get her warrant card before she headed home. She woke the car's navigation and tapped in her postcode in London. The route was displayed, a two-hour drive that would take her north-east until she reached the M25. She enlarged the early part of the route and saw that she would pass just to the north of Broughton. It would only add a few minutes to her trip to divert to the south. She could stop at the farm, collect her warrant card and be on her way.

She tapped the screen to start the navigation, put the car into gear and pulled out.

61

Mack knew that they were going to have to tread carefully from now on. Atticus was too full of his own sense of brilliance to acknowledge that the case had just become much more sensitive, but that had been Mack's first thought. The fact that Salisbury's sitting MP was now the prime suspect in a murder investigation changed everything, and she knew, for the sake of her career, that she was going to have to proceed with the utmost caution. She had gone to speak to Beckton immediately after Atticus had dropped his bombshell, and had ended up in his office for the better part of half an hour. Beckton, like her, had instinctively grasped how the landscape had changed. She had watched as Beckton had passed through disbelief, then shock, then horror, eventually finishing somewhere – she guessed – that involved the knowledge that he was going to have to proceed with the most extravagant care in order to protect a career that had taken him years to build. He had suggested that she convene the full team in the incident room and had insisted upon attending himself.

She had told Atticus to wait in her office while she was with Beckton and, when she returned to collect him, he was standing behind her desk with a piece of paper in his hand.

Her stomach dropped. 'What are you doing?'

He looked up. 'Sorry,' he said. 'I was just clearing up, and I saw this.'

He laid it on the desk. She saw that it was the divorce petition that had been served on her by Andy's solicitors.

'You didn't think that might be private?'

'He's divorcing you?' he said.

She was ready to tell him to mind his own business when she saw Beckton pass by the door in the direction of the incident room.

'We'll talk about this later,' she said.

She beckoned him to come with her and followed the chief superintendent to the conference room. The team was waiting for them.

Mack rapped her knuckles on the table to bring the room to order.

'Settle down,' she said. 'We've had a breakthrough. Atticus has identified one of the men in the photograph that we recovered from Alfred Burns's flat. Atticus?'

He stood up and ran through the identification that he had made of Miller, illustrating his conclusions by way of the print-outs that he had shown to Mack and setting out the evidence that the MP was familiar with Alfred Burns.

'And what do you think that means?' Mike Lewis asked.

Atticus looked at Mack as if annoyed that he had to answer such an elementary question.

'It means,' she said, 'that there was a connection between Burns and Miller that most likely began in Northern Ireland and then continued after they returned to this country. It's possible that Burns was blackmailing Miller with it.'

'Likely,' Atticus corrected. 'The other two people in the photograph were murdered.'

'And now Burns is dead, too,' Nigel Archer said.

'Buried in a graveyard with the remains of four teenagers who shouldn't be there,' Beckton said.

Archer shook his head in disbelief. 'And we think Miller is involved in that?'

'I really hope not,' Beckton said.

'It doesn't look good, does it?' Archer said.

'No,' Beckton said. 'It does not.'

'He at least has questions to answer,' Mack added.

'Are we bringing him in?'

'I don't think we're too far from that,' Beckton said. 'I've spoken with Mack, and we've agreed that we should treat this with sensitivity until we know more. She'll go and speak to him today, and if we feel that there's a case to answer, we'll arrest him and bring him back.'

Robbie Best raised his finger. 'Want me to come with you, boss?'

'No thanks, Robbie,' Mack said. 'Atticus connected the dots on this one. I want him to be there when I speak to Miller.'

Best turned to Beckton. 'What happened to sensitivity?'

Beckton made no attempt to hide his discomfort. 'You're going to behave, aren't you, Atticus?'

'Of course,' he said, as if affronted by the suggestion that anything else was possible.

62

Broad Chalke was one of the prettier villages in the vicinity of Salisbury, and the house that belonged to Colonel Richard Miller, DSO, was in its most pleasant lane. It was difficult to find, and it took directions from a villager to rescue them from a series of wrong turns.

Mack pulled over in front of an iron gate that opened onto a gravelled courtyard. Atticus got out and looked over the roof of the car at the view. The house was gorgeous. It was constructed in Flemish brick on a limestone plinth with stone quoins, a hipped tiled roof with a large gable end and panelled brick chimney stacks at either side. Weathered stone pilasters merged with the centuries-old brick to give a warm, inviting appearance.

'*Look* at this place,' Mack said. 'He didn't get *this* on an MP's salary.'

'He set up a corporate intelligence operation after he left the Army,' Atticus said. 'He sold it for fifteen million before he went into politics.'

'I'm in the wrong job,' she observed wryly.

'You and me both.'

She narrowed her eyes as she looked over at him. 'Is there any point me telling you how we're going to play this?'

'As in will I keep my mouth shut? Not much point.'

'Let me lead. Ask anything you think is relevant, but at least let me pretend that I'm in charge. Okay?'

'It's your case, Mack. I'm just here to help.'

She smiled at him. 'Thank you.'

Atticus nodded and reached for the gate. 'Ready?'

She nodded. 'Let's see what he has to say for himself.'

* * *

Atticus opened the gate and paused to allow Mack to lead the way across the courtyard, their feet crunching over the gravel. The house was even more delightful the closer they came to it. Wisteria grew up across the walls, and the front door was framed by rose bushes, the blooms absent for the season but the plants well tended.

Mack knocked firmly on the door.

It was opened by an older man wearing a pair of walking boots and with a Barbour jacket draped across the crook of his elbow.

'Yes?'

'Colonel Miller?'

'That's right,' he said. 'Who are you?'

Mack took out the wallet with her warrant card and held it open. 'I'm Detective Chief Inspector Jones, and this is Atticus Priest. Do you think you could spare a few moments to have a chat with us?'

Miller looked down at the warrant card, then up at Mack's face, as if comparing one with the other.

'I'm just about to go out for a walk,' he said. 'What's this about?'

'Alfred Burns,' Mack said. 'I'm sorry to impose, but it's important.'

Miller straightened up and gave a little harrumph of displeasure. Atticus could see that the irritation was an act, a reaction that he probably thought Mack might expect from a man of his position. It was a deflection, too, because Atticus caught the flicker of fear in the older man's eyes.

'Sir,' Mack pressed, 'can we come inside?'

'What's happened?'

'I'd rather not do this on the doorstep.'

He opened the door wider and stepped aside. Mack went first, and Atticus followed. The entrance hall looked like something out of the Italian Renaissance. It was grand yet neatly proportioned, stone-flagged with columns; a table in the centre of the small space held a pitcher that was full of sweet-smelling lavender.

'We'll go into the winter sitting room,' Miller said. 'This way.'

He led them into a room that was dominated by four pieces of furniture: a vast sofa, two recessed oak bookcases on either side of a marble fireplace, and a fruitwood writing table. A fire had been lit in the grate and then banked; Miller took a poker and prodded the logs until the flames were revived, then tossed in fresh wood from a large tin bucket. He took the chair from the desk and turned it around, indicating that Mack and Atticus should sit on the sofa. They did. Mack reached into her handbag and took out her notebook and pen. Atticus watched the colonel carefully.

'Thank you,' she said.

'Now then. What's this all about?'

'As I said – Alfred Burns.'

He shuffled on his chair. 'Who?'

'I believe you served with him,' Mack said. 'He was a soldier in the Royal Green Jackets, and I understand that at the time you were an officer in the same battalion. I checked the records – the battalion was on a resident tour of Northern Ireland, based in Londonderry.'

He paused, then nodded. 'That's forty years ago.'

'But you remember him?'

'Yes,' he said. 'He was badly injured in the Ballykelly bombing.'

'That's right,' Mack said. 'He lost his leg.'

'He did,' Miller said. 'I remember. He was a bit of a rascal before that, as I recall. What's he done now?'

Mack reached into her bag again and took out an A4 envelope. She slid her finger into the open end and withdrew a printout of the photograph that Atticus had found on the drive in Burns's flat. She laid it on the table; Atticus watched the colour leach out of the old man's cheeks.

'Right,' he said quietly. 'I see.'

'Have you seen that before?' Atticus asked him.

Miller turned his head to glare at Atticus. 'I have.'

'Probably best if you told us about it.'

Miller swallowed. Atticus saw discomfort, fear and anger. The old soldier had made his career on his reputation as a stern, straight-talking man with impeccable morals, and now, Atticus could see, he was frightened that the façade would be peeled away to reveal whatever rancidness had been concealed beneath.

'That photograph shows a mistake I made as a young man. I'd rather not discuss it.'

'I'm not sure you have that luxury,' Atticus said. 'Burns blackmailed you with this, didn't he?'

'Alf . . .' Miller paused, a vein pulsing angrily in his temple. 'Yes. He extorted me.' He waved a hand at the photograph. 'You got that from him, I presume?'

'We found it at his flat,' Mack said. 'He didn't give it to us.'

'I don't understand.'

'He's dead.'

Atticus watched the man's face carefully. It was difficult to decode his reaction: there was shock there, but, for once, he couldn't tell whether it was because he had been found out or because it was an artful confection.

'What?' he stammered. 'How?'

'He was murdered.'

'What? *Murdered?* By whom?'

'We don't know the particulars yet,' Mack said. 'His body was found buried in a shallow grave on Salisbury Plain.'

'The story on the news?'

'That's right,' she said. 'His was one of the bodies that we found. The second body, as it happens.'

'My God.'

The confusion on Miller's face had curdled into fear. Atticus knew why that might be. It was obvious. With a blackmailer found dead, the finger of suspicion would point at the black-mailer's target.

'Excuse me.' He stood. 'Could you ... could you give me a moment?'

He left the room before Mack or Atticus could say anything.

Atticus got up, then spoke quietly. 'Look around. See if you can find anything useful.'

He went back into the hall. Miller was already out of sight, but Atticus heard the sound of a door opening and closing to his right. A short flight of stairs descended to a second hall, with doors to the right and left and one straight ahead. Atticus followed. The door to the left was open, revealing a breakfast room. The door straight ahead led into the kitchen and the door to the right to a cloakroom. Atticus looked inside and saw two more doors; the one to the right was closed and, through it, Atticus could hear the sound of running water. He waited, out of sight should the door to the WC be opened yet close enough to hear the sound of conversation over the noise of the running tap. He could only hear one voice – Miller's – but he was too far away to discern any of what was being said.

The tap was turned off, and the lock on the door turned. Atticus went back to the sitting room, where Mack was inspecting a photograph on the table. They shared another look, and she gave a tiny nod to indicate that Miller was returning.

Atticus turned as Miller came back into the room. 'I'm sorry,' he said. 'That was a terrible shock.'

The colonel had mastered the surprise that had apparently led to his dash to the bathroom. Atticus was sure that the reaction had not been manufactured, but now could not help but wonder whom he had been speaking to on the telephone and what had been said. The panic that had accompanied the news of Burns's death had gone, to be replaced by something approaching accept-ance; but of what? Atticus wasn't sure.

'You can see now why we need to talk to you,' Mack said.

'You can't think that I had anything to do with that?'

'We don't know who was responsible, Colonel. We're inves-tigating it now. Please – sit down again, would you?'

He didn't. 'You think I have a motive.'

'Well,' Atticus said, 'you do.'

Mack flashed an irritated glare in his direction, but Atticus didn't see it.

'I didn't do a bloody thing,' Miller said. 'I had no idea. I haven't seen him for weeks.'

'Sit down, sir,' Mack repeated, and, this time, the colonel did. 'Now, before we go on, I'm going to caution you. You do not have to say anything. But it may harm your defence if you do not mention when questioned something which you later rely on in court. Anything you do say may be given in evidence. Do you understand, sir?'

'Is this necessary?' he said.

'I think it's best we do things by the book, Colonel. For you and us.'

'Fine,' he said.

'Do you want to have a solicitor present?'

'No,' he said.

'Are you sure?'

'I'm happy to go on without one.'

'Tell us everything,' Atticus suggested. 'From the start.'

63

Miller took a breath, laced his fingers in his lap and exhaled.

'Fine,' he said. 'I met him in the Army, like you said. We were both in the Green Jackets. I was in Northern Ireland with him.'

'You were friendly?'

He laughed, softly and with bitterness. 'I wouldn't quite go *that* far.'

'Why are you laughing?' Mack asked him.

'Because getting to know him was one of the worst decisions I've ever made. He was bad news. Always has been.'

'How did you meet?'

'We met because we were in the same unit. I was a captain, and he was a rifleman. I doubt either of you have served — have you?'

'No,' Mack said. 'We haven't.'

'No, of course not. It'd be hard for you to understand what it's like to be in a situation like that. Londonderry, back then? You go out on a patrol and there's a good chance a sniper tries to pick you off. Or maybe you get back and you go out for a beer and the Provos blow up a bomb.'

'Like in Ballykelly,' Atticus suggested.

'Yes,' Miller said. '*Just* like that. We were both inside that bar when the INLA detonated their bomb. Seventeen people died. Eleven soldiers. We were both injured. Alfred lost his leg below the knee, and I had lacerations and a broken arm when the roof fell on top of me. They put me back together again, and I was back on the job in six months, but Alfred wasn't as lucky. Never recovered. Got a medical discharge.'

'But you kept in touch?'

'No. I didn't see him until a couple of months ago. He showed up with that photo and asked me for money.'

'Tell us about it,' Mack said, pointing to the photo. 'What happened?'

Miller looked away and, when he looked back, little dots of scarlet had formed in his cheeks. His lips were bloodless. 'It'll ruin my reputation. My career. Everything.'

'I'm sorry about that, sir, but you still need to tell us.'

'We were in Londonderry. I'd just been promoted, but I was broke. My parents died when I was very young, and it was down to me to get my brother and sisters through school. They were at Bishopstrow. My parents had left us a little money, but it was all gone, and the only way they would've been able to keep going there was if I found the money to keep paying the bills, and they were bloody, *bloody* expensive.' He shrugged helplessly. 'I didn't have it – there was nothing left. I was on watch with Burns one night, and we got talking about it. He said he might have something that would interest me and, stupidly, I listened.' He exhaled. 'I don't know how much you know about Burns, but he was always involved in things that he shouldn't have been. He stole things. He was violent. There was this one time he assaulted another rifleman. It was more than just the boys scrapping – the other bloke was badly hurt, but he kept his mouth shut. Burns must've had something on the poor bastard.'

'He was a frightening man,' Atticus offered.

'You knew him?'

'I investigated him.'

'For the child pornography?'

'That's right.'

'I should thank you, then,' he said bitterly. 'He said that was the reason he needed money. He couldn't work after the case.'

'Get back to Londonderry,' Mack prompted.

'Alf told me that he knew about a local criminal who had robbed a building society and had the cash at home. He said we should go and help ourselves to it, and, like a fool, I agreed.'

'What happened?'

'There were three of us,' he said. 'Me, Alf and another soldier.'

'Name?'

'I don't know,' he said.

'You must have known.'

'He was in a different unit. Alf didn't tell me, and I didn't ask.'

Atticus didn't believe him, but, before he could press, Mack waved for him to go on.

'We went to the house after dark and kicked our way in. Alf had said the robber lived on his own, but his girlfriend was there.'

'That's them in the photograph?'

He nodded. 'I held them in the bedroom while Alf and his mate searched the house and found the money. We were ready to go, but the man threatened us. He said he was connected to the IRA, that he'd remember our faces, and he'd make sure that we all got slotted the next time we were on patrol. I thought he was bluffing, but Alf lost it. Lost it. He told the two of them to get down on their knees. We'd found a Polaroid when we were looking for the cash, and Alf said we should get a snap to remember a job well done.'

'Who took the photograph?'

'The third man.'

'What happened next?'

He looked away, clenching the arms of the chair so tightly that his knuckles shone white through his parchment-thin skin. 'Alf shot them both.' He looked away and swallowed. 'I had no idea that he was going to do that. I thought he just wanted to frighten them.' His voice cracked. 'There'll be a court martial.'

That would be the *least* of his worries, Atticus thought. There would be a trial in Belfast Crown Court for murder; what the colonel was describing was a classic joint enterprise.

'This is going to ruin me,' Miller said.

Atticus had no time for his self-pity. 'Did you report it?'

'At the time? I was going to, but he threatened me with the photo. He said that I had to keep my mouth shut if I didn't want it to be sent to my CO. He said the other man—'

'Whose name you can't remember,' Atticus cut across.

Miller scowled. 'Alf said he'd back *him* up. My word against theirs. That's when the blackmail started. I've had this hanging over me for forty years. There was another job. Alf said that we'd do that one together and then that would be that.'

'And did you?'

'No. The bomb put a stop to that. Alf and I were sent to Musgrave Park to recover. I carried on with my career, but it was obvious that Alf was finished. He couldn't be a soldier after that. He was bitter about it all. Can't really blame him, but, in the end, it just got to be too much. I never saw him again.'

Atticus pointed at the photograph. 'Until he came back with this and asked for money.'

'Yes,' he said. 'He said he'd been in Thailand after the trial but that he'd run out. He said he couldn't get a job – he said no one would even interview him after the trial – and he said that if he couldn't work, then *I* needed to look after him. He said he knew I had money and it was only fair that I return the favour – those were the words he used – from when I was broke and had needed his help.'

'How much did he want?'

'Ten thousand.'

'And you paid it?' Mack said.

'What choice did I have?'

'You didn't think that he'd come back again and ask for more?'

'They usually do,' Atticus added.

'I did think about it. My wife had cancer, and she only had a few months to live. I decided that I'd pay him to stay away until . . .' He swallowed. 'Until it wouldn't matter. I couldn't bear the thought of her witnessing my disgrace. She died just after Christmas. I decided that if Burns came back, I would tell him no and take responsibility for what I did. But he didn't come back.'

'Because someone murdered him,' Atticus said.

'So you say.'

'When was the last time you saw Burns?'

Miller frowned at his brusqueness. 'When I paid him. I met him in the lay-by near to the Army Flying Museum in the Wallops. I had a bag of cash. I handed it over, and that was that.'

64

Atticus found it difficult to assess how much of what Miller had said was true. He held eye contact for most of the time that he was speaking, and his breathing and voice remained steady. His hands stayed in his lap and did not touch his face or fiddle with anything in a way that might suggest a lie. The story was full of details, suggesting either that it was true or that it had been prepared and rehearsed in advance. Overall, his story and behaviour suggested veracity, but there was still the matter of the phone call that he had made before delivering his confession.

To whom had he spoken?

Mack got up. 'Could you give us a moment, Colonel?'

'Of course.'

She signalled for Atticus to follow and led him back to the hall, where they could talk without fear of being overheard.

'What did you make of that?' she asked him in a low voice.

'I think some of it was true.'

'But?'

'But he's holding something back. He spoke to someone on the phone when he went to the bathroom. I couldn't make out what he said, but, whatever it was, it changed him. Did you notice the difference when he came back?'

'He was terrified before,' she said. 'And then resigned afterwards.'

'You think he did it?' Mack said. 'Killed Burns?'

'I don't know. But he's just confessed to conspiracy to murder. You're going to have to arrest him and take him back to the station.'

Mack said that she agreed and led the way back to the sitting room.

The colonel was looking out of the window onto his garden. He swivelled as he heard their footsteps.

'Colonel Miller,' Mack said, 'I am arresting you on suspicion of conspiracy to murder.' She cautioned him for a second time.

'I understand,' Miller said. He did not look surprised.

'I'm going to take you back to the station in Salisbury,' she said. 'We'll go over some of the things we've spoken about again.'

'Of course,' he said.

The colonel led them back to the front door and opened it for Mack and Atticus to step out. He took a set of keys from a dish on the hall table, stepped out and locked the door, and walked with Atticus and Mack out to Mack's car. She opened the back and waited for the old man to lower himself inside, then closed the door.

'We need to search the house,' Atticus said. 'No need for a warrant. We can do it under Section 32.'

'Agreed.' Mack opened the rear door again. 'Excuse me, sir – we'd like to search your house. Could we have the key to the front door, please?'

The colonel nodded. 'I don't have anything to hide.' Miller pulled out his keys, removed one from the ring and handed it to her.

Mack thanked him and closed the door. 'I'll drive him back,' she said to Atticus. 'I'll get Francine or Mike Lewis to come out.'

He put out his hand for the key.

'You'll wait for them?' she said sceptically.

'Of course I will.'

He knew that she didn't believe him, but, nonetheless, she held out the key and allowed him to take it.

65

Atticus waited for Mack to drive the colonel away and then went back to the house. He unlocked the front door and went inside. He turned right rather than left, taking a half-flight of stairs that led down to the kitchen and then a flight that led up to the first floor. There were four bedrooms, each with an en suite bathroom. There was no way he could search the house himself and even pretend to be thorough, so he looked through the rooms in the hope of finding something that might be relevant. He opened drawers and wardrobes and medicine cabinets, unpacked and then repacked an ottoman that was full of blankets, found an airing cabinet and rifled through the towels that were stacked on the shelves. He checked in bedside tables and reached beneath beds, ran his finger along the spines of rows of books, opened a humidor and took out the cigars inside. He found black bin bags full of women's clothes and realised that the colonel was sorting through his dead wife's things.

There was nothing of interest.

He looked at his watch. He had already been inside the house for twenty minutes, and he doubted that it would take much longer for whomever Mack had sent from the station to arrive.

Atticus took the stairs back to the ground floor, passed the open door to the breakfast room and turned right into the cloakroom. The bathroom was to the right, with another door to the left; Atticus opened it, continued through a small vestibule into a utility room and then, beyond that, to what appeared to be another sitting room.

He looked around. The room was opulently furnished, with generous sofas loaded with cushions, a footstool that held a large book dedicated to the photography of Cecil Beaton, ornaments on several small tables and more pitchers full of sweet-smelling lavender. There was a pair of French doors to the left and a large stone fireplace with a wood burner. He crossed the room and looked down at a low table that carried a thicket of photographs in matching silver frames. He looked at the photographs; they appeared to be of the Miller family: Miller himself, his wife, and children in their early twenties.

He crossed over to the mantelpiece and looked at the photographs that were displayed there. Once again, they were bland: Miller at a regimental event; with his wife at a wedding; smiling for the camera as his daughter held a newborn baby. A copy of the order of service for his wife's funeral had been propped up against one of the frames. Atticus took it, intending to flip through the pages, but stopped.

The photograph in the modest wooden frame behind it caused him to gasp in surprise.

He heard the sound of a car in the road outside and, quickly, he took out his phone and fired off three photographs. He stuffed his phone back into his pocket and put the order of service back so that it was as he had found it and then hurried back to the front door. He closed and locked it just as Mike Lewis and Francine Patterson came through the gate.

Lewis whistled. 'Nice place.'

Atticus held out the key. 'You'll want this.'

Patterson took it. 'Are you coming in?'

'No. I've got something I need to do.'

66

Jessica pulled up at the gate of the farmhouse, got out and pressed the button for the intercom.

James York answered, 'Hello?'

'It's Detective Constable Edwards. I was here earlier.'

'Yes, hello, Officer. You've come for your identification?'

'Yes,' she said. 'Did you find it?'

'It was on the ground. It must've fallen out of your pocket. I'll open the gate – come in.'

The gates clanked as they parted. Jessica drove through them, followed the drive to the parking space at the front of the farmhouse and pulled in. She got out of the car and took the path to the stables. James York stepped out of a door at the side of the house and made his way across to her.

'Afternoon,' he said, holding out the wallet with her warrant card. 'Here you are.'

She took it. 'Thank you.'

'Did you find Jordan?'

'No. He wasn't there. But I found Shayden Mullins. He's in London.'

'And Molly?'

Jessica shook her head. 'I'm afraid not.'

York looked crestfallen. 'This is a nightmare.'

'I'm sorry.'

He put both hands to his head and massaged his temples. 'This is going to lead me to an early grave. What do you think I should do now?'

'I'd call Atticus.'

'Yes,' he said. 'I'll do that. Bring him up to speed.'

'I'm sure Molly will turn up.'

She offered her hand and York took it.

'Thanks again,' York said.

Jessica opened the car door and was about to slide inside when her phone rang in her pocket. She took it out and saw a London number.

She held the phone up. 'I think this might be Shayden.'

'What does he want?'

'I asked his mother to have him call me. I'd better take it.'

York nodded. Jessica accepted the call and put the phone to her ear. 'Hello?'

'Officer Edwards?'

'Hello, Shayden.'

'My mum said you wanted to speak to me.'

'I do – thanks for calling. She says you've been in Salisbury.'

'Yeah.'

'When did you leave?'

'Yesterday. Came back last night and stayed with a friend in Camden. Got home this morning.'

'Why were you there?'

'Do I have to say?'

'You're not supposed to have left London.'

'I left my PlayStation at the place I was staying.'

'Did you see Molly York?'

'I tried.'

'But?'

'She ghosted me. I've been calling and calling. Straight to voicemail.'

'You've really got no idea where she is?' she said. 'Her dad's worried about her.'

He laughed bitterly. 'I bet he is.'

'What does that mean?'

'How much do you know about him?'

'Not much.'

Jessica looked up. York was watching her closely; she smiled in as noncommittal a way as she could.

'You want to know why Jessica ran away from home? She's scared of him. She's *terrified.*'

She picked her words carefully, aware that she had two audiences. 'Why?'

There was a pause, as if the boy was deciding whether or not this was something that he ought to share. 'Because she says she saw him kill some geezer at their farm.'

Jessica spoke too quickly, her surprise much too obvious.

'*What?*'

'Says she saw him put some kind of gun they use to kill cows against the back of this guy's head and shoot him.'

'When?'

'Didn't say. But now Molly thinks *he* knows that *she* knows. That's why she ran.'

'Thank you, Shayden. I'll want to talk to you about that a little more if that's okay.'

'I ain't going anywhere.'

Shayden ended the call. Jessica stood with the phone held to her ear as she tried to weigh the importance of what she had just been told.

'What did he say?'

She turned too quickly, lowering the phone and fumbling it as she tried to put it back into her pocket.

'Nothing,' she said.

He smiled and took a step forward. 'It didn't sound like nothing. What did he say about Molly?'

'He hasn't been able to get in touch with her,' she said.

She felt a knot of bile in her stomach. York was still smiling at her, but there was something in his eyes that she hadn't noticed before.

She held up the wallet. 'Thanks for this. I'd better be going.'

She opened the car door and was about to get inside when she heard the sound of a telephone ringtone. It was muffled, and it took Jessica a moment to place it. It sounded like it was coming from inside the gilet he was wearing. There was something about the sound that she recognised. It took her a moment, but she picked out the tune: 'Blinding Lights.'

She had heard that ringtone before.

York smiled at her. 'What is it?'

'Molly has that ringtone.'

She should have run, right there and then. Perhaps, if she had done that, she would have been able to put some distance between herself and him and get away. But she didn't, and, as the words tripped out of her mouth before she could think to stop them, so she saw the expression change on James York's face. His chummy affability took on an edge that was part suspicion and part determination. He must have seen the confusion on her face, watched as it changed to shock. He maintained his smile, but his lips whitened as they were pulled back against his teeth. There was animal cunning in his eyes.

He took another step towards her.

Jessica raised her hands to ward him off. 'No further, please, Mr York.'

He stood a little straighter, clenched his fists, and, instead of retreating, took a third step.

'Stay where you are.'

'We have the same ringtone,' he said. 'Family joke. Look – I'll show you.'

He reached into his pocket.

'Stay *there*. Not another step.'

Jessica felt exposed and vulnerable. She had told Atticus she was coming here on her way home, but what if he didn't check his voicemail?

'Please, Officer,' York said. 'This is just silly.'

His emollient words might have been plausible save for the fact that Jessica *knew* what she had heard. There was that, and the fact that as she took a step to her left to get around him, so York stepped to his right to block her against the car. She retreated into the car, but, before she could get all the way in, he lunged forward and grabbed her right shoulder and tried to pull her out. She held onto the side of the seat as York yanked at the top of her arm. She fumbled open the compartment in the centre console and reached inside, her fingers closing around the plastic canister she kept there. York dragged harder, and, unanchored, she was hauled out of the car and onto the gravel.

York knelt beside her, one hand pressed down on her sternum, the other clenched into a tight fist, cocked and ready to strike. Jessica fumbled the canister around, stretched out her thumb until it was over the stippled applicator, aimed up at York's face and pressed. The can hissed as the propellant and liquid were ejected through the valve and into York's eyes, nose and mouth. The liquid was a solution of CS and a solvent, and Jessica was so close that it was impossible to miss. The liquid splashed into York's eyes, forcing them shut almost at once. Jessica reached up and shoved him, rolling out from underneath his body as he crashed down onto the gravel, his hands pawing at eyes that were streaming with tears.

She backed away and took out her phone. It felt slippery in her hand, like a bar of soap, and she had only just managed to wake the screen when she saw York on his feet again. He had something in his hand and, as she backed away, she stumbled enough for him to close right up to her. He reached for her neck; she heard the unmistakeable crackle of electricity and felt a sharp pain, the sensation running into her right shoulder and then all the way down her arm. Her knees buckled and she collapsed, her left shoulder taking the impact and her head slapping into the muddy ground.

York loomed over her, his eyes still streaming. She tried to scramble clear, but her legs were weak, and she could do nothing to stop York from jabbing down with the thing in his hand. She felt a sharp pressure against her neck, the electricity crackled again, and Jessica went rigid as her muscles locked.

67

Patterson and Lewis went inside the house. Atticus called a taxi and waited impatiently for it to arrive. He took out his phone and called Mack.

'How's it going?' he asked.

'Fine.'

'Did he say anything in the car?'

'Not a word, and he wants to speak to a solicitor before I interview him. We're waiting for them to get here. What about you?'

'Just waiting for a taxi.'

'You didn't go inside?'

'I thought I'd leave it to the police,' he said.

She paused, then spoke again. 'What are you doing tonight?'

'I want to work on the case.'

'What about?'

'Some things that Miller said. I just want to cross-reference them with the notes I have on Burns from before.'

It was a lie, but adjacent enough to the truth that he was able to say it without Mack picking up the falsehood.

'That won't take all night, will it?'

'I hope not.'

'I'm going to need a drink after I'm done with Miller,' she said. 'Fancy it?'

He was impatient to get back so that he could start to work. 'Can I call you later?' he said, then, sensing her disappointment in his equivocal reply, realised that might have sounded like a snub. 'That came out wrong. I'd love to. When would be good?'

'Can you be flexible? Maybe eight thirty?'

'That works.'

The taxi arrived.

'Come to the hotel,' she said. 'I'll see you there.'

He ended the call.

'Where to, mate?' the driver asked through the open window.

Atticus opened the door and got in. 'New Street in Salisbury. As fast as you like.'

* * *

Atticus paid the driver, unlocked the door and hurried up the stairs. He took out his phone and transferred the photographs that he had taken at Miller's house to his computer. He opened them in Photoshop – three photos, each taken from a slightly different angle – and arranged them on his second screen. He selected the one with the least glare on the glass and blew it up to full size.

He examined it. It was an official photograph from what appeared to be some sort of military event. There were nineteen men in uniform, arranged in three rows: a row of seven, sitting down at the front, and then two rows of six standing behind them. They were dressed in peaked caps and dress tunics with red banding around the collar and epaulettes on the shoulders. All of the men wore medals with green and purple striped ribbons over the left breast pockets of their jackets; Atticus zoomed in and, with a bit of googling, identified the decorations as General Service Medals that were awarded after thirty days' continuous service in an operation. There was a building in the background, but, despite zooming in as far as he could, Atticus could not identify it nor find any clue that might give him an idea what, or where, it might be.

He zoomed out again and concentrated on the men in the photograph.

Three of them were of particular interest to him.

Atticus zoomed in on the man in the middle of the front row. He had medals on his lapel and a braided lanyard that ran down from the epaulette on his right shoulder. Atticus opened the photograph that Burns had used to blackmail the colonel and compared that man with the man in the front row.

He was sure: it was a much younger Richard Miller. He zoomed out.

The man on the far-right side of the second line had no medals or lanyards. He was big and broad of shoulder, standing straight with his chin jutting out. Atticus drew a box around his face, zoomed in again and clarified the image. He referred to the photograph from the house in Bogside and compared the two.

Again, he was sure: it was Burns.

He drew the focus back again and then closed in on the man in the middle of the back row. He was the shortest of the six who stood there, but, thanks to the way that the rows had been arranged, his face was easily visible between the two men who stood in front of him. Atticus stared at the man for a long minute; his eye had been drawn to him as soon as he had seen the photograph in Miller's house. He went onto Facebook and found the profile of the man he wanted. There were twenty points in a person's face that were unique. The ears would have been best, but the man was facing forward. Atticus scaled the two pictures and then measured the spacing between the eyes, the distance between the bottom of the nose and the top lip, the rough size of the ears.

The photos were not perfect, and the comparisons were inexact, but they were good enough for Atticus to know that his gut feeling had been correct.

It was James York.

He closed his eyes and allowed his thoughts to unspool. There had been a third man in the bedroom in Londonderry.

He had taken the photograph, and Miller had confirmed that he had been there, although he had pretended not to know his name.

Burns had been blackmailing Miller.

Could he have been blackmailing York, too?

Atticus inhaled and held his breath, trying to find the clarity of thought that he would need to start identifying those facts that, when knotted together, would allow him to see the truth.

Molly York seemed determined to run away from home. Why? What had prompted it? What if it wasn't because she had wanted to be with Shayden Mullins? What if Mullins was a means to help her to get away, rather than the reason? Was it possible that the reason she had run had nothing to do with what York had suggested?

A man who might have been blackmailing York had been murdered.

York's daughter had run away.

Coincidence?

Lots of coincidences.

Atticus could see some of the threads he needed, but not the others. He started to extrapolate, to speculate and test the strength of the connections that he had created, and then stopped as a thought crashed through to the front of his mind.

Jessica Edwards had gone to see York this afternoon. Atticus took out his phone and called Jessica's number.

Voicemail.

He held the phone out and stared at it.

He breathed in and out and hoped against hope that he hadn't been stupid enough to have been used.

He called York's number.

68

James York drove the detective's car up onto Fifty Acre, the field to the north of the house, and bumped it along the muddy track until he reached the barn.

He opened the boot and dragged her out. He had wrapped her hands and ankles with tape and then stuffed a rag in her mouth to keep her quiet; the latter was unnecessary since she was still unconscious after he had knocked her out. He hauled her from the car into the barn, then opened the trapdoor and dropped her into the cellar, closing the door and padlocking it. He backed the car inside until it covered the trapdoor. He would have to get rid of it eventually, but that was something that would have to wait.

He found her bag on the passenger seat. He opened it and emptied out the contents: a purse, a packet of tissues, some make-up, a box of breath mints. He opened the purse and thumbed through her bank cards and driving licence, flipping through them one by one. Nothing of interest.

He tucked the purse under his arm and walked back to the house, stopping at the blackened oil barrel that he used when he wanted to burn waste. He took a jerrycan of petrol from his shed and some kindling from his wood-store; he dropped the kindling into the can, poured the petrol over it and lit it with a match. The fire caught at once, the flames reaching up over the sooty rim. He flipped the woman's cards into the barrel, then her purse. The cards began to warp and then melt, plumes of acrid black smoke unwinding into the night.

He went into the house and took off his boots. He was hungry; he would make himself something to eat before he went out to dig a pit in the field. He took the detective's phone out of his pocket and laid it down on the kitchen counter. He was just setting the microwave to heat his dinner when the phone started to ring. He squinted at the screen. The display showed the name of the caller: Atticus Priest. He let the phone ring three more times until it went silent.

Why was he calling her? They had been working together. Perhaps he was checking in on her. He powered down the phone to ensure that the GPS was off, and left it by his boots so as not to forget it. He would bury it with her.

The microwave had just beeped that his food was ready when his own phone rang. He cursed, took it out and saw that now Priest was calling him. He bit his lip. He knew he would have to speak to him eventually, but the prospect of it was not something that he was looking forward to.

He took a moment to compose himself and then accepted the call.

'Hello?'

'Mr York?'

'That's right.'

'It's Atticus Priest. How are you?'

'About as good as could be expected under the circumstances.'

'I hope I'm not disturbing you.'

'Not at all. I've just got back from the field – had a cow get tangled up in barbed wire. Silly sod's cut her legs. Got blood all over me. Do you have any news about Molly?'

'No, I'm sorry, I don't. I was just calling to see if you'd heard anything.'

'Not a word. But the detective from London stopped by.'

'Jessica?'

'That's right. She said that the lad from before was in London. She said he'd been in Salisbury again.'

'Molly's not with him?'

'Apparently not.'

'When was this?'

He closed his eyes and concentrated on what he needed to say. 'She's been twice, actually. Once this afternoon and once this evening.'

'Why did she come back?'

'She left her identification here. She came to get it. She was only here five minutes.'

'I'll call you if I find anything else out.'

'I appreciate that.'

York said goodbye and the line went dead.

He paced. Had Priest believed his story? There was no reason why not. It would check out if he – or the police – were minded to investigate it.

The conversation certainly clarified one thing: he had to get rid of her sooner rather than later. He had decided to put it off until tomorrow, but that seemed like an unnecessary risk now. There was no reason to wait. It was the same for Molly, too. He had been delaying *that*, knowing that it would be more difficult when it was his own flesh and blood, but he was just going to have to pull himself together and get it over and done with. He didn't have a choice. Molly had been in the cellar since they had returned from London. He could have kept an eye on her, kept her under lock and key, but that couldn't last for ever. York knew that she would run again as soon as she saw the chance, and how could he risk that? She had told the boy in London about what she had seen, and he had told the detective. York was going to have to think about whether he would need to do something about him, too.

First things first, though.

He collected his meal from the microwave, peeled the cellophane sleeve away and picked at the pasta with a fork. He looked at his watch. It was getting late. He would eat and then go back up to Fifty Acre and dig a grave big enough for the two of them, plus the lad who had come around last night. That had been a nice touch. York had taken Molly's phone and sent a message to Jordan Lamb about how much she wanted to see him, and, true to form, the lovesick idiot had turned up in his car an hour later. York had used the stun gun to disable him and then, while he was still spasming from the shock, had finished him off with the bolt gun. Him disappearing at the same time as Molly gave him the chance to muddy the waters; the two of them had run off together.

It was time to tidy everything away. He'd find a spot in the copse by the fence; no one went up there. He had the bolt pistol in his Land Rover. He would use that on Molly and the officer, then drive them up to the field and bury them. It would take two or three hours, he estimated, but once it was done, it was done.

69

Atticus put the phone down on the desk and stared at it. York was lying to him. He had stammered and left a long pause before telling him that Jessica had been to the farm on two occasions. Lying was a complicated business, and York had found himself caught in the crux of what he had said and what he thought Atticus might know. A pause was often an indication that a conversational partner dealing in untruths was trying to think of something safe to say.

He looked, again, at the photograph of York, Burns and Miller.

York was lying; what was he lying about, and how deep did those lies go?

Atticus was worried: why wasn't Jessica answering her phone?

He grabbed his jacket and set off for the street.

* * *

Atticus pushed his way through the doors into the hotel lobby and, ignoring the staff member behind the desk, made his way straight up the stairs to the first floor. He jogged down the corridor to Mack's room and rapped his knuckles against the door.

She opened the door. 'You're early,' she said; then, when she noticed the frantic cast to his face, she frowned. 'What is it?'

'We have a problem. It's DC Edwards.'

'Why? What's wrong?'

'She's in trouble. Mack – I missed something about Burns and Miller.'

She paused, looking at him quizzically, before stepping aside to let him in.

Atticus had printed out his copy of the photograph that he had taken at the colonel's house and laid it on the bed.

'What's this?' Mack said.

'This was in the sitting room at Miller's house. You should recognise these two.' He stabbed his finger against first Burns and then Miller.

'So? We know they knew each other. Miller admitted it.'

'He did. But look here.' He dragged his finger up to the middle of the back row. 'What about him?'

Mack looked at the man and shook her head. 'Who's that?'

Atticus took out the printout of the photo from Facebook and laid it on the bed.

Mack compared the two photographs and frowned. 'James York? The father of the missing girl?'

'Burns, Miller and York all served together in Northern Ireland in the eighties. They were in Londonderry together, and I'll bet you whatever you like that York took the photo in the bedroom. And then they all ended up back in Salisbury. All three of them. We know that Burns was blackmailing Miller.'

'And you think Burns was blackmailing York, too?'

'It's possible. Molly York ran away from home within a month or two of Alfred Burns's murder. Why did she do that?'

'You think York was involved?'

'I'm starting to think that.'

'But what does it have to do with Edwards?'

'Molly went missing for a second time on Friday night. I called Jessica to ask if Molly had gone back to London to be with the boy she was seeing there. But *he'd* come down here, and I thought it was likely that he was here to see her. Jessica came to find him, but he's gone back to London, and Molly isn't with him. Jessica left her warrant card at York's place by mistake, and she was going to stop and pick it up on the way home.'

'And?'

'And now she's not answering her phone. I called York, and he said that she had been there, but she'd left. The problem with that is I don't believe him. He's lying. I'm *sure* he's lying. It is at *least* possible that York was involved with Burns and Miller, and that he had something to do with Burns's death. What if Molly ran away because she found out about that? What if I was employed to find her because York was concerned that she might give him away? What if Jessica found something out that threatened him? I don't know, Mack – it's *all* possible, and I can't get through to her to check that I'm wrong.'

'So what are you going to do?'

'I'm going to go out there now. I just wanted you to know – just in case.'

'You can't go barging onto someone's property, Atticus. You're not police.'

'So you keep telling me. But I can't just sit here and wait.'

'No, you can't.' She got up and unhooked her jacket from the back of the chair. 'Are you going to drive, or shall I?'

70

Jessica was woken by the throbbing in her head. It pulsed from just above her ear, arcing down her neck and into her right shoulder. She felt nauseous, too, a curdling in her gut that she knew would rush up her gullet the moment she moved. She was lying on her side against hard ground. Her legs were bent, with her feet pressed against her backside, and her arms were behind her back. She tried to straighten out, but couldn't. She felt a tightening around her wrists and ankles as she strained and realised that she had been hog-tied.

Something had been stuffed into her mouth. It filled her cheeks and pushed up against her teeth and, when she probed at it with her tongue, it felt rough and fibrous. She opened her mouth as wide as she could manage and pushed with her tongue, forcing whatever it was out bit by bit until she was able to get rid of it completely.

She gasped for breath. It was dark; so dark, in fact, that she had to blink her eyes to make sure that she had not imagined opening them. Her stomach settled a bit, enough for her to move a little more. She waited for her eyes to adjust; there was a little light filtering in from somewhere overhead, and she was able to see enough to tell that she was in an enclosed space of some sort. Whatever was above her looked as if it had gaps, enough for slivers of the very faintest light to pass through.

'Hello?' A girl's voice came from close by. 'Are you awake?'

'Yes,' Jessica mumbled through dry lips. 'I'm awake.'

'Are you okay?'

'I think I banged my head.'

There was a pause; Jessica could hear the sound of water droplets nearby, a regular *tick, tick, tick* as they fell to the floor.

'Where am I?'

'In the cellar,' the girl said. 'Under the barn.'

Jessica felt the panic bubble up and, before she could stop herself, she yelled, 'Help! Someone – help!'

'Don't,' the girl said. 'No one can hear us here, and you'll just upset my dad. He'll punish you if you don't behave.'

Jessica's breath was ragged. She stopped shouting and focused on her breathing, inhaling a deep breath through her nose and then letting it out as steadily as she could through her lips. It helped; after a moment, the panic subsided a little.

'Are you Molly?'

'How do you know my name?'

'My name's Jessica. I'm with the Met Police. I've been looking into county lines drug dealing. I've been getting information from the private detective who found you in London.'

Jessica tried to flex her arms, but the ties were too tight. She grunted with the effort, but the edges of the plastic cuffs dug into her skin.

'What are you doing?'

'Are you tied up, too?' Jessica asked.

'Yes.'

Jessica tried again, but it was futile; she arranged herself so that she wasn't leaning back onto her shoulders in an attempt to find a little more comfort. She tried to think how long she had been down here. It had been early evening when she had arrived at the house. It was difficult to know how many hours had passed since then. The minuscule amount of light that reached them through the gaps above could have been artificial, or, equally, it could have been moonlight. It was impossible to say.

'What time is it?'

'I don't know,' Molly said.

Jessica shifted her weight again. 'What happened to you?'

'Dad put me down here when we came home.'

'Why?'

'Because he's a bad person. He knows I'll run away again otherwise.'

Jessica felt a quiver of fear. 'How is he bad?'

The girl didn't answer.

Jessica heard the sound of something scratching away to her left. She looked, but couldn't see anything.

'There are rats here,' Molly said.

Jessica thought she could make out a shape in the darkness next to her. The tiny amount of light fell onto something that looked solid, more substantial than the gloom around it.

'Molly,' she said, 'do you know what that is over there?'

'His name was Jordan.'

'Jordan Lamb?'

'Do you know him?'

'I went to see him today. He wasn't there.'

'He's been here since last night.'

'Jordan!' Jessica called out.

'He's dead,' Molly said. 'Dad told me what he was going to do. He took my phone and sent Jordan a message, pretending to be me. He shot him with the bolt gun and dumped him down here with me.'

Jessica felt bile rising in her throat.

'I told you – my dad's evil.'

'What else has he done?'

'He kills people. There was another person. A man. I saw it. I don't know his name. I hadn't seen him before. Dad thought I was out, but I wasn't. I was smoking a joint in the woods. There was an argument. I saw it. Dad shot him with the bolt gun.'

That term again. 'The what?'

'He uses it when he needs to kill one of the cows. Dad put it against his head and . . .' The words petered out.

Jessica tried to speak, but her words were lost in the white-hot flood of panic that swept over her. She tried to free her wrists again, ignoring the pain as the cuffs sliced into her skin, yanking against them so that she might loosen them enough to slide a hand through. It was a waste of time. They were too tight.

'You're wasting your time,' Molly said. 'You'll just hurt yourself, and even if you did get out, what then? We're locked in the cellar. There's a bolt that fastens the trapdoor, and Dad usually puts his truck over it as well. There's no way out.'

71

Atticus tried Jessica's number again as they pulled out of Salisbury and again as they arrived at the outskirts of Broughton.

'Nothing?' Mack said.

'Voicemail. She should have been back in London hours ago.'

'She couldn't have lost her phone? Or it's out of battery?'

'Possible, but unlikely.'

'Maybe she's had an accident on the way home.'

'I checked. Nothing's been reported. No, Mack. York lied to me. Something's wrong.'

'All right. We'll check it out and see what we can find.'

'And what if we don't find anything?'

She shrugged. 'What do you want to do? We don't have enough to arrest York. All we know is that he served in the same regiment as Burns and Miller.'

'There *has* to be a connection.'

'Find the evidence. We can go from there.'

Mack switched off the lights as they turned onto the lane that led to the farm. 'Where is it?'

'Down there.' Atticus pointed. 'Pull over. We'll go the rest of the way on foot.'

Mack pulled over and parked in a passing space that was still a good fifty yards from the gate. She reached for the ignition and killed the engine.

She swivelled around to face him across the cabin. 'How do you want to do this?'

'I'll go and look around.'

'Not on your own.'

'We can't just ring the bell.'

'And we can't trespass, either.'

'*You* can't,' Atticus corrected. '*I* can. As you keep reminding me, *I'm* not a police officer.'

He opened the door and stepped out into the cold, damp night. There was enough of a glow from the moon to see that there was no one else outside with them. Mack got out, too, and quietly shut the door behind her. They set off. Atticus walked briskly, a sickening feeling in the pit of his stomach. They reached the entrance with the black iron gates. The drive was as he remembered it, wending its way through the neatly cut trees to the farmhouse. The windows were dark.

'Looks quiet,' Atticus said.

Mack checked her watch. 'It's midnight,' she said. 'He might be asleep.'

'I don't think so.'

He had already decided that he would break into the house if he had to. He knew Mack would protest, but he would ignore her. Something had happened to Jessica, and he knew that waiting for everything to be done by the book would not be tenable. She might not have the time for that and, he reminded himself, it wasn't as if they had grounds for an application for a warrant to go inside; a bad feeling on the part of a disgraced ex-policeman was not one of them.

They continued down the lane. The perimeter of the property was marked by a yew hedge on the right that was thick and tall, perhaps ten feet high. An old rusted iron fence had been subsumed by the yew over time, the two creating a boundary that would be difficult to breach. They walked on, following the gentle bend in the road until they came to a second gate. This one was agricultural, with barbed wire wound around the top rail to discourage people from clambering over it. A dirt track led into the broad field beyond.

'Here,' he said. 'I'll go in and look around. I'll call you if—'

'Shut up,' she said, cutting him off. 'I'm coming with you. Come on.'

72

Atticus took off his jacket and used it to cover the barbed wire. He climbed over and waited for Mack. They were in the field that lay to the north of the farmhouse. The moon was directly overhead, and the light cast the open space in a silvered glow. The field was empty and, to the right, the house looked as peaceful as it had when they had looked at it through the bars of the gate.

'Look,' Mack said, pointing.

Atticus had already noticed it: the light of a torch jerked around in the gloom in the direction of the farm buildings to the north.

'What's he doing out there this late?' she said.

'Nothing good.'

They heard the sound of an engine firing up, and then saw a blue Ford Ranger edging out of the open door.

Atticus set off at a jog. Mack caught up, the two of them splashing through ankle-high ruts that were filled with muddy water. The barn was a quarter of a mile away from them now, and they slowed to a careful walk when they drew near enough to think that the sound of their approach might betray them.

Atticus could see more now. The doors had been pulled back, and two vehicles were parked next to one another: the Ford Ranger and a BMW.

'See the BMW?' he hissed. 'That's her car.'

'What about the other one?'

'York's.'

The torchlight was inside the barn now, a steady beam that suggested that the source had been set down somewhere. Atticus crept ahead, Mack close behind. Atticus heard the creak of something moving on unoiled hinges, and the beam of the torch was interrupted as a trapdoor was opened, blocking it from where Atticus and Mack were standing.

Atticus heard the sound of a voice.

'Did you hear that?' Mack hissed.

Atticus held up his hand for silence.

Not one voice: there were two.

The first was female and panicked; the second was male and stern.

He started forward again, stepping through another puddle, and, over the quiet susurration of his boots through the water, there came the sound of a scream and then the thud of an impact.

'Go left,' Mack whispered, pointing to the left of the Ranger.

They split up. The fear that had sat in Atticus's gut was worse now, curdled into a dread that they were too late. He reached the side of the Ranger before Mack and was afforded a view into the interior of the barn. The trapdoor was in the middle of the space, pulled all the way back so that it was resting against the Ford's front bumper. The torch was on the floor behind it, its glow pooling against the wall to the left and providing enough illumination for Atticus to see the body that lay sprawled on the floor. It was a woman, hog-tied and with a rope looped around her waist that looked as if it might have been used as a tether or a leash.

He recognised the jacket that Jessica had been wearing earlier that day.

A man was standing between Jessica and Atticus. He had his back turned, but Atticus could see that it was James York. He had the rope in his right hand and was looping it through a metal ring that had been concreted into the floor. Jessica's head hung down low, and Atticus could see blood running freely from it. York must have struck her.

York walked over to a table at the side of the barn and picked up what looked like a very large handgun. Atticus knew what it was: a captive bolt gun of the sort used to kill cattle. He had seen one before. It fired a retractable bolt into the animal's head, killing it immediately. York checked the gun and, evidently satisfied, walked back to where Jessica had fallen.

'*Police! Stop!*'

Mack had come out around the other side of the vehicle.

York turned to Mack.

'I'm a police officer, Mr York. You need to put that down – *right now.*'

York took a step towards Mack. She was unarmed and, if York hadn't already realised that she was here without backup, it wouldn't take him long to reach that conclusion.

Atticus edged around the Ranger and broke into a flat run before York could notice him. He threw himself at the older man, wrapping his arms around him and tackling him to the ground. They both slammed down onto the rough concrete floor, mud smearing across them as they rolled first one way and then the other. Atticus wrestled himself on top and tried to pin York down. York was heavier and fit and strong for his age. Atticus locked his fists in the shoulders of York's jacket and shoved down, trying to press him in place until Mack could get over to help. York slithered left and right, opening up enough of an angle to drive his knee up and into Atticus's groin. The pain flashed, causing Atticus to loosen his grip for just long enough that York could punch up, his fist connecting with Atticus's cheekbone. He fell off York and onto his back and, before he could do anything to stop him, York was on top of him. Atticus stared up into his face, and then across at the bolt gun in York's right hand as he tried to force it down. Atticus tried to block his arm, but York punched him with his left hand, and then again. Atticus bit down on his tongue and tasted the blood in his mouth.

York pushed down until the bolt gun was inches away from Atticus's forehead.

'Mack!'

He tried to push York's arm away, but he didn't have the strength. York's eyes bulged, and a line of spittle dribbled down from the corner of his mouth and landed on Atticus's chin.

'*Mack!*'

He heard something – the crackle of static – and York spasmed and then went limp. Atticus bucked his hips and shrugged the older man off, then staggered to his feet. Mack was holding a black and yellow device in her hand: a stun gun.

'Where did you get that?'

'From his truck.'

York was still twitching helplessly. Atticus flipped him over, put his knee between his shoulder blades and pressed down with all his weight.

Mack helped hold him down. 'Are you okay?'

'Yes,' he said. 'Thank you.'

'You're making a habit of this,' she said.

'Of what?'

'Me saving your arse.'

She gave Atticus the stun gun and went to check Jessica. 'Is she okay?' he called over.

'She's breathing.'

Mack was loosening the rope around her wrists when they both heard a desperate voice from the open trapdoor.

'*Help!*'

Mack tossed the rope over to Atticus. 'Who's down there?'

'Molly York,' came the weak reply. 'Please – help me!'

'Hold on,' Mack said.

York had begun to struggle beneath Atticus's weight. 'Get *off* me.'

Atticus pressed the prongs of the stun gun against York's bare neck and pulled the trigger. York gasped and stiffened once more. Atticus took the opportunity to tie the rope around his right wrist and then his left, pulling the knots tight, and then, just because he could, shocked him for a third time.

Mack knelt down next to Jessica. 'You okay?'

The blood was still running from her nose. She nodded weakly.

'What's down there?'

'A space. Not big.'

Atticus stood, picked up the torch and aimed the beam down into the maw of the pit. He saw walls that had been braced with wooden planks and a rough dirt floor that glittered as the light reflected in puddles of water. There were two people below: Jordan Lamb lay on his back, face up, lifeless; Molly York stared up at him, her eyes blinking in the glare from the torch.

PART VIII
MONDAY

73

Jessica Edwards was wrapped in a blanket and drinking coffee from a paper cup when Atticus found her. She was in an empty interview room on the ground floor of the building. A PC had just delivered the coffee, and Atticus waited for her to step outside before he put his head through the door.

'Morning.'

Jessica looked up at him and smiled wanly. Her face was pinched and pale, and she looked exhausted. There was a nasty bruise on the side of her face from where York had struck her. She glanced down at her watch. 'So it is. I've completely lost track of the time.'

'How are you feeling?'

'Sore. And done in.'

Atticus took his hip flask out of his pocket and held it up. 'Want a nip of this?'

She held the cup out for him. 'Yes, please.'

He unscrewed the lid of the flask and poured a generous measure into the muddy brown coffee. He held up the flask once he was done. 'Cheers.'

She raised the cup in reciprocation of his salute and took a long draught, exhaling with satisfaction as she set it down again. 'I needed that.'

Atticus took a sip himself, then screwed the lid back on the flask and stood it on the table between them. 'Are you sure you're okay?'

'Just shaken up.'

'What happened?'

Jessica recounted her misfortunes from the previous day, explaining how she had gone to York's house to pick up her warrant card and how Shayden Mullins had called her while she was there and explained why Molly had run away from home. She said that she had heard the girl's ringtone coming from her father's pocket, and how – realising that his crime was exposed – York had attacked her.

'Did you speak to Molly when you were down there with her?'

'Yes.'

'What did she say?'

'That her father put her in the cellar when they got back from London. She says she saw him kill someone else and Jordan Lamb.'

'And that's why she ran?'

'Yes. She's terrified of him. Have you spoken to her yet?'

'Not yet. She's still with the doctor. And I wanted to check you were okay first.'

Jessica took another sip, then held out her cup again and gestured to the flask. 'I'll be even better with another of those.'

Atticus poured out another shot.

'Do you believe Molly?' she asked him.

'I do. I think her father was being blackmailed.'

'And the blackmailer . . .?'

'Was the man she saw being murdered.'

'What a mess,' Jessica said.

'That's one way to describe it.' He held up the flask. 'One for the road?'

'Go on, then.'

He poured a third measure, screwed the lid back on and dropped the flask into his pocket. 'I'd better go and see if I'm needed. I'm glad you're okay.'

'Can you ask them to send someone down to take my statement?'

'My guess is that they'll do it in the morning.'

'I'm not waiting here. I need to get some sleep.'

'Where are you going to go?'

'I'm too tired to drive home. Plus . . .' She held up her empty cup. 'A hotel, I suppose.'

'Crash at mine,' he suggested. 'My dog's there, but he'll just make a fuss of you and then curl up and go back to sleep.'

'Are you sure?'

'I'm going to be here all night. It's not a problem.' He took out his keys and gave them to her. 'Remember how to get there?'

'I do,' she said. 'Thanks.'

'I'm sorry about how I behaved before,' Atticus said. 'You're right. I was out of order.'

'Forget it,' she said.

'Leave the keys with my upstairs neighbour if I'm not back in time.'

'I will.' She got up, came to him and kissed him lightly on the cheek. 'Goodbye, Atticus.'

74

Atticus took the lift to the third floor and crossed over to the incident room. It was busy, with most of the team called in. The kettle had been boiled, and chipped mugs of strong coffee had been handed out. Mack was at the front of the room, watching a video that Mike Lewis was playing on his phone. The video finished, and she looked up and noticed Atticus. He gave her a nod; she reciprocated and then called the room to order.

Detective Inspector Best handed a mug of coffee to Atticus. 'Well done,' he said. 'Mack told me you worked it out.'

Atticus nodded; Robbie Best had never been his biggest fan at the nick – not that any of them had been – and he couldn't recall receiving praise from him before.

'Quieten down, everyone,' Mack said again. 'Take your seats. We've got a lot to get through, and the custody clock is ticking.'

They all did as she asked and settled down around the table. Atticus took out his flask and poured a measure of the whisky into his mug. He took a long sip, appreciating the heat of the alcohol. He was tired, too, and had been getting by on adrenaline for too long.

Mack quickly updated the detectives on the events of the last few hours and said that they had James York and Colonel Richard Miller in the cells downstairs. Molly York was also waiting to be questioned so that they could have a formal record of what she said her father had been doing.

'We've got twenty-four hours before we need to think about charging or applying for an extension, and there's still a lot we don't know.' She pointed to Atticus. 'Do you want to run through it?'

Atticus cleared his throat, collected the mugshots of York and Miller and the historic mugshot of Burns that he had pulled from his file and stood up. 'I'll start with what we *do* know,' he said, taking the mugshots of Burns and Miller and pinning them to the wall. '*One*: we know that Alfred Burns was blackmailing Miller with evidence that he was involved in the murder of two locals in Londonderry in the early eighties. *Two*: we know that Burns was killed. *Three*: we know that Burns's body was buried in a graveyard with the bodies of five teenage girls.' Atticus took the photograph of James York and pinned it next to the other two. '*Four*: we know that *this* man, James York, was an acquaintance of both Burns and Miller during their time in Northern Ireland, and that all three settled in the area after leaving the Army. *Five*: we know that York's daughter has named him as Burns's killer. *Six*: we know that York paid me to find his daughter and then, once I'd located her and reunited them, imprisoned her in a cellar underneath the floor of his barn. *Seven*: we know that York murdered a local lad in an attempt to make it appear that his daughter had run off with him. Finally, *eight*: we know that York attacked and imprisoned a Metropolitan Police officer after she found out that he had been lying about his daughter.'

Robbie Best raised a hand. 'That's a good start. What are we missing?'

'We know Burns had form for child porn. Young girls. It doesn't seem unreasonable to suggest that he's connected to the girls who were buried at Imber. But who killed them? Burns on his own? Or were Miller and York involved? We know that Burns was blackmailing Miller. Was he blackmailing York, too? If not, why did York kill him?'

'What about Miller?' Patterson said.

'Mike Lewis has a team at his house now. He's searching it.'

Best shook his head. 'Are we really ready to accuse an MP of murder?'

'We had more than enough to arrest him for what he said happened in Londonderry,' Mack said, taking over. 'This, though, with Burns and York? We don't have enough for that.'

'*Yet*,' Atticus qualified. He sat back down. 'I'd start with York's daughter. Find out what was going on in that house. Fill in as many gaps as you can with what she can tell us, and then take that to her father. Tell him that she's cooperating, then let him know that we've arrested Miller, too, and tell him that the colonel's going to talk. Then you take what York says and go to Miller. Make the colonel think that York is putting the knife into *him*. Turn each against the other – if you play it right, you get them to incriminate themselves and you find out whether anyone else was involved.'

Mack finished up, deputing Robbie Best to lead the search of York's property. Best picked the officers who would assist and left the room. Atticus waited where he was until Mack came over and sat down on the edge of the table next to him.

'You know you can't interview them,' she said. 'It's got to be a detective.'

'I know. But I can still help. Speak to Molly first. She's not a suspect. I can sit in on that.'

'You can.'

'And then set me up in a room where I can watch the live feed of the interviews. Do York first and then finish with Miller. Come and see me after each. I'll tell you what I think, the areas where you need more, different directions you can take. We'll set them at each other's throats and bag them both.'

75

Molly was waiting for them in the interview room that was decorated specifically for young or vulnerable witnesses. There was a sofa with brightly patterned cushions and two matching chairs facing it, and the walls were painted a gentle eggshell blue rather than the utilitarian shades that were found in the rest of the station. The girl had been joined by an appropriate adult, a woman whom Atticus recognised as a social worker who was called to the station when children needed to be interviewed. She sat on the other end of the sofa from Molly. Molly had been given a cup of coffee and a bar of chocolate from the vending machine at the end of the hall. She had a blanket around her shoulders and was staring dumbly into her drink.

'Molly,' Mack said, smiling, 'I'm Detective Chief Inspector Mackenzie Jones, but you can call me Mack if you like.'

The girl looked up from the coffee. She was pale and had red rings around her eyes. There was a purple bruise across the right-hand side of her forehead and lurid abrasions around her wrists from where the rope her father had used to secure her had chafed against her skin.

'I'm in charge of the investigation that has led to the arrest of your father tonight,' Mack said. 'This is Mr Priest. He helped find you in London.'

'I'm sorry about that,' Atticus said. 'I had no idea why your father wanted you back so badly. I'm afraid he fooled me.'

'He does that,' she said, her voice flat and emotionless and heavy with fatigue.

Mack and Atticus took the empty seats facing the sofa. Mack told Molly that she was going to record their conversation; the girl did not object. They started by asking her what had happened to her. She answered with the same lack of emotion, confirming everything that Jessica had recounted about her own conversations with the girl while they were both trapped in the cellar. Mack steered the conversation skilfully, building rapport and then gently prompting her with questions that enabled them to construct a picture of what life had been like for her with her father.

'You said you saw him murder someone,' Mack said. 'Is that right?'

She nodded.

'And that's why you ran away?'

'He realised I knew. I was frightened of what he would do to me.'

'Can you tell us what happened?'

Molly nodded and took a sip of her coffee. She swallowed, then paused before beginning to speak. She told them that her father had been arguing with another man, and that, although she was too far away to hear, she thought that it was about money. She told them about the bolt gun that her father had used, and how she could still hear the noise that it had made as the trigger was pulled.

'Could you describe the man who was killed?'

'He was around the same age as my dad. He walked with a limp.'

Mack had a folder on her lap. She opened it, took out the file picture of Alfred Burns and handed it to Molly.

'Is this him?'

She looked at the photograph and gave a little shrug. 'They weren't that close to me.'

'But it could be him?'

'It could be.'

Mack reached back into the folder and took out the photograph of Richard Miller that was on his website. She gave it to Molly.

'Have you ever seen this man before?'

She stared at it and gave a hopeless shrug. 'No.'

'Take another look,' Atticus urged.

She did as he asked, exhaled and then shook her head again. 'Try to remember.'

Molly blinked back sudden tears. 'I'm sorry. I can't . . .'

Atticus ground his teeth in frustration.

Mack glared at him and then turned to smile at the girl. 'It's fine, Molly.'

'It's one in the morning,' the social worker said. 'I think Molly's tired. Perhaps this could wait until the morning?'

'That's a great idea,' Mack said. She reached out and laid her hand over Molly's briefly. 'You've done amazingly well. Thank you.'

76

Mack led the way down to the interview suites where James York and Richard Miller were waiting. There were four rooms dedicated to that purpose at the station; York was waiting in room one, and Miller was in room three. Mack pointed to room four, and Atticus went inside. One of the civilians who managed the tech was setting up the monitor that Atticus had requested.

'You're good to go,' the woman said, stepping aside.

Atticus looked at the screen. There were two cameras in the corners of room one, and the feeds from both were displayed on the monitor. James York was sitting down with his solicitor next to him. The chairs on the opposite side of the table were empty. Atticus sat down. There was a pad of paper on the table, and he took out a pen and laid it across the first page.

Mack pointed to the screen. 'What do you think of him?'

'He's a good liar. He pulled the wool over my eyes. He won't be a pushover.'

'No,' she said. 'But we've got a lot of evidence against him.'

Atticus laid his finger over the lawyer. 'What about him?'

'Sam Aikenhead,' she said. 'He works for Corbetts.'

'I don't know him.'

'He only joined a month ago. Came down from London. I had him representing a burglar I had in. He's all right.'

'This is a bit more than burglary.'

Atticus watched the screen. York and his solicitor were talking.

'Who's doing the interview with you?'

'Nigel,' she said.

Atticus would have preferred to be in there himself, but, knowing that was impossible, he agreed with the choice. DS Archer was an imposing man, and he had a knack of looking at a suspect and inspiring fear. Having him in the room would be a good way of distracting from the fact that, beneath Mack's affability, she was as sharp as a needle.

'I'd better get to it,' she said.

'I'll text you if there's anything I think you need to know.'

'Fine. I can always step out for five minutes.' She clapped her hands. 'Right, then. Wish me luck.'

* * *

Atticus settled down, removed the cap from the pen and jotted down a few of the points that would need to be covered. He watched as Mack and Archer came inside and sat down opposite York and his solicitor. There was a microphone on the table next to a bottle of water and two cups of instant coffee from the machine in the corridor. The mic was switched on, and Atticus heard the scrape of the chairs as the two detectives arranged themselves.

'Good evening, Mr York,' Mack said.

'Good *morning*,' he corrected her.

Mack looked up at the clock on the wall. 'You're right. Good morning. For the purposes of the recording, I'd just like you to identify yourself with your full name and give us your date of birth.'

He started to speak, but was overtaken by a hacking cough.

'Are you all right, Mr York?'

He held up a hand to indicate that he was. 'Sorry,' he said. 'Something in my throat – I'm fine. My name is James Alexander York, and my date of birth is 9 September 1957.'

'Thank you. I'm Detective Chief Inspector Mackenzie Jones, and this is Detective Sergeant Nigel Archer. This interview is commencing at one thirty in the morning on 17 February. You do not have to say anything, but it may harm your defence if you do not mention when questioned something which you later rely on in court. Anything you say may be given in evidence. Do you understand this?'

'I do.'

'Good – thank you.'

York looked to Aikenhead and then back to Mack. 'I want to make a confession.'

Atticus sat forward.

Mack did, too. 'What do you want to confess to?'

'The murders of Alfred Burns and Jordan Lamb.'

Atticus's mouth fell open.

'And the murders of the five girls that you've been digging up at Imber.'

Atticus stared at the screen in stupefaction.

Mack was stunned, too, but mastered it quickly. 'You understand what you're saying, Mr York? You understand the consequences?'

'I do.'

'And you've spoken to Mr Aikenhead about this?'

'He has,' the solicitor replied.

'Why are you telling us this now?'

'Because I've had to live with unbearable guilt for twenty years. And I don't want to do that any more. It's ruined my life. It's ruined my relationship with my daughter. It's enough.'

Mack turned her head to glance up at the camera, as if she might be able to check that Atticus was watching.

'Start from the beginning,' Archer said.

'It started with Alf,' York said. 'Alfred Burns. I knew him from the Army. We were both in the Green Jackets. Served in Northern Ireland together. Patrolled together. I got to know him pretty well. We spent a lot of time on OP duty.'

'What's that?' Archer said.

'Static, overt surveillance. We'd both be in a sangar on four-hour stags, scared shitless but bored shitless at the same time. You get talking to the bloke you're with in a situation like that and we talked about anything and everything. There was this one time when we were on stag together and the conversation turned to money. I asked him where he was getting all his, since he seemed to have so much more than me. He said he'd been moonlighting and that he'd earned enough to buy a brand-new Cortina. I didn't have a pot to piss in back then – I was *completely* broke – and when he asked me if I wanted to earn a little extra, I was interested. He said he knew a bloke who knew a bloke who was selling drugs to kids in Londonderry. The IRA were kneecapping anyone they suspected of dealing, and Alf's plan was to pretend to be them, kick our way into this bloke's house and rob him.'

'Just the two of you?'

'To start with. It was just like he said. We went in, pointed our guns in his face, took his money and ran. I regret what happened now. It was a stupid idea, but when you're stuck in a place like that, getting shot at most days, always wondering if you'll make it through the end of a patrol without getting blown up or sniped . . . it's a pressure cooker. An atmosphere like that can make you do things you'd never normally do. It's not something I'd expect a civilian to understand.'

'No,' Archer said. 'I'm sure you wouldn't.'

'Just the one time?' Mack asked.

He shook his head. 'It was so easy that we agreed to do it again. Alf got information on another pusher. The word was that he had his stash hidden under his bed. He was a bit more of a serious proposition, though, not likely to give up the money without a fight, and Alf said he was worried enough about being robbed that he had a sawn-off shotgun. Alf said we needed a third man on the team, and he had someone in mind.'

'Who?'

'Richard Miller.'

Mack pretended to be surprised. 'The MP?'

'Yes. He was an officer then. A captain.'

York went on to recount the same story that Mack and Atticus had heard from Miller earlier that day. Mack took out the photograph that Atticus had found in Burns's flat and laid it on the table.

'You took this picture, didn't you?'

York nodded. 'I did.'

Mack scribbled notes. 'What happened?'

'The man had a woman living with him, and they both laid into us. The woman especially – she said that as soon as we left, she was going to tell her brother's mates what had happened and that we'd end up getting shot before we knew it. Alf lost it. He shot the boyfriend, raped the woman, and then, when he was finished, he strangled her.' York shook his head. 'I remember what Alf told me the first time we met. He said he was born with the devil in him. At the time, I thought he was just saying that for effect. I knew he was crazy, but what he did to those two was . . . I didn't see it coming.' He paused. 'We cleaned up and left the bodies where they were. We got back to barracks and waited for something to happen – it never did. The case made the newspapers, but they put it down to the loyalists. There'd been a murder the week before, and the man Alf had shot was supposed to have been involved. The police said it was tit for tat and closed the investigation.'

'What about you?' Archer said. 'You didn't think to say anything?'

'I was there,' York protested. 'I'd been involved with Alf for six months by that time. I knew what would've happened if I'd said anything – Alf would've said it was me, and not him, and it would've been his word against mine. Alf knew I'd been in trouble when I was younger, too.'

'What kind of trouble?'

'A girl I was seeing before I enlisted accused me of assault. It wasn't the way she said it was, but I got a record for it. I joined the Army to put it behind me.'

Atticus noted down that they would need to check that.

'And then?' Mack prompted.

'The Ballykelly bomb. I just got cuts and bruises. I was lucky compared to Alf. They had to take his leg off.'

'Miller was there, too, wasn't he?'

'He was. The roof fell on top of him. They shipped the two of them to Musgrave Park to recover. They patched Miller up okay, but it was obvious that Alf was done. He got a medical discharge six months later, and I thought that would be that. I didn't think I'd ever see him again. I certainly had no plans to.'

Atticus was rapt.

York coughed again and took a sip of his water.

'I got out of the Army in 2000 and took over my dad's farm. I met my wife, and we had our daughter a few years later. I hadn't seen Alf for twenty years – I'd almost forgotten about him.' He chuckled humourlessly. 'That's the thing with people like him, though. You can never get away from them completely.'

'When did you see him again?'

'Just after Christmas in 2001. I was in Sainsbury's car park in town. I tried to get away, but I had a trolley full of shopping, and he'd already seen me. He came over and started chatting, telling me about what he'd been doing since he'd got out, asking about me and what I was up to. He said we should go for a drink, but I made an excuse and managed to get away from him. I put it down as a lucky escape until he turned up at the farm the next day. He said that we really did need to catch up properly, and that he wasn't going to take no for an answer. I told him I wasn't interested, and then he threatened me. He brought up what we'd done in Londonderry. I remember what he said:

"Wouldn't you love to see those pictures of what we used to get up to in the good old days?" *The good old days.'* York swore under his breath. 'Anyway – he said he had something that I needed to see, and I had no choice – I had to go with him there and then. I got into his car, and he drove me out to Imber. Alf worked for the Ministry of Defence after he was discharged. He was in charge of the range there, and he had keys for all the buildings. There was a cottage near to the graveyard where you've been digging. Alf opened it up and took me inside.'

Atticus had stopped writing. He stared at the monitor, fearful of the direction he suspected the confession was about to take, yet doubtful of it at the same time.

York took a sip of his water and then straightened his posture. 'And?' Mack said.

'Alf had a girl there. Couldn't have been more than fifteen or sixteen. He'd tied her to a chair. Dead. He said she'd been there for three days and that he needed someone to help him get rid of her. I knew that wasn't why I was there. There was nothing to her – even with his leg, he would've been able to get her into his car and take her wherever he wanted.'

'So why did he take you there?'

'He told me later – he wanted a partner. That was the way he always was, the way he did things – he took me out there and got me into the same room as the girl. He knew how easy it would have been to say that I was involved. He knew I already had the assault on my record, and he could have brought up what had happened in Londonderry, too.' He sighed. 'He told me that we had to bury her. He'd had the idea to put her in the graveyard. I remember what he said: "No one's going to notice another body in there, are they?" Probably fair enough. It was dark. I carried her across the road, and we dug a grave for her and put her in it.'

Atticus could see the tension in Mack's posture, even from above and behind. 'What was her name?'

'He didn't tell me.'

'You didn't ask?'

'What would've been the point?'

Atticus gripped the edge of the table.

'She was someone's daughter, Mr York.'

'She was already dead.'

There was a moment of silence, interrupted by the hiss of static from the microphone.

'Okay,' Mack said, her voice taut with suppressed anger. 'We'll have more questions about that, but I'd rather press on. What happened next?'

'I didn't see him for another couple of weeks, and then he turned up at the farm for the second time. He told me that I had to go to Imber with him again. I did. We went to the same cottage as before, and there was another girl there. This one was alive. Alf said I'd been loyal to him and she was his gift to me.'

'And?'

York looked away. 'And the same thing happened to her as happened to the other one.'

'Who killed her?'

'Alf did.'

'But you were involved this time?'

'I was.'

'How?'

He breathed in and was silent for a moment. 'I'd rather not say anything about that.'

'You raped her?'

York paused and then nodded.

'For the benefit of the tape, Mr York is nodding,' Archer said.

Mack looked down at her notes, her disgust evident.

Archer took over. 'How many times did this happen?'

'I'm not sure. How many bodies have you found?'

'I'd rather you answered the question.'

'I can't remember. At least five.'

'You think more?'

'Yes, I do.'

Atticus listened and watched as York answered Mack's questions. York was right-handed, yet he was emphasising his points with his *left* hand. That was an unnatural gesture for him, and he made it *after* he had delivered his points rather than at the same time. His mind was too busy telling the story, assessing whether or not it was being believed, and then adding to the story depending on that. It was artificial and, although he was good – well rehearsed – Atticus could see the effort that was required to manufacture a sense of credibility.

'You said you killed Burns,' Archer said.

'That's right. Alf was arrested and charged. They found porn on his computer.'

'Images of young girls,' Mack said.

'I remember Alf's reaction when it happened. He thought it was *hilarious*. "If only they knew," he kept saying. Over and over, he kept going back to that. "If only they knew."'

Atticus bit down on his lip so hard that he drew blood.

'But then he had the trial and he got off. He told me he had to leave the country. Thailand, he said, for obvious reasons. It didn't matter that he'd been found innocent, he said. The stink would stay on him. He was worried that what we'd been doing in Imber might be found out, too. He had no money – that was the problem. He asked me, but the farm was doing badly, and I didn't have anything to spare. He went to his brother, I think, and then he left. I thought that might be the last I saw of him.'

He shifted uncomfortably in his chair.

'Don't stop,' Mack said.

'No,' he said. 'I need a break.'

77

Mack came into room four and took the seat opposite Atticus.

'Holy *shit*,' she said.

'I thought something similar.'

'What do you make of it?'

'It's hard to say from here.'

'Is he telling the truth?'

'I'd need to be in the room for that, Mack.'

'Your educated guess, then.'

'His body language is consistent with telling the truth. Not much grooming, no playing with his hair or touching his lips. He doesn't sound uncertain or vague. Most people are light on details when they lie, and he's been the opposite. It's either the truth or it's a story that he's had time to cook up.'

'What would you do?' she asked him. 'To tell whether it's the truth?'

'There's one technique you could try.'

'What?'

'Go back in and ask him to recount the story in reverse. Lying is more mentally taxing than telling the truth. Make it more difficult for him. Increase his cognitive load and see if he trips up. I'll watch for behavioural cues – he'll be less able to suppress them.'

She said that she would. 'What do you make of what he said about Burns?'

'You mean, is Burns capable of murder?' Atticus said. 'Definitely. I always said so. That's why I didn't stop working his case. But I would've said that he was building up to it rather than already having done it ... Still, much as I hate to admit it, it's not impossible I was wrong. You know what he was like when we had him in here – very hard to read.'

Atticus saw movement on the screen, and first Aikenhead and then York took their seats again, setting two fresh plastic cups of coffee down on the table. 'They're back,' he said.

'Right.' Mack stood up and smoothed out her shirt. 'I'd better get back to it.'

'Make him tell it backwards,' Atticus said. 'I'll text you if I think he's lying.'

* * *

Atticus put his phone on the table and opened a text to Mack. He watched as Mack and Archer took their seats opposite York and his solicitor once more. She started the recording again and then asked York to repeat what he had just said, but, this time, asked him to work backwards. Atticus watched carefully, still frustrated that he was having to make an assessment remotely, but hopeful the camera might reveal the body language that might indicate the truthfulness of York's testimony. A liar would exert much more mental energy towards controlling his behaviour and evaluating the responses of the person to whom the lie was being told.

York was a little slower in the retelling, but not dramatically so. His hands fluttered a little more than they had before, but Atticus couldn't tell whether it was just from an increase in stress from the interview itself, or whether he was having greater difficulty in keeping his facts aligned. Atticus watched the interview as his phone's screen faded off; he didn't do anything to keep it awake.

'So,' Mack said, 'you said Burns went to Thailand.'

'That's right. He was gone for months. I'd almost forgotten him, but then he called me. He said he'd come back again because he'd run out of money. He wanted me to give him some. I still didn't have anything to spare, so I told him no. It didn't make any difference. He said that I was lying. He told me that I should sell some land. "You've got enough of it," he said. "You can spare some to help a mate." When that didn't work, he threatened me again. He said he'd follow Molly to college and tell her what we'd been doing. The girls at Imber. I was out of my mind with worry.'

'You thought he'd do something like that?'

'Of *course* I did. Look at it from his perspective – his life was over. He had nothing more to lose.'

'Did you pay him?'

York took a moment to breathe and then continued. 'I didn't have anything left, and, even if I did, I knew he'd keep coming back. I told myself it had to stop. I told him to come to the farm.'

'When was this?'

'Two months ago. December. It was dark – five-ish. He turned up. I had a bag that I'd filled with newspaper. I told him it was the money he wanted and gave it to him. He bent down to look at it, and I used my stun gun on him. I took a bolt gun that I use for euthanising cattle, put it against the back of his head and pulled the trigger. He wouldn't have felt a thing. I knew I had to get rid of him, so I put him in the Ranger and drove to Imber. There was no one around, so I dug a grave, buried him and drove home. I burned my clothes, cleaned out the car, showered, and then had a drink. I thought that might finally be it. I just wanted it to be over.'

He took the plastic cup and sipped the fresh coffee.

'At first,' he continued, 'it seemed as if everything was fine. Burns has a brother, but no other family and no friends. No one came to ask if I knew where he was. Why would they? I didn't think anyone knew that I knew him. I tried to forget about it, but ...' He stopped and drew the back of his hand across his eyes as if wiping away tears; Atticus couldn't see whether he was crying or simply embroidering the moment.

'Please,' Mack said. 'Carry on.'

'Molly,' he said. 'Her behaviour started to change. She's always been a difficult child, but we've always got along, especially since her mother left. Not any more. She became disobedient. Stopped talking to me, and, when she did talk, it was all attitude and sass. I started to suspect she was using drugs. She was seeing a young lad in the city who I found out was dealing from his flat. I confronted her about it, and we had a row. I said she couldn't see him any more, and she told me that I had no right to tell her what to do. I remember her words exactly: "Who are you to tell me what to do after what *you* did?" I made her tell me what she meant, and she said that she'd been home when I'd killed Alf. She said she'd been smoking a joint in the field and that she saw me use the bolt gun on him. She saw all of it.'

'What did she do?'

'She ran away. I thought about going to the police, but I knew I couldn't. What if she told them what she'd seen? But then, on the other hand, what if they didn't get her back? She could tell someone else what had happened – the result would be the same. I remembered seeing a local private investigator on the television after that big case at Christmas.'

'Mr Priest.'

'Yes,' he said. 'I decided that was my best option – tell him that I was worried about Molly getting a criminal record so he wouldn't involve the police. I went to see him, and he found her for me in London.'

York looked down at the table, and Atticus caught the sound of his snivelling.

'Have another drink, Mr York,' Mack said, indicating the plastic cup in front of York.

He finished the coffee and set it back down.

'I drove up to London, and Molly came outside as I was waiting for her. I was able to get her into the car and drove away before she had a chance to say anything.' He stopped again, biting his lip. His eyes were wet when he continued, but, this time, he did not wipe them dry. 'We argued again. She made me stop – we were in a lay-by just off the M3 – and she got out of the car. She told me that she couldn't live in the same house as me, and that if I tried to make her stay, she'd go

433

to the police and tell them everything.' He stopped, his shoulders shuddering.

'What did you do?'

'Hit her.'

'A little louder, please.'

'I *hit* her. I didn't mean to, but I lost control. She fell, and . . . she banged her head against the side of the car. She didn't move – I thought she was dead. I . . .' He paused. 'I wasn't thinking. I panicked. I put her in the boot and drove home. She was awake again when we arrived – but she was hysterical. I took her up to the barn and put her in the cellar. I couldn't control her. I didn't know what else to do.'

'How long was she in there?'

'It was Tuesday when we got back from London.'

'And it's Monday today. So *six* days?'

Atticus watched the screen: Mack was writing in her notebook; DS Archer was hunched over, his fists clenched; Aikenhead didn't appear to know where to look; York was biting his lip to stop from crying. Atticus felt uneasy. Something about the confession bothered him, and he couldn't say what it was. He couldn't shake the feeling that there was something in the shadows, something important, something that York had not revealed.

'What were you going to do with her?' Mack asked him.

'What choice did I have? I took her phone and texted the lad she'd been seeing in the city before she went to London with the other one. I pretended to be her and told him to come over to the farm. I used the bolt gun on him. I thought that if he disappeared at the same time as Molly, it'd look like they were together. Then the detective who had been working with Priest—'

'DC Edwards,' Archer said.

'Yes. She came to the farm yesterday afternoon, and I told her the story I made up about what had happened. I thought she believed me, but then the other lad from London phoned her. I'm not sure what he said.'

'Your daughter had told him what you'd done,' Mack said. 'He told DC Edwards.'

York nodded his understanding. 'That's what I thought. And then Molly's phone went off in my pocket, and Edwards knew what had happened. She tried to leave. I had to do something. I couldn't let her go. I shocked her and put her in the cellar with Molly.'

'What were you going to do with them?' Mack asked him. 'Tonight, I mean, before we interrupted you.'

'What I had to do. I was going to bury them in a wood on the edge of the farm. Molly used to play there as a child. I thought it would be a nice spot for her.'

It appeared that York was at the end of his confession. Neither Mack nor Archer spoke, until Mack checked her watch – it was two fifteen in the morning – and announced that she was going to stop the tape, and that they would continue later.

'Up you get,' Archer said. 'I'll take you to the custody sergeant and get you in a cell for the night.'

'Will I be charged?'

'You've just confessed to multiple murders,' Mack said. 'You'll be charged.'

'Thank you,' York said.

Mack slipped her notes into a folder. 'For what?'

'For listening. I've been wanting to tell someone my story for years. It's a relief that it's done.'

Mack and Archer stood.

Atticus stared at the screen as York looked up into the camera. His cheeks were wet with spilled tears, but, for a fraction of a second, his eyes shone with a wariness that should not have been there.

York was lying; Atticus was sure of it.

78

Mack came through into room four again and sat down on the opposite side of the table to Atticus. 'What do you think?'

He massaged his temples, kneading them with his fingers. 'I suspect that *some* of the story is true. Molly, for example. I think that's probably not far off what happened. The story about Londonderry feels authentic; plus it'll be easy enough to corroborate with the PSNI. He'd know that. The rest of it, though? I don't know. Something about it is off.'

'It's a confession,' Mack countered. 'And it's tallying with what we know so far.'

'Could Alfred Burns be the killer of the girls in the cemetery? Definitely. I'm just not sure that we've been told the full story, and I can't put my finger on why. I wish I could be in there with you. It's difficult trying to read him from here.'

'We can't do that,' she said. 'You know we can't.'

She pointed to Atticus's hip flask. He unscrewed it, poured a shot into his empty plastic cup and slid the flask across the table. Mack poured some into her own cup and sipped. 'Thanks.'

'We need to see York's medical records,' Atticus said.

'Why?'

'Did you notice him coughing?'

'Yes. He's got a cold.'

'It's not a cold. Compare what he looks like today with the pictures on his Facebook page. He's lost weight. I didn't really pay attention to it, but now I wonder if it might be relevant. Get a court order and go to his doctor. I bet he's being treated for something nasty. I think that might be very relevant.'

'Because if he's sick, he might not have anything to lose by confessing?'

'Exactly.'

'You think he's protecting someone?'

'Maybe. Miller, perhaps.'

Atticus poured out the last of the hip flask, splitting the alcohol between their plastic cups.

'I'm tired,' Mack said.

'You need to speak to Miller,' he said. 'You can't postpone it. Don't give him any more time to think than necessary.'

'I know that,' she said. 'I'm just fishing for sympathy. How would you do it?'

'Give him a prompt about what York said, but not too much. He won't be able to deny that he knows York and Burns – he knows we've seen the photo of them together. Tell him that York has explained what happened in Londonderry and see where he goes after that. We need to establish a connection between the three of them here, when they got back.'

Atticus saw movement on his monitor and turned to see Richard Miller as he lowered himself into the chair that York had just vacated. His solicitor was next to him, a woman from a local firm with whom Atticus had had dealings in the past.

Mack stood and smoothed down her shirt. 'Same again,' she said. 'Buzz me if there's anything you think I need to cover.'

Atticus said that he would, wished her luck and waited as she made her way back to the interview room.

* * *

Atticus watched as Mack started the interview.

'You've told us about your relationship with Alfred Burns,' she said. 'Tell us about James York.'

'We were in the Army together in Londonderry. You know that already, though, don't you? Your colleague saw the regimental photograph with the three of us when he looked around my house during your visit.'

Atticus stiffened, surprised by Miller's perspicacity and wondering whether he was going to make an issue of his search of his property. He didn't.

'I was a senior platoon commander and York had just been cross-posted into my platoon. I knew him as a soldier in the battalion, of course, but obviously I knew the rest of my platoon much better. He wasn't an easy chap to get acquainted with, to be honest.'

'Did you know he was in Salisbury?'

'No – is he?'

He spoke with an assuredness that had not been there to quite the same degree before; he had had time to consider the situation in which he'd found himself.

'Are you sure?'

'Why do you ask?'

'Burns was blackmailing you.'

'Yes. I already told you that.'

'He was blackmailing James York, too.'

'I didn't know that.'

439

'We arrested Mr York this evening, too.'

'For what?'

'The murder of Alfred Burns. He's admitted to it. He's also admitted to the murder of at least five young women whose bodies we found in the graveyard at Imber.'

Atticus stared at Miller on the screen, looking for signs of the surprise that would be there if that really was something that was unexpected. But the colonel had turned his face, and all the camera could catch was the side of his head. 'My God,' he said. 'You think . . . Please, Chief Inspector, *please*. That's ridiculous. You think I could have been involved in murdering him?'

'You had the motive,' she said. 'Just like Mr York.'

Atticus heard the sound of feet running down the corridor. They went past his room and continued. He heard a knock and, turning his attention back to the screen, he saw Mack look behind her and invite whoever it was to come inside.

It was Francine Patterson. She looked panicked.

'I'm sorry, boss. I didn't want to disturb you, but this is an emergency.'

'What is it?'

'It's York.'

Mack told Archer to take care of the procedural niceties for pausing the interview, got up and followed Patterson out of the door. Atticus stood quickly, his chair scraping against the floor as he pushed it away, and went to the door just as Mack and Patterson were passing.

'What is it?' he said.

Mack didn't stop.

'Come with us,' she called back over her shoulder.

79

They hurried to the custody suite. The corridor was painted in a neutral white with an alarm strip on the left and doors on either side. DS James Boyd was the sergeant on shift. He was pacing the corridor, his hand pressed to his forehead. The door to the cell at the end of the corridor was open, and the first-aid case that they kept behind the reception desk had been discarded on the floor, the lid open and the contents spilling out.

Mack went into the cell, and Atticus followed behind her. It was a small space that was also painted white, with a thick blue stripe between the floor and the ceiling. James York was sitting on the blue mattress with his back to the wall. He was dressed in a standard-issue replacement tracksuit, his right arm hung loosely, and his left hand rested on the mattress. His face was slack and pallid. Blood had pooled on the waterproof surface of the mattress, and there was a puddle of it on the floor beneath the dangling right arm, a shocking red against the white.

PC Dave Betts was sitting on the edge of the bed by York's knees, holding a piece of gauze against the man's right wrist to staunch the blood.

'Is he still alive?' Atticus said.

'I don't know,' Betts said.

Atticus swore under his breath, stepped around Mack and went over to the bed, shoving Betts aside. He reached down and pressed his index and forefingers to York's neck. There was no pulse. He moved his fingers a little and pressed harder, but there was still nothing.

'Gone.'

'Shit,' Mack said.

Atticus saw the glint of metal on the floor next to the bed. He took a piece of gauze and, with the material pinched between his fingers, knelt down and picked it up. He held the object up so that Mack could see it.

'A razor blade?'

Atticus stood. 'Betts? *Betts!*'

Betts was fidgeting by the door. Atticus held the blade up so that he could see it. 'Where did he get this from?'

'I don't know.'

'Didn't you search him?'

'Of course I bloody searched him.'

'And you missed a *razor blade?*'

'I didn't miss anything. The doctor checked him, too.'

'You say that, yet there it is—'

'Stop it,' Mack said. 'Both of you.'

Atticus bit his tongue, aware enough, for once, that there was no profit in an argument.

'When was he searched?' Mack asked Betts calmly.

'When we booked him, boss. It was a full strip-search, his clothes were bagged, and the doctor body-mapped him. There's no way he had a blade on him when he came in.'

Atticus looked at the razor, the sharp edge sticky with blood. 'Has anyone been close enough to hand him something?'

'No,' Betts said. 'Not since he was brought down here.'

'His lawyer?' Mack said.

'Where is he?' Atticus said.

'He left after the interview finished,' Archer said.

'Find out where he lives,' Mack said. 'Send someone to pick him up.'

'Where did York speak to him?'

'In one of the empty interview rooms.'

'Was the camera on or off?'

'It's his solicitor,' Archer said. 'It's confidential. Of *course* the camera was off.'

Atticus closed his eyes and took a breath. The corridor outside was busy with the sound of urgent conversation, and it distracted him. It was *possible* that York could have killed himself after his confession. He would have known that he faced life in prison, either for what he had admitted to doing during his time in the Army or especially for his murder of Burns. He had been distressed during the interview, but suicidal? Atticus hadn't seen anything to suggest that. His mind raced with competing ideas and possible explanations, but there was too much clamour for him to be able to unravel the one thread that would bring him to the truth.

He needed quiet. He needed to think.

PART IX

ONE WEEK LATER

80

The roads through the New Forest were unusual for their beauty and, more, for the animals with which the traffic had to contend. Atticus dabbed the brakes and crawled between two wild horses that were walking on either side of the road. Ahead, a family of wild pigs snuffled in the undergrowth for morsels to eat. Bandit was alert in the back of the car, standing up to his full height and staring through the rear window, his tail pointed straight out behind him. Atticus pulled off the road and into the car park next to Godshill Cricket Club, slotting his beat-up old Volvo next to Mack's similarly dishevelled Range Rover. He looked over and saw that it was empty, as expected; Mack had told him that she would meet him on the trail.

He got out and opened the back so that Bandit could vault down. The dog was itching to run and, after assuring himself that there were no other horses in the vicinity that he might worry, Atticus slapped him on the hindquarters to send him on his way. Bandit sprinted off at top speed, blasting through the gorse so that he could barrel down the slope that led to the bottom of the gentle valley. Atticus set off after him. The track wound down, crossed a brook by way of a wooden bridge, and then climbed up to the other side. The view was spectacular, with miles of open lowland heath fringed in the distance by forests of ancient trees. The last week had been unseasonably warm, and the first spring flowers were stirring. Atticus saw early flowering orchids, wild garlic, lesser celandines, bluebells, primroses and snowbells sprouting amid the gorse and bracken.

Atticus continued down the track, splashing through puddles of standing water and patches of thick, sticky mud. He saw Mack waiting by the bridge, leaning against it as she held up a pair of binoculars. She enjoyed watching the birds and the other wildlife and, as she swung the glasses around, he raised a hand in greeting. Bandit had seen her, too, and set off towards her at a flat sprint. Atticus grinned as the dog reached her and reared up, planting his muddy paws on her coat so that she might be persuaded to rub his ears. Atticus jogged down the slope to the bridge.

'Sorry,' he said, gesturing to the mud that had been smeared across her jacket.

'Worth every stain,' she said, ducking her head so that Bandit could press his snout into her neck.

'He likes you,' Atticus said.

Bandit lowered his paws to the ground and dashed away again, splashing through the brook and starting up the slope that led into a wooded enclosure.

'So?' Atticus said.

'So,' Mack replied, exhaling. 'It's been busy. Where do you want me to start?'

'York,' he said. 'Anything on how he got that razor?'

'No. We interviewed the solicitor, and he swore blind it had nothing to do with him. We looked into his background, and there's nothing to suggest that he would ever have done something like that.'

'So York had it on him?'

'You were there – Betts swears he searched him thoroughly.'

Atticus was minded to suggest that the search had not been thorough enough, but there was no profit in sniping at the sergeant now.

'We've reported ourselves to the IOPC,' she said. 'There'll be an independent inquiry.'

'What about York?' Atticus said.

'There'll be no charges against him now that he's dead,' she said, 'but the coroner will get all of the evidence that we've put together. His confession and everything else. The families of the victims will get answers.'

'But not justice,' Atticus said. 'He took the easy way out. And Burns is dead, too.'

They climbed through the wood and up to the top of a tumulus that offered a panoramic view of the countryside in all directions.

'Burns,' Mack said. 'We've got a little more on him. He started work at the youth club in 2000, right after he left the MoD. The thing that we can't quite figure out is how he got a job working with kids. He didn't have any experience, at least not as far as we can make out.'

'He wouldn't have had a CRB check, would he?'

'No. Those kind of background checks only started in 2002. He would've been checked off against List 99 for any offences against children, but he hadn't been investigated for anything back then – his record would have been clean. We've spoken to some of the other staff who worked there then. They said it was all a bit of a mess. Record-keeping was non-existent, and no one noticed that some of the kids who went there had disappeared.'

'Why would they? It was spread out over time.'

'And it wasn't the sort of place that had regulars. Kids dropped in and dropped out again.'

Bandit checked back to make sure that they were still following him before racing off again. Atticus and Mack walked on.

'What about IDing the victims?' he asked.

'Francine's been busy on that. We've got three of them from their dental records: Abbie Ross, seventeen when she went missing; Orna Foster, nineteen; and Lindsey Alexander, twenty.'

'And the last two? Catherine and Evelyn?'

The girls had been given the names as they had been the third and fifth to have been found.

'Not yet. We'll keep looking.'

Atticus knew there was a good chance that the two would never be identified. The teenagers who visited the youth club were often drawn from the fringes of society, and there would have been many who passed through its doors who would not have been fortunate enough to have loved ones who would miss them when they did not return home. They had been waifs and strays who had found an evening's distraction from the sadness and difficulty of their day-to-day struggles, only then to find that they paid for their transitory fun with their lives.

'Are the parents still alive?'

'Some,' she said. 'I went to see the Fosters this afternoon. They'd never been able to get over the fact that Orna didn't come home. They've been grieving for her for fifteen years. I don't know whether knowing what happened to her will make it easier or harder to deal with.'

They continued downhill again, towards Blissford Hill.

'Have you seen Molly?'

'She came in the day before yesterday,' Mack said. 'She's been placed with foster parents until something more permanent can be sorted out for her.'

'How was she?'

'Surprisingly well given what happened to her. Her evidence is strong. She also said that she thinks her dad might have had something to do with her mother's disappearance. She says she left and never tried to get back in touch with her. She said that York told her there was someone else involved, but she never really believed him. It'll be hard to prove anything, but we're looking into it.'

They climbed a stile over a fence and followed the track up into another wood.

'And Miller?' Atticus said.

Mack sighed. 'That's going to be very difficult. He's only admitted to being in the bedroom in Londonderry with Burns and York.'

'He couldn't very well say he wasn't – he's in the photograph.'

'But that's *all* he'll admit. He says he left the house immediately after the picture was taken and that he had no idea that Burns was planning to murder the couple they robbed. The only witnesses to what happened that day – the two victims and Burns and York – are dead. It's going to be difficult to prove that he's lying. We've passed our file to the PSNI – it'll be up to them now.'

'What'll he be charged with?'

'I don't know,' she said. 'That's for the PSNI to decide. He's out for now, though.'

'And Imber?'

'We're searching the buildings. Nothing useful found yet, but there's a lot to check. We'll keep looking.'

Bandit sprinted back to check on them and, after ensuring that they were still where they were supposed to be, flashed down to a stream and splashed through it. Mack and Atticus followed, stepping carefully through the clear, icy water. Mack lost her footing on a lichen-encrusted rock, and Atticus put out a hand to steady her; she grabbed it, and, even after fording the stream, did not attempt to take her hand away.

Atticus had been interested in finding out about progress in the investigation, but that was not the subject that had occupied him the most since the last time he and Mack had been together. He had told himself that he wouldn't ask her, that he would let her tell him when she was ready, but he couldn't stop himself.

'What about you and Andy?'

'What about us?'

'What have you decided to do about the divorce?'

'I don't have a choice,' she said.

'You could contest it.'

'I can't *make* him stay married to me,' she said.

They walked on for a moment, her hand still in his.

'Do you want to?' he said. 'Stay married, I mean?'

She thought about that for a beat. 'No,' she said. 'I don't think I do. I was thinking of the kids before, but I had things the wrong way around. We weren't happy, and I don't see how they could be happy when we were arguing all the time. It wasn't doing them any favours.'

She stopped and tugged on his hand. Atticus stopped, too, and turned to face her. She stepped closer to him, let go of his hand and reached up with hers to cup his cheek. She pressed herself against him and kissed him on the lips.

'I'm going to do what I want to do for a change,' she said.

Atticus felt a nudge on his hand. Bandit was back, watching them, his tail wagging enthusiastically.

81

Richard Miller drove through the open gate and into the wood that formed a natural boundary around the big house. It was eleven at night, and the thick banks of cloud overhead blocked out the moon and stars; it was as black as tar, and he could see no further than the reach of the car's headlights. The trees on either side grew close together, the darkness between their trunks absorbing the glow as the car drove on. Miller gripped the wheel a little tighter, fancying that he saw the flash of an animal's eyes in the undergrowth to the right. A fox, perhaps, or a badger. A predator in search of prey.

He had been here many times, ever since they had moved the private broadcasts from Imber. Summers had regaled him and the others with the history of the estate, how the tools that had been excavated from the grounds in the 1920s proved that Woodyates had been occupied since Neolithic times. He had taken them to the ancient Roman well in the Well House and had pointed to the handful of coins that were displayed in a case on the wall, explaining how they had been dated to the reign of Constantine I, eighteen hundred years earlier. The coins were fine, Miller thought, but he had been more interested in the axe-heads and laurel-leaf knives, the blades that might, at some point in the past, have been dipped in blood.

The road passed out of the trees and descended into a depression, and then, as he crested the hill, the house was revealed. It sat in a hollow, with the hills rising gently all around it and with open farmland to the front and the oak forest of the Cranborne Chase to the rear. It was secluded and offered privacy and security; that was important, given the business that took place there.

Miller parked his car. He drew in a deep breath, composing himself for what he suspected might be a difficult conversation, and then got out and made his way to the side entrance. The door was open, and Miller went inside, making his way along the hall, passing the darkroom and the cloakroom, crossing the empty dining hall and library and reaching the door to the drawing room.

Harry Summers, the owner of the house, sat in his leather armchair by the fire.

'Richard,' he said.

'Harry.'

Summers gestured to the Chesterfield. 'Please – sit.'

Miller lowered himself into the chair as Summers picked up a bottle of what looked like an exceptionally fine red and offered it. Miller nodded. Summers poured out a glass and handed it to him.

'It's very sad about James,' Summers said. 'Very unfortunate.'

Miller sipped the wine, then placed the glass on the table next to him. 'He knew what would need to be done if he was discovered. And he didn't have long left – not with the cancer.'

'Both true,' Summers said. 'But his sacrifice is still admirable.'

'There but for the grace of God, and all that.'

'Quite so,' Summers said, nodding his agreement. 'What have you heard about your own situation?'

'The case has been passed to the authorities in Northern Ireland.'

'And what will you say when they question you?'

'I can't very well deny the armed robbery charge. But my story is that I left before the two of them were shot.'

'How do your lawyers rate your chances?'

'They tell me it's hard to predict. I'll get time for the robbery – I can't say that I wasn't there; I'm in the bloody photograph. But there are no witnesses to the murders. Alf and James and the two Micks are all dead. I'll say I left before that happened.' He shrugged.

'Whatever the verdict,' Summers said, 'we'll make sure that the sentence is as brief as possible and that you can serve it in a pleasant establishment. I suspect you'll spend a month or two somewhere insalubrious, but, once the attention is off, you'll be moved and looked after properly. We have some levers to pull over there, as you know.'

'I do.'

'It'll be fine,' Summers said.

'I know. You don't need to worry, Harry. I'll do what I have to do.'

'I know you will.'

He raised his glass. Miller raised his, and they touched them together.

Miller gazed into the flames. 'What about Priest?'

'A minor irritant,' Summers declared with a downward curl of his lip. 'It was bad enough with his *crusade* against Alf. If it weren't for him, I doubt he would have made the foolish decisions that he did. But we all knew that Alf was weak. Weak and venal and a problem waiting to happen. I should've realised much sooner that he couldn't be trusted.'

'Will anything be done – about Priest, I mean?'

'We're watching. The concern is that he'll keep digging, pardon the pun. We won't allow that to happen.'

'What about Alf's brother?'

Summers tutted. '*That* was irritating. Doyle missed him by minutes. He's looking for him now. I doubt he'll be resourceful enough to stay out of the way for long.'

'Do you think he has anything damaging?'

'We didn't find all of Alf's material, did we? So I think we can assume that he has that, at least. But there's no reason for him to threaten us with it. He'll see it as insurance to keep us away.'

'He won't be tempted to blackmail us?'

'Alf tried that. I find it difficult to believe that his brother would be that stupid.'

Summers spoke with the confidence of a man with the resources and disposition necessary to eliminate threats. It had been a bumpy few months, one way or another, and Miller had found a little peace of mind knowing that Summers was on top of everything. Alf had damned himself and had eventually brought York down with him, but there was a firebreak now between them and the rest of the business. Miller would serve time for the crimes that could be proven, but that would be that.

He sipped his wine. 'What about Jones?'

'The detective chief inspector has family problems,' Summers said. 'Her husband wants a divorce. She might be open to being reassigned away from Salisbury. But, either way, it's in hand.' He finished his glass and stood. 'There's no need to dwell on it. Come on – we need to get down to the chapel. There's a lot to do tonight.'

* * *

Summers led the way to the chapel in the grounds of the house. It dated back to the fourteenth century and was small and simple. The timber door was ajar, and Summers pushed it open and went in.

The room inside had been equipped as a film studio. The stone walls had been draped with sound-absorbent material that shone red in the glow of uplighters set around the floor. Several cameras were arranged on tripods that, carefully positioned around the mattress on the floor, offered coverage of the action from all angles. There was a table with various lenses laid out on it and LED lights set on tripods that could be moved around to accommodate the requirements of the scene being recorded. There were microphones on stands and booms, a mixing desk and two large monitors that allowed them to view the live feed.

The operation was overseen by Adam, a technician who was paid generously in return for his discretion. Apart from the sating of his greed, Adam's continued obedience was guaranteed by the fact that Summers had made it plain that he knew everything about him and his family: his wife's place of work, the schools that his kids attended, the fact that he had taken money to work on these broadcasts for months.

'Is everything ready?' Summers asked.

'We're good,' Adam said. 'There was a problem with the uplink, but that's sorted.'

Their films had been much less sophisticated when they had started making them more than twenty years earlier. They had used the Manor House in Imber, a spacious property that offered additional privacy thanks to the tall brick wall that surrounded it. Miller remembered it fondly. He, Burns and York had transported their equipment in the back of an old Ford Transit that Burns had bought, set up and filmed scenes in accordance with the orders placed by their customers, and then removed all evidence of their presence by the time dawn broke. Burns had edited the films and supplied them to the customers on DVDs. The Manor House's proximity to the cemetery had been another bonus, especially when it became obvious that there was a demand for content that pushed the boundary, and that patrons were prepared to pay through the nose to satisfy the most taboo of kinks.

Summers had been a customer himself back then, but, having seen the potential of the business, he had become involved in it. It had been his recommendation that Imber be abandoned and his suggestion that they make the chapel their permanent studio. The business had become known in the darkest corners of the internet as the Red Room, on account of the lighting that they had incorporated in their first shoots; they used the same lights, to the same effect, today.

'What are we doing tonight?' Miller asked.

'MFF,' Summers said. 'The two from before and the junkie. Doyle's getting them now.'

They didn't have long to wait. The actors in their films were kept in one of the old servants' cottages, the door secured with padlocks and the windows barred. Doyle arrived, pushing three teenagers – one male and two female – into the studio. Doyle was a big man, with a barrel-like chest and arms as big as Miller's legs, and a disposition that did not brook disobedience. Miller did not know anything more than his surname – and doubted that even *that* was real – but York, in an unguarded moment, had suggested that he was a soldier that Summers employed to clear up the occasional mishap that threatened his businesses. Miller knew that someone had been sent to Alfred's flat in Andover when Atticus Priest had been inside, and suspected that it had been him.

Miller watched the trio as they came inside and looked around. The first young woman was slender with dark hair that hung over her face as she bowed her head; the second was a redhead, younger, her face scattered with freckles. Miller hadn't seen her before; she was, to use the term that Summers preferred, 'fresh'. The young man was rail thin, his arms marked with tracks that identified him as an addict. Miller knew that Summers had found him in a shooting gallery in the Priory and tempted him here with the promise of free smack. His habit would kill him, although not in the way that he might have feared. All three of them were dressed in clothes that had evidently not been changed during the time they had been kept in the cottage.

'Over there,' Summers said, pointing to the mattress in the centre of the room. 'Get undressed.'

Doyle nudged them forward, and Miller saw the fear in their eyes. He had seen that same fear countless times before. Some of those who had been in the Red Room had been allowed to leave. Others – those selected for a particular type of feature – had not been so lucky.

Adam set the cameras to record and opened the live link to whichever customer was paying for tonight's show. They used the dark web to hide their activity, and there was never anything in shot that could identify them or their location. It was convenient, secure and remunerative.

The three actors were naked. They stood around, nervously looking at each other and at Doyle.

'What are you waiting for?' Summers said. 'Go.'

* * *

It was three in the morning by the time Miller left the house. The shoot had lasted two hours and, by the time the party following the shoot had finished, he had been tired and ready to go.

There was a car parked on the lane next to Miller's house. The passenger-side door opened, and a figure stepped out and started down the road to him. Rain was falling heavily, but the figure – Miller thought it was a woman – didn't seem to be paying it any heed.

'Mr Miller?'

Miller stopped with his hand on his gate. His first thought was that it was the police, back to question him again. 'Can I help you?'

The car's headlights flicked on, shining right at Miller. The sudden illumination blinded him, and he had to look away and blink until the streaks and smears of brightness disappeared.

The woman drew nearer. 'Remember me?'

It was dark and she was silhouetted by the lights. Miller could see that she was of average height and build, but not much beyond that.

'I can't see you very well. The lights—'

'Doubt that'd make much difference. It was a long time ago, and I was a lot younger then.'

'I don't know who you are, and I don't appreciate being bothered at my home at this time of night.'

The lights flicked off. Miller heard footsteps behind him. He turned – too late – and saw the smudge of movement coming out of the thick dark. He saw motion, something swinging at him, and, when it hit him – hard and fast and sudden – the night drew around him like a fist.

82

Atticus and Mack had come back to the office. She was asleep in the room next door, but he had been unable to relax. His mind raced with thoughts and, unable to quieten them, he had got out of bed and crept through into the office. He had read Bronstein's book on the Zurich chess tournament for an hour and then, inspired, had woken his computer and checked whether any of his online opponents had taken their moves. He opened the game with Jack; Atticus had moved his kingside knight, and now he saw that Jack had responded by bringing out his second knight. Atticus mirrored that with his queenside knight and submitted the move.

A message appeared in the chat box.

> *I need to talk to you.*

Atticus typed:

> *We're talking now.*
> *It's not the same.*

Atticus looked up from the screen, then stood and went to the window. He looked out into the street below. It was deserted. The rain had been falling all night, and now even the road was awash with it, run-off pooling around drains that were already in full spate. He had the uncomfortable feeling that he was being watched, yet could see no evidence to suggest that it was more than just a premonition.

He went back to the desk and saw that another message was waiting for him.

> *I need to speak to you. Properly.*

Atticus reached for the keyboard to reply, started to type, then stopped. He didn't know what to say.

Another message flashed up at the bottom of the chat box.

> *It's about James York.*

Atticus stared. His fingers rested on the keyboard, lifeless.

> *And Richard Miller.*

His mouth was dry. He reached for a plastic bottle of fizzy water that he had left next to the keyboard and drank down the tepid half-inch that was left in the bottom.

> *Come to the cathedral. I'll meet you under the tree on the path between the visitor entrance and West Walk.*

Atticus frowned.

> *The gate will be locked.*

Another message flashed up:

> *I've unlocked it. I have a key.*
> *When?*
> *Ten minutes. Please don't be late. It's cold, and you'll want to hear what I have to say.*

*   *   *

Atticus grabbed his leather jacket and put it on and wrapped a scarf around his neck. He glanced into the bedroom and heard the gentle breathing that told him that Mack was still asleep. Bandit looked up from his position on the sofa, one ear cocked quizzically.

'I'd better do this on my own,' Atticus whispered. 'Stay here. I won't be long.'

He made his way down to the passageway. The door that opened onto New Street was closed, and Atticus unlatched it and stepped outside. He looked left and right, expecting to see someone watching him. The street was still empty. The rain fell heavily.

He set off, walking briskly through the rain towards the junction with the High Street. He reached the junction and turned left. The North Gate was locked every evening at eleven. Residents of the Close were given a key to unlock it, but ingress and egress were otherwise restricted. He raised his hand and found that the gate swung back at his push. He opened it far enough to pass through and continued inside.

The floodlights that lit the cathedral at night had been switched off. Atticus walked into the grounds and made for the West Front, the Gothic frontage populated by statues of religious figures: angels and archangels, Moses, King David, Isaiah, Jeremiah. He waited there and looked about: it was late, coming up to half past three. There was no one about. The buildings that faced the cathedral from the West Walk loomed in the darkness, a handful with their windows lit, the others shapeless and foreboding.

There was a footpath that led from the West Front to the West Walk, and Atticus made his way along it. A large tree stood at the edge of the cathedral grounds, its naked boughs spread out in all directions, the rain slicing through the leafless branches. Atticus slowed his pace, looking for someone who might be waiting for him, but saw no one. He was alone.

He zipped his jacket all the way up to his neck and then shoved his hands into his pockets. He was starting to feel a little foolish. This had all the makings of a wild goose chase, and he started to wonder who might have been inventive – and bored – enough to have pranked him so thoroughly.

He was about to turn back when he heard the buzzing of a phone.

He looked around, expecting to see someone nearby, but still there was no one: he was all alone.

The phone continued to ring.

He searched left and right, trying to place it, until his eye alighted on a rubbish bin next to the wall. He walked towards it and looked inside: the bag for collecting the rubbish had recently been replaced, and there was just a small collection of discarded newsprint, drinks cartons and other detritus inside it. He ignored all that, for a clear bag had been fixed to the inside of the bin with a length of tape. There was a phone inside, its screen glowing. Atticus yanked the bag away from the tape, ripped it open, and took out the phone.

He answered the call. 'Hello?'

'I'm sorry to have put you to this inconvenience, Atticus, but I really wanted to speak to you properly. You know what the internet can be like – it's so difficult to appreciate nuance.'

The words were distorted and robotic. There were dozens of apps on the market that could change the sound of a person's voice, and Atticus guessed that one of them was being used now.

'This seems like a very complicated way to do it,' he said. 'You could have made an appointment like normal people.'

There came a laugh. 'I would love to meet you – really, I would – but I don't think that would work for either of us. Not now, anyway. Perhaps another day.'

The voice sounded male, but Atticus knew that that meant nothing. The software could make a woman into a man and a man into a woman.

'Well, here I am. What do you want?'

'Richard Miller,' the voice said.

'What about him?'

'You know what he would've got if his case went to trial, don't you? A light sentence and a pleasant place to do the time. An open prison, after a while. Somewhere he can come and go. How would you have felt about that?'

Atticus noted the use of past tense with unease. Something bad had happened. 'How do you know about Miller?'

'Never mind that. Answer the question.'

'I wouldn't have felt great,' Atticus said. 'But it is what it is. It won't be easy to prove he was involved in the murder. All of the other witnesses are dead.'

The answer was quick and impatient. 'Come on, Atticus. You don't think that's *all* he's guilty of, do you? *Really?* I had hoped for more from you.'

'Okay, fine – you tell me. What do you think he's done?'

'It's not what I *think* – it's what I *know*. Miller, York, Burns . . . what happened in Londonderry was just them getting started. What about the kids at Imber?'

Atticus looked around. He was still alone. 'What about them?'

'Haven't you looked into that at all?'

'Of course we have,' Atticus said. 'York confessed to it. He said he and Burns killed them.'

'And you believe him? You think it was just the two of them?'

Atticus paused. 'I'm not convinced.'

'Good,' the voice said. '*Good*. It wasn't just them. There were others.'

'Miller?'

'Yes, but not just him.'

'Who, then?'

'They were being paid to abuse those kids. I don't know the names of the customers. I was hoping you might have been able to tell me, but maybe I'm asking too much.'

'There's no evidence that anyone else was involved.'

'Aren't you listening?' the voice spat. '*I* was involved.'

Atticus looked around again, itchy that he was being watched. 'What does that mean?'

'I'd give you more, but I need to think about whether you're the right person for the job.'

'Fine. Don't tell me. Tell the police.'

'You think I can trust them? I know you're not naïve enough to believe that.' There was a pause. 'I can see that you're trying to do the right thing. You were the only officer who made any effort to investigate what Burns had been doing. You *knew* it was more than just the pornography they found. I had hoped you might have realised how much more, but ...' The voice paused. 'Never mind. You have an open mind, and I appreciate the work you did. You lost your job because of it. That and ... well, your drug use. And the situation with the detective chief inspector.'

Atticus had the impression that whoever it was on the other end of the line was making a point, demonstrating how much he or she knew about him.

'Do you have proof that Miller was involved?'

'Don't worry about him. He's been taken care of.'

'What does that mean?'

'It means he won't hurt anyone else.'

Atticus turned and started to walk back to the office, taking the most direct route straight across the lawns. He started to jog.

'There's no need to hurry,' the voice said. 'I won't be there when you arrive. I'd like us to work together, and we wouldn't be able to do that if you handed me over to your girlfriend. That really wouldn't work at all.'

Atticus reached the gate and passed through it onto the High Street. 'Where's Miller now?'

'I'm giving him to you. I want you to take me seriously.'

Atticus reached the crossroads and turned right onto New Street. He saw a small black car parked down the road on the right-hand side. The rear lights were on, their red smudging against the rain-slicked tarmac. The car was opposite the multi-storey car park.

It looked like it had been left outside his office.

He tried to breathe normally as he lengthened his stride, fighting the urge to run.

'It's the system, Atticus,' the voice said. 'The institution. That's why I've had to take matters into my own hands. It's either incompetent or corrupt. Often both. I have no faith in it and neither do you.'

Atticus passed the Cosy Club and could see the car more clearly. It was a black Vauxhall Astra.

'Do you know your Bible, Atticus?'

'What?'

'Proverbs, chapter 106, verse three.'

'I'm sorry, I—'

'"Blessed are they who observe justice, who do righteousness at all times." It's one of my favourite verses. I've left a copy in your postbox. I took the liberty of highlighting some of my favourite passages. You should read them. Give them some thought.'

Atticus reached his office as Mack came out of the passageway and onto the pavement. She was wearing her jeans and one of his shirts.

'What is it?'

Atticus ignored her. He reached the car. The engine was running. He tried the driver's door.

It was unlocked.

He looked inside. It was empty.

Atticus pressed the phone to his ear. 'Hello? Are you there? *Hello?*'

The line was dead.

'Atticus?' Mack said. 'What's going on?'

Atticus backed out of the driver's side and looked down the road to the junction with Catherine Street. He squinted and saw a figure standing outside the old court building. There must have been a hundred and fifty feet between them, but, as Atticus watched, he saw the figure raise an arm before walking around the corner and out of sight.

Atticus covered his fingers with the sleeve of his jacket, reached back into the car and pushed the button to open the boot. The lock disengaged with a thunk. He went to the back of the car, pulled the lid up and pushed it back so that it stayed open.

Mack joined him. They both looked inside.

'Jesus.'

Richard Miller was curled up in the compartment. His knees were drawn up to his chest and, were it not for the sickle of blood on his throat, it might have been possible to mistake his posture for one of peaceful repose.

Atticus hurried back around the car. He ran down the pavement, his feet splashing through puddles of standing water. Mack followed, but Atticus quickly outpaced her. He reached the corner and turned, blinking into the wind that whipped at him from St John's Street.

There was no one there.

No cars.

No pedestrians.

Mack caught up with him.

'Who was that?' she asked, breathless.

The street was empty.

'Atticus – *answer me*. Who were you talking to?'

He turned back to the car outside the office, the headlights glaring down the street at them, a dead body in the boot.

'I don't know,' he said. 'But I'm going to find out.'

Acknowledgements

Thank you to my wonderful advance readers for helping me make this book as enjoyable as possible. Special thanks to detective sergeants Neil Lancaster and Nick Bailey for making sure the police work stands up to scrutiny.

Mark Dawson
Salisbury 2023

MARK DAWSON is the bestselling author of the
Beatrix Rose, Isabella Rose and John Milton series
and has sold over four million books. He lives in
Wiltshire with his family and can be reached
at www.markjdawson.com

www.facebook.com/markdawsonauthor
www.twitter.com/pbackwriter
www.instagram.com.markjdawson

A message from Mark

Building a relationship with my readers is the very best thing
about writing. Join my VIP Reader Club for information
on new books and deals, plus correspondence dealing with
Atticus's departure from the police. Find out what really
happened with this exclusive reader content.

Just visit www.markjdawson.com/AtticusPriest

WELBECK

PUBLISHING GROUP

Love books? Join the club.

Sign-up and choose your preferred genres to receive tailored news, deals, extracts, author interviews and more about your next favourite read.

From heart-racing thrillers to award-winning historical fiction, through to must-read music tomes, beautiful picture books and delightful gift ideas, Welbeck is proud to publish titles that suit every taste.

bit.ly/welbeckpublishing

WELBECK

ANDRE
DEUTSCH

MORTIMER

MORTIMER

WELBECK